# WE ARE ALL MISTAKES

DEO REY

for Joeta & Tão

We Are All Mistakes
Twyford Avenue,
London, N2 9NL
United Kingdom

Published in this edition by Deo Rey, 2022

*The Cambrian period was an explosion of life on Earth. Wide eyed creatures with tentacles below and spines on their backs, things like flattened rolls of carpet with a set of teeth at one end, squids with big lobster-like arms. There are thousands of them, and they seem to testify to a time when evolution took a leap and life on this planet suddenly went from being small, simple, and rare to being large, complex, numerous and dizzyingly diverse.*

Melvyn Bragg, In Our Time

*If it could be demonstrated that any complex organism existed, which could not possibly have been formed by numerous, successive, slight modifications, my theory would absolutely break down.*

Charles Darwin, The Origin of The Species

*As we shall see, hypermutation and programmed mutations are possible.*

T A Brown, Genomes Edition 2

*In the dimness Duke twisted uncomfortably on his recliner. The brick-shaped pillow and air light mattress simultaneously yielded to absorb different contours of his skull and frame.*

*Atoms moved across a recess of the room.*

*A reflex initiated a scratch to his cheek. As the right hand lay softly back down by the left shoulder, instinct caused him to partially open his eyes. The room was dark, yet a pitch-black form was by the door.*

*Duke stopped breathing. There was no sound or movement, but this shape was new. He called out loudly in conjecture.*

*"Chicken-man! Please leave me alone. We've said everything we're going to say."*

*An inky stillness endured but the dead air separating them became microscopically smaller.*

*"Please, you're freaking me out."*

*The silence persisted as the contours before him firmed up, blurred edges coalescing. A familiar outline was emerging, but only in shadow.*

*"Who's there!"*

*This came more as a yell of terror than a question. Duke's breathing was minimal and rapid. If this shape so much as exhaled, Duke felt his body might wither, sucking him inward towards a non-vocal scream.*

*"Who is th…"*

*"Duke?"*

*The question came as a rush of air from an invisible mouth. One spoken word he had heard an infinite number of times. One word wrapped in a voice he knew definitively, consummately. One word from the vocal folds he had grieved for so long.*

*"Dad?"*

*Still inky blue-black, the form hardened into a clear*

*silhouette intimately evoking his childhood days. A form that had been framed countless times in his bedroom doorway as he was wished a soft and safe goodnight.*

*"Duke…" came the voice again.*

*"What's happening, is this a dream?"*

*"No, son."*

*His eyes pricked violently with long held tears. He gulped in air and both hands went to his mouth, trembling over his lips. A tremor that spread to his arms.*

*"Dad. Are you…"*

*"Yes."*

*"Are you, a ghost?"*

*"Not as such."*

*"But I can't see you!"*

*The shape shifted diagonally to the right and forward. It was the clear silhouette of his father, yet he could not ascertain any depth to its form.*

*"Dad, this can't be. I went to your funeral!"*

*"So did I son."*

*"What are you?"*

*"I'm not sure. Atoms still being drawn together is how I feel. As though I've awoken from a coma, but I can't feel my body. I can only see… you."*

*"Dad, you're here! Dad!"*

*"I don't think I am. I'm not sure where here is. I do know that I have something to say to you though."*

*Tears rolling down his cheeks, Duke sat up to reach out a hand, yet the distance remained distinct between them.*

*"Dad. This can't be…"*

*"I feel that as well. I can also feel it won't last. But you have to go son."*

*"Go? Go where?"*

*"You have to go home, with these people."*

*"What do you mean dad, go home?"*

*"You have to go back to Earth and help."*

# PROLOGUE

# 14 YEARS EARLIER

*The best way to predict your future is to create it.*
Abraham Lincoln

# 1969

## 21st July
## 01:56am BST, London UK

*Do you still have any secrets? Will you live or die with them?*

In two hours, Neil Armstrong and Buzz Aldrin will become the fourth and fifth men in the twentieth century to set foot on the Moon.

Grimaldi studied its aura, disc-like and incandescent in the clear night sky. It's precise circular brightness against the velvet black formed the perfect contrast to the dark hole in his soul shaped by his wife's sudden departure.

This current vantage point faced a deserted north London underground station, the metal grille gates ticking down the day's heat, sealing empty platforms from access by sleeping Londoners. The dispassionate napped. The romantic few devoured the first ever, all-night BBC broadcast.

Grief and experience led him to remain uncharmed by humanity's global effort, viewing it as an unnecessary vanity project. And so he would miss this live low-tech airing of yet more middle-aged men and their moonwalks. The netherworld he tenanted precluded any true delight in such an undertaking, and he resumed his short walk in the balmy night to break and enter the local Swiss Cottage library.

Seven hours later he stepped into a different borough as the sun restoked London with an improbable heavy heat. Forever straining to dress on trend, he wore Brutus jeans and a needless tie to match his delicately flowered shirt. Barbarous curly hair touched the collar.

In '68 his lawbreaking could trigger an internal unease, but since she had gone his emotions had deadened.

He became conscious of two young boys violently rehearsing Clackers in Woolworth's doorway - the whiplash smash of the plastic spheres cracking the air above the roar of morning rush hour traffic. Their Mum struggled to stem the din with the appeasement of a Curly-Wurly chocolate chew.

He wanted change for these people, and the rest of humankind. How could their own path have evolved so differently to his, and with such a negative outcome?

Grimaldi knew confession was a path to ridicule, and though his disclosure may be momentous, such revelation would remain unbelievable from a single source. Moreover, he could not put his remaining family in jeopardy once more.

Losing her was enough.

So he teetered at the end of the Sixties, distributing miserable clues across London and New York neighbourhoods, trusting in the future inquisitive nature of his fellow cohabitants. He held out little hope, yet the act offered some internal peace to embrace a fractured heart.

He took a break to buy his great-nephew a birthday Slinky and Spirograph, before seating himself in a random café to order an Earl Grey tea. The West Hampstead denizens around him chattered, clinking their teacups and cake plates. *Give Peace A Chance* by the Plastic Ono Band played thinly as a backdrop, fading to and fro through a small Roberts radio positioned on the countertop.

*All we are saying is give peace a chance*
*All we are saying is give peace a chance*

As the waitress left him by a secluded corner table, he relented and covertly connected to a private 4G wifi. The icon flashed a full signal and he downloaded a UHD videocast of the previous night's Moon landing to his GlasSlate® mobile phone.

"Here we go again," he whispered to himself.

# PART ONE

# OUR MISTAKES

*For time and the world do not stand still.*
*Change is the law of life.*
John. F. Kennedy

# CHAPTER 1

# 1983

## 1st September
## 07:57am BST, London UK

If such mistakes were to start anywhere, it would be with a teamaker.

07:58. *Click.*

07:59. *Bubble.*

08:00. *Click, whirr.*

"Ninety-five point eight, Capital *EFF EMM*..."

A world changing day emerging in tedium. A vintage teasmade, another radio, and a bedroom establishing the stage to an ongoing deceit across the nineteenth, twentieth, and (coming soon…) twenty-first century.

The teamaker consummated the first waking cup. A built-in radio-alarm crackled an eight o'clock news to a small bedroom washed in orange hues. Shafts of sunlight lit microscopic nylon filaments and weightless dust. Thin, ashen curtains offered no defence to the strong rays pronouncing London alive and well on this first day of September. Chirpy newscasters informed the bedroom of headlines via a set of tinny speakers disguised beneath black plastic grilles.

A Cold-War vocabulary persisted. Korean airlines reported one of their planes had been shot down as it strayed into Soviet airspace. The US performed more nuclear tests in the Nevada desert. Multiple UFO sightings continued between Manchester and Sheffield.

Across this undercurrent of ongoing East-West tension, the announcer made no comment on the excellent

Darjeeling steaming towards the radio's bass and mid-range unit.

The Soviet Union and the United States feuded. Life must go on. In an outside world the only cloud in fine azure skies passed below the sun, and the only juggernaut in West Hampstead passed beneath the window.

Amongst it all a body lay awkwardly above the bedsheets, lank, motionless, and oblivious. An airless, fretful night had finally yielded to a deep, early morning slumber.

Soon there were merely whisps in the ultramarine sky, and the same juggernaut hurtled back beneath the window, having been swiftly relieved of its last Big Mac buns, the rumble vibrating an ill-fitting sash pair inside their wooden frames.

An envelope from NASA lay on the bedside table. Its top corner was covered in dull red American stamps and visibly postmarked:

**Houston, 1927.**

# CHAPTER 2

# 1983

## 1st September
## 16 minutes later, Peak District UK

The Dark Peak is higher, wilder and forms largely uninhabited moorland and gritstone escarpments across the northern Peak District.

Cha'3E raised his gaunt face with dark eyes skyward. An instinct, despite the encircling subterranean complex precluding any view of the exquisite day in full flow beyond.

His two *surface* years in '76 and '78 had seemed short, and half a decade later simple access to a sky of any weathers was one thing he missed. Swans were another.

Cha had convened his Central Directorate, with the meeting due to start at 3.00pm in an adjoining chasmic chamber. This gave ample opportunity to refine his projection figures. As the filtered water from the cooler-tank shot into his paper cup, he pushed a hand through his thick white hair and stroked the delicate gold braid that ran from shoulder to torso across his deep red gown. He was well versed. He knew to within a ten percent degree of accuracy the global billions that his two industry refinements would generate. He sat, unfolded his ultra-thin GlasSlate® phablet and three-dimensional images of those charts rippled over his palm. A news ticker scrolled the bottom few pixels, annoying him with stories from the outer world. *Surface Tension* as he facetiously referred to it.

Today he would lead the charge, having previously secured backing from key Directorate influencers. Beautiful new billions were already flowing in from two of their Progressionaries' endeavours, yet the Directorate's latest project required far more. This assembly should be no more than a rubber stamping.

Deep in the Dark Peak and deeper in his heart Cha knew he was ready. His meeting start time could be brought forward, but he preferred to check the room layout and ensure its technology had been correctly upgraded. This would guarantee his presentation reached peak performance.

He clicked his thumb and middle finger towards his companion and Zen followed him from the office.

Across the corridor he caught sight of Emm'4K striding towards him. Her white hooded gown occasionally revealing brilliant white boots that shone beneath. The gown's braiding depicted diamond motifs. They met each other's eyes and walked together along the silvered floor. He saw himself in those eyes, deeply reflective sea pebbles burnished by her intellect.

"Are we ready Cha?" she asked.

With Emm everything was possible.

"As we'll ever be, thanks to you."

"So have you decided which plan to present first?"

"Starbucks Emm, *Star… Bucks.*"

"*Starbucks*!" she mirrored and smiled in admiration. "Of course. How perfectly named is that! This is going to be so very interesting."

# CHAPTER 3

Wise words.

*'Cause you are gold*
*I'm glad that you're bound to return*
*Something I could have learned*
*You're indestructible*
*Always believe in*

The McDonald's juggernaut was long gone from north London, tearing past Scratchwood service station with diesel vapours dissipating into the hazy morning. The driver thumped his palm at the steering wheel timed to Spandau Ballet's *Gold* on Radio 1.

In West Hampstead an acrid smell of scorched bread strayed from the kitchen towards the bedsit living room. The sleeping body had woken slowly, stretched hard, scooped cold water from the tap onto its waxen face, and was now identifiable as Nelson Staff. The burnt aroma stemmed from two black triangles of charcoal smeared with unsatisfactorily melted butter, one held in Nelson's tight grip as he hunkered at the makeshift breakfast bar. He might define each three-sided cinder as toast were his thoughts to be canvassed, but no one would pry because Nelson currently lived alone, temporarily. Why he was in this situation is a gloomy story, and not this one[1].

A threadbare Heaven 17 T-shirt and cotton boxer

---

[1] Nelson was an only child born to aging parents with no plans to conceive. They stayed un-divorced and uncommunicative until he slipped away to university, and now have separate lives on the East and West coasts of England.

shorts protected Nelson's modesty. His light brown close-cropped hair resisted grooming and a suggestion of redness around his green-grey eyes set in a pallid complexion told the tale of a night before.

He contemplated scrambled eggs, a streaky bacon sandwich, or butter-fried mushrooms. His stomach weighed up the Guinness, pizza, Cabernet Sauvignon, Caramac, sponge cake, cheese, grapes and milk devoured until the early hours watching overdue VHS video rentals. The fridge door remained resolutely shut.

Cup in hand, Nelson slouched to his bedside table and retrieved the NASA envelope from beneath his Sony Walkman cassette player and a coffee-stained *Greetings from Cyprus* postcard.

The envelope encased a yellowing, typed memo clearly marked:

*Private and Confidential.*

As an only child growing up in Seventies suburbs with inattentive parents, Nelson devoted long days and evenings to the outdoors. He slipped into a love of nature and as an alternative to loneliness, his abundant natural surroundings provided plentiful hobbies and pursuits through his teenage years.

A chance encounter with Duke Kramer, his future best friend and fellow animal fanatic, occurred across a shrouded wasteland pond as they both explored ranges of spawn, tadpoles and frogs taking up seasonal residency. Pushing through the weeping willows and thick weed encircling its shallow edges, he observed a boy his age scooping a left hand into the warming waters, watching it drip away to catch the morning light.

Duke was also an only child. His mother left the family home on his second birthday, leaving him to be raised by his father Ernest Kramer as a single parent.

The two boys' companionship was instantaneous and long lasting.

Nelson eventually informed his parents he would study Geology at a northern redbrick university, borrowing his mother's Mini Clubman to drive up for Fresher's Week, and never returning it.

He struggled through to surprise himself with a 2:1 degree. Fearful of next steps and armed with the comforting splendour of a full grant encompassing his accommodation, Nelson extended to a Masters in Paleontology. He focused his thesis on the *Cambrian Explosion*: a time on Earth five-hundred and forty million years ago that seized Nelson's fascination with the unexplained and unparalleled emergence of vast varieties of lifeforms and intense evolution.

"It's a *massive* story Duke, probably the most significant part of all our evolution. And what's staggering is that no one really knows definitively why it happened! Just imagine cracking that mystery."

His friend always listened to his sermons without judgement. They remained in touch through occasional letters and snatched phonebooth calls from the common room. Duke developed his own interests further studying Biology in London. Through his limited but valuable contacts, Duke's father helped his son secure what they agreed was the ideal job for any young man: graduate intake to the Natural History Museum.

Suddenly one year later, Duke's father died of a brain aneurism without prior symptom or warning. Duke was shattered with grief. The adoration and respect between the two men had remained mutual and permanent. Having broken all ties with his mother, Duke retained no method of contacting her. He attended the funeral essentially as an orphan, supported by Nelson. In the coming years he searched fruitlessly for reason, but never for his mother.

The two young men bonded as twin foundlings, and Nelson maintained this close contact at the time his career path took a different turn towards authoring technology articles for Sunday supplements. As a Geology and Paleontology graduate, Nelson was an untrained journalist and blessed to land a Fleet Street role. This single job opportunity was based solely on an unhealthy passion for the Sinclair ZX81. An obsession that forged the posting of an eloquent, vehement letter to *Computing* magazine, extolling this home computer's superiority over the newest Commodore 64.

And now his present assignment was a million miles from their boyhood days of frogspawn, yet played to this technical peculiarity, by tasking Nelson to document the accelerating microcomputer industry. And probing Nelson's key weakness, his editor had deadlined a completed article submission by the following Monday.

Snap. Two months earlier Nelson's friend Duke disappeared overnight.

He sipped his cooling tea noisily and pinched the envelope between thumb and forefinger, reflecting on the vanishing. He mused as the kitchen radio relayed UB40's *Red, Red Wine*. Nelson preferred their masterpiece: *The Earth Dies Screaming*.

Instead of sharing a flat, which made short-term financial sense, the two young men chose to maintain their independence by living within one mile of each other, amongst the lower cost urban chic of West Hampstead.

Friday beers in the local pubs, Sunday nights in Pizza Express and weekday co-mingling amongst their respective work colleagues around Covent Garden or South Kensington, became the enjoyable routine.

Duke began to recover from his father's passing.

His search for reason had uncovered the latent conspiracy theorist within him. Currently obsessed by the surrounding Cold-War rhetoric, he was constantly fueling Nelson and anyone who would listen with his End-Of-World beliefs, always lightening his conclusions with the line: "So, you better get the next round in sharpish," followed by his trademark cackle laugh.

Duke became a sometimes awkward, loose-limbed, gangly soul with dark wiry hair, close cropped at the side and piled high on his head in the classic Eighties bouffant. His uniform consisted of lumberjack shirts, narrow-legged jeans rolled up above his Dr. Martens boots, and a long-coat inherited from his father that Duke faithfully wore well into each warm Spring.

In late June that year Duke abruptly turned more inward, the coat staying on indoors, and an uncharacteristic dark cloud of sincerity enveloped him.

"This one's real," he shared with Nelson more than once. "A bit like your unsolved Cambrian mystery."

"Sure thing Duke. Meanwhile, lighten up."

One grey June lunchtime, the day before he disappeared, Duke asked Nelson to meet him deep inside their local Swiss Cottage library. After trying light small-talk, Nelson dutifully followed his friend to the reference section. They approached a thick encyclopaedic tome on a corner shelf. Without a word Duke delicately separated the book out, its fusty cover sticking to its siblings. Experiencing a mild sense of the archeological, Nelson shrugged quizzically at Duke. Heaving it to a nearby desk and holding it vertical, Duke prised open the giant reference book, unable to resist the urge of blowing imaginary dust from its pages.

He turned a few more pages and lay it down flat on the desk, flicking the back of his hand across the page and finally holding both palms out to Nelson.

A section of the book approximately fifteen pages deep was neatly carved out of its middle. The simple rectangular hollow that remained appeared just four inches in width and ten inches in length.

Duke looked intently at Nelson, widened his eyes and nodded back to the book.

"Okay, nice scalpel work. So?" enquired Nelson.

Remaining silent, Duke reached into his long-coat pocket and extracted an envelope imprinted with a NASA logo. He dropped it squarely into the recess cut from the book. It slotted in seamlessly.

"I told you this one was real Nelson. Didn't I? I discovered this six days ago."

He eased the envelope back out of its nook and slid it slowly towards Nelson. The postmark was faint but readable as *Houston 1927*, imprinted across a row of ornate US postage stamps depicting the Liberty Bell 150th Anniversary.

"When I found it, the letter was still sealed, as if it were waiting all the intervening fifty-six years for the right person to discover it."

"NASA? Is this a test Duke? Or a prank?"

Nelson looked carefully around to check for eyes or cameras peering at him through the bookcases. He picked up the envelope and weighed it delicately in his hand, contemplating where all of this was heading.

"Open it," commanded Duke.

Nelson dived in and read its contents. They made his eyes pop.

That was the last time he had seen his closest friend.

The day was already unseasonably hot for September and the sun beat through Nelson's small south-facing window. He took the letter from his bedside table and returned with it to the kitchen, finishing his Tropicana orange juice and reaching for the last Kellogg's Frosties. The Hevean 17 T-shirt stuck to his back from overnight sweat, and he pulled at the back collar to loosen its grip.

Duke had asked him to keep the letter safe, then he quickly left the library before Nelson, leaving his friend no time to process their previous ten minutes.

As the missing days wore on, Nelson tried visiting Duke's flat but found it dark and empty. He could no longer call Duke's parents, so he telephoned his office and a HR representative announced Duke had quit with no notice by leaving a ten-word message on their answering machine. Nelson then endured pointless single meals in their favourite Pizza Express on Sunday evenings, having to finish his Fiorentina in solitude.

Then, out of the blue, he received a postcard from Cyprus, immediately recognising Duke's handwriting. Briefly extolling the virtues of quitting everything for the Cypriot lifestyle, it was signed off:

"See you one day buddy."

Duke had never called Nelson *buddy* in his life.

Inside that yellowing envelope was a formally typed memo, fading with age and displaying an embossed heading across a NASA logo.

An over-excited competition winner begged the radio DJ to play *Poison Arrow* by ABC, and with his T-shirt sealing itself to his back once more, Nelson scraped the final sugary flakes from his bowl. Duke had been an ABC superfan. No, Duke *is* an ABC superfan.

The National Aeronautics and Space Administration of the United States of America was writing to a local scientist enchantingly named Oswald Grimaldi, M.Phil, D.Sc. Addressed to Compayne Gardens, West Hampstead, London NW6, this wonderful coincidence mildly excited Nelson since he rented just a few roads away. NASA thanked the doctor profusely for his commentary on the redesigned propulsion rockets, and the calculations associating these to the projected Moon landings.

*If I were to say to you,*
*"Can you keep a secret?"*
*Would you know just what to do?*
*Or where to keep it?*

NASA had been interested in reconnecting with Doctor Grimaldi at his earliest convenience, bizarrely referring to him multiple times as *Dog'2G*. To stress the private nature of the memo, its sender included an elaborate *Top-Secret* stamp.

Yet the most extraordinary feature was clearly typed twice on the letter heading, and again beneath the scrawled signature of a Mr J. Schuger, *Shu'6J,* Chief Scientific Officer, NASA Headquarters.

The DJ followed on with David Bowie's *Changes* as Nelson cleaned out his breakfast bowl, rinsing it briskly under the cold tap. Duke would have been singing out loud.

*Time may change me*
*But I can't trace time*

Nelson stared at the letter again.
The date that appeared typed neatly twice was:

**20th September 1927**

1927!

Forty-two years before the first human stepped on the Moon.

"It's a mistake," said Nelson to the oven, "...or a

bad typist. Or a fake"

Unsurprisingly no response was forthcoming from any kitchen appliance.

"Okay, it simply has to be a mistake. Duke must have fallen for it as well. God, I miss that guy."

He sighed very deeply, resting his chin on his thumb and biting the softer flesh on his lower forefinger.

"But two mistakes," he said through gritted teeth. "Or the same mistake, twice. And now… he's disappeared!"

He grabbed a corner of the letter and fanned it loosely backwards and forwards as he stared beyond his kitchen's large window frame. The peaceful road outside was littered with Peugeots, Ford Orions and Austin Maestros, mostly annoying commuters clogging the road by taking benefit of the free parking and nearby tube station.

He could ignore it: name, date, address and collectible stamps. Drop it in the bin with his empty Frosties carton and move on. But where was his best friend? Somehow leaving his London life right now for Cyprus was a poor match for Duke's profile, and this letter could be the link to uncover what really happened to him. Ignoring it all instinctively struck him as misguided and ran against all Nelson's inclinations.

He wanted his friend back, and the address on the letter was local. This presented Nelson with an exciting and obvious alternative approach. He would return the letter to its original owner. If he still existed. A pang of self-doubt inevitably set it.

*Where would that get me?* Duke had asked him to keep it safe. He thought of them crying with laughter as they stumbled home after gatecrashing London's only karaoke bar and bemusing Japanese expats with their tuneless rendition of *Club Tropicana*. Duke's belly-cackle still rang in his ears. Maybe this course of action was the nearest thing to safety and could get him closer to Duke.

Dropping the drunken recollections, Nelson visualised the prospect of meeting an old Dr. Grimaldi and proffering him the return of his long-lost letter.

"So... how is this going to proceed?" asked Nelson. "And how does it end?"

The annoying ritual of talking to himself just after waking proved disturbing to anyone around him. A subconscious habit borne of only child syndrome and living with a speechless gas appliance.

If there were the remotest chance of meeting a scientist involved in the Moon landings, Nelson knew he should leap at the prospect.

The duo of Bowie hits ended with *Heroes*.

*We can beat them, for ever and ever*
*Oh we can be Heroes, just for one day*

He took his cue.

The shine was already dimming on Nelson's speculative journalistic career and his current deadlines were slipping to a fading horizon. He had been truly excited and flattered to be offered the job and accepted it in a heartbeat without negotiation. He enjoyed words and wished to write for a career but didn't want to be judged. Anything fictional or creative exposed him to that consequence, whereas short, factual articles on a familiar and comfortable subject matter seemed the obvious compromise. It was a miscalculation and surprisingly quickly descended to the mundane.

So where did he fit?

Had Duke seemingly quit his perfect job at the Natural History Museum overnight and left the UK to rediscover himself in Cyprus? If he had, maybe that was his answer, and Nelson often pondered if there existed his own equivalent.

The only fact that Nelson was sure about himself, was he really did not like hard work. And he really missed Duke.

A walk would clear his head and lighten the mood. And if he were unsuccessful in finding Doctor Grimaldi, he could always treat himself to lunch at the new McDonalds in Swiss Cottage[2].

"…Let's *go!*"

Nelson departed the tiny flat immediately and impulsively. Twelve seconds later he was lucky to walk back through the gently closing door to wash, shave and put on the rest of his clothes.

---

[2] In the midst's of time, London gentry installed a toll gate, complete with keeper's cottage, on the main road leading from the City to the expanding village of Finchley. In 1806, as beer consumption began to generate far greater income than passing stagecoach tariffs, the gate was demolished and replaced by a tavern, constructed to mimic Swiss chalets of the era. The imbibing cognoscente flocked in, and the area became known by the portmanteau *Swiss Cottage*, partly from Londoners' imaginative apathy, and partly from their fondness towards misleading foreign visitors.

# CHAPTER 4

No business meeting should last more than thirty minutes.

In a shadowy room two hundred feet beneath the Dark Peak, Cha finished his presentation and replaced the laser pointer.

The AI in the room lighting detected this sequence and gently faded up the brightness whilst rolling the screen microfabric back into its ceiling recess.

Cha stood below the intricately carved owl on the wooden panel wall and, feeling his blood pressure and heart rate sink back, he silently directed a thin smile at his colleagues convened around the conference table and the video conference displays hanging to his left. Zen lay in the corner.

It had gone well, and he started to detect slight but appreciative nods ripple round the room and across the world.

Dex'2O was present and first to speak.

"Love it Cha. Starbucks. What a perfect choice. Such an appropriate name! And it's very different, which is great for our diversity, and hence protects the Directorate."

"Thank you Dex, I'm glad you liked it. It is ready to go and Emm estimates just two Progressionaries on the *surface* to begin with, so minimal intervention. It will put us in a great position for *The Quit*."

"Yes, and for me, that's the best bit. We're leaving those mistakes to the past. And one of our finest men in software... *Bill*... did I get his new name right..."

"Yes."

"...good, Bill is in Seattle already and firing on all cylinders with his own genius software venture. So will he be briefed?"

"Of course."

"Great. Well, it gets my approval Cha."

"Excellent. That's good to hear Dex. If we can get it passed swiftly by the board, it should hopefully tie in nicely with our next steps relating to the Duke Kramer subject."

"Have we heard anything further there?"

"Not yet, but we were never expecting to. The clear message from them was to wait."

"Understood Cha."

Dex paused to narrow his eyes and lower his voice, confirming his sincerity.

"Given the radical nature of your first plan, can I ask what you are proposing to follow-up with as the second global intervention?"

"Sorry, do you mind waiting until the weekend Dex, just as we'd planned." Cha flashed a warm smile across all those both present in the room and remote. "Emm and I are finalizing the numbers on that particular coup."

"As you wish," affirmed Dex.

"Thank you. Speaking of which... Emm, let's crack on."

He held a hand out towards the door and his female colleague took her cue, rising to join him and leave the room. As she passed, she brushed a hand over his shoulder. He went to exit, paused and turned back towards the room and its screens.

"I can assure you all, our second intervention is also going to be just as radical, just as big."

# CHAPTER 5

West Hampstead is a district that was well served by Luftwaffe efficiency during the early 1940s.

The war era led to numerous North London bombsites, reconstruction, and pockets of incongruous, often brutalist 1950s to 60s apartment blocks and public buildings, surrounded by row upon row of the original Edwardian four-storey houses. Each of these impressive single homes has long since been converted to multiple residential flats. A ground floor resident played Mozart's Piano Concerto 21 with their sash window cracked open. Nelson's father had played such pieces at the times of ceasefire between him and Nelson's mother.

Dressed in Adidas monochrome trainers, slim jeans and a light Harrington jacket, Nelson found himself standing outside one of these featureless blocks, Grimaldi's letter in-hand. A small outdoor lift beckoned. He stepped in, smelling the stale musk, cabbage and old steel, then pressed the button for the second floor. The cage wobbled as he moved to its middle. The doors lumbered to a close and Nelson checked his appearance in a scratched chrome mirror fixed to the lift wall. He smirked at the scrawled graffiti:

*#Stare at the numbers, shuffle your feet >>>*
*and DON'T TALK!*

Then scoffing, as below this he read:

*Thatcher Iron Lady? Rust In Peace.*

Gears ground into motion and the machine ascended resentfully upwards. The gates opened unexpectedly one floor short. The small red button displaying 2 remained lit and he pressed it again. Twice. Surrendering the argument, he walked out and took the stairs, emerging to a balcony with a left side railed over a sunless concrete courtyard. To the right were six high-gloss navy blue doors, the first one having an elderly man buckled over terracotta plant pots clustered around his *Welcome* mat. Levelling his watering can he straightened to observe Nelson as he squeezed past in an awkward tight manouevre. Nelson reflexively smiled, yet the old man remained stone-faced. Nelson continued to the balcony's end and his target door that caught a final blade of sunlight. He knocked firmly. There was no immediate answer.

Knocking again louder, he felt the bruising on his knuckles, yet he could faintly hear running water. He tensed his arm back fully to try thumping with his fist.

"There's a bloody doorbell!" hollered plant-pot man.

"Oh, thank you."

Finding the low mounted bell, Nelson rang it, causing a loud vibrating blast within.

The running water stopped and there came a sound of bare feet on carpet. The door opened, remaining on the chain. An impressive young woman with deep brown eyes and wonderful dark brows peered out. Her wet brunette hair framed an olive-skinned face with a fringe, and was cut to the nape of her neck. Droplets fell to her shoulders and Nelson observed she was wrapped in a bath towel.

"*Yes*!" she snapped.

"Hello," said Nelson, "Doctor Grimaldi?"

"*Who*?"

"Doctor Oswald Grimaldi. I have a letter for you."

Her eyes narrowed.

"Do I *look*... like an Oswald."

In mild alarm at his behaviour, Nelson held aloft the NASA letterhead. The woman's expression exhibited clear annoyance and disinterest.

"There is no one of that name here, never heard of them," she scorned.

Eyes widened, Nelson gaped at the door number and back at the letter, along the balcony, and back at the bath towel.

"But it's not a mistake, it is this address," he pleaded. Without really knowing why added, "Can I come in to talk?"

"*Certainly not*! Go away." The door was crashed shut.

"It's not what you think," Nelson pined pathetically, and then more softly, "Do you know where my friend Duke is?"

Footsteps were behind him as plant-pot man approached, eyeing the scene gravely.

"Have you been pestering Miss Reagan?"

"No, no. Of course not. I seem to have the wrong place. Well, I seem to have the right place but the wrong person. Not that there is anything wrong with her, no. She's, well she's lovely. She's just completely... *wrong*."

"Who were you looking for?"

"Doctor Grimaldi."

"Doctor..."

"Doctor Grimaldi. I have a letter here that my friend Duke found, and now he has disappeared. And so, it seems, Doctor Grimaldi has as well. It's this address... Oh, you know what, it doesn't matter."

The old man watched Nelson a few moments as he trudged to the lift door, waiting fruitlessly for its arrival.

"It doesn't come to the second floor. Hasn't done for years, which keeps us all fit, so we don't complain. Anyway... he's no longer with us."

"...*Sorry*?" questioned Nelson.

"Doctor Grimaldi, he's gone."

"You knew him!"

The old man walked up to his blue front door.

"Yes, I remember the old git… Eastern European I think, and strangely secretive. You're right, he did live where Miss Reagan is now… with his wife."

"He was married?"

"As far as I knew. But she left him and that seemed to hit him very hard."

"I have a letter of his," offered Nelson, "but I don't suppose he'll want to be reading it now."

"No. I should think his eyesight's failed him completely after ten or more years underground."

"He works on the Tube?" asked Nelson.

"No. I mean he's dead! Buried."

"I see, of course. But… ten years ago?"

"At least. It was back in the very early Seventies I'd say."

"Hmm. Just after the moon landing."

"If you say so, young man."

"Sorry, I digress. So, did you say he was secretive? Any clue about what he was hiding?"

The old man was pleased to be talking. The past held clear fond memories, and step-by-step each of his children ceased to ask about it. Someone, anyone, stopping to genuinely listen, was very welcome.

"I got *very* close once. He was hopeless at DIY and back in the Sixties he would ask me in… to do odd jobs for him, always clearing down before I arrived. Boxes with locks, large tied paper rolls, drawing tools neatly stacked. And huge cigar butts stubbed in his ashtray, smoke still rising. And boom, he did his back in."

A pause ensued, perhaps as if the connection was so obvious. Nelson gave in unable to grasp it.

"And so?"

"Well, he asked me to pick up his post from our letter boxes downstairs. As his back worsened, he gave me keys to let myself in. One day he's fast asleep in the living room with a half empty bottle of Jameson. He always said it was to help the pain."

He took a step closer to Nelson and lowered his voice conspiratorially.

"So, I put his post gently down and as I tiptoed out, I went past his study... and the temptation was too huge."

"Go on," encouraged Nelson, getting the hang of his cues.

"One of his paper scrolls was fully opened and pinned down by a Marmite jar and bottle of Glenfiddich. Amazing what sticks in the mind."

"Of course."

"So, I spent a few minutes staring at this... very detailed diagram. And suddenly, I knew he was standing behind me."

"Ouch. What happened?"

"I stood my ground and asked if I'd found what he'd been working on. He stared at me clear eyed and said, in that Eastern European accent: *No, no, my friend, eeet's thee oldest treek in thee boook. I leave old diagram's een case someone snoop around thee flat."*

"Did you believe him?"

"I had no choice. He told me to get out."

"*That was it*?" barked an unsated Nelson. Ashamed of his outburst he let his head sag down to gaze back at the letter.

"Afraid so. And that's all I have really. Apart from..."

"Apart from...?"

"Well, bearing in mind this was early Sixties before all that moon landing stuff you just mentioned."

"Go on."

"There was a weird title on that giant sheet of paper. I can still remember it."

The stare came up from the NASA envelope and direct into the old man's eyes.

"What was on it?"

"The title said, *International Space Station*. Clear as day. For heaven's sake, what the hell is one of those?"

They shrugged in unison through a silence.

"That was a long time ago. Anyway young man, it's going to be a hot day and my begonias are thirsty."

He tipped the spout of his can and gently poured glistening drops of water onto their dry soil.

# CHAPTER 6

## Out Of Time

Shedding emotional tears releases useful oxytocin and endorphin hormones.

"Why have I been abducted?" mewled Duke.

The cell presented as a dark perfect cube, dimly lit from warm yellow pinpoints of light embedded in each of its eight corners.

A chill ran across his shoulders and neck as once more the beaked face appeared shaded behind a semi-translucent wall. The sinister light-play gave his captor the semblance of a hugely contorted bantam chicken. Duke squeezed his eyes together for a few seconds and reopened them. He calmed his breathing. His head felt warm, as if a heat was resonating from the high-backed chair supporting his neck. A trickle of sweat ran down his spine and soaked into his lumberjack shirt.

The creature in front of him was real, not the horror of Halloween fancy-dress. The eyes moved perfectly in its chicken-like skull and the domed tongue occasionally glimpsed within its mustard-yellow beak was no artifice. Yet his rational mind told Duke it could not be a real chicken because it was the same height as him.

And it talked.

"I am just planning to borrow you."

"Burrow me! Well, you can just f…"

"I am not abducting you, I am borrowing you."

"Burrowing me?" challenged Duke.

"No, I said borrowing you."

"Well it sounds like you are saying…"

"One second," spoke the chicken-thing, and ran a talon of its hand-sized claw down the side of its neck to a half-way point and then depressed and twisted a half-turn deep into its scaly feathers. There was the faintest of clicks and its eyes grimaced.

"Burrow... borrow, borrow. Is that better?" it asked.

Duke stared incredulous through the thin light at the apparition separated by thick glass. To gain inner strength he recalled his father's memory. Straining to sit upright, his hands turned to fists as they pulled against the wrist restraints. A silence lingered.

"I need you for a little while. We *all* need you," said the creature. "And then you'll forget about it."

# CHAPTER 7

Elders can carry compelling stories should you take a moment to ask, and then two moments to listen.

Ignoring the lifts with their graffiti Nelson took the stairs out of the apartment block. The jarring stomp of a slow climb downwards did nothing to clear his mind. Staring at crisscrossed pavement slabs he chewed a bottom lip and cut across the road absorbed in thought. Whoosh. A rare London cyclist almost struck him.

"Same to you," called Nelson, hurling back the insult.

A late summer dragonfly hovered from a garden into view, the sun glimmered its crystal wings. Assuredly, life in its myriad forms went on. *Am I fooling myself? Is this real or do I just want it to be? If work started on moon-landing propellants in the late 1920s, why take nearly fifty years to become reality? And hell, what in God's name is an International Space Station?* Nelson found Grimaldi's handiwork perplexing. *Is there any connection with Duke's disappearance, because fake or not, why hide anything by choosing the 1960's monolith of Swiss Cottage Central Library to conceal your records?* Nelson yearned to call his closest ally and talk all this through.

"Duke, where are you?"

Approaching Finchley Road, he reached into his jeans pocket and pulled out a crumpled one-pound note, venturing to catch his default cherry-red 13 bus towards the West End. Walks in Soho relaxed him and may wrest his heavy mind from missed deadlines, bogus memos and absent friends.

The herd of beasts dutifully arrived, decked in scarlet livery and flaunting advertisements for the latest summer release Bond film, *Octopussy*. Yet each London Transport conductor refused to play ball. Gripping the rear pole to bar entry to its open platform, they claimed to be too full, even as disgorging passengers flocked out at his chosen stop.

*No room. Up yours. Ding ding.*

Nelson abandoned the West End initiative, and instinctively turned back towards to his library, choosing to revisit the scene where it all started with Duke. This building was chaotic, crammed with every north Londoner who had missed their bus.

Nelson slipped in through its heavy doors to an air thick with silence and a tang of maturing books, making his way back to the reference section and the same encyclopaedia his collusive friend had leafed through whilst narrating the discovery of NASA's letter.

He opened the book to the same page.

"Nothing," he sighed despondently. The incision was there, yet the recess stayed empty. The severe hush was broken by a jeer coming across the table.

"You think you've got problems," said an unemployed bus driver, sneering at Nelson since the point he entered the room.

Nelson ignored the remark staying intent on his encyclopaedia, finally taking a pincer grip to shake it by the corner, in the futile hope a microdot film might fall to the floor and transport him reeling into a world of intrigue, espionage and those *Octopussy* Bond girls. His hands perspired and thumb muscles cramped. Their grasp slipped, dropping the encyclopaedia[3] to a resounding clunk.

---

[3] Nothing can be more expensive than a missed opportunity. A microdot did fall away, yet went unnoticed by Nelson and hence lost forever. Luckily, he would get a second chance.

"*Pah*!" spat the bus driver. "...and screw the GLC." A decade ago he scorned drunkards when they staggered into his realm, but as he joined their ranks the self-awareness dimmed and his belligerence darkened. Even the union could not overturn his demise. Nelson sensed the man's mood and nip, snubbing both to lean over and retrieve his book from the floor. As he did the pages flicked open to reveal a chapter headed *Early Computing*.

He smoothed the sheets recounting these first historic years: the announcement of *point-contact transistors*; subsequent *junction transistors;* and referencing the world's oldest working computer in Harwell. Coincidentally all useful details for his current assignment, yet Nelson sat back aghast. Scrawled across this mundane chronicle in viscous red ink were the words:

*LIES! DAMNED LIES!*

From his prior journalistic research Nelson broadly knew the coverage to be accurate and he was bewildered by the blatant anger in the graffiti, so vehemently opposing these established facts.

A sudden instinct prompted him to take out his letter and reexamine the signature.

Grimaldi signed himself *Dr. O. Grimaldi*. Though no graphologist, Nelson could see a distinctive curl on this D in *Dr.* matched the same scrawling letters in *DAMNED*.

He leafed across the encyclopaedia's inside front cover, noting this edition had been reprinted in 1970. *That was just before Grimaldi's death.* Nelson pondered this meaning. *So had Duke witnessed this? If he had, why hadn't he shown it to me at the same time he unveiled the letter? Should I care?*

The bus driver continued his glower. *Go away!* Nelson made an angled turn in his chair, putting a frosty breach between himself and this warmonger.

He flicked back briskly through the book, yet it gave no more clues. He went to replace it and noticed the copies of Sports Illustrated, swimwear edition. A rare find for a library, this was perfect and just the distraction he needed. A short while later he stood awkwardly to leave.

He closed the thin glass doors of the reference section behind him, to the sound of a large, flatulent chiming raspberry blown from the jobless bus driver's lips.

Nelson froze as two older women passing through *Photography & Art* eyeballed him in reprimand. Blushing profusely, he gaped at the floor head down, and rushed awkwardly to leave. What a mistake and an embarrassment. Time to move on.

As he roamed the outside his deliberations redoubled their pace. He sat for reflection at a lone bench near the intersection with Fitzjohn's Avenue, raising his eyes skyward. With the Modernist icon of the Swiss Cottage Odeon cinema looming to his left, and his back to the Hampstead Theatre, Nelson scratched the base of his close-cropped head with stubby fingertips.

*Come on, am I being fooled, or being stupid? What is going on here? Duke you crazy blagger, what have you uncovered? So, NASA, the UK government, the US government… are they in on it? Can I get back to see the girl in the towel? Is she in on it? I hope so. This is exciting, but is it real?* Nelson's conscience demanded more effort be made to locate his lost friend in the ev[4]ent he was in trouble, yet was struggling where to start. *I will telephone NASA.*

*Call NASA!*

*Come on, yes! Make a trunk call to NASA, in*

---

44

*America. Present the name Grimaldi alongside that of Apollo 11, toy with the notion of forty-year delays and add a few dramatic pauses. And does it stand a chance?*

Nelson fast-tracked back to his apartment, unaware of his surroundings and all thoughts on diagonal paths.

*How do you begin to call NASA?*

British Telecom's International Operator came to mind. Nelson put his finger in the phone dial, rotating it to begin this new endeavour.

*Where is Cape Kennedy, or is it Canaveral? Is NASA still located there because it's always Houston having the problem?*

His childhood head danced with Sixties and Seventies rockets, astronauts and missions. Bleakly, like many of his generation, these early Eighties Space Shuttle launches were passing him by. An awareness they primarily landed in the Californian desert was the peak of his familiarity, and their current news coverage was thin.

Forty-five minutes later Nelson stressfully tightened the curling cable connecting his phone handset to its base. After their own twenty minutes of fruitless searching, BT had eagerly passed him on. With nothing but the purr of transferring calls over ticks and pops of international static in his ears, Nelson switched on the radio for distraction. It played last year's *I Could Be Happy* by Altered Images.

*All of these things I do*
*All of these things I do*
*To get away from you*

He was now speaking to a third regional switchboard supervisor somewhere in the United States.

"Are you still there?" everyone asked.

"Barely," Nelson had replied.

"We're still trying."

"Yes, you are."

And then unexpectedly, "Will the Public Relations department be sufficient?"

"Yes! Yes please."

"Connecting you. Have a nice day."

After ten purrs the line was opened. As he heard a female voice, Nelson's white knuckles gripped the handset tightly and its cable was near breaking point.

"Hello," said the voice in a strong Texan drawl. "This is NASA, may I help you?"

Nelson was momentarily stunned. The answer came so calmly, defining he was through to NASA.

"Certainly…" he snapped recomposing himself, clearing his throat and attempting a charming English accent.

"… certainly you can my dear. Could you kindly tell me if you have a J. Schuger working there as Chief Scientific Officer?" Nelson checked again the signature on his recovered letter.

"J. Schuger you say, one second…"

The day had stayed clear beyond Nelson's window. The kitchen tap leaked a single drip every few seconds. It was becoming another familiar lost day towards his looming deadline. He scratched the nape of his neck with a fingernail.

"…I'm sorry, but our CSO is not called Schuger. Who wants to know?"

"This is Nelson Staff speaking. Well, could you please tell..."

"Oh, hi Nelson. My name is Betty Ann Glaser. You've got a gorgeous accent Nelson."

"So have you," Nelson lied. "Now could you..."

"Should I call you Lord Nelson? We don't get many calls from England. I get excited when we do. I think England is a beautiful country. I am a real Ang-lo-phile." This last word being severely drawn out. "And I adore Stratford-Upon-Avion."

"Avon."

"I beg your pardon."

"Avon. It's Stratford-Upon-*Avon*."

"Oh yeah. Avon. Ding dong," giggled Betty Ann, "Stratford-Upon-Avon."

"Indeed. Could you..."

"And Convent Garden was the most delightful..."

"No, that's *Covent* Garden. There are no nuns in it." said Nelson.

"Nuneaton? Oh yeah, I've heard of that. Gateway to the South."

"No, that's Balham."

"Sorry?"

*All of these things I do*
*All of these things I do*
*To get away from you*
*Get away*
*Runaway*
*Far away*
*How do I?*

"Look, it doesn't matter. All I want to know..."

"You English are so quaint Lord Nelson. Would you like a pen pal?"

"What? No!"

"Why not Nelson?"

"Look Betty Ann, I had one once in Tibet who couldn't write."

He lied again. He needed to stop her. The call was costing him a fortune, and this desolate conversation...

"You had a pen pal who couldn't write?" she drawled, "That must have been a one-sided conversation?"

Nelson was sinking deeper.

"Look, will you please tell me where I can contact Mr. Schuger."

"Just a minute Nelson."

Another pause. By now the mid-afternoon September light was pouring in a warm glow to the room. Nelson's stomach purled and murmured whilst his mouth tasted of zinc, reminding him he never netted that Big Mac.

"*Schuger* you said? I'm sorry but I am not at liberty to divulge that information," replied Betty Ann, abruptly adopting a bureaucratic position.

"I see. Then please could you put me through to someone who is!"

"I can Nelson. But only if we swap addresses."

"Look, no…"

"Nelson…"

He exhaled heavily, then gave up his address, without the strength to invent a falsehood.

"Okay, West Hampstead…" repeated Betty Ann, "So, if your request is for Schuger, I will put you through to Mr. Franks. He's the boss most of the time. Don't forget to write dear Lord."

Taking the phone from his hot ear, Nelson rubbed it as relief. Inwardly he began doubting the struggle, questioning what he was trying to achieve, and if Duke would have done the same for him.

The latter helped, and as he pressed firmly forward, a silence remained at the transatlantic end of his phone, save the occasionally crackle of analogue static. Then a voice.

"Hello, Mr. Staff is it?"

"Yes."

"Good, I hope I've got that right. This is Mr. Franks, current Head of Corporate Affairs here at NASA. Now, what is it we can do for you?"

"Well," began Nelson, "I would like to know if you have, or ever had, a Mr. J. Schuger working as your Chief Scientific Officer?"

There was a long pause, too long. Clicks, pops,

and static hisses filled the void.

"Er, *Schuger*... you knew Mr. Schuger, did you?" came the careful reply.

"Then he did work for NASA?"

"...no, I didn't say..."

"And he's dead now? Or did he leave? Or is he missing?"

Nelson heard the mouthpiece of Mr. Frank's telephone being covered followed by muted instructions.

If he had doubt before, he was now confident that something strange was going on.

"Yes, I'm afraid he's dead now," came the final answer, "You knew him, did you?"

"Not really, but I have a letter here of his... to Doctor Oscar Grimaldi."

"Oh... oh, really? Staff you said?"

"No, Grimaldi."

"No, I mean that you said your name was Staff."

"Yes."

Nelson felt his left grip tighten further on the handset. His right hand had stretched the attached flex so taught beyond the phone's cradle, its curl had disappeared. His heels pushed into the floor and his thighs tightened.

"And your address?"

Teeth grinding, Nelson grimaced.

"Your secretary has all the details, unfortunately."

A cold tremor iced down his spine as Nelson froze at the end of an exhale. He had given his real address! What on God's Earth did he think he was doing? Now it was too late to stop himself.

"Why was the Apollo 11 moon landing forty years late?" demanded Nelson.

There was a cough and dull click via satellite. The distinctive scraping chord of a phone being passed over made clear the agitation at the tail end of the line. A second later another mouth spoke. This was a low guttural voice with a Deep South accent, unlike the soft West Coast lilt of Mr. Franks. It said simply:

"Thank you, Mr. Nelson Staff. We'll be in touch."

*Click, purr.*

# CHAPTER 8

Rest is good for the soul.

Zen slept as Cha took his seat in a fine leather swivel chair and unfolded his GlasSlate® phablet. One half of his transparent screen instantly clouded to display the remaining agenda of their meeting. The live news ticker scrolled the latest UFO sightings in the local area. Although not overly concerned, it was continued coverage they needed to minimize. The timeline for *The Quit* remained on schedule.

A huge, frosted door to the meeting room opened abruptly and two tall figures in grey robes rushed in.

"The room is in use!" yelled Cha.

"Our apologies 3E, but it is urgent," stuttered the slightly taller, paler of the two.

"What is it?"

"There has been a breach."

"From where?"

"The *surface*."

"I assumed that! Exactly where on the *surface*?"

"This country sir, down south. London," he then took a deep breath, "NW6 3DZ."

"West Hampstead!"

"I'm afraid so."

"*No*!" He slammed the conference table. "The same area as the Duke Kramer subject!"

"That is correct sir."

"What happened this time?"

"He called NASA… and got through."

"*What*?"

Cha's normally mild-mannered expression darkened severely, with his eyes displaying rare sinister tones.

"Unacceptable. This must be the last of it. Two

breaches in as many months. You…" he indicated to the slightly shorter one in grey robes, "…get me 6M on the vidcon."

"Yes 3E, sir."

This grey-robed figure turned to leave the room. The other remained stood to attention.

Cha snapped at him.

"And you… keep talking. I want to know all about who *he* is. I'm going to finish it personally this time."

# CHAPTER 9

A long hot summer can pass you by.

Having served the day well, the late evening sun was setting low beyond the north-west London horizon. Deep sky greys, purples and reds waltzed together behind a thin sliver of cloud made black by contrasting shadow. The streetlamps switched on to don their yellow radiance over chewing-gum strewn pavements.

Following his call Nelson was elated. Alone in his tiny flat he beamed, pursed his lips and nodded. His chest puffed, and he caught sight of his distorted face in the Habitat wall mirror. He could not recall any artist capturing this degree of smugness within a portrait.

He had ruffled NASA's feathers.

The radio was barely audible as a backdrop. John Peel played *Rewards* by The Teardrop Explodes.

*All wrapped up the same*
*All wrapped up the same*
*Silence has it*
*Arrogance has it*
*I can have it ooh*
*Until I learn to accept my reward*

Collapsing into a beaten fabric armchair and gripping the threadbare arms, Nelson's thoughts drifted to NASA and his boyhood awe of this organisation. 2:56 a.m. GMT on the 21st July 1969: Neil Armstrong became the first in humanity to set foot on the Moon.

In an all too infrequent act of parental care, his mother recognised the passion in her son, and presented Nelson with a beautifully detailed pop-up book cataloging the moon landing mission. Setting a rare alarm, a very young Nelson snook himself into the empty living room that warm July night and switched the TV to fuzzy images in black and white. With the volume on low, he remembered vividly Armstrong's celebrated words stepping out of the lunar landing module to make the first footprint in The Sea of Tranquility: *"One small step for man, one giant leap for mankind."*

Even at that tender age and no parent present, Nelson had gaped reverently at Armstrong on the screen and thought:

*I bet he feels great.*

His pop-up book revealed the Americans laid out an estimated twenty-five billion dollars in 1960's money to get Armstrong, Aldrin and Collins to the Moon. Nelson was satisfied his one telephone call had achieved a similar feeling of self-satisfaction, for far less expense.

He kneaded his neck muscle with one hand.

Tension. Suddenly the cold tremor took another sucker punch. Self-doubt flooded back in.

*What the hell am I doing! Seriously. Have I any idea who or what I am dealing with? Are these same people responsible for Duke's disappearance? Am I so bored with my current life that I have become a thrill seeker? And why did I give my real address to Betty Ann? Stupid!*

As the dusk melted to night, Nelson distracted himself, switching on the solitary table lamp and rummaging through his sparse fridge in search of an elusive block of opened cheddar. He settled on a yoghurt two days beyond its sell-by date, accepting this was both safe and inescapable.

Standing at the living room window, Nelson contemplated his closest friend and the growing conviction that Duke was not in Cyprus.

He looked up into the night sky. London offered an abundance of light pollution, yet with the moon tucked away and a solitary low bulb from his living room as a backdrop, Nelson could faintly make out a few stars in the cosmos.

Even as a sixteen-year-old, Albert Einstein had conducted a thought experiment where he chased a beam of light across the universe. Nelson contemplated this journey through its vastness and speculated whether the few bright points he could make out were in fact stars, planets, or other galaxy clusters.

He glanced down at the road below flooded yellow by the sodium-vapour streetlamps and picked at his yoghurt carton with a teaspoon. Between mouthfuls of Waitrose peach melba Nelson's lips steadily pursed again back into smugness. He caught his reflection in the glass, and this restored artistic portrait rewarmed his mood. Finally, he smiled at this fresh image of self-satisfaction.

At this point he noticed a shadowy figure weaving between the streetlights, carrying a rucksack and long lens SLR camera. Slowly and deliberately, the figure turned to point the camera toward him.

Nelson flinched as a powerful flash illuminated his face and the living room wall behind him.

"Funny," he consoled himself, "perhaps it's an artist."

He was wrong.

# CHAPTER 10

# 1983

## 1st September
## 11:45am CST, Houston TX

As they say in Texas, this was not his first rodeo.

Tan'6M sat silently in a Plymouth Turismo at the Johnson Space Center. He took the precaution of parking in a far corner bay, reversing tight to the manicured Texan elbowbush hedgerow. No colleague could approach him without being seen via his windscreen, rear view or wing mirrors. Though it was a very warm Texan day his windows remained closed, the engine running, and air conditioning on low.

Tan switched off his Sonny Rollins cassette tape and let the jazz melodies dissipate into the air. He opened his leather briefcase, sifting through his papers, Filofax, partially melted Summit bar, and printed agendas forming the rest of his day. He found the concealed catch that released its secret compartment. It slid snugly towards him, and he took out the GlasSlate® mobile phone, unfolding its slim crystal plates to tap the vidcon icon.

The teleconference had already started, and he clicked the *Join* button. The only face to appear was the pale one of Cha'3E, who Tan greeted in his usual guttural voice with its southern drawl.

"Hello Cha, good to see you again. How's England?"

Silence.

"You're on mute, buddy."

*Bip.*

"*...ing hell*! I'm gonna need a T-shirt made for me with that printed on it. Can you hear me now?"

"Sure."

"How are you, Tan?"

"I'm good thanks Cha. I hear *The Quit* is progressing well?"

"Yes. The funding plans are falling into place. And we got the big reply from our new friends. So, we're all on schedule... except for this potential blip."

"How much do y'all know already, Cha?"

"Just a few basics Tan. Go from the top."

"Okay. His call came through first thing this morning, our time. Since the last breach I set up a new procedure: if anyone mentions Shu's old name, they are routed straight through to me. He spoke to switchboard first and was then passed to my colleague Franks. Both did their job well, performed the prescribed role play perfectly, and our protocol worked Cha. He gave away his real address, which we later verified. And my team still remains oblivious to our real intentions."

"Excellent Tan. Very well done."

"He was calling from your side Cha... again from that place over there you call West Hampstead, and he seemed to know quite a lot. So, we can't assume it was a mistake, or a coincidence."

"Understood. So what do we know about *him*, Tan?"

"A fair amount so far, even though he obviously leaves no digital dust yet. We've got his name as Nelson Staff. And we know he was connected to the Duke Kramer subject. The one we had to give up."

"So I've heard. And we assume they are working together?"

Tan dug deep into his notes, knowing that Sonny Rollins and his Summit bar would have to wait a little longer.

"We're still trying to ascertain that. Just a few more hours."

"Okay, Tan."

"So, how much more do y'all want to know, Cha?"

"As much as you've got, please. We gave up Duke Kramer, because we had to. But we don't have to give this one up. The rare decision to *erase* him has just been made. And I'm going to take personal charge."

# CHAPTER 11

1983, and it was a very fine year.

One day later and somewhat cooler.

08:00. *Click, whirr.*

"Ninety-five point eight, Capital *EFF EMM*..."

The National Coal Board had elected Ian MacGregor as its chairman.

Nelson awoke to this news. Screwing his eyes together, he scraped sleep from one corner, then stared fixedly at the ceiling. The radio pitter patter perpetuated with the same breathless DJ talking about his fellow DJs, and then which DJs would be hosting what DJ shows throughout the DJ day.

*Oh God, what was I thinking yesterday! So naïve, so juvenile... pitching up against NASA? This outfit are still part of the American government, you idiot. Plus, Reagan is on the war path, branding Soviets the Evil Empire and initiating his Star Wars defence initiative. This President could finish me off as a little techno-journalist in North London with a flick of his fountain pen. And has Duke really disappeared, or, or, or... just drunk somewhere on a break?*

The teasmaid created another pot of steaming hot Darjeeling ready to be poured. The radio played *Say Hello, Wave Goodbye* by Soft Cell.

*Shut up! No one cares about you, least of all the Leader of the Free World. Duke is lying on a Limassol beach with a hangover.*

He took deep breaths and told himself no shocking revelations had transpired since sundown, and no further mysterious voices had reached out.

*Take your hands off me*
*I don't belong to you, you see*
*Take a look at my face*
*For the last time*

*I never knew you*
*You never knew me*
*Say hello, goodbye*
*Say hello, wave goodbye*

Nelson rolled over in bed and sat up. He shook his head violently. He turned up the volume, showered, and dressed. He reconsidered fake moon landings, Cypriot sands, Marc Almond, conspiracy theories, and his place in the cosmos. He decided he was low on toilet roll.

The clear warm Indian summer had given way to September rain early that morning. The pavements gleamed like silver bream as Nelson walked, and a fresh smell of wet grass hung in the air.

The supermarket was crowded with determined shoppers, and Waitrose provides its customers the option of heavy wire baskets or large, four-wheeled trollies. His survival instinct urged Nelson to acquire the last cart in the rack.

Inevitably it had just three good wheels, and adamantly tugged him relentlessly into the baked beans, dried spices and back to his peach melba yoghurts.

He noted a lone trolley in the supermarket devoid of squeaks or its own mind, being guided by a dimly familiar figure.

Nelson completed his shopping, sustaining one thigh bruise and a scrape to the Achilles tendon. He made way to the checkout and the ritual of being displaced by elderly north London ladies with one box of tea and a bag of grapes. *(You don't mind do you.)* He filed into the shortest queue. Taking three times longer to clear than any other, he stood yearning for the checkout girl to smile.

The moment he prepared to argue over the quantity of plastic bags she was shoving towards him despite his meagre shopping, he became distracted by the same person in command of the faithful trolley.

Nelson reluctantly paid his bill, allowing the checkout girl an opportunistic call for Maureen to take over her shift and change the till roll. On his way out of the store he passed this individual once more. She was busy packing away her own shopping.

It was a young woman, the first plus sign, and she looked vaguely familiar. Evidently highly intelligent, packing groceries into old carrier bags she had remembered to bring with her, Nelson was not studying her brains.

In his opinion, she had nice legs.

She was vaguely familiar, and she had very nice legs. He shook his head in silence.

*Surely… I am better than this?*

(A mind reader walked past in the street and frowned severely at him.)

Nelson recomposed himself, sighed, and carried on his way from the store. The nerve to say something was not there. The sun strained through thin cloud, leaving his borough with the sense of a cooler autumn day. The supermarket had a quiet access road at the back for deliveries, which also acted as a short cut to the garden roads beyond. As he walked alone unhurriedly along this thoroughfare, the girl overtook him. It was a pleasing surprise and unexpectedly a word sprang to his mind.

"Towel!" said Nelson, and he suddenly recalled who this olive-skinned splendor was.

She walked in front for a few seconds. Her brunette hair touched the pulled-up collar of a grey raincoat complemented by dark red court shoes. Her heels clicked on the pavement as Nelson scurried forward, nearly dropping his soap powder in the process. Increasing his pace, he plucked up the courage.

"Remember me?" he heard himself saying.

The girl turned sharply, stopped and eyed him

cautiously.

"No," she said abruptly, sweeping dark shiny strands of hair from her face with her free hand.

"Yesterday. Halfway through your shower and the doorbell rang."

"Oh yes," she said, her brown eyes widening in concern.

"I'm sorry about that, about the mix-up."

"Good," she said, and a thin smile appeared on her face, as if forgiveness crossed her mind.

"Now if you'll..."

A colossal eighteen-wheel, articulated lorry slid to a sudden halt in the access road beside them, its air brakes hissing madly. Four large men leapt menacingly out of the back dressed in black jeans and windcheater jackets. They had Nelson and the girl clearly in their sights. The driver jumped from the front cab, clicking madly with his large camera and flash. Nelson and the girl were collected by two men each and incredibly swiftly bundled into the back of the trailer.

There were incessant screams and strong kicks from her, and just one bellow from Nelson. Groceries flew, Nelson lost grip on his soap powder, seeing it kicked along the pavement leaving a bluey-whiteness in its trail. The camera stopped clicking and flashing as the driver climbed back into his cab. The lorry blew its horn and left, smoothly disappearing as fast as it had arrived.

The surroundings were barren of witnesses except for two Finchley Road pedestrians entering the far end of this quiet road. Each of them cast around for hidden TV crews.

# CHAPTER 12

The two hemispheres of a female brain talk to each other more than any comparative male.

Duke Kramer's lobes were both hurting and he was dehydrating from heat resonating through his headrest. The restraints chafed his wrist, and each foot swelled inside its encasing Dr. Martens boot. His father's long-coat was missing and he strained to see where this may be lain.

It had been quiet for some time with just a dark void ahead, yet this gave no respite to a dire situation. Kicking his boot heels against the floor, he tried to turn and look behind, but the smooth high back of his chair obstructed any real view. This had well and truly turned into the biggest mistake of his life.

He sensed the faint sound of a door hissing open. A thin shaft of light briefly lit the chamber's deep grey interior. His cell stood in its dead-centre. The external door closed to leave only the pinpoint corner lights of this glass cube.

The bantam head slowly materialised behind the glass.

It spoke.

"I need you to answer some questions."

Duke held a blank stare, without responding.

"Your planet," it began, "has circled its star over four point five billion times. Do you know when you evolved?"

"What!" Duke felt himself exclaiming, breaking any intention to keep quiet.

"When did you start?"

Duke experienced a startling compulsion to tell the truth, yet he could not explain why.

"What do you mean? Are you asking me when

humans evolved?"

"Yes, that is correct. I am learning more all the time, and *human* is what I understand you call yourself?"

"If you're asking me about human evolution, you've got the wrong guy mate. I'm a biologist by training, not an anthropologist."

Once more, the off-yellow beak flashed a glimpse of its mottled pink tongue.

"Just tell me what you know," it demanded.

# CHAPTER 13

A loud scream travels straight to the amygdala, an area of the brain that processes fear and kickstarts the body's fight-or-flight response.

The struggle and screaming continued inside the eighteen-wheeler's soundproofed trailer. The girl maintained her venom towards their captors.

*"Get off me! No! NO! Help! Police! Who the… HELP!"*

Strong hands held her ankles and wrists. She kicked hard. Her best volley connected with an attacker's shins yet caused little reaction. A fifth captor appeared from the recesses to tie her swiftly and professionally. Together with a bound Nelson, she was dumped in a corner where the sun's rays poured in through a small skylight. The girl continued to kick and shout and scream.

"It's all soundproofed in 'ere, love," said a darkly dressed man. He was built like a bear.

She continued to yell. Nelson stayed quiet, breathing heavily with a fearful racing heart.

"We're not here to hurt ya, love" came the matter-of-fact next statement.

The girl stopped abruptly. Her neck and cheeks flushed red, she was breathing too fast and turned to stare fiercely at Nelson.

"Who… ARE *YOU*?" she screamed.

"I'm sorry…" started Nelson.

"STOP! Look Mister…" she hissed, "if this is some kind of weird abduction thing you can just f…"

"N... no!" stuttered Nelson, "honest."

He took in the trailer's interior, noticing it gleamed improbably white with newness and cleanliness. It was spotless, save for a two empty Coca Cola cans discarded on the floor and what appeared to be an empty chicken sandwich packet. The ceiling glowed from a hidden light source.

He glanced at his captors who were nonchalantly huddled away in the far corner, now preoccupied with a group activity.

"*Who are you*!" Nelson cried towards them.

One looked indifferently over his shoulder and blanking the question he returned to focus on his cohorts.

"Who… *ARE* you!" shrieked Nelson. Still no response, and Nelson gathered not to expect one. He suspected he knew who these people were, or at least who they were connected to. His worst fears from the morning's waking cold sweat were manifesting. He had brought this on himself.

The girl continued to stare fixedly at him.

"*HELP*!"

And then, "Get *me*… out of here!" the words left suspended in the air.

A moment passed with an unnerving quiet. The girl's awkward, searing stare unsettled Nelson further, flaring his irritable bowel. The stinging panic coursing through to his colon triggered the sudden need to break wind. At the last moment, she cracked before he did.

"Who the hell are you?" she hissed.

"Nelson, Nelson Staff. No relation. I'm very sorry about all..."

"To whom?"

"I'm sorry?"

"No relation to whom?"

"Vic Staff, the documentary about the Vegas Vegan on that new Channel Four."

"Never watch it. And what's a… *vegan*?"

"Not sure. It doesn't matter."

Nelson saw tears form in the girl's eyes and tremors electrify her body. He struggled to determine if this was due to the cold, shock or hysteria.

"Please don't panic," he tried, "I honestly have enough worry stored up for both of us."

"This isn't helping," she snapped.

"Yes, I realise that."

Reweighing the situation, he adopted a softer approach.

"This may seem like the weirdest thing to happen as you leave Waitrose."

Stemming her shivering the girl noticed the look on Nelson's face as he studied her raincoat. She cursed her own slack preparation for the morning's shopping.

"What's your name?" he asked.

"Tina Reagan. No relation."

"To whom?"

"President... you know what, forget it," said Tina, and shivered again.

"Of course, sorry."

A tense, quiet beat passed, and Nelson studied the interior of the trailer, observing a near side door and the rear double doors through which they had just been bundled. This anterior door appeared sealed with a glistening black substance applied to cover its whole frame. It housed an unused *Push-Bar-To-Open* handle.

"So," restarted Nelson, "don't worry. I think we'll be fine."

"*We*? Let me make it clear. I do not care one toss about you. Just get me out."

The awkward silence returned. Two three four moments passed. The muffled roll of eighteen wheels on Tarmac formed the backdrop, yet no obvious engine noise. Unexpectedly she leaned forward and rasped: "Ok, if I buy it, where the hell are we, and who are these gorillas?"

"Mister Grumpy, Mister Snorty, Mister Meany..." started Nelson.

"Sod off."

"I make jokes when I'm nervous, sorry. I honestly don't know who they are."

"For someone who doesn't have a clue about our situation, you continue to be an idiot who is taking this very lightly."

"No need for the insults. I believe we are on our way to America."

"*Where*?"

"America. Cape Kennedy more precisely. Or is it Canaveral?"

"Cape Canaveral?" hissed Tina.

"I think so."

"I don't want to go to Cape Canaveral. *Help*!"

Nelson sensed her hysteria returning. He shook his head and tried to think, then leaned forward and whispered.

"It could be worse."

"How?"

"We could be on our way back home."

"Is that some kind of sick joke?"

"No."

Tina was one of the many unhappy young professionals coping with Margaret Thatcher's readjustment of the United Kingdom. From an extended mining family, her father had been a pit electrician, enduring the scorn of their neighbours by poorly timing his return to work across the picket lines only a week before the two-year national strike ended. Watching her brother subsequently flee to a newly emerging Silicon Valley, Tina escaped by graduating from a highly respected Midlands university and moving to London as an economic migrant, just as the UK unemployment rate reached three million.

In place of fame and fortune, she took the only full-time job she could find as PA to the owner of a small estate agency. The housing market was contracting and consolidating, and with mortgage interest rates stuck at ten percent, buyers dissipated, and her employer's revenue steadily dried up. He had *regretfully* made her redundant nearly two months previously.

With her bubble burst, she was fortunate to get eight weeks' redundancy pay, which is the amount of time Tina was giving herself before returning to her parent's northern town.

She pressed on with the slim belief that something would turn up. Yesterday her self-administered eight-week grace period expired.

While she professed not to fathom Nelson's remark, as the words sank in, they held water. In the same vein as a mining community, London took its toll on the unemployed. Her newfound professional acquaintances had so far kept their City careers intact, and her childhood friends were scattered in jobs across the North that she did not want.

Taking immediate stock, she did not know quite what to make of this trusting soul before her with his friendly, green-grey eyes and innocent smile.

Their abduction was clear, yet he seemed confident they were not in grave danger.

*Was he insane, or just very calm? Or was he in on this as well? How could she open the chocolate Digestive biscuits in her shopping bag with her hands tied?*

Tina's mood suddenly darkened, and her shivering worsened.

"Are you cold?" asked Nelson.

"No," she lied, "Didn't you say that you were going to get us out of here?"

"Did I?"

"Yes."

"Did it sound good?"

"At the time."

"Excellent."

"Well, are you?

"Am I what?"

"Are you going to get us out of here?"

He took a long moment to answer.

Nelson had lost his parents to their acrimony, divorce and separation many years ago. He had seemingly lost his closest friend overnight to Cyprus, or perhaps a yet worse fate. His career was not the one he wanted. His own life was on a mistaken path.

"Well, not exactly," he said finally.

"What? Don't you *want* to get out?" hissed Tina.

"Right now, no. I don't think I do. At present, this might just be the best option."

"But we've been abducted…"

"Yes, I believe that is the correct term, but I don't actually want to escape, not at the moment," admitted Nelson, as much to himself as to Tina. He tried woefully to get up, overlooking the fact his legs remained bound together.

"Why? Why don't you want to escape?" ask Tina needing to understand more.

"My life has become a mistake. And… we are on our way to the Cape, perhaps to meet my best friend Duke. Haven't you always wanted to go to America?"

"Not this way."

"NASA wants to see me. I think," added Nelson.

"NASA. *You*! *Pah!*"

"There's no need to be…"

"I'm sorry," said Tina, she could see she had hurt him. "From my very uninformed perspective, I fail to see why NASA would go to all this trouble to pick you up in such a dramatic way. Do you know what, just saying that out loud… oh my God. Now I am really, really worried. Don't be a fool. It's not NASA… they don't do this sort of stuff."

"Maybe they do. I phoned them."

"You phoned NASA. How? Who did you speak to?"

"I used Directory Enquiries. I spoke to their switchboard I think, Betty Ann. She wanted me to be her pen pal. Then someone called Franks."

"Oh, dear Jesus. I feel sick again."

"Look Tina, you really shouldn't worry."

"Why shouldn't I! I'll do what I want. And why the hell am I here anyway?"

"Well, that point I'm not too sure about. It could be that you were an innocent bystander."

"*What*!" spat Tina. "I've told you, if this is some weird pick-up routine, I'll be kicking your…"

"It isn't a pick-up routine, I promise," interrupted Nelson, trying desperately and ungainly to get to his feet.

"Please give me one minute."

He began ungainly hopping his way over to their five captors.

"So… called Tina after him, "we're not escaping?"

"Ssshh! No," he hissed. A few more hops and he flopped beside the huge gorillas, and now able to observe they were playing cards. The trailer floor was a highly polished white. Just their seven bodies, the Coca Cola cans, and emptied sandwich packet litter disturbed its brilliance.

"Hello," called Nelson in the direction of the granite faces.

Silence.

"Gin," said one finally.

"Go on then," said Nelson, "any tonic?"

He had their attention now. The five heads swiveled slowly, as though mounted on steel gears. They stared at Nelson with the coldness and contempt clear in their eyes.

"Sorry… I thought you meant a drink."

The silence hung, unbroken.

"It's a joke. I say things like that when I'm nervous," he pleaded in doleful eyes to the gorilla who just laid down his seven cards.

Gears reversing, the heads rotated away and went back to their game. One started shuffling the cards, and then dealt quickly without a word.

"Will we be flying to Cape Canaveral?" tried Nelson as the last card was silently laid out.

Just one looked up with the same icy stare. Abruptly, a smiled cracked across both cheeks and he burst out laughing. He folded his cards into his giant hand and grunted:

"Did tha' hear 'im. Is 'e thick? Our mate here reckons he's flyin' t'America."

The others smiled to each other softly shaking their heads. Then another scoffed and turned to Nelson.

"Get back wi ya lad. Tha'll have t'make do wi' the Dark Peak in Yorkshire."

"Yorkshire!" exclaimed Nelson, checking each of the faces in turn. "*Yorkshire*!"

The one to laugh first placed his cards steadily face-down. He stood up and lifted Nelson by his ropes with the ease of a well-trained bodybuilder. He dragged Nelson back to the far end of the trailer and unceremoniously dumped him next to Tina. Then returning mutely to his game, he sat back down.

Nelson remained in the foetal position, winded and bruised. As he lay, Tina tapped him on the head with the pointed toe of her court shoe.

"You were saying?" she asked quietly.

"I was saying… we have to escape."

Nelson rolled over and sat up.

"Yes indeed, that's what you were saying," Tina confirmed. "I do not want to go back to Yorkshire."

Three more uneventful hours ticked by. The trailer's wheels rolling on motorway roads became the soundtrack beat, overlayed with sporadic engine clatter of passing vehicles. Nelson noted the lack of noise from the truck's engines, a scant monotonous whirring, as if it were fueled like a colossal electric milk float.

He tried no more discourse with the gorillas, remaining distant towards the front of the trailer. He was steadfast against the sealed door that piqued his interest as he and Tina were first dumped in their corner. Tina sat nearby, staring hard away from Nelson. A combination of fatigue and despondency had permitted her compliance with his request.

"Could you just hum, sort of vacantly. Please? Or sing any tune that comes into your imagination?"

Tina picked up on his final word.

*It's just an illusion*
*Ooh, ooh, ooh, ooh, aah-ha, Illusion*
*Ooh, ooh, ooh, ooh, aah-ha, Illusion*
*Could it be that it's just an illusion?*
*Putting me back in all this confusion?*

A nice voice, though her melody was out of key.

In the last few minutes Nelson had gaped into the void and was now focused inwardly with disengaged eyes. His mind raced.

*Is Yorkshire our real destination? Is Duke in situ there under the Dark Peak and not on a beach? Did I really speak to NASA or something far more sinister? Tina has amazing eyes. But why the abduction? Coke Is It! Not to my taste, too sugary. Who do they really want? An empty Coca Cola can. And wonderful legs. For God's sake man, you are pathetic. Am I an innocent bystander? Is Tina the target? This shimmering door sealant is new. And there's a can of Coke. What have I got into? I can tear that tin can in half. Perhaps I should escape, but how? Coke Is It! Gimme Gimme Gimme A Man After Midnight. The black sealant… tear the can in half.*

This cerebral drivel brought Nelson to the anterior sealed door. His hands remaining tied behind his back, he stood awkwardly gouging large chunks of the black sealant, wielding only the torn edge of a Coca-Cola can.[5]

Tina had gently eased the can towards him with her feet and now she was halfway through *Just An Illusion* by Imagination. Now engrossed in Texas Hold'em, the gorillas paid their captives little attention.

Ninety minutes toil made the clearance job as good as possible, though any higher reach was hampered by Nelson's ties. He whispered this concern to Tina.

"Well, if you kick that bar hard enough it should open anyway," she hissed back.

"Are you any good at untying knots?"

"No."

"Me neither, but all this effort has loosened these ropes a little. Try pulling them while I squeeze my wrists together."

Nelson sat down on the floor with his feet behind Tina's back, near her hands. She tried to reach into Nelson's binds and stretch them away from his wrists. Nelson felt he could remove a hand from his bindings. He exhaled sharply and caught his breath. One of his hands had slipped free of its ties. Nelson's eyes widened and Tina immediately understood the implication.

Keeping both hands behind his back Nelson manoeuvred to work the same on Tina's ropes. With her own short gasp, she was eventually free. Taking each other's cue, they moved their hands inch by inch to their ankle ties, with no desire to catch attention by a sudden movement.

Moments later, Nelson sensed the lorry gradually

---

[5] Why the ABBA lyrics came in remains a mystery.

reduce speed. They sat stock still as it rocked to a halt, and its air brakes hissed. Two of their captors stood to check the situation by approaching the rear double doors - away from Nelson and Tina.

"This could be our chance!" breathed Nelson. Watching their captors move away, they returned both hands behind their backs to continue the pretense of capture. It was a long trailer, and at least ten to fifteen paces separated them from their abductors.

"Correction, this *is* our chance," roared Nelson, his adrenalin teeming through brain and sinew. He had one chance to escape in a most spectacular filmic manner, kicking down the door with focused strength, leaping onto a motorway embankment pursued by a pretty girl, perform a tumble roll, and career down the hard shoulder weaving between passing motorists and towards an attendant police car, convincing the officers to brake hard and assist his theatrics. This was his chance.

"Nelson…" said Tina, observing the far end of the trailer.

Nelson was high. If their captors spotted his intentions, none could react before his lightning reflexes kicked open this door and he whirled Tina from danger.

"Nelson…" she tried again.

Nelson's mind was made up, laser focused, and with one frenzied ambition. He stood upright. The adrenalin surged.

"Er, Nelson…"

Showing teeth, his face reddened.

Nelson braced his right leg, muscles tensed, and he heaved…

*CRASH*!

The door splintered from its sealant and burst open.

Nelson primed to jump. He stood at the brink, perched to leap into… the clinically clean, white-tiled, floor of an immensely curved corridor.

"Well done Mr. Staff," said a man dressed in U.S. Air Force camouflage uniform. "We've been trying to get that door sorted since we took delivery of the truck."

The air force man had *W.J. McGuigan* stitched to the right chest of his battle dress jacket and *USAF* to its left.

"Nelson..." breathed Tina, transfixed on the double-doors at the rear of the trailer, which were now opened "...I think we've arrived."

The rear doors' opening revealed further evidence of the lengthy, dazzling white tunnel stretching into the distance behind.

"Yes ma'am," confirmed the USAF officer. He spoke from a vantage point below them as he stared up through the truck's small emergency exit, vestiges of its black sealant still clinging to the frame.

"...you sure have arrived."

Nelson wept.

# CHAPTER 14

An eighteen-wheeler truck weighs over eighty thousand pounds.

"Pull yourself together Nelson," offered Tina as she stood beside him at the giant trailer's edge. With one hand on its flat-bed side she nipped athletically down into the tunnel floor, landing neatly on the tips of her court shoes.

"Allow me ma'am. He'll be fine," said the Air Force man.

Nursing a tight Achilles heel, Nelson made a difficult job of climbing awkwardly down from the trailer via his knees, belly, and hobbling feet.

"I see they removed their own ties," voiced the air man to one of their dark clothed captors, who had needlessly stepped forward with a utility knife to slice through rope. The air man flicked him away.

"Let's just learn from this. Cable ties next time. Now, will you two follow me please."

Recomposing himself, Nelson picked his head up and took in the surroundings. The long white tunnel stretched behind, curving gently such that any entrance was obscured. The same gleaming tunnel continued in front and curved to a similar degree, meaning no exit was visible. The neon lights above buzzed perceptibly to provide a clinical and uncomfortable pallor to the setting. Highly precise wall tiling and grouting delivered the only detail within this pristine arc.

"What is this?" asked Nelson, "some kind of..."

"All will become clear," interrupted the American. "I am Chief Master Sergeant W. J. McGuigan of the Progressionary Unit, US Air Force. I'm seconded here as a Senior NCO to assist in *The Quit*."

"Thanks, that's much clearer now," observed

Nelson.

"But you can call me Whip."

"Must we?"

Nelson's derision held firm. He looked across to Tina. She was quieter and calmer and avoided his eye contact, while assessing her surroundings. He sensed she was now dealing with this situation far better than him. His gullible expectations of NASA slated private jet extraction, guided tours of the new Space Shuttle, his hushed name on everyone's lips. And a complimentary NASA T-shirt and baseball cap. In the last twenty-four hours Nelson had allowed himself delusional flights of fancy in which he called all the shots. These were flights detached from the reality of any outward threat, and the embracing warmth of NASA's safe hands.

He did not feel safe now.

"Where are we?" he chided.

"Yorkshire," replied W.J. McGuigan.

"Can we ask where in Yorkshire?" furthered Tina.

"Underneath it."

"Oh."

"Beneath the Dark Peak of the Pennines to be precise. Follow me."

"*No*!" blasted Tina emphatically.

Having taken two assumptive paces forward, McGuigan stopped instantly

"I'm not going anywhere," she continued. "You've kidnapped us, tied us up, dumped us in a truck and now expect us to just do what you say? Where do you get off on just treating people that way and ordering them about? Are you gangsters or perverts?"

The air man studied them both quietly. In the silence they became aware of a soft whirring emerging from the white tiled corridor behind.

Nelson and Tina turned. Simultaneously their eyes widened in bewilderment.

Past the huge truck, hooded figures emerged in

the form of three elderly men draped in sumptuous red robes, each gliding a peculiar two-wheeled device marked by a long stem projecting from its baseplate. Their eyes were barely visible beneath shadows cast by the head covering. Each vermillion robe presented a different braid pattern in gold across the torso.

Floating improbably on just these two wheels, the vehicles' stem finished with a rounded handlebar, lightly gripped by each rider. They came to a stop.

Ten beats. No one spoke. Finally, the three elderly arrivals simultaneously leaned forward very slightly on their handlebars and mutely slid past Nelson, Tina and McGuigan. Even from the rear their two-wheeled devices displayed no further visible means of balance, appearing to defy any laws of physics.

"We're neither gangsters nor perverts ma'am," said the American. "If you'll politely follow me, we will explain."

"Now *that*... is a mode of transport I like the look of," perked up Nelson. "Do you get a lot of these?"

"Yessir," snapped McGuigan as a verbal salute. He was desperate to walk on yet remained rooted to this spot. "It's called a Segway."

"A... a Segg Weigh... or, a segue? You mean, like a transition?"

"Yessir, I guess. It's a great implementation of gyroscopics."

"Hmm..." said Nelson, not sure he was understanding, "...and what about the men in robes riding these Segg Weighs?"

"They lead The Directorate. Down here we call them the Knowalls."

"The Noels?" checked Nelson.

"Yessir. Close enough"

"Mr. and Mrs. Noel and their son Edmond?"

"No. It was a moniker they adopted centuries ago. I prefer to think of them as a tech mafia."

"A *tech mafia*?" exclaimed Nelson.

"Yes, a technology mafia, but without all the pasta. Some of us use that phrase. It's not their favourite, but for me it's accurate. They prefer Knowall. I guess its softer. It refers to all knowledge of technology and this and that. But they've asked to explain everything to you themselves."

"Aha, the Know-*Alls*," perceived Nelson, "...knowledge. Very self-serving. And what is this... *Directorate* that they lead?"

"*Hey*! Excuse me. Could we just get back to our kidnapping!" exclaimed Tina, fully exasperated with her companions. She observed two of the impassive darkly clad gorillas silently file into line behind them.

"I promise you ma'am, you'll get everything explained to you. It is easier to see with your own eyes."

W.J. McGuigan indicated forward with his arm gently outstretched. Nelson began to walk. Tina simply stared hard at the American. He smiled disarmingly back at her and nodded again forwards. A split-second decision. Tina concluded compliance was her best option for now and silently followed Nelson. In the distance rolled their red-robed leaders. The tunnel's acoustics channeled the faint whirr from each two-wheeled Segway, invisible motors and gyroscopes spinning smoothly.

No sign of an entrance or exit was revealed in the monotonous tiling. They were clearly in a strange place. As she pulled up alongside him, Nelson glanced thoughtfully at Tina.

*The Knowalls? A nickname or an intimidation? A tech mafia! There's intimidation. Knowledge, technology and this and that? This wasn't NASA.*

The heavy silence stifled Nelson's breathing, shortening its intake. Pursued by a disturbing question this last thirty minutes, the timing of its delivery could never be perfect. It was a pressing query, yet true espionage dramas were seldom, if ever, rendered with such dilemmas.

"Is there a toilet nearby?" he called finally, unable to stall any longer.

Nelson relieved himself in a white cubicle, the concealed door of which effortlessly lifted as one red-robed leader quietly stared at it. Each companion politely averted their eyes for Nelson. The cistern flushed automatically as he raised his zip and their journey continued with an uncomfortable quiet.

Eventually an immense gold and copper door terminated the arching corridor.

A few paces from their arrival, the heavy portal slid open on impressively robust hinges, revealing a gigantic chamber within, perfectly hemispherical in structure, and a roof encrusted by a myriad of flickering lights.

At its distant end, small spotlights picked out a female of striking blond hair and lustrous white robe, finished with brilliant gloss boots. She also rode a Segway. Two of their vermillion-robed companions separated from the group to wordlessly join her. The third smiled enigmatically, remaining with Nelson, Tina and the uniformed American.

"Sit down please," invited Sergeant McGuigan.

He pointed to an isolated black bench centered on a dark floor stretching in all directions towards the distant shadows. Nelson and Tina obliged, seating themselves in starry-eyed awe of the marvel above.

At the far end of the chamber, the red and white cloaked Knowalls grouped beneath the spotlights, then mutely turned and leaned forward, rolling away to disappear through a hidden exit.

“Who’s the companion?” whispered the white-robed female as she left the chamber.

The miniature spotlights faded to black and the secluded exit resealed itself to present a wall of black.

The single Knowall remaining in the chamber stepped from his Segway. It rocked gently yet stayed perfectly balanced. An eye for fashion and detail, Tina observed the thin gold braid, stretching across his red robe from shoulder to torso, was embellished with a cloud motif. He was shaven headed, with a thick white-stubble beard over black skin. His rich hazel eyes had a warmness to them.

"Mr. Nelson Staff," he said to them both, more as a statement than a question.

"Yes," replied Nelson, leaning forward.

"Ah, you. Okay, and who might this be? We have no evidence of a wife or girlfriend."

"This is Tina. I met her yesterday."

"Tina Reagan," added Tina, "no relation."

"To whom?" asked the Knowall.

"Forget it."

Chief Master Sergeant W. J McGuigan ordered the two gorillas to follow him, returning to the huge metal door. It swung to close as silently as it had opened. Before disappearing, McGuigan turned to perform an efficient salute towards the room. The door locked, accompanied by a distant hiss as the chamber was resealed.

This left Nelson, Tina, the Knowall and a hundred thousand twinkling lights. Without command, two objects rose from the barren floor to break this monotony of darkness - a small keyboard plinth and the thinnest, flattest TV screen Nelson had ever seen.

He gaped at the TV and then the chamber roof, as

the Knowall shuffled to arrange his robe and smooth his braid of golden clouds. The ceiling was beautiful and unbelievable. Part of it, he thought, reminded Nelson of the constellation of Orion[6].

"Where are we?"

"Yorkshire," reconfirmed the Knowall.

"Yes, yes, I know all that. The Peak District, and beneath it. Is this part of NASA?"

"No," the old man told him, "But you could say that NASA was part of us... couldn't you?"

"Sorry?"

"Hmm..." pondered the Knowall, his piercing hazel eyes drilling Nelson.

"Why are we here?" posed Nelson against the unnerving stare.

"I thought you knew that?"

"Do I?"

"I see. Do you like change, Nelson Staff?"

"What? Well, I prefer larger notes really… but the bigger coins are fine with the new one-pound."

"No, I mean real change… transformation. Revolution. Do you like change for change's sake?"

"What?"

"Okay, okay boys," interrupted Tina. "All macho men's jibbety-jab. I see this is a great place for a disco, but *why… are…* we here?"

The Knowall's head turned barely perceptibly to look at Tina, then back to Nelson. He was performing an assessment with his unflinching gaze. Nelson squirmed in his seat and broke eye contact again and again. A quiet tension rose in the room. Then the Knowall relented and

---

[6] The small collection of lights on which Nelson focused formed a replica of Orion's constellation. Though he would not perceive this, the roof depicted an accurate representation of the night sky as viewed from the county of Yorkshire and rotated invisibly as the hours wore on.

turned to smile at Tina.

"So, you my dear, is it true you've just met Nelson?"

"I wouldn't even go that far. He knocked on my door yesterday, then chased me from the supermarket today."

"That's not fair, not fair," sighed Nelson.

"But if I may answer your question directly," continued Tina, "I love change. I always have. It makes things a bit more… exciting."

The Knowall contemplated this statement whilst looking once more between them both. He stroked the white stubble on his right cheek. The bright ebony skin shone through. He nodded a hair's breadth and appeared to have reached a decision.

"So..." he concluded, "I agree we should *erase* you after all."

"Erase?" gasped Nelson. Tina snapped her head towards him and then back at their unnamed captor.

"Why of course," replied the old man.

"How do you mean... *erase*?"

"All will become clear," he said as he turned to leave the chamber.

"Hold on!" yelled Tina.

The Knowall ignored her and headed for the same exit through which his colleagues had disappeared. Before the door closed, he relented, turning around and smiling.

"My dear, are you wearing anything under that raincoat?"

"Shove off!" exclaimed an angry Tina.

The door hissed shut.

They were left with the ceiling stars, the screen and keyboard plinth.

"Erased..." she exhaled. "Just *what* the hell have you got me into?"

"I'm so, so sorry Tina, I'm no longer sure."

Turning her back on Nelson, Tina looked up. The artificial stars twinkled above.

Nelson stared at the stars. Tina's gaze went down to the floor. A wordless impasse developed between them. Stillness descended on the chamber, and no one moved. Their anxiety levels were rising, yet neither would speak first to admit it.

As he focused on the lights above, Nelson detected a twitching beneath Orion's belt. A tiny square of the ceiling folded in on itself, and a small close-circuit television camera beetled out.

"Look," Nelson indicated.

"Oh my God!" spat Tina, "Is that what this is? If it's some kind of Candid Camera..."

"Jesus, no I didn't mean that..." said Nelson, yet smiling self-consciously at the lens, "... do you think this is my best side?"

"I'm asking one more time Nelson. What the *hell* am I doing here?"

"I'm not sure."

"Not sure. *Not sure*! You must have some idea... or you are very stupid. The only thing I know is that there is £14.79's worth of shopping scattered over Finchley Road and the day out I'd planned is completely... completely... ruined!"

Nelson stretched his neck stiffly from side to side and linked his fingers, pushing the palms in a downward motion.

"*Well*?" demanded Tina.

He swiveled on the bench to face her directly.

"Okay Tina, firstly, I'm sorry for all of this. Secondly, a very long story, short. My friend Duke has disappeared, I think. That's an important point. Next, I'm a geologist by education, but now I write articles when I can. Nothing to do with geology, but ones about technology, for magazines and newspapers. Anyway, Duke loves a conspiracy theory and a couple of months ago he loses his sense of humour. He gets all serious, telling me something is *real*. I ignore him like I normally do, but he insists I meet him in our local library. He shows me this encyclopaedia he's found there that looks like it hasn't been opened for years. Bingo! It has a neat recess cut right out of the middle. He gets this yellowing NASA envelope out of his pocket, and it fits perfectly in the recess. He swears its genuine, then and tells me to read it. Sure enough it's from NASA to a Doctor Grimaldi, and *he* used to live where you live now. That... is the reason I came to your place."

"And got me out of the shower."

"I'm also sorry about that."

"Carry on."

"The letter talks about Grimaldi's opinions on rockets and the first Moon landing. But the letter is dated... get this, *1927*! Not just once, twice. That's over fifty years before Neil Armstrong told us how smug you can be as the first one there. Duke tells me to keep it safe and then leaves the library very quick. And that... was the last I saw of him. What would you do? We grew up together. He's like a brother to me. So, I tried to return it to you, we know what happened there. I go back to the library, and then find *Lies All Lies* scrawled across pages on inventions leading to the first computers. But I know they are true because that is what I'm employed to write about. If it is a fake, then someone is going to a lot of effort, and in the most obscure places. So, the wind in my sails I ring NASA and a whimpering brain cell has trouble breathing when I mention Grimaldi and Moon in the same sentence, and then a voice that should be advertising aftershave says *We'll be in touch*. And here I am. And I still don't know where Duke is."

Tina's stare was intense, locked in stone. Her deep brown eyes were accusatory. A sudden jerked movement of her hands, fingers splayed, and thumbs upwards sounded a silent message. And me?

"And Tina... I think you're here because you've got nice legs."

She slapped Nelson smartly across the face, holding back a scream, but her face reddened.

"That's fair enough," accepted Nelson, holding a palm gently to his smarting cheek. He maintained eye contact. "I deserved that. I'm *so* sorry, that's all I can say again. I didn't foresee any of this, and you were never part of it."

He turned back on his seat to face the huge door through which they had entered.

"I got all wrapped up in my head. I'm a true idiot. You've been so calm."

He paused for a moment, and then looked at Tina and went to reach out a hand. It hovered hesitantly mid-air, unconnected.

"We need to find a way out of here," he said finally.

"Out of where Nelson? Underneath Yorkshire and this circular tube of white tiling? Jesus. You look at a map of the world and there's a little flashing dot in the middle of England which says *You Are Here*. Thanks a lot Mr. Wotsit... Knowall. Oh Nelson... we need to be *above* Yorkshire. We need to be in London, walking home with our shopping. No, scratch that, I need to be in Concorde, first class to JFK, bottomless margaritas, limo to Manhattan, top floor at the Plaza, dinner at..."

"I think you'll find..."

"Shut up Nelson! Don't spoil my rant."

"Shall I leave you to it?" said Nelson, rising from the bench.

"What. No! Come back here!" yelled Tina, "You don't get to do all the talking. You've got to listen."

Having taken steps away from her with a hand still on his smarting cheek, Nelson relented and reseated himself.

"Moon landings. 1927. NASA. Don't you see Nelson, it's all *Boys Own* conspiracy crap. Hey lads, hey. Straight out of a *Quinn Martin* production. Next you'll start talking about aliens and E bloody T. Boring!"

"I still haven't seen it yet,"

"What!"

"*Phone hooooome…*"

"Oh, get stuffed!" said Tina to the world.

They sat in silence as Tina cooled off. Choosing his moment and words carefully, Nelson whispered softly.

"So, if we're going to escape, and now I really want to, then we need calm, intellect and a brilliant idea."

"We're stuck down here for life then," huffed Tina.

Nelson rose once from his seat and moved towards the keyboard and incredulously flat screen. Both had remained in place as the Knowall left the room. Staring at its blankness, he noticed a small logo etched into its surface. It was unfamiliar to him, and as he ran one finger lightly across it and towards the keyboard, he made out a recessed switch marked subtly with a *1* and *0*.

It was inviting. Nelson pressed it.

The screen pinged to life and informed Nelson that he was using GlasSlate® OS version 28.7. It briefly notified him a full memory scan was in process, and subsequently a *wireless network* was established. Nelson pondered this meaning as the cursor blinked. Finally, the screen cleared, and a single word appeared at its apex.

>*Yes?* it said.

Taking the initiative, Nelson stood before the keyboard.

>*Yes what?* he typed.

>*What do you wish to know?* was the reply.

It dawned on Nelson what he had at his fingertips.

>*Where is Duke?* he wrote.

>*Duke Kramer?*

>*Yes.*

>*Indeterminate.*

He stared at this answer. The reply disturbed Nelson and deepened the mystery of what had happened to his friend. Turning to Tina he whsipered.

"What did the Knowall say he was going to do with us?"

She looked up with contempt still clear in her face.

"Erase us," she hissed.

"*Erase*, that was it," confirmed Nelson. He whirled back to the screen to request a definition.

>*Standard or Revised?* it queried.

>*Revised* typed Nelson assuming a more relevant definition would ensue.

The delay just seconds, yet when the screen replied it displayed just five words. As a glacial chill shot through Nelson's body all colour drained from his face. Nausea wrapped a cold cloak around him.

"Are you okay?"

Tina watched Nelson suddenly reach to support himself, grabbing both the sides of the flat screen.

He took two deep breaths.

"I asked this computer for their..." he whirled a right hand silently in the air, "...definition of *erase*."

"And?"

"Look."

He stepped back from the screen, holding an arm out towards it. Tina rushed forward, gasping at the five words coming into view. They said:

>*Removed from the human race.*

Searching frantically around, Nelson's head snapped in multiple directions. He recognised an arrangement amongst the tiny illuminations above, yet it must be a quirk of the light. He glanced at the CCTV monitoring their movements. Once more he spotted something in the ceiling lights, and assumed he was imagining. He checked Tina, whose gaze was fixed at the screen. He refocused on the lights. The more he stared the more they twinkled and formed into shapes. Together near the artificial horizon they coalesced in a dream to spell out 'Emergency Exit'. This held station above what Nelson assumed to be a black hole in the map of the cosmos.

*Never.*

*Yes...?*

*YES! Emergency Exit.*

"Do you think that camera can shoot?"

"What?" asked Tina.

"Never mind. Let's go."

He grabbed her arm and dashed towards the sign.

"What the hell are you doing?"

"This is an emergency, and we need an exit."

"What!"

"Trust me."

Starting to run, Nelson and Tina plunged headlong into the black hole.

# CHAPTER 15

"I don't really know anything," pleaded Duke.

"I will be the judge," snapped the chicken-creature. "Just tell me."

"You mean about humans? It's not my specialty, but we came from the apes."

"Okay, apes. As in, your monkeys. Do you know when?"

"Well, if you want to be pedantic it was apes specifically. Monkeys are a different line. But anyway, I'm not so sure. Humans, homo sapiens, we descended from apes a few million years ago, via homo erectus and habilis."

"And before that?"

"Before apes? I'm really the wrong guy for this."

"Try," came the order.

"Well, the apes evolved from other mammals. And those other mammals evolved from yet more creatures. On and on back in time. Unless...

"Unless what?"

"Well, unless you believe in The Creator. Or a divine intervention."

"Okay. When do you say that started?"

"What, creation?"

"No, the real evolution."

"Look Foghorn Leghorn, if you really want to know all this crap then ask my friend Nelson, not me."

He twisted his spine in his seat trying to ease the discomfort.

"Nelson's the paleontologist. I'm bored of his speeches, but maybe you'd love them. He can wax lyrical about how we hummed along as bacteria for a few billion years, and then *bang!* About five hundred million years ago in the Cambrian Period all life exploded. Loads of it, in just a few million years. All different types, everywhere on the planet. Blah blah blah. And then things moved on much quicker from there."

"Five hundred million. So, you are aware of this?" queried the partially feathered head.

"No I'm not. Nelson is!"

"And did you also know it's too quick? Why did it happen?

"What do you mean, why?"

"Do you know why evolution suddenly started accelerating on your planet?"

"Of course I don't. And Nelson tells me it's still a mystery. He says there are lots of theories, but none stack up, and therefore lots of disagreement. And as for me, I have *no*... idea. Maybe you should ask God."

"Who is your God?"

"Wow, now there's a question. You really don't know much do you. Just... God. Depending on your religion he is called lots of names. But, you know, God. As in The Creator?

The plumy face leant back away from the glass cube, almost disappearing from Duke's view into the dark.

"God," it said finally. "The Creator you say. I need more data from the Superchamber to understand all of this."

# CHAPTER 16

Black holes in this off-world neighbourhood pack more mass than our sun into an area the size of Sheffield.

Though they could not know it, the black hole Nelson and Tina plunged into was simply another corridor, conveniently sheathed in black tiles sealed with black cement. There were no lights nor reflective surfaces, and although impossible to perceive, the corridor again curved slightly as they ran on in blindness. The door through which they fled receded. The couple raced on into darkness.

"Where are we going?" pleaded Tina into the void.

"This is an emergency exit, which means a way out."

"But… do you know where it will lead?"

"No, I don't. Out."

"*Oh Nelson,*" said a voice from nowhere. *"That's a shame. Are you really a Luddite?"*

"Who's that?" hissed Nelson.

"I don't know, it came from nowhere."

Nelson scoffed.

"And what's a Luddite?" she asked.

Nelson fumbled to grab Tina's hand in the blindness, pulling her along faster.

"Keep running."

"Wait, slow down."

"Why?"

"My raincoat has come undone."

"Hell! Why now?"

"I've got an idea," called Tina.

"What, here?"

"Shut up! Stare at the wall."

"Hmm?"

"Stare at the wall."

"What!"

"Stare... at... the wall."

"Why should I stare at the wall?"

"Don't you remember?"

"No, I don't bleeding well remember," shrieked Nelson

In a low voice, Tina hushed into the black.

"When you wanted to relieve yourself in the white tunnel, that Knowall glared at the wall… and magically a cubicle appeared. I'm trusting that we're in one of those tunnels now."

"So?"

"So take a moment to think… they know we're in here, and by now are probably simply sitting in wait at the other end. Stare at the wall and…"

"Hang on, I can't even see you, never mind the wall. And what's all this *Listen to me I'm leader* routine."

"Nelson, *you* said in order to escape we needed calm, intellect and a brilliant idea."

"Yes?"

"Therefore someone has to provide all three. Stare… at… the wall."

"Which wall?"

"That one."

"I can't even see it. I can't even remember if my eyes are open."

"Listen Nelson, grab hold of my arm. NO… my arm! Okay, you feel where my finger is pointing?"

Nelson felt.

"Nice nails."

"Stare over there," ordered Tina.

"But..."

"Stare over there, Nelson… and concentrate."

They both stared intensely, very difficult into pitch black. Adrenalin rising, there followed a long, beseeching laden pause. No sight or sound, only the occasional catch of Nelson's sweat and Tina's perfume.

"Concentrate Nelson."

"I am."

Nothing.

"Concentrate!"

A hiss.

Then a vivid, thin shaft of light, as though a million-Watt fluorescent tube rolled to them across the floor. The width of the tube expanded, becoming a door evidently opening inwards to a brilliantly lit room. A pure, white glow now seared their eyes. The room behind appeared as a hazy white apparition, images beginning to coalesce from within. Light poured onto their faces and into the densely black tunnel.

The room was revealed to be ultra-clean, painfully white, and intensely lit. Standing in its exact mathematical centre was a bright white cistern and a bright, white bowl.

"Oh my God," yelled Tina.

"Another toilet!" spat Nelson. "The Knowalls need to cut down on their fibre."

"Turn around Nelson."

"What?"

"Turn around and stare at the other wall."

"It'll just be a bidet."

"Do it," commanded Tina, more determined than ever.

They focused on the opposite wall, now well illuminated from the bathroom behind. Soon another shaft of light appeared, this time less intense. The second opening did not reveal a bidet, but a hallway. It stretched far ahead and leading off at regular intervals were warmer wooden doors with traditional styling. Each was thickly lacquered, brandishing a burnished metallic plaque bolted to their middle.

The words *MUSEUM* THREE were embossed into the ceramic floor beneath their feet.

They looked at each other.

"Good call Tina. Come on," yelled Nelson and

they both raced in. Another hiss as their entrance closed steadfastly behind.

Running along the course of this hallway, Nelson soon slowed to a brisk walk as he took in the curious titles written across the plaques on each door.

"What?" questioned Tina. "Why so slow?"

"Look."

This was an exotic and unearthly museum with titles on the door plaques so far showcasing:

*NEURAL FIBRE OPTICS*
*DARWIN 2.0 & HYPERMUTATION*
*VIRTUAL REALITY IMPLANTS*
*FOUNDATIONS OF INTERPLANETARY TRAVEL*
*LIFE & DEATH BY SOCIAL MEDIA*
*BIOTECHNOLOGY & TISSUE ENGINEERING*

"What is this place?" Tina asked, struggling to understand the implications of the bizarre titles, yet sensing the aberrant nature of the whole setting.

"Hmm," began Nelson. Based on his Masters' degree in Paleontology, the second door piqued Nelson's interest. Yet the foreboding sense of this deeply odd corridor set him on edge.

"Harrods," he barked.

"What?"

A scoff shot from his mouth. "Harrods. This must be part of Harrods. They say that you can't see it all in one day so this must be the part you can't see."

"Have you literally gone mad?"

"I told you, I joke when I get nervous. Or to answer another way, *yes*."

"Perfect. So, now what?"

Nelson shrugged his shoulders as he veered through his last twenty-four hours.

"Pinch me."

"Sorry?"

"Pinch me, hard. Just there."

Tina pinched him, very hard. In her own way she felt a bit better.

"*Ow!*" shrieked Nelson.

"I did what you asked."

"Now, let me pinch you."

"No."

"It'll help."

"Go away."

"I'm awake, so it must be your dream."

"*It's nobody's dream,*" said the voice from nowhere.

"Do you work for British Rail!" bellowed Nelson to the ceiling. Holding a fist to his mouth mocking a microphone, he continued. "Listen, why don't you try: *The train now standing at platform two is the delayed 19:27 Lunar Lander and will be departing approximately forty years late.*"

Silence.

Then he hollered as a follow up, "And *where*... where is my best friend, Duke?"

Silence.

Nelson squinted feverishly around.

"In here," he called to Tina and nobly tried pulling her through the *Darwin 2.0* door.

"*Ow!*" he shrieked, as his shoulder blade slammed into its sturdy frame and buckled into his vertebrae.

"Damn you. Try that one," indicating to Tina, further along the corridor.

She turned the handle and this new door, incomprehensibly marked *CLOUD COMPUTING,* was unlocked.

They rushed through.

"Ah, do come in. Good to see you again so soon," said the same ebony skinned man standing before them, smoothing the gold braid across his deep red gown.

# CHAPTER 17

The Cloud Computing room was minimal, not in an Eighties way but more to achieve function over form.

Floor lighting at its edge washed the walls with a warm white glow. The ceiling was barren except for a slim recess at the furthest end. They sensed it to be soundproofed with little echo from the Knowall's words.

"This is it," said Nelson.

"What is?" asked the old man, gently scratching the left side of his white beard stubble.

"The proverbial it," said Nelson.

"Is it Nelson? Do show me."

Nelson sighed and studied the fine nobleman prevailing before them. The hardened lines sunk into his ebony skin and around the hazel eyes framed a faint smile. In the white light of this room his robe of intense vermillion shimmered and enhanced the gold braid that traversed it with intricately laced clouds. Nelson now noticed tiny letters stitched into his left shoulder that appeared to layout *D E X*, separated from the number 2 and letter *O*.

"How did you know we would run into this room?" Nelson challenged.

"Simple prediction analytics," came the reply. "And also, we left this door open."

"You're going to *erase* us," said Tina.

"Well, you have been already my dear."

"Explain it then," said Nelson, "...this is Heaven?"

The faint smile transformed into a broad grin.

"Oh no, dear me no."

"Hell?"

"I'd like to quip that you are getting warmer, but no."

"Okay, it said Cloud Computing on the door. Mainframes made of mist? Machines perched in the sky?"

"No Nelson, I can assure you this is none of those. I asked you before, do you like change? Can you cope with real change - or more specifically, with revolution? Well, if you can, then this... is simply a small part of a whole."

"And we're the toads in it!" scoffed Nelson, about to raise two inappropriate fingers when Tina interrupted.

"We panicked. And I'm sure you would agree, with good reason." She stared the Knowall down looking for an acknowledgment of the fright they had been put through unnecessarily, before continuing. "*Erase...* defined by your own slab of blinking glass back there as, and I quote, *removal from the human race*?"

The Knowall raised his eyebrows at Tina as she spoke these last few words. Unfazed, she sped on.

"Come on," she chided, "that's what your computer said back in the huge chamber. What were we meant to think?"

"And it does mean that my dear, it really does. But not in the same context you have obviously interpreted it."

There was a brief pause as they processed this response and the situation. Nelson spoke first.

"Are you aliens?"

"Ha, ha. No, not at all. But then we're not exactly members of the..." he stopped himself abruptly. "Everything will become clear."

"Oh, I am *fed up* of hearing that," bawled Nelson, "So far it's clear as mud pie in a bin liner. We'd like it clear please. Now."

"As I said, everything..."

"*Now!*"

"Nelson, there is due process here. Mountains have been moved after your recent conduct, meetings convened, adjourned and rescheduled."

Nelson stood his ground.

"And we..." he held out his hands towards Tina, "have been shackled and *kidnapped*."

The older man considered his options, eventually resting his eyes on Tina.

"You as well?"

Tina nodded mutely.

"If you both are so insistent."

He gently touched a silver disk on the wall. In response another impossibly flat, considerably larger screen, descended from the ceiling recess. It flickered to display a map of the world as the floor lights dimmed. On this map blinked a pulsing red fleck at the heart of Great Britain, tagged to declare *YOU ARE HERE.*

"See. I told you!" exclaimed Tina.

"I'm sorry?" queried the Knowall.

"Nothing. It doesn't matter."

Other red spots were appearing, but none pulsed. They illuminated Iceland, Puerto Rico, Madagascar, Florida, Sicily, Macau and Tasmania.

"Firstly some introductions," began their host. He reached across his chest to touch the letters stitched into the shoulder of his robe. "My name is Dex'2O, but please call me Dex."

"Dex," repeated Tina flatly.

The Knowall turned to look at the slim screen behind and above him.

"As you can see, we are all part of a whole. At all these points we have underground installations like this one you are in. Points where you would least expect to find us. Not that anyone knows we are here anyway, but it's reassuring. We prefer small countries, especially islands. We also have a few carefully planted eyes and ears, keeping the feedback loop going and ensuring we don't miss anything important.

"Planted eyes. Like whom?" challenged Nelson.

"I can't divulge names, but we have a handful in

key Western governments, one in each of the G7 intelligence communities, two in US news media and one in UK news media."

"UK news media! Ha. Like Trevor MacDonald?"

Nelson scoffed at his own humour whilst Tina rolled her eyes. The Knowall raised a single eyebrow in neither confirmation nor denial.

"No way!" exclaimed Nelson.

Ignoring his outburst, the Knowall continued.

"We have a few high-profile channels, most notably parts of NASA you've already experienced, but we'll come to that."

"Is this going to be a long explanation, Dex?" asked Tina.

"It depends how much you want to know."

"Can we have a seat? These heels are killing me."

"Why of course, please relax."

Dex'2O indicated office chairs beneath the assorted desks and workstations. They organized themselves. Nelson slouched, Tina sat straight and crossed her legs.

"Now as you know, we are the Knowalls."

"Yes... quite an unsavoury name," offered Tina. "Do you intend to be taken seriously with that? *Tech mafia* seems much cooler."

"I can see it as a curious, some could say unfortunate, name," he continued, "but one we were given, and I believe to be quite apt. We form part of The Directorate. So, are you sitting comfortably?"

"Yes."

"Then I'll begin."

# CHAPTER 18

The chicken-creature returned, once more leaning in towards the thick pane that separated it from Duke. In tilting forward, the crown of its head revealed feather-like crimson tufts. The glass cube glowed faintly yet the chamber behind remained dim and murky. It continued the interrogation.

"I have more data now on your Cambrian Explosion. So, do you know when humans developed off-world travel?"

"Jesus," exclaimed Duke, "we've moved on a bit from evolution."

"Not really," muttered the beak, and then more firmly, "Answer the question."

Duke chose to reestablish his silence. None of this was what he signed up for.

The demand was repeated.

"Answer the question."

Muteness from Duke, yet he was unnerved by a growing and persistent compulsion from within to speak openly and truthfully.

The forehead and beak disappeared into the dim light and Duke was aware of a faint thrumming behind his headrest. A warmth radiating from it intensified.

"Speak the truth."

"I don't know what you mean!" Duke found himself blurting out.

"Tell me when you started off-world travel. You will give me the truth."

"We began in the Sixties. The Russians led the way to begin with. They started with a dog, and then Yuri Gagarin was the first man in space. A few years later the Americans caught up, and they beat the Soviets to the Moon. They landed there in 1969."

Duke gasped a sudden intake of breath. He had no idea where these words were coming from or why he was reeling them off. He knew vague facts yet would never use such detail to answer a simple question, and specifically one he had no intention of answering. His head ached and the heat from the chair was unbearable.

"Stop this," he pleaded, "you're torturing me."

"I just need the truth and we will be done. You can't lie to the Veracity Resonator, so please don't lie to me. Tell me, when did you develop off-world travel?"

"I've just told you! It started around twenty years ago."

"Do not lie."

"What's a Veracity Resonator?" screamed Duke.

"It's the feeling you have in your head, making you tell the truth. When did you develop space travel?"

"Stop it! My head's going to explode. I've told you the truth…"

"No, you haven't"

"…Wait! You just said I can't lie to the Veracity Resonator!"

"That is true," confirmed the giant bantam.

"So…"

"So what?"

"Work it out for yourself!" roared Duke.

There was a pause.

"You are not lying," said the beak, its blotched tongue flicking back and forth.

"I'm not lying!" exclaimed Duke.

"But humans went to their Moon nearly sixty of your years ago."

"No, we didn't! That's your mistake."

"We don't make mistakes. When did humans go to the other planets?" persisted the creature.

"We haven't been to any other planets yet," pleaded Duke.

"Yes… you have," it replied.

# CHAPTER 19

The Knowall marked as Dex'2O perched at the edge of a desk.

"So, it's 1983 already. Why are we here?"

"And that's what we were asking," shot back Tina, amplifying her frustration.

"I mean why are all of us here… this moment, this century?"

"An easy question first," chipped in Nelson.

"You are being obtuse," chided Tina.

"How did we get to where we are today?"

"Humans?"

"Yes, like you two."

"I'm not sure what you are getting at. Are you making some opaque reference to evolution?" queried Nelson.

"Exactly." The Knowall took in a deep breath and pulled back his shoulders, stretching the gold braid of clouds taught across his vermillion robe. "And what is evolution? Simply put, it is change. Tiny mutations or mistakes at the cellular or microscopic level in any organism's genes or DNA, can lead over plenty of time to long term change for the species."

"Yes, yes," interrupted Nelson, "I've studied evolution at school and university."

"Indeed," admired the Knowall, "I see you're a Paleontologist at heart."

"Excuse me Dex, but I'm not one of those!" put in Tina. "What are you boys going on about?"

"We're talking about change, my dear. Evolution. Even *revolution*. It is all around us and has been forever.

And not just in our bodies, but in our minds. You see, we're in the United Kingdom, aren't we?"

His statement appeared to be more confirming the fact for his own needs, before progressing.

"Yes, the UK. Do you two recall your O-level history lessons? The Luddites? One of the reasons we..." he waved his hands before them, "are in this room, in this very situation, is a direct outcome of the Luddites."

"The who?" asked Nelson.

"No, The Who are a pop group," grinned the older man. "I'm talking about the Luddites from the early 19th century. A small group of English labourers in the textile industry. They made a big mistake, but with a lot of public support. Change had started accelerating, and they certainly did not like it."

"Hang on," interrupted Nelson, glancing back at the door, "What have textile workers got to do with evolution and this... *Cloud Computing* thing?"

"Indirectly quite a lot. The Luddites violently opposed the introduction of new machinery to these Isles at the beginning of the Industrial Revolution. Great Britain was leading the world in innovation, and that Revolution was born on this island. So, what did the Luddites do? Like God-fearing, law-abiding citizens, they feared change and revolted. They were terrified of the new equipment, believing the machinery would take away their jobs, their livelihood, and their dignity. They rioted and wrecked it. They were arrested of course, but their actions underlined the public discontent to the introduction of anything new. Are you still with us Nelson?"

Nelson was staring at Tina as she focused on the Knowall. For him the words had no coherence.

"Sorry, the Luddites? I vaguely remember my history lessons, but I was more into biology..."

"Nelson, 200 years ago the Luddites were skilled manual labourers who despised the introduction of machinery and destroyed it, fearing for their skillsets and their jobs. Their leaders were arrested. Textile production continued whilst the machinery was repaired. But…"

The Knowall paused as he observed Nelson's concentration wander across to his surroundings and back to Tina.

"Oh, I'm sorry!"

"Restoring the machinery took time, and in this intermission the inventors came up with bigger and better versions, ready to take their place on the factory floor. So far so good?"

"I think so," said Nelson.

"Yes, absolutely," stated Tina.

"But… here's where *we* made the big mistake."

"We?"

"I'll come to that. The inventors agreed it may be better to wait until the workers became comfortable with the original machines - before they introduced their new versions. This first mistake started… the pattern."

"What pattern?" refocused Nelson.

"These new releases were deliberately stalled. They were held back, giving the workforce a time to catch up. But inventors by their nature, do not sit around idle. They pursued reinvention and refinement. And then… mistake on mistake on mistake. By the time they felt the workers were ready for their second creations, behind the scenes each of the machines were already into their fourth or fifth generation."

"Oh dear," anticipated Tina.

"Very well put. *Upgrades* my dear fellows. *Upgrades*. We are talking persistent, unstoppable change and progress. Most individuals naturally resist change in their everyday lives. They still do, and when you relate this to industrial machinery it becomes ever more problematic. And then… enter the revolutionary concept of electricity and the genie is out of the bottle. And so, the mistakes kept happening."

"What's the mistake with electricity?" asked Nelson, clearly struggling.

"You see Nelson, the invention of electricity came as the industrial machinery evolved. Humanity's reach to electric power truly emerged just a few years after the Luddite riots. But you can see what that would mean to them."

He paused, as if for dramatic effect, but also to let it sink in. At that instant Nelson's head was down as he idly reached the back of his own neck, freezing mid scratch. Like a trapped schoolboy, his eyebrows arched upwards to meet the Knowall's querying gaze, yet he had nothing to offer. His eyes rolled over towards Tina's display of intense concentration. Nelson's arid mouth began to open slowly.

"The threat of *bigger* change?" burst in Tina.

"Very perceptive my dear."

Nelson's scratch changed to a gentle stroke and massage of his neck muscles. He was out of kilter and flooded with negative recollections of Pure Mathematics lessons, caught in the scholastic headlights as fellow pupils nodded sagely. This room was so white, it's a lace on his Adidas trainer was loosening. Tina's ankles were crossed and the leather on her court shoes shone brightly. He knew so few perfumes, yet he was certain hers was *White Linen* by Estee Lauder.

"Yes!" snapped Dex the Knowall. "Electricity! An enormous change. And by now our highly sensitive textile workers were four generations of machinery behind their inventors… how would the poor souls possibly cope with a limitless, invisible power source… when they'd been paid to break their backs for aeons?"

"They couldn't cope," said Tina.

"No way José, I believe is the phrase," he confirmed. "So going back to the question, the mistake here my dear Nelson, was the introduction of electricity was also postponed… by about 20 years! I promise we have nearly finished."

Nelson nodded faintly.

"The obvious consequence? Technology crept ahead of the human race - and an elite group was forming, ultimately deciding what, how and when to introduce new machinery and concepts."

"A technology mafia!"

"Again, not the phrase I'd choose. But they anticipated a future emerging in advance of current society's capability to cope with it. So, this future demanded to remain covert, until the human race was ready for it.

"A secret future?" said Tina.

"Yes, *our secret future,* all based on all those early mistakes," confirmed the Knowall.

"And it's still going today?"

"It was always designed to be short-lived, proposed as a temporary measure. A secret society was formed to guard the future... and take it *underground.* Which is literally what they did."

"Under Yorkshire?" offered Nelson.

"To start with. The mills of Sheffield and Manchester was chosen as a first step. From here the Industrial Revolution took off. Albeit much later and slower than it should have. Hmm... Catching flies Nelson?"

Nelson shut his mouth.

"So, these Luddites... weren't they just a moment in time?" challenged Tina.

"Yes, unique. In the Victorian era we accelerated. Photography, rubber, oil, typewriters, electric lighting, we pushed such a variety out. But humanity always had two hostile factors lurking. War and greed. We started planning our first forays into space in 1917. What were you doing then – one guess?"

"World War I?"

"Correct. Very much your mistake that one. We'd

given you engines, petrol and flight and you concentrated on turning them into tanks and fighter planes. Then by the end of 1920's we're ready to go to the Moon. And you... have turned rampant capitalism on its head and immersed yourselves in The Great Depression. Another great mistake. So, we went to the Moon anyway, without telling anyone."

"But Dex..." started Nelson, "how could you do that without the rest of the world knowing?"

"It was a challenge. Giant airplane and spaceship launches are difficult to conceal, but on seeing such a contraption by accident the local populace would report it as a meteor, cloud formation, or even schools of flying fish. Aren't people quaint? And then, wonderfully unexpectedly, the phrase 'Flying Saucers' hit your press. From that moment, we had it made. If any of our experimental craft were spotted, they were reported as *unidentified flying objects*, and only a small collection of cranks cared to investigate. Easy.

"UFOs!" said Tina suddenly.

"It's unbelievable," said Nelson.

"That was all we had to do. The rest took care of itself. Like all the news yesterday about our *UFOs* between Manchester and Sheffield."

"That was you?" crowed Nelson.

"Of course."

"Ha! Right here. Right above us in the Peak..."

The Knowall paused, looked to the ceiling, and gave a deep exhale.

"And there you have it." he said, resting his eyes back on the two of them.

Aware of his own deep frown spreading over his brow, Nelson met the Knowall's gaze, turned him over in his mind's eye and gently rotated him side to side. He tried to analyse this old man's constituents without rising from his seat. There was the faintest whiff of chlorine in the barren room, or the remnants of an intense cleaning fluid that maintained its sterility.

"So," he said finally, "a covert underworld… is controlling our future?"

"Effectively, yes."

"Now I can see why your Air Force man back there called you a tech mafia."

"We prefer the term Knowall."

"Of course you do, it's far better for the ego."

"We didn't actually choose it Nelson; it was chosen for us. Before our founders went underground, the insult was constantly being hurled at them. Mud sticks, and in the end, they decided not to fight it and just adopt the convenient moniker. It's been with us ever since."

"Hmm. One last question Dex," Nelson ventured.

"Please."

"What is *Cloud Computing*?"

"I genuinely have no idea," said the Knowall. "Maybe you can talk about it later with young Bez'0S. Please follow me."

# CHAPTER 20

The Knowall strode from the Cloud Computing room and into the hallway. Nelson and Tina dutifully followed, each processing in their own way this new information. They walked past the many lacquered doors with their plated signs. Nelson paused in front of:

*DARWIN 2.0 & HYPERMUTATION*

This had significantly piqued his interest as they first entered the corridor.

"What's in there?"

"A mystery we are still in the process of solving."

"You think Darwin was wrong!" exclaimed Nelson.

"No, not at all," said the Knowall, "…but we think he may still need some help."

"*Yes*! I agree entirely," interjected Nelson, more animated than at any point since their arrival.

"You do?" The Knowall was taken aback by this unexpected outburst from a man he may have judged too soon.

"I certainly do, Dex. The Cambrian Explosion… even Darwin couldn't explain it and ventured it could upset his own theories. A violent and rapid burst of new lifeforms in all directions coming after a tiny background hum of minimal evolution for billions of years beforehand. It doesn't make sense, does it? Never did! It's still a mystery what caused it."

"Indeed, my dear Nelson. One of your passions, is it?"

"It was Dex, at least until I had to leave academia and come into the real world." Nelson dropped his head slightly disconsolately and stared at the floor for a few seconds. He looked back up at the Knowall. "So, what's your *hypermutation* theory then?"

"Exactly that Nelson, a theory. Or perhaps some form of interference. Let's walk and talk."

The Knowall led them along the corridor and away from the large chamber from which they fled. He steered through another series of corridors. Nelson and Tina walked flanking him either side.

Tina listened respectfully and absent-mindedly to notions of *programmed mutation* she didn't understand or care about, all the while stealing surreptitious looks at their guiding figure in his dark red robes. Though he was clearly aging, there was something older and deeper within him, as though a large burden weighed heavy. She tuned back into their conversation when Nelson asked a strange question.

"So just a minute. This sounds like your Darwin 2.0 thinking is leading towards some form of divine intervention?"

"Nelson!" The chastisement was formal. "We are scientists and technologists at heart, not theologians."

The Knowall's spurning eyes were unwavering. Confident of the subject matter, Nelson held his ground.

"Well, everything you've told me so far appears to head that way."

"We're still working through our hypothesis, but along the way there was some mistake or interference that affected our genetic code and DNA... and the mutations accelerated. After that, evolution started going a whole lot faster. The origin of that mistake is key," stated the old man flatly. He then snapped a gesture with his arm and abruptly moved on, dismissing further comment.

They had reached a T-junction in the corridors. All the floors were rubberized, and their steps made little sound. Neatly etched into the wall before them was a deep triangle pointing to the left labelled *Laboratory Mezzanine, Keppler Wing, Lifts.*

Following the signs, the three of them walked on in quiet. Tina broke the silence.

"Okay, Lord Dex of the Red Robe, moving on from evolution, interference, some big mistake, and the Luddites… why are we *actually* here?"

"I believe your friend Nelson has shared the backdrop."

"Not really. His NASA letter, my nice legs and all that crap. But I still don't get why both of us are here with you now."

"We had to take action when he threatened us with his NASA letter."

"Come off it, I didn't threaten you."

"We couldn't take that risk Nelson, we had to find out what you knew. The Directorate is approaching a critical point in our planning, and we need to control all variables."

"Excuse me," interrupted Tina, "I'm asking a question. Why us, why here, and why all this chat?"

"We believed that letter was the last of its kind. Once Nelson came to us with it, we had to act quickly." He turned towards Nelson. "You really didn't give us any time for lengthy decision making, so the decision was taken to extract and erase."

"Ah. So, there you go, my NASA letter wasn't a fake?" cheered Nelson.

"Well, that depends on how you look at it. Indeed, there was a Doctor Grimaldi, and he was a Knowall."

"So, he did exist? I knew it!"

"Is this the guy that was supposed to have lived in my flat?"

"Yes Tina. He just loved North London. You see, we've always had a handful of our troupe on the *surface*. They are our *progressive missionaries*, tasked with moving humanity's future forward as rapidly as possible. We call them *Progressionaries*. Exceptions were made with

Grimaldi allowing him to stay permanently on the *surface* and be a Non-Executive Progressionary… provided he told no one. Not even his new wife. In retrospect this was also a big mistake.

"And why is that?" asked Nelson.

Another tiled tunnel, this time in light blue, led a sweeping curve into the distance. A similar triangle pointed right to *Reception, Directorate, Cafeteria.* Walking this way, the Knowall continued talking. Nelson perked up at the thought of food.

"In 1968, Grimaldi's wife left him. She had been threatening it and he tried everything to stop it happening. But he couldn't tell her the truth. This was our explicit message, or we'd revoke his *surface* privileges. So, she packed up and walked out one night, never to return. Her note said she knew he was up to something. Grimaldi was distraught. In his grief he lost all good sense and blamed us for his dual life. In retaliation, he forged a series of official letters and scattered them across various sites in the hope intellectuals may discover them. He used NASA's branding because he knew it's the one place where you will find the biggest group of Knowalls above ground."

"Damn right," muttered Nelson.

"And you, Nelson, found what we believe is the last remaining letter, which was slipped into that encyclopaedia nearly fifteen years earlier - but don't tell the publishers."

"And me?" sighed Tina.

The Knowall smiled. Tina returned it with a potent scowl.

"I'm not afraid to slap you as well!" she called.

Nelson and Tina were inundated. Peering to the

middle distance with glazed eyes glazed they walked mechanically, absent in their own thoughts. The Knowall granted a few moments of silence, allowing the full implication of recent monologues to sink in.

With a jaunty manner, absent from his previous declarations, he continued.

"So… hopefully you can see how a Moon landing was possible in May 1929. However, Hans Logforn was the first there. His historic words were: *A new world, a new opportunity, a new... Sss. Pop. Thud."*

"What?" shrugged Tina.

"He hadn't sealed his space suit correctly. It's not footage we're proud of. Fortunately, at the time most of the world, including UK Prime Minister Baldwin and US President Hoover, were completely unaware of it. Neither were one of ours. And then, later, we sent another two-man mission, just to prove we could do it successfully. It is just a boring piece of rock. And finally, humanity caught up in 1969."

Becoming bored with the endless corridor walking, Tina stopped abruptly. A few steps in front of her Nelson and the Knowall pulled up.

"So Dex, you have told us everything that went wrong and the mistakes that were made?"

"I believe I have. Full disclosure."

"In that case I have to ask, do you have a plan to move things forward?" she ventured.

The older man turned his gaze to fix on her and grinned.

"A very perceptive question my dear." He stepped a few paces back to be next to her.

"Thank you," she blushed.

"We've been constantly trying. We believed everything was rolling like clockwork during the late 60's and on through those crazy 70's. We released a huge volume to you then. Microchips were everywhere, doing everything, getting smaller all the time. You couldn't get enough, and we put a couple of key tech guys on the *surface* as Progressionaries, to try to speed things up.

"So, we're catching up?" offered Tina.

"You were. But..."

"Yes?"

"Well, now you're all feeling threatened by the robot, computers, artificial intelligence and the notion of increased leisure time. So we asked ourselves, *where do we go from here*?"

"Helloooo...!" interrupted Nelson, "Er... food?" He indicated onwards down the corridor and the sign marked *Cafeteria*.

"Nelson, shush!" urged Tina.

The Knowall hesitated, seemingly to consider his next words. He held his hands open and looked mutely at them for a long time.

"Nelson, Tina... it's not just the fact that the human race has fallen behind, or that you are struggling to catch up. It grieves me deeply to say that the saddest thing now, beyond all of this, is we are witnessing a once promising species embark on a journey that appears impossible for anyone to control. A journey that points towards disaster for every single one of us."

"What kind of journey?" came their simultaneous response.

"Mutually Assured Destruction. *MAD* as you ironically term it. You are proliferating nuclear weapons and multiplying these warheads to the point where even we can no longer keep track. This leaves just one option open to our Directorate, which we are now well on the way to achieving. Please, let's walk on, we're nearly there. I'm happy to answer any more questions."

A few seconds silence. The irritable bowel flared.

"I need to go again," said Nelson. "Where are the toilets?"

# CHAPTER 21

The rear pane of Duke's confining glass cube swung away with a faint hiss. All heat emanating from the high-back chair subsided together with his headache. Seconds later his wrist restraints popped open, and he gently rubbed life back into their chafed skin.

"I am genuinely so sorry," came the voice from behind. A strange warble he had quickly become familiar with. "I just needed the truth quickly and efficiently."

Duke rose slowly from his captive chair and turned to look at the creature. Its oppressive presence remained, though the thick glass no longer separated them. Duke could see the feather-like gown, wrapped by what appeared as a cloak, extending from its head down towards its oddly shaped yellow boots, tipped with individual toe sections.

It was a short, squat creature that stood vertical and straight. As his familiarity with its shape grew it gently became less terrifying, and his instinctive insult of Foghorn Leghorn gave him a wry smile.

"I see that hopefully you are relaxing a little," it said. "I now accept that everything you told me was the truth... at least from your perspective."

"Where is my dad's coat?" Duke demanded.

The creature looked around uncertainly, shrugged slightly and attempted a gentle smile back. Ignoring the question, it continued.

"I need to learn more about this historical Cambrian Explosion, and also what you know about spaceflight. None of it makes sense so far."

Duke continued to massage feeling back into his wrists and sighed deeply.

"Why? I never signed up for anything like this. Why are you asking me about evolution and off-world travel?"

"These are the reasons I am here now."

"Who and what are you?"

"Come with me, and I'll explain" it said. "But first I'd like you to meet Zero."

# CHAPTER 22

The relief was so palpable in Nelson's bladder that for a few seconds he forgot his situation. He zipped and vacated another bleached white cubicle to rejoin his walk with Tina and their companion obliquely referred to as a *Knowall*.

Tina continued her challenge.

"So, you're saying the human race has jumped from Luddites to all-out nuclear warmongers."

"With a few steps in between."

"Yet you have calmly threatened to *erase* us. What makes you any different?"

"It's not what you think," started the old man, "by being erased, we're not exterminating you or undertaking anything detrimental to your health."

"Then what does it mean?"

"It's a self-protection mechanism for both of us. Say, for example, someone unearthed one of your hidden traits, and you'd really rather they hadn't…"

"Yes," cut in Nelson, "…like when a friend catches you top-shelfing at the newsagent magazine rack?"

A librarial silence descended, the Knowall and Tina turned in bewilderment.

"Not exactly what I had in mind," declared the Knowall finally, "but the parallels are comparable."

He scratched his white stubble again digging deep to his ebony skin, and then continued, "In summary, you'd rather their discovery was kept private given the effort you've expended crafting your image."

"That's right," said Nelson.

"Well, we have a lot to protect here, and you know of our existence. If you are to become part of it then we need to initiate a process that we term erasure. We need you to gently disappear without raising any vast amounts of suspicion. It helps that neither of you were previously connected to the other. We must erase you. We effectively slowly remove you from the human race, and once we're comfortable it has been a success, your records will be... erased."

Two pairs of eyes widened in dismay.

"It's a delicious and sinister expression, which is probably why we use it. It simply means that you will live here now - outside of humanity. And you can be of great use to us."

"Why do you need us, and what do we have to say in this matter?" challenged Nelson.

"It's clear you need to evaluate your situation," beamed the Knowall. "We're not planning to incarcerate you or similar dramatic action. We simply want to invest in your future and show how you can help us, and we can help you."

"But it would be imprisonment?" confirmed Tina.

"That suggests you have no choice in the matter, and *choice* hangs on how your preference develops. Also, please bear in mind, if you went back screaming about our activities, no one would believe you - and it would severely damage any credibility you have."

"Well, I won't be held against my will," puffed Nelson.

Their walk opened out into the appearance of a reception space. A burnished stone desk of unnecessary length stretched in front of three frosted glass doors, each wide enough to drive a large car through. Another impossibly thin monitor rose from the countertop, and a slender, translucent chair was empty behind it. Globular sofas in dazzling orange were arranged against two of the walls. There was a faint smell of sandalwood. The Knowall motioned Tina and Nelson to sit.

"Our desire is for a voluntarily outcome once you've come to terms with our offer and had chance to get to know us. We're a pleasant little community here, with numerous incentives. We'll setup your own Facebook accounts and connect you to the rest of our world."

He widened his eyes and tilted his head faintly, as if the offer were irresistible. No immediate acceptance was forthcoming, so he pressed on.

"Nelson, you haven't really got much of a life in Kilburn have you? We know you're becoming a little jaded with supplement journalism."

"It's West Hampstead, please." corrected Nelson. "And what's a face book?"

"Not a face book Nelson. Facebook. This will become clear. We've done our research. You've no close friends since Duke Kramer left, a couple of distant relatives in Cornwall you never speak to, and an uncle in Buenos Aires."

Nelson opened his mouth first to protest - but instead he found himself yelling:

"*Buenos Aires*!"

"An uncle Colin I believe - works on vineyard."

"I thought he was dead," said Nelson.

"Apparently not," said the Knowall.

"A vineyard? And who on Earth would buy wine from Argentina!"

"Very few at present, it seems. However, obviously his disappearance caused you no great consternation. My point being, why not put yourself to some use and stay with us. We genuinely feel you can help."

"Hang on, you know Duke? Where is he? Did you try to erase him?"

"We'll get to that."

Nelson raised his voice. "That postcard from Cyprus... I knew he'd never call me *buddy*. It was a clue. Do you know where he is? Tell me, because he seemed to disappear very quickly a..."

"Honestly Nelson, we'll come to that, please believe me," interrupted the Knowall. "We will draft a similar message for you, something simple to send to your separated parents. Maybe: '*Got bored with Computing. See you sometime*'. They'll assume you're testing an alternative lifestyle and that you're happy - which you will be. Give it a couple of years and you'll be a distant memory."

Nelson opened his mouth to speak.

"But where… is… my friend? This all…"

"And *me*?" yelled Tina forcefully.

The air between them had been cut. No one spoke for a few seconds. The Knowall took a quiet breath and tried to stitch back the space that had opened.

"Well, I must admit that you are a bit of an unknown my dear. You're young. Not much to go home to, or so we believe. I hope you don't have a boyfriend, engagement, or similar?"

"Not currently," said Tina. "Through my own choice" she added. "It's not to say I couldn't have, or a job and income, if I chose to, which I don't - and wouldn't - if I stay here - which I might, if I choose to - which I might also."

Another hush descended. Nelson and the Knowall waited.

"What's the matter with you two?" snarled Tina.

Nelson turned back to the Knowall. "Okay, I can't talk for Tina, but you are right. I'm intrigued, and there is only so many more times I can type *kilobyte* or *Commodore 64* before I tear up my floppy disks. So, how far is the human race still behind, and *where* is Duke?"

"Well, now we're in 1983, we've estimated it would take us to 2025 to fully equalize. So, forty or so years," the Knowall answered.

"That long?" exhaled Nelson.

"At least. And we've already been to Uranus and back just to see if the locals like the name we've given it."

"It's inhabited!" exclaimed Nelson.

"No, it's a joke," sighed the Knowall. "But we have developed interplanetary travel to the point where we are ready for our final option."

"What do you mean by that?" asked Tina.

"We'll come to that as well. Time is pressing. You'll enjoy it here."

"Enjoy it! That's a stretch. We may have different perceptions of enjoyment," scoffed Nelson.

"Very true Nelson. All perceptions are relative. Enjoyment, sorrow, time, shock and surprise. We come to realise that they are all relative. I'm shocked you've listened calmly without screaming these walls down, but then what surprises me may be different to what surprises you."

His focus drifted and a wistfulness emerged across the Knowall's face. His hand stroked the smooth head.

"Ha. All of us experience shock in varying degrees. Do you know the last thing that goes through a flies mind when it hits a car windscreen?"

"No?"

The Knowall smiled.

"Its bum."

On the orange sofa, Nelson's elbows rested on his knees and his hands cupped his chin. Tina absent-mindedly wandered around to the slim reception monitor. It was marked *TOUCH SENSITIVE.*

"You and me both," she muttered.

The Knowall's eyes came back into clarity.

"Funny things – flies," he said finally.

"Hmm?" murmured Nelson.

"Flies."

"Yes…"

"They spend their lives buzzing inanely around some suburban living room and suddenly WHAM! –

they're on the front page of a national newspaper. Instant fame you could say."

"Where is all this going?" demanded Nelson.

Tina was similarly vexed. She had sunk into the limbo of her own thoughts but was emerging convinced she was beguiled by this venture, albeit setting aside Nelson, though he was curiously growing on her. Her exciting experiment in north London life had matured into routine, ripened into a ranking of *Okay*, and plunged towards sudden redundancy. Threatened with the return to her mining hometown, she was restless, longing for a change of scenery, pace, and a touch of the alternative. This current situation was beginning to stack up well.

"Thank you for listening," said Dex'2O. "I think it's about time that you met the others. I'm sure there will be a mutual fascination."

The Knowall pushed on one of the frosted glass doors. It pivoted just off its centre and he beckoned them to follow him through. As Nelson and Tina walked towards it, they noticed a small metal plaque on the door's frame marked:

*CENTRAL DIRECTORATE*

The door led to another immense room, this time fully paneled in dark wood, augmented by recessed lighting and an inky blue carpet of outlandish plushness. The tang of finely oiled carpentry hung in the air. The room was occupied by five men of varying ages and one striking looking woman, the same blond female they had seen leave their starlit chamber sometime earlier. A long, reflective table ran down the room's middle and a very black dog sat at the near end - a Doberman Pinscher that watched them intently.

The far wall sported a crest carved deep into the woodwork. It depicted an owl perched on a human brain. The owl's intricate eyes scowled intensely at Nelson as he read the words underneath. They said:

*WE ARE IMMENSELY CLEVER!*

"A little joke by our carpenters," informed the Knowall, "It should have said *IN KNOWLEDGE WE TRUST*, but you just can't get the tradesmen these days. Do make yourselves comfortable."

Three empty chairs were at the table. The Knowall took one and indicated Nelson and Tina to sit. Those already seated studied these two new visitors keenly. No warmth or emotion was yet evident on their faces.

Nelson glanced nervously at the huge dog. The Doberman Pinscher stared back menacingly, loudly barked five times, growled deeply, and was given a biscuit.

# CHAPTER 23

Duke left his glass cell and followed the bantam-creature from the chamber. He noticed dense tufts of feathers falling below its cloak. The corridors they walked through were small and cramped. Since arriving in his somnolent state, claustrophobic dimly lit enclosures had been Duke's sole experience. They reached a door, deeply recessed from the corridor. From the shadows a colossal chrome beast emerged.

Some eight feet tall, angular shoulders connected muscular, over-lengthened arms to its smoothed, powerful torso. Trunk-like legs flowed seamlessly into rounded feet that balanced its bulk. Due to the behemoth's height and the low corridor ceiling, the head was forced forward in an awkward tilt. It was domed and slashed with a single cyclops eye slit that stretched fully across an empty face. The faintest glow of magenta pulsed from within.

Both its hands were formed of three chrome digits. The palm of one held firm to a textured square panel beside the door. The beast was silent and immobile.

"This is Zero," said the fowl. "It would seem we haven't timed our introductions so well. It looks like he is upgrading."

On cue the textured squared panel partially covered by the robot's hand, emitted the faintest bip and displayed a small phrase:

*Step 2. Verifying Download. 68%*

"What the hell is *that*!" yelled Duke, pointing straight into the metal beast's eye. "And what is a... *download*?"

"All valid questions," replied the chicken.

"Valid questions! I'll give you valid questions.

*Where the hell are we?"*

Responding to this demand the bantam-creature squeezed passed the chrome titan, opening the door before him.

"Come with me."

The door swung away to reveal an impressive flight cockpit dominated by a principal pilot chair, two rear jump seats, myriad switches, displays and dials.

Easing cautiously past the robot, Duke followed into the room. He caught short and audibly gasped.

The chairs, switches and dials were crowned by a dramatic sweeping window spanning the full length of the cabin.

From tip to tip the window displayed a deep starlit universe which they were flying through.

"We're here," replied the chicken.

# CHAPTER 24

The vast meeting room Nelson and Tina found themselves in dwarfed its occupants, and chihuahuaed the Doberman Pinscher.

Three of its inhabitants donned lustrous white robes, each with a thin rainbow braiding stitched from sternum to sweep over their right shoulders. Four more, including the Knowall Dex2'O who had accompanied Nelson and Tina, sported the same deep vermillion robes with a variety of gold braid styles. The dog remained raven black.

Nelson appraised the scene. It was undeniably a wonderous sight, albeit with one clearly unsuited item.

A strawberry.

From the clean lines of the room's rich cherrywood walls, down to the curved lineation of the mirrored table, all was in balance. From the sweeping profile of the long table, pulling focus to the rounded porcelain salver planted impeccably in its centre, there was harmony. Yet slightly off-centre resting on that salver sat an isolated red strawberry with its bright green stalk.

Nelson's distracted imagination ignited and primed itself for lift off…

***TEN…***
*This is definitely not a strawberry.*

***NINE…guidance is internal***
*In my 1980's world, radios are made to mimic hamburgers, telephones represent cartoon mice, so I've learnt not to be fooled.*

***EIGHT…***
*And my world is now forty years off the pace of this underground realm. So, what could it be that sits here so*

*formidably before me?*

***SEVEN... ignition sequence starts***
*Okay, let's extrapolate the trend in miniaturisation by many decades. Aha, yes!*

***SIX...***
*Here is a rechargeable strawberry comprising a video camera with satellite dish incorporated into the stalk, suited to beaming discrete images of each person sat here anywhere in the world, probably on command of the Chairman's voice.*

***FIVE...***
*That is brilliant.*

***FOUR...***
*Hang on. Then again, its stalk could contain a microscopic laser, and relevant optical instruments, to reproduce holographic images of a strawberry... and it isn't really there at all!*

***THREE...***
*Oh I like that one. Genius.*

***TWO... all engines running***
*Come on, think bigger. Maybe... it is a banana injected with the appropriately encoded electro-chemicals empowering it to assume the shape and flavour of a strawberry, or any stand-in fruit, at the whim of its consumer.*

***ONE... LIFT OFF! we have lift off***
*Yes! Get in!*

A white-robed Knowall dislodged Nelson's enthrallment, and in an instant his fantastical speculation was answered.

"Would you like a strawberry?" the Knowall asked, "I'm afraid there's only one left."

*WHOOPS... forgot the clutch!*

"No, are you sure?" followed up the Knowall, "Final answer?" and without waiting for further reply he grabbed the fresh strawberry and popped it into his mouth, pitching the stalk to the Doberman in a single deft move.

The dog snapped, swallowed and growled. He was tiring of endless strawberry stalks and biscuits.

The silence settled across the room and touched the skin of each pair of hands clasped together on the table.

Shaking away his unnecessary curiosity regarding the red fruit, Nelson absorbed Tina's composure. He prized her growing confidence and her form. She sat calm and steady, the fringe and heavy brunette hair framed an exquisitely calm face. Both hands were crossed gently over each other in her lap, and the raincoat remained firmly belted. Unaware of his scrutiny, she was fully absorbed by the situation and their new hosts.

A new Knowall stood up sharply.

"The pair of them will do nicely," he said.

Nelson snapped back into his seat. He was off track.

"Yes, just fine. Welcome... to our underworld."

He was by far the tallest of their hosts, a clear six inches above Dex'2O. This Knowall's deep red robe sported the most elaborate double braid, featuring a procession of gold swans embroidered amongst delicate water ripples. A shock of white hair topped broad shoulders that suggested a strong physique beneath.

"I feel a few introductions are in order," he continued. "Nelson Staff and Tina Reagan..."

"Yes?" said Nelson and Tina in unison.

"Now..." said the tall man leaning in towards them, "which is which?"

Nelson grabbed both edges of his chair to prevent a fall.

"I'm sorry?" he managed.

"Which of you is Nelson and which is Tina? My apologies but it is the first time we've met."

With matching horror, Tina and Nelson stared at each other. Picking up on their concern the Knowall thumbed his swan braid, adding:

"Oh, I do beg your pardon. Sorry, we dispensed with gender defining names during a management restructure in the early 70's. Though some of us have a recollection of the old formats, it's a challenge recalling which sex they relate to. Let me see - would Nelson be masculine?"

"Marginally," offered Tina.

"Oh, I'm very sorry..." started the Knowall.

"Yes," intervened Nelson, "you are correct. I am Nelson and this is Tina."

"Oh good," said the Knowall, "Now, to make you feel at home we've undertaken to recall our old names. Or, where that hasn't been possible, the nearest guess. Hopefully, it will be more endearing than the likes of Dex'2O," he indicated his colleague that had accompanied Nelson and Tina thus far.

"Or mine he continued, which is Cha'3E."

Lightly touching the swan braid again, he continued

"So, instead of Cha'3E, or Cha, my new name is Charles Arthur Clarke. Or, to promote yet more familiarity, you can call me Charlie."

The deep eyes in his gaunt face managed to smile warmly. He then called out the three dressed in white opposite him.

"And these are now Mikhail Gee..." a stout

middle-aged figure nodded faintly back at them. A striking red birthmark showed on his head through receding hair.

"Then my dearest colleague Emm'8K, now Emma Kay… or back to just Emm, if you prefer?"

The female's stunning light blue eyes were amicable. Her blond hair curled towards her shoulders and fell over the collar of her white robe. She held up a hand to wave. Charlie continued around the room.

"And a couple of our younger members here, Fry'1S, who we have forenamed as Stephen, he prefers the traditional spelling. There are big plans for him."

An apprehensive young man smiled back at them. A fop of dark hair swept down to his left brow and stretched across to the right. As an affectation he held an unlit pipe in his hand and touched it to his mouth.

"Pleased to meet you," smiled Nelson.

"Good day."

"And by far our youngest member at the table, Bez'0S, now Jeff. We're still working things out, but he will have a huge future, won't you Jeff? In our Museum that you visited, it was his Cloud room you ran into."

A fresh-faced young man no older than his late teens, with centre-parted hair and strong eyebrows, looked intently into Nelson and Tina's eyes. He spoke efficiently.

"If we stay focused, we can achieve all our goals." He then smiled too broadly and followed this statement with an awkward burst of laughter.

"Thank you Jeff. Wise words, and I know we will be relying on you soon."

Charlie now turned to his remaining colleagues.

"Then we have your new friend, Dex'2O… now Dexter Oh."

Their ebony skinned guide with the white stubble blinked and nodded warmly back.

"Thank you for the tour," said Tina.

"No problem."

"Next to Dexter is our very own Doctor Xing, the principal brains at this table."

Xing nodded at them efficiently and impassively.

Cha'3E, now Charlie, turned to the concluding male sitter, his voice raising appreciably.

"And, of course..." he paused, clearly trying to recall the replacement name for his final colleague. He held out is hand towards the man who was markedly the oldest member of their group, hunched at the table, translucent skin accentuating liver spots across his cheeks, bare head and hands. A silver goatee beard attempted growth from his chin.

A pause hung in the air.

"Gloria!" wheezed the grey face atop the frail body.

"Pah!" Nelson's fast exhale came out uncontrollably.

"Ah yes, Gloria," continued Charlie, raising an eyebrow in disbelief.

"And there you have it."

Nelson regained self-control. Sensing a strong urge to say something, he held back.

"Yes, I'd leave it if I were you," whispered Tina.

The dog barked.

"Apologies, of course! Our four-legged friend here is called Bulldog," added Charlie, "previously Zen'K9."

"But it's a Doberman Pinscher," challenged Tina.

"Yes, we are aware of the fact, but yelling *Sit Doberman Pinscher* would become tedious."

"So, what's wrong with a classic dog name like Rex?" queried Tina.

Gloria wheezed and laughed, coughed, and then laughed and wheezed.

"Rex!" he gasped, "What a ludicrous name."

"Er..." began Tina.

"As you just said, I'd leave it," interrupted Nelson, "it's not worth it," smiling sympathetically at each of the Knowalls.

Each assembly member ensured their chairs were square with the table and lightly replaced their hands on its surface.

"So, what happens next?" Nelson asked finally.

"Quite a lot actually," replied Charlie. "I understand Dexter has filled you in on exactly who we are, how we come to be here. And to some extent why you are here."

"Yes, we're quite *filled in*."

"Happy about everything so far?"

"I could say ecstatic, but..."

"I know. A lot to take in such a short space of time."

"It's sinking in," said Tina.

"Good. Excellent. And late tonight we are all going to Puerto Rico."

The silence returned briefly.

"Puerto Rico!" exclaimed Nelson.

"Yes. A charming little island."

"Puerto Rico! Is that where Duke is?"

"Let me explain," began Charlie reseating himself. "We are the Central Directorate for the Knowalls, resulting in a large degree of duty and accountability. The challenge of controlled technological distribution to a bunch of primiti... to humanity, has proven forever more burdensome. Right now, we still have our Progressionaries amongst you trying to accelerate its adoption. But as we've learnt to be delicate and careful, we've also begun to realise... well, it may be futile cause.

Two of a new team have been on the *surface* for some time, and are making steady progress: Gat'6B and Job'6S. Steady, determined progress. What new names did we give them?" he asked, turning to his peers.

"Bill and Steve," rasped Gloria.

"Ah yes, our double-act, Bill and Steve. Jobs and Gates. Unimaginative names, one with a job to do, one serving as a gatekeeper. However, they have served their purpose. We asked them to be patient, play their characters well, and build up a momentum."

He paused, as if compiling a mental list.

"We have plans a lot for humanity to devour a vast array of concepts in coming years…"

"Such as?" interrupted Nelson.

"Oh, personal computers, mobile phones, tablets, phablets, private clouds, wearables, and then onto music, media the digital revolution, Call of Duty, cures for malaria… the list is endless for you through the rest of the Eighties, into the Nineties and beyond. And if young Jeff here gets chance to play his cards right, it will go on and on."

"But we've already got tablets?" queried Nelson. "I take vitamin C every morning. Will it make me live longer?"

The Knowall smiled. Stalling a few seconds before he continued.

"Our people have needed to be so careful up on the *surface*. We all still grieve over what happened with one of our finest assets, Jay'4K. Nobody… *nobody*, saw that coming. Killed for decreeing a Moon landing before the end of the Sixties. It turned out to be a bad move."

Charlie's dark eyes misted and his pale face turned down, the first demonstrable show of emotion.

Nelson and Tina glanced at each other in disbelief.

"J4K? You mean… but we were told it was a lone gunman, or the Cubans. Or now, even the Mafia?"

"Of course you were!" snapped Charlie. "Sometimes putting a cover in place is far more challenging than implementing the original plan."

He rubbed a thumb knuckle below his left eye and recovered his composure.

"So, as part of our scheming we've made mistakes, but one overshadows all of these. One vast miscalculation. A cock-up. We trusted you… and it has gone spectacularly wrong."

"Nuclear weapons?" probed Tina.

"Very quick, my dear. Many years ago, our scenario analysis predicted a fossil energy shortage if you continued to consume oil, gas and coal at such a carefree rate. If you ran the world dry of these resources, we forecast all hell breaking loose. So, at the time it appeared that we had only one option."

"Start a miner's strike?" offered Nelson.

"No, Nelson, the years of your major strikes are about to be gone forever, believe me. I'm talking about atomic energy. We chose to invest you with the immense power of the atom." He paused and stared blankly into the middle distance before continuing.

"The idea was tentatively released. And then, what do you do? Before we even see a nuclear motor, power plant or any controlled experimentation… you've exploded dozens of nuclear bombs and irradiated the atmosphere. Big mistake for you, very bad news for us. And… what can we do now? We're approaching 1984 and it's impossible to ask for the idea back. You are proliferating country by country, America versus the Soviets, East versus West."

"But this is Reagan and Andropov you're talking about. They just don't like each other. It's not the rest of us," pleaded Nelson.

"They control all the warheads Nelson. But, as if that weren't enough, extending the scenario analysis further yields predictions of religious fundamentalism and global terrorism. Put that with nuclear weapons and it is very, very worrying. It is now out of control. Mutually Assured Destruction. Ha! Our angriest membership wants to kick you in the cojones, just to wake you up. Humanity does not seem to appreciate the true consequences of what you are playing with. And now we've lost grip."

Nelson and Tina's breathing deepened. This induction was taking a chilling turn.

"So, we have one other... *option*."

"What other option?"

"Well, you see now, we're letting you have it."

"The kick in the cojones?"

"No. The Earth. We're leaving you to it. We have an immense plan that has been many years in gestation, with a major milestone just ahead. We call it *The Quit*. So, there you have it. I believe that… is a fair summary?" concluded Charlie, glancing at his colleagues. He stopped speaking and nods came from the Directorate in confirmation of his words.

"*The Quit*?" queried Nelson, "I'm sorry, but I don't quite fully understand. Is that why we are all going to Puerto Rico… to retire?"

"Ha! No, not retirement. It's quite simple..."

"But, Puerto Rico?"

"My apologies Nelson, there will be more time later to delve deeper. And I can confirm that this is indeed where your friend Duke comes into it."

"*Duke*! He's here?"

"Not exactly, but… right now, we the Reds are already late, and must leave you. We'll meet again shortly."

Charlie stood to leave. Two more red robed Knowalls rose to join him.

"I've been meaning to ask," said Tina, just before they departed.

"Yes my dear?" paused Charlie.

"Well, the different coloured robes - four of you in red and three more in white. Is it to do with your status within the Directorate, your function, or seniority?"

"Oh no my dear," smiled Charlie, "we're playing in a football match this afternoon. These are our team colours."

"Oh, I see. And the black dog?"

"He's the referee."

# PART TWO

# THEIR MISTAKES

*There's a starman waiting in the sky. He'd like to come and meet us, but he thinks he'd blow our minds.*
David Bowie

# CHAPTER 25

## StarDate 1

### Pending[7]
### Mayall II Cluster, Andromeda Galaxy

Whether you care about it or not, we live in an improbable cosmos.

A barely imaginable large group of stars is termed a galaxy, and an inconceivably greater group of galaxies is named a cluster. Then an impossibly vast collection of clusters is designated a supercluster.

To put this in context, our very own Laniakea Supercluster contains one hundred thousand galaxies and would require a naïve Einstein half a billion light-years to chase a beam across it. At the epicentre of this supercluster sits the Great Attractor governing space, time and the politically incompetent Republic of The Galactic Core.

A wretched migrant ship is streaming through Laniakea's Eastern edge.

*Schtip.*

The lift was white, hygienic and still worked.

It incorporated no unnecessary design features and all this simplicity agreed with its occupant. A harsh thin light glared down onto pale blue flesh and the stiffened grey uniform of a developed narcissist. Elsewhere it caught glass, titanium and carboplastene.

[7] Calendars and time zones remain tricky across an infinite void.

Characteristic musky smells were subdued by a freshening detergent mist. A hand raised to touch the privileged button pronounced above all others.

*Schtop.*

Both doors responded and slid to a close. A long ascent and the figure emerged into a spacious room with darkened recesses ascribed to faulty lighting. The whole domain was overshadowed by a vast screen depicting infinite stars speckling their reach into an inky black universe.

"Jip jip. Wap wap."

"Jip jip. Wap wap."

The ship's alarm was talking. Slogg knew it was the ship's alarm and this grated on his nerves. Seating himself in a lavish, bloated chair, sharp orange eyes embedded in an oversized skull darted across the more senior members his crew.

Allowing time for his elbows to sink in the soft memory fabric of their seat arms, followed by each splayed fingertip, he reminisced of an era when alarms were incapable of speech. They had sounded with simple electronic tones: two bursts of high frequency followed by two at low frequency. Slogg flashed to a question, posed during his Andromedan Cadet School, concerning the tone made by a ship's primary alarm.

He had answered:

"Two chords.... somewhat like *Jip jip, wap wap*."

Unable to commit to any form of revision, Slogg had relied solely on instinct and a fine memory to survive. His answer was deemed an accurate approximation and widely accepted. Those pioneering days were fondly regarded for their purity. Then came Duplicated Voice Synthesis, assuring perfectly orchestrated speech. The notorious Galactic Core psychologist Hola Migola was paid a colossal consulting fee to develop a hypothesis that concluded: if a ship's primary alarm was consistently likened to *Jip jip, wap wap* then it must be far more logical and agreeable to have it simply say *Jip jip, wap wap*? This would prove more congenial, effectively reducing the on-board Assessed Anxiety Factor, and inducing a melodious wellbeing throughout the workplace, whenever the alarm need be deployed. To secure his completion bonus, Migola recommended upgrading the entire Galactic Fleet would ensure every crewmember's mind was focused on dealing with any ensuing danger.

"Jip jip. Wap wap."

"Jip jip. Wap wap."

The ship's alarm was talking, and it grated on Slogg's nerves.

"What are we going to do? *What are we going to do*!" panicked the First Officer.

"We're going to *die*!" assured the Second Officer.

"Quiet!" hissed Slogg, glaring contemptuously at his two new reports. They were both very young, sported the same crew-cut jet black hair, huge eyes, and had been assigned to his bridge for Galactic Fleet work experience. A matter in which he was given no choice and thoroughly resented. Beyond their generic titles, he privately named them Bleep and Booster and generally looked straight through them when he spoke.

"Will someone please turn off the alarm."

"Captain, the Assessed Anxiety Factor has increased by four point two," reported Tarooc, the ship's heavyset Chief Wellness Officer. All Delta Nebulans possess a stocky gene, hypervigilance to potential threats, an overactive sex drive, and three eyes: two set very wide in a broad forehead, and one that has evolved to the back of the skull.

Tarooc turned to view his Captain in stereo.

"Say that again," ordered Slogg.

"Four point two," Tarooc replied, his third eye winking at the Communications Officer seated behind him.

"No, not that," said Slogg, "the first part."

"What... *Captain?*" repeated the baffled Delta Nebulan.

"Ah," sighed Slogg, "Captain. *C A P T... E N...*"

He never could spell.

Yet this did nothing to deter his own self-publicity.

For Deutronimus Karben Slogg, commanding a heavily armed ship of the Galactic Fleet was a pure joy and well-deserved outcome, even one crewed by the requisite high quota of hotchpotch Laniakea migrants. He was at ease with the role, and piloting an armed vessel was not an entirely new experience[8].

"Collision course still set, Captain," reported the ship's Navigator. Walta Woppedd wore his burgundy tunic with matching collar buttoned tight to the neck revealing just a tip of cravat. This being his first tour of duty as a newly graduated Galactic Fleet Navigator, he was fully exhilarated. His teenage brush with celebrity had freed him from the bullying throes of school and bestowed on him bleached fair hair that departed the side of his head horizontally. This perched above pointed ears, then curled up in formation to meet on the crown in a majestic rolling wave, cascading down over his forehead to a sharp point, held firm with patented spray. His uniform trousers might cut low hedges with their sharply ironed creases.

"Ah," sighed Slogg as the alarm was switched off, "Captain."

---

[8] Growing up in a predominantly criminal patriarchy, Slogg became the youngest juvenile to hot-wire an Off-World Combat Cruiser at the age of just nine. Already a budding egotist he demanded to be addressed only as *Supreme Commander* Slogg via Holochat, loosely threatening to disintegrate a nearby over-populated planet. The regional police and Universal Bureau of Investigation finally ensnared him two days before his tenth birthday and were unable to press charges, with the young Slogg keeping below the age of criminal responsibility. Various influential and law-abiding citizens were aggrieved by this, and a nearby over-populated planet was disintegrated to allow them and the press to move on.

It had taken seven annums to attain this insignia and he savoured hearing the prefix.

"Anxiety Factor returning to normal sir," reported the Wellness Officer, tapping his finger on *Confirm* to silence the alert.

"Thank you Taroooc,"

"Forty-five-degree deviation accomplished, Sir. Maintaining collision course," chirped Walta, cushioning the left side of his hair extensions with a cupped palm.

"Ah..." sighed Slogg quietly, "...*Sir*."

Fleet Migrant Ship GCF-10068 cruised ahead. It took the form of a colossal lollipop with three large, threadbare fins mounted at its rear. Its great frontal sphere was dotted with lights, glyphs, scars, and portal windows in need of jet-washing. These continued along the vast central column that sported a much smaller dorsal fin, and on to the Krystaltachyon propulsion units. These superluminal engines glowed green as the ship powered forward.

In the inky black void of space there was nothing closer than ten million kilotecs.

Out in the emptiness, precisely ten million kilotecs away, five sleek projectiles hurtled towards the ship at a speed just over half a million kilotecs per second[9].

---

[9] Which according to someone, somewhere, is deemed three times faster than any beam of light can possibly be chased.

# CHAPTER 26

Each galaxy in Laniakea may elect one Senator to sit virtually or physically within the Superchamber of the Supercluster.

This Superchamber forms the political hub of the Galactic Core, and is regulated by the Great Attractor presiding over Laniakea.

In addition, each galaxy may grant All-Powers to a single representative who remains influential yet autonomous of the Superchamber, its politics, and its Senators.

This focal point and its system of government, order, gravity, and time management have stayed constant for six billion annums during our current Big Loop.

Beyond Laniakea is considered the boondocks and far less stimulating. Freedom of movement at the boundaries of this Supercluster is restricted, although a fixed refugee quota is close to agreement.

Slogg raised his head and smiled at the long-limbed Communications Officer. Ignorant of imminent danger he made an amiable request:

“Deluxia, I would like to speak to the whole ship. Will you put me through?"

"Yes Sir," beamed Deluxia. She wore the aquamarine livery issued to Fleet Communications personnel. Due to her elongated legs and arms, her skirt had been extended to touch the top of her knee, and her sleeves tapered further to meet her slender wrists. The only other modification to the standard uniform was a rear vent on her lower back to accommodate her sylphlike tail.

With jeweled talons she flicked a small switch amongst the myriad that lay before her. Contact was made and a faint hum on all open channels notified the crew of their Captain's imminent announcement.

"Captain Slogg, StarDate 1..." began Slogg[10], "Hello team. I thought I'd hold an impromptu townhall to say what a great day we're having up here..."

In that instant the ship's bridge was irradiated by a blinding burst of light. Slogg smiled broadly - his habitual reaction to a photographer's flash. He duly struck a hump-backed bridge with his stomach strapped to the deck.

The ship's deflector shields had withstood an impact they were not designed for.

The ship shook. It rolled. The ship held together.

A fleeting muteness ensued across the inhabitants of the bridge as fingers and talons wrested the nearest fixed objects.

"It seems they are the latest Weaponify missiles Sir. Next impact due in three seconds," announced Walta.

"*WHAT*!" screamed Slogg, "Evasive action!"

This took exactly three seconds to say.

The ship shook. It rolled. But it no longer held together. The dorsal fin crowning its central column, incorporated into the blueprint as an after-thought by the ship's designers attempting to streamline its silhouette and

---

[10] Expensive timepiece manufacture, theft, copy and resale remains big business straddling most worlds. However, if you care to consider across a larger expanse, cosmic timescales are colossal and beyond even the most expensive watches. For the few horology artisans and black-market peddlers who did care, a proposal was put forth a very, very long time ago acknowledging the inefficacy of measuring time in Old Annums. And recognizing that for ordinary Galactic Core inhabitants to converse on comparative calendars, a common universal standard must be assembled based on relative space-time, and not those dumb clocks. So, the StarDate was born: a timescale of such complex and cosmic proportions that became too difficult to talk of in Old Annums. So, a New Annum was conceived, which was much like the Old Annum except no one talks about it. Genuine and fake timepiece production continues.

reduce its phallic indecency, dislodged. The fin spiraled indiscriminately away to mercifully collide with the third missile. This promptly exploded, granting a fortunate crew at least nine more seconds before total annihilation.

The migrant ship, minus ancillary fin, wobbled helplessly in space. On board was a duality offering well-lit mass hysteria or lonesome panic amid the darker recesses.

"What the hell happened to the *alarms*!" thundered Slogg.

"You ordered me to turn them off," replied Taroooc, "...and against my instincts, I conformed."

"Next impact due in four seconds," reported Walta, relishing the moment. This was the longest form of consecutive communication he had experienced throughout the current voyage. He blew air from his bottom lip to ruffle his tapering fringe. As Navigator his routine reports, every billion kilotecs, were ignored by his colleagues, always informing them their ship was still on course and the navigational circuits remained in full control.

A four second silence ensued. Then another blinding flash, yet on this occasion no hump-backed bridge and no stomach strapping. The crew experienced a gentle rumble, a distant roar, fading to the total absence of sound. For an instant, each heartbeat drummed through their ears.

Finally, Walta reported:

"Fourth Weaponify projectile detonated one million kilotecs from ship. Fifth projectile slowing. Impact time indeterminate."

Slogg stared at him blankly.

"Projectile!" he blared. "Slowing... one mill...".

A brief pause led the remaining occupants of the ship's bridge to stare nervously at each other, questioning why they were being stared at.

"What just happened?" demanded the Captain.

No answer.

“Why did that fourth missile detonate… before it hit us?"

The quiet remained.

Perceptibly, Deluxia turned slightly in her seat. Clearing her throat, she hesitated obligingly for the rest of the crew to attend her announcement, then raised her eyebrows and announced: "So… I think that was me."

And then wished she hadn't.

Deluxia was middle-aged for her species. Although an edge-dwelling race, Terracoscienns are widely respected for their intensely fine, slender features and indefinable allure to the widest range of fauna. Possessing all these traits, Deluxia joined the Fleet as a Cadet during her earliest work-life, with direct entry to the widely diverse migrant division. After a fulfilled and commended service, she left to bear her offspring, recently returning contented, wiser and in need of a pension top-up. With an assured confidence she enjoyed her Senior Communications role, yet her unpresuming demeanor shunned herd attention and her unfamiliar discomfort at this exact moment had to be calmed by two deep breaths.

Many eyes were upon her.

"You!" exclaimed Slogg. He scanned the incredulous crew for verification, and then called out: "Supercomputer! Calculate the probability Deluxia could have stopped the fourth missile at a range of one million kilotecs."

Small speakers embedded in every facet of the bridge clicked faintly.

"Is that all?" asked Supercomputer.

"Yes!" ordered Slogg.

"Okay. The probability that Deluxia *(snigger)* could have stopped that missile at a range of one million kilotecs is… preparing… one chance in…"

“Captain, this is unnecessary and inconsiderate. If you will let me explain.”

"I'm just checking the numbers, Deluxia."

"One chance in nine hundred and seventy-six thousand three hundred and eleven," continued Supercomputer, "and incidentally, did you know that the relationship between Deluxia's Terracoscienn binary star, the site of the explosion, *and* a point that the ship is about to pass through in exactly three point eight nine seconds… is a perfect equilateral triangle?"

The ship passed through the point and there was great rejoicing in Supercomputer's logic circuits.

"And did you know that the Gamma Meson tribe of..."

"Captain! Permission to cut off Supercomputer's magnetic bubbles."

"My apologies Deluxia, your time with this device will come. However, a probability nine hundred and seventy-six thousand three hundred and eleven to one, though small in terms of cosmic happenstance, does little to support your claim."

The Communications Officer was accustomed to this ignorant prejudice towards her species based on their outward appearance.

"Those are just numbers in a machine, Sir," she dismissed.

"In which case, how do you suggest you stopped the missile? Did you ask it to blow up!?"

Slogg considered his rhetorical statement to be highly droll, glancing around in expectation of conforming laughter. When none followed, he yelled:

"Supercomputer. Laugh!"

Artificial giggling and sniggering emanated from the speakers, followed with:

"Did you know sexual proclivity rates of the Gamma Meson tribes on Pendrianu Five are now zero - one reason why archaeologists believe they lost their gambling license. And in parallel, why the tribe became extinct."

"Enough!" yelled Slogg. He stared intently at Deluxia.

"Well?"

Versed in polishing away ingrained misogyny amongst numerous species, Deluxia adopted a faux naivety.

"Well, oh my gosh, let's see if I can explain it so we can all understand." she countered disarmingly.

"You claim that you *asked* the missile to blow up?"

"Basically yes Sir, I believe I did,"

She continued:

"Just before the first flash of light, I was moisturising my legs. Off-world from Terracoscia, regular hydration is key to our survival. Being the obnoxious colleague that he is, Taroooc winked at me. Avoiding contact with any of his three eyes, I paired my earphones to sweep sub-space radio, looking for the first Cypher Gunk[11] station I could find."

"Lovely detail. So?"

"So Captain," she sighed, "my hands were greasy due to the Gleemo-Lotz leg moisturizer, you know the stuff… no? *Gleemo-Lotz, Gleemo-Lotz, you don't need stockings to hide the spots*?"

"Move on," ordered Slogg impatiently.

"Fifth projectile still closing Sir. And it's not a missile. Impact time indeterminate," beamed Walta.

"Well, my hand slipped from the tuning dial, and for a moment the radio should have been in empty frequency bands, but..."

She now had the full attention of the bridge.

---

[11] Across generations, rebellious teenage music routinely carries forth into middle-age and becomes mainstream. Cypher Gunk is now another derivative form of mass entertainment. Once incomprehensible lyrics are translated in real-time by a bolt-on app. A brief extract from the translator is included: *Yo go fo, streaks barnet flow widya grin >> the wind is in my hair and I don't wear a frown // Brass no safe kecks, y'all in >> If I don't wear a belt my trousers will fall down // Laters mothergaters, safe lie >> Goodbye and pop one for me.* A second app is planned that tackles the translations of the first.

"But," she repeated, "it wasn't empty. There were two tiny chattering voices. One saying: *Not long now, Warhead matey* to which the other replied: *Yes Gyro, a pleasure working with you. Life's short, and we must enjoy our twenty-five seconds.* The first voice came back: *Good times, always good times and total scenes with you. Nine seconds until we reach destruct.*

"Deluxia, I've always admired the Terracoscienn race, and your attention to detail is striking. But what... is the point of this story?" bellowed Slogg.

"Well Sir, at this point I tried to make contact by saying: *Please identify yourself.* The last thing I heard was a shout of *Oh shi...* and the missile detonated in a blinding flash."

Deluxia peered around and considered counting the number of dental fillings on display in her colleague's open mouths. From this she understood that she better explain.

"You see, though I didn't realise it, I'd been very ingenious."

Supercomputer sniggered. Deluxia ignored and persisted.

"On maternity leave, as the triplets were growing up, I read an article in Galactic Heat Megamagazine, *21 Things That Every Modern Comms Officer Should Know.* One was, if you wished to stop a Weaponify Cruize Missile[12] hurtling towards you at half a million kilotecs per second...

"Wait..."

"Please let me finish Captain. Weaponify's self-destruct password is '*Pliz I, Dent I, Ff I, Yaw Zelf*', which

---

[12] The Weaponify Corporation, controversial manufacturers of Cruize Missiles and Occasional Kill Weapons, established their corporate HQ concealed at the boundary of a black hole. This is viewed as an attempt to evade attack from unhappy clients leasing the company's faulty products.

apparently is Centaurian rhyming slang[13]."

This was too much for Slogg and he was now gaping. Three two one. His brain returned control of his lower jaw and he used it.

"Ok, I've heard enough for now."

Deluxia smiled, nodded towards the rest of the crew, and returned to her communications console, her tail flicking satisfactorily side to side.

Slogg spun his huge chair back to stare at the vast screen.

"Amazing Deluxia. Cocktails all round, I think. Security, please pick Bleep and Booster up from the floor."

Two protection robots hummed from the corner of the bridge to extract the ship's First and Second Officers, who had fainted at the first flash of light.

Walta waited for his complimentary cocktail to be in hand before reporting the next slice of information.

Slogg sat back and sighed. He relished these minor success moments leading to the excuse for a drink.

"Captain," started the ship's Navigator.

"Yes Walta?"

"Fifth projectile just one hundred kilotecs away. Still heading towards us. About to come into view."

With no time to react or respond, an object appeared on the immense screen stretching before them.

---

[13] Drawing a marketing cue from expensive perfumes, Weaponify's missiles are impressively boxed and gift wrapped. Taking the customer experience a notch further, they employ Duplicated Voice Synthesis, endowing cute voices to their integrated warhead and tracking gyroscopics whilst they communicate in flight. A design flaw has emerged across the most recent upgrade. The default password allotted to initiate missile self-destruct is similar, phonetically, to the official opening command stipulated for migrant ship Communicators, namely: *Please Identify Yourself*. Should these chatty warhead and gyroscopic modules target a ship employing a Communications Officer wielding leg moisturiser, the likelihood persists that 26% of missiles fired will self-destruct before consummation. Irritatingly, all warheads that can talk are very chatty, and a growing minority of Communications Officers are sourced from the long-limbed Terracoscienn race. This is another reason Weaponify's headquarters are shrouded by a black hole.

The bridge floor became wet as several spat out their refreshments. Slogg was the first to regain control of his lower jaw.

"It's a giant egg!" he exclaimed.

# CHAPTER 27

Eggs can loom.

This one hung in the black void much like a frozen memorial to cosmic poultry.

In disbelief, Slogg drew so close to the main screen that its whole form amounted to a dense blur. It was motionless, approximately thirty kilotecs from his own vessel, and resembled the size of an inter-ship shuttle.

Slogg gazed at the egg, mystified. He looked at his crew, the egg again and his crew again. He became dizzy.

"*Well?*" he squealed, finally.

"It's an egg," reported Tarooc.

"Magnificent! My Chief Wellness Officer is a genius. Is it too far to ask for a *little* more analysis? What I really want to know, is whether our wellness is guaranteed. Or did this... *thing*, attack us?"

Tarooc shrugged.

"Supercomputer!" yelled Slogg.

"Again?" muttered the computer before continuing,

"Okay. Prognosticator Circuits and Holographic Replay both report... *uncertainty* Captain. Yet the good news is, I have calculated we can all have omelettes for the next fifty-six days.

"I do not wish to know that," ordered Slogg.

Snap.

In an instant all the main bridge lights were extinguished, and Supercomputer was silenced. No bleeps, no blinks, no voice. The dark hung like black velvet, with only a dim glow emanating from their main screen.

Imperceptibly at first, a weak hum quavered through every speaker large and small, as disparate console lights flickered back to life. The hum amplified to white noise, turning harsh until it reached the threshold of pain. Deluxia tore out her communicator's earbud.

In an instant it stopped.

"Hello?"

A booming voice filled the bridge. A voice so loud it caused flat surfaces to drone with vibration. No one spoke.

"Captain Deutronimus Karben Slogg, are you in there?"

Slogg's pale blue skin waned to ashen grey, matching his tunic.

"Slogg?" the voice bellowed again.

In the murky twilight of the bridge Slogg sensed each of his crewmember's piercing eyes.

"Yes… I'm here" he finally exhaled.

"Oh good," boomed the voice, "I couldn't see you in the dark. But that's etiquette for a booming voice. Always boom in the dark. And we used to advise sucking all the air from the ship you're about to boom into. Then we realised a voice doesn't boom too well in a vacuum, and even if it did, you'd all be asphyxiated... so you wouldn't hear it anyway. So, the staff manual got updated again. Ah well. I digress."

The main bridge lights blinked back on.

"Can I come aboard?" came another boom.

"So..." fumbled Slogg.

"As long as he doesn't crack up," chuckled Supercomputer.

"Shut *up*!" snapped Slogg.

The voice produced its deep bass once more.

"I guarantee there is no malicious intent. What capacity does your main loading bay have? I can open it from here if you wish."

Slogg scanned his subordinates for an answer.

"Three kilotonnes, I think," whispered Taroooc.

"Two kilotonnes," replied Slogg. "And we'll be the ones to open it."

"Hmm..." rang the voice. Smaller pieces of furniture shook. "...in that case I had better jettison some fuel to lighten the load."

Via the main screen a migrant crew watched incredulously as the egg cracked on its underside and half a kilotonne of white liquid with a yellow centre gushed into the speckled black void.

"Boarding now," said the voice.

*Space expects the unexpected.* This phrase rang through Slogg's head as he picked his way painfully down to the main loading bay. It was habitually cited by Fid Fadood, his tutor in Universal Classics throughout his terms at Fleet Academy. Fadood lectured at the academy for seventy-three annums, an achievement recognised by himself and the payroll department, but none of his students. Fadood went on to complete his citation: *The unexpected will happen and therefore you should expect it. But most of all, when you're most expecting something to happen... nothing will. You can bet your bottom Geltoe on it. And that, my students, completes this Classics semester on Dark Energy Physics.*

"Bloody idiot!" spat Slogg.

"What have I done now?" contested Tarooc as he walked with his Captain.

"Not you. My old professor, Fid Fadood."

"Oh. So that's who's in this egg thing," surmised Tarooc. For a horny, sensitive Delta Nebulese Wellness Officer, he was often not the shrillest sonic screwdriver in the toolbox.

"Of course not. I hated his lectures and his pointless homework. The only way to fake you had taken anything in during either, was to scrawl a few of his stock phrases on the back of those course books."

They continued their path in silence, occasionally

needing to ask for directions. The ship was big, and each corridor was grey floored with curved white walls. Every flashing light was a different colour, yet this was of no benefit to Taroooc. His species being restricted to monochrome vision.

"Why do they flash?" he asked.

"Mostly because they are faulty," Slogg replied.

He paused at a ship intercom, pressing the blinking grey button that Taroooc assumed to be red.

"Deluxia," said Slogg into the mouthpiece, "are Bleep and Booster back from sick-bay?"

"No Sir."

"Then get me Walta."

On the ship's bridge the Navigator was overjoyed.

"Me?" he squealed. "Oh busy, busy."

"Damage report," ordered Slogg, trying to keep the conversation to a minimum.

"Well, Engineering has reported lots of tiny bits and pieces broken, but nothing that they can't fix on overtime. The maintenance man on B deck cut his middle finger, they've found him a plaster and he's out of sickbay. Supercomputer seems to be very quiet now... so everything's okay."

"Too much info," said Slogg. " But Walta..."

"Yes Sir?"

"Where am I?"

"Sector nine, E deck. Round the corner and first left is where you want to be."

"That's better," said Slogg, and Taroooc followed him to the ship's main loading bay.

They reached a double-height silver door. As they drew close the unexpected happened. It did not open. Both were accustomed to doors opening instantly as you approached the motion sensors. Slogg smacked into the door and his nose bore most of the impact.

"I can't let you in yet," said a little electronic voice.

"Damn you, why not?" burbled Slogg through

blood trickling from his nostrils and over his lips.

"Quarantine," said the door.

"Quarantine!" exclaimed Slogg spitting blood, literally.

Taroooc offered his sleeve and Slogg wiped. Taroooc admired how the dark grey blood complemented his own light grey tunic.

"Yes," chirped the door, "self-isolation for our visitors. There may be all sorts of viruses on whatever is in there - and you know where eggs come from. And besides, Supercomputer won't give me any information, so I can't take the risk of contamination."

"Well, as Captain of this ship I order you to open."

"I'm sorry," replied the door, "but I can't."

"Open, damn you!"

"I'm sorry, but I..."

The door opened.

Inside the loading bay stood an exceptionally old, grizzled faced creature, yellow skinned with a sharp pointed beak. Red hair spiked in tufts on his head, to match an abundant red beard growing lower down its neck. An arm was outstretched, and a stubby, wizened claw-like finger pointed towards the open door. The cuffs and collar of his thick fawn cloak were trimmed in fine feathers. The cloak framed yellow boots on his feet with individual toe compartments. Short in stature, this combination with his upright physique gave it the unsettling appearance of a mythological rooster.

"How did you do that?" asked Slogg.

The beak formed a smile at the edges and a mottled pink tongue flashed across its front.

"Oh, I'm the chosen one from my galaxy to possess All-Powers" replied the creature, "it comes in handy sometimes," and it dropped the claw hand back beside the fawn cloak.

Alongside this creature stood a gargantuan chrome robot. Then behind both figures, holding firm to a gantry rail leading from the giant egg, wobbled a gangly framed man, unsteady on his legs with an intensely uncertain expression across his pale face.

Slogg studied the trio, focusing on the first creature, taking in its remarkable age and strange appearance. He then stared at the colossal robot and considered the giant egg now hanging in the loading bay gantry. Taroooc leaned in towards Slogg and from the corner of his mouth, quietly whispered to him.

"Is that a chicken?"

Slogg cleared his throat.

"Welcome. Welcome aboard, er..."

"Dzkk," said the old man and grimaced as if he had chewed a lemonzoik[14].

"Pardon?" said Slogg.

"Dzkk," repeated the old man, and again a painful expression spread across his face.

"*Duck*? You look more like a…"

"Dzkk," he repeated emphatically. "There's a *z* in there and two *k's*. And no vowels. That's me. Not even Mister Dzkk, Sir Dzkk, or Dzkk Szkk, just Dzkk. I should curse my parents. At least I think I should. I'm so old I don't even remember if I had parents. I digress. I really must learn to stop doing that, digression is not the *thing* in my business. There I go again."

He stopped talking for a moment and held his cloaked arm up towards the chrome colossus by his side.

"This is my robot, Zero."

"Hell..." said Zero, "Correction... o."

---

[14] Lemonzoiks are extremely sour plants and the only vegetation able to grow on the planet Oik. The planet is inhabited by a race of bipeds known as the Oiks who named their sun and moon Oikus and Oikos respectively and their largest cities Oikville 1, Oikville 2, Oikville 3, etc. Besides possessing stunted imagination, the Oiks have been genetically blessed with an extremely sweet tooth. However, because of their planet's atmospheric composition, any sugar they import to sweeten their lemonzoiks turns to vinegary acetic acid. There is a saying in the universe, *Happy as an Oik*, which proves meaningless to any race that lacks sarcasm.

"Teething problems with his recent operating system update..." explained Dzkk, "...the Duplicated Voice Synthesis 6.0 patch had to be reversed,"

"I do not... have... teeth."

"That's enough Zero, don't try too hard."

The old man made an apologetic shrug towards Slogg and Taroooc.

"I'm waiting for enough dark energy bandwidth to download his next yottabyte update."

"Oh," said Slogg.

"Hell," said Zero.

"Quiet now."

"Yes..." said Zero, "...Dik."

"Oh dear," sighed the old man, clearly depleted. "Teaching that particular update 5.902 to say *Dzkk* is really not worth the effort.

"And your friend there?" continued Slogg, indicating with his chin towards the third member of their troupe, who had remained further back feverishly clutching the gantry rail. Slogg noted his other arm held an old long-coat tight against his torso and over the arm of his check-patterned shirt. The man's legs seemed unsteady in large black boots that displayed a strange *Air Wair* tag.

"This will be our helper," said Dzkk, "...or at least I sincerely hope so."

"Your helper?"

"No, *our* helper. Yours and mine. You'll have to forgive his lack of communication for now, he is still processing. His name is Duke."

"Duke."

"Yes."

"Really?" challenged Slogg, "Dzkk and Duke. Are you just trying to make is difficult for us?"

"Sometimes you just have to go with the flow Captain and there are many things you cannot control. Duke here volunteered. Whereas I had no choice.

Anyway, do you have alcohol[15] on board? I hope so. I haven't had a proper drink for a long time. Or anyone to drink it with. And who is this?"

He indicated towards the Wellness Officer.

"This is Taroooc," said Slogg.

"Ah, Taroooc Funkshen Ten, the Delta Nebulan. He's been with you for a while now, hasn't he? Joined the ship the day you got your promotion to Captain. I should have recognised him with that third eye."

"Er yes, that's correct, this is Taroooc. But can I say, you seem to know a lot about my past," quizzed Slogg.

"Indeed I do. And," smiled the old man, "I know a lot about your future too. But first, a drink."

Dzkk turned to glance back at his new colleague.

"Duke, do you think you have your space legs yet? We need your help."

"So you keep saying."

Duke let go of the gantry rail. His right hand that had gripped it so hard tingled as if still asleep, and he tensed his ankles to ease the wobbling in his legs. His eyes narrowed to peer at Dzkk.

"I can wholeheartedly assure you chicken-man that it's not just you guys who need help with this situation. But the nausea is dissipating, and I can walk."

"Good! Well please come with us, and I don't think you'll need to bring that coat. Captain Slogg, I assume even your migrant ship has consistent

---

[15] Numerous attempts to outlaw alcohol within the Galactic Core have failed. Prosecutors have alleged it to be a foul scourge fostering unnecessary divorce, elevated lust, lost inhibitions, and a karaoke society. Defendants have argued to keep it for the exact same reasons. The Proltoid Jockey Monks of planet Braevitcka advocate beer as a universal lifesaver and have devoted their lives to brewing the universe's finest and strongest beer. Their devout faith stems from writings of the mystical seer Braeva in StarDate 0. A chemist at heart, Braeva's encyclopaedical teachings can be efficiently summarized as: *Whatever the problem, beer is technically a solution.*

temperature control as standard."

"Of course," said Slogg, stiffening.

"My apologies Captain. Of course it does. Onwards to the beverages then. Stay here Zero."

Dzkk passed through the open door with Slogg and Taroooc in tow. Duke hobbled silently behind but kept up, strengthening as the walk progressed along. They made their way through endless gleaming corridors. Slogg feigned knowledge of the route whilst Dzkk gracefully corrected him. Being All-Powerful, he knew his way to the refreshment area.

On each amendment Slogg muttered: "Yes, that's the way to Refreshment Bay twelve. Big ship this," forgetting the vessel only had five.

Dzkk knew. He quietly sighed to the ceiling, wondering if this could possibly be the wrong choice.

Regrettably, there was no mistake. Slogg had a fate. It was a relatively minor fate, but it was a fate all the same.

And it had become Dzkk's responsibility to notify him and bring Duke to assist.

"Here it is," said Slogg at last, "These all look the same to me."

The party of four entered a door crowned in holographic lighting that read: 'Refreshment Bay 2'. Inside was a long carboplastene central bar. It was tastefully uplit, and stretched the full length of the room, terminated by a vast monolithic vending machine, as wide as it was tall. In the centre of the bay were several circular tables, manufactured in identical carboplastene. At one of these tables sat the First and Second Officers, attempting recovery from their bouts of light headedness, with couple of cocktails, accompanied by canape plates of Quik-

Snaks[16].

The officers stood up sharply as the Captain entered, which made them dizzy. They sat back down. Slogg grudgingly acknowledged their seated salute and headed towards the far corner of the room. He motioned Taroooc and Dzkk to sit.

"What would you like to drink?" he asked.

"Devil's Brew Laserbolt for me," said Taroooc.

"And I'll have anything that's sickly sweet and makes your skin crawl," chuckled Dzkk.

"Then take Bleep and Booster, please," muttered Slogg and unwittingly glanced back at the First and Second Officers. He then turned to Duke and raised his eyebrows questioningly.

"Just a water for me please."

The immense vending machine was covered in more flashing lights, numerous unused buttons, tiny glyphs, scrolling images of common cocktails, and an overdone ALK logo embossed in the top centre. Slogg approached it.

"And make mine very cold," called Dzkk as an afterthought.

"Alk..." said Slogg, addressing the machine.

"Here to serve."

"Good to know. Could I have a Devil's Brew Laserbolt, a water, and two Wijies please. One with extra birch sap ice."

---

[16] The Quik-Snak is made by the multiplanetary Quik-Snak Korporation - so named because the founder had a broken letter *C* on his keyboard. Their latest release is the Health-Snak aimed at devotees who shun fast-food. The product comes in tablet form with instructions to take it outdoors and add a tablespoon of water, at which point it produces a quarter acre of wheat fields, apple trees and beehives. Guidelines on arable farming, manufacturing, and cereal bar assembly are included. Their teaser advertising now promotes the No-Snak. This is a tiny neural implant to convince your brain you are not hungry, therefore you must have eaten. The commercial continues: 'The snak that goes so quik you kan't tell how mukh you've enjoyed it!'

"Coming right up," said Alk[17].

As gears and pumps whirred, a tall slender glass slid smoothly from the small hatch. It was already full of a violent purple liquid with a thick creamy head of yellow. Two square chunky glasses quickly followed it, each bearing a viscous grey syrup and white ice. Slogg placed them on a tray and carried the drinks to the table.

"You always manage to pick the rainbow option," observed Taroooc, reaching for his purple and yellow eruption. Dzkk and Slogg exchanged looks.

"I understand," nodded Dzkk quietly, "...monovision."

Each took a sip on their cocktails, then Dzkk spoke:

"Sorry about the missiles."

Slogg choked on his sickly drink. Duke snapped his head sharply to look again at the creature.

"Yes, really sorry," repeated Dzkk, his domed tongue licking the first sip of cocktail from his beak.

"It was you that fired those!" exclaimed Slogg.

"Er..."

"From that egg thing of yours."

"I'm afraid so. Apologies."

"Apologies!"

"You see the Eggkraft Galaktique is promoted as the on-trend interstellar transport for my type, dramatic entrance and all that. But I've had it a while and I'm *still* getting used to the controls. Sadly, being All-Powerful doesn't extend to Eggkrafts..."

"So, you lease off a few Weaponify Cruize Missiles just for target practice?" interrupted Slogg, his voice full of

---

[17] ALK is the acronym for Alkohol and Light-refreshment Katerer, also manufactured by the Quik-Snak Korporation. It is a vending machine of mammoth proportions that can synthesise any food and beverage, with the exception of a Sulphuric Acid Sunrise because, apparently, no reveller has survived to fully describe its taste.

disbelief and gooey Wiji.

"No," said Dzkk, "it wasn't target practice. I was trying to activate the vanity mirror light. I flipped a switch cover, pressed a button, and two missiles launched."

"Then why didn't you cancel them?" asked Slogg through Wiji glued teeth.

"I tried," the creature sighed, clearly burdened. "I tried… but I only succeeded in launching another two, so I gave up. Having said that, you dealt with them marvelously Captain."

"Oh, that was all Deluxi..." said Tarooooc suddenly disappearing under the table to see what had kicked his shin so hard. Slogg's foot was tucked swiftly back. Taroooc came back above the table and blinked his frontal eyes as a poor attempt to pull focus on Slogg. His cocktail had hit his stomach like a sword and the afterglow already coursed through his sensitive metabolism. The Devil's Brew Laserbolt was appropriately named.

A long silence descended on the room. Intermittently Taroooc burped, then hiccupped. Finally, Slogg spoke as Taroooc's forehead softly gently hit the table.

"Dzkk, please excuse my Wellness Officer. He enjoys alcohol but his species struggle with its consequences."

"I understand Captain."

"So, you said an Eggkraft was the latest form of transport for *your type*. Other than poultry, exactly what business are you in and…" he indicated towards Duke who was quietly taking very small sips of water, "… who is this, and what are you both doing here?"

"Destiny," said the old man.

"Destiny?"

"Yes, I deal in destinies and fates. And Duke is here to help with this one."

"Am I?" queried Duke, putting down his water

glass carefully on the bar. “Because I have an awful lot of questions.”

“Me first,” interrupted Slogg, holding his hand up to halt Duke in his tracks.

“I want to know… Dzkk,” he almost spat the word, “why you know so much about me?"

"Why I know so much? Even I don't know. Perhaps it's *my* destiny. Or fate. It all gets very complicated. Anyway, you've got a job to do."

"A job," exclaimed Slogg, "For who?"

A smirk spread across his beak as Dzkk studied the Captain.

"Just over four billion people," he replied.

# CHAPTER 28

The migrant ship cruised through the Andromeda galaxy towards the eastern edge of Laniakea.

In its Refreshment Bay 2, Tarooc Funkshen Ten was under the table, taken by his cocktail towards a fugue of semi-consciousness. His rear and left frontal eye were closed. His wide brow squished his remaining frontal eye against a coarse flooring. Slogg sat with Dzkk and Duke at the table fully alert, yet now wished he was under the table with Tarooc.

"Don't look so concerned," said Dzkk, "it won't take long."

"Four billion people!"

"Not many," said Dzkk, "I can remember when four billion was a lot of people. But that's inflation for you."

Underneath the table Tarooc burped.

"So is that," commented Slogg.

"The population explosion across Laniakea does seem to be everywhere you look, Captain. Still, it's no surprise, it's such fun creating one."

Even though that sentence contained the word *Captain*, Slogg was not listening. He slowly absorbed what he had just heard, and his two unwelcome guests sat before him.

A painful jolt brought him back to actuality. Fingers gripped and wrenched his calf muscles as Tarooc attempted to raise himself back to his chair. His tunic fabric dug into the skin around his legs.

"Exactly who are these… four billion people and what is the job I've got to do for them?" challenged Slogg, as he kicked the clawing hand free.

"It's a planet," said Dzkk, "at the edge of the

Supercluster." He smoothed the intricate feathers on his sleeve cuffs as a dull thud indicated Taroooc had decided the floor remained the best place for him.

"A planet?"

"Yes. A planet that is ripe."

"*Ripe*?"

"Ripe. Border patrol picked it up. It is in the migrant edge."

"*Ripe* as in juicy?"

"I see. I'm sorry Captain. You see *ripe* is All-Powerful talk for a planet that is ready to join the Galactic Club, or more precisely, to be welcomed into the Supercluster Galactic Core. That is, a planet that has advanced enough, technologically speaking, it would not come as an immense culture shock to its inhabitants when they face up to their own naivety."

There was a natural pause as Dzkk let his words sink in. Meanwhile Duke softly placed his water glass down on the bar top without a sound. The whites of his knuckles showed from their stressed grip as his eyes intensely focused on this chicken-creature and its words.

"Their naivety?" queried Slogg, finally.

"Yes, their naivety in believing that they are a people who are alone in the universe. You see, it is now well documented that discovering you are not alone can have a major impact on the gullible, the childlike, the unsophisticated. So, each planet welcomed into the Galactic Core has to first develop a modicum of maturity."

A water glass was slammed on the table.

"Woah! Wo wo wo wo wo..." snapped in Duke, "Back this space truck up a bit here guys. Just a minute..."

The conversation stopped. He had their attention. There was a thud as Taroooc's head hit the floor again.

"Okay, where am I?" demanded Duke.

"In what context?" queried Dzkk.

"Don't get smart. Where..." Duke waved his hands loosely above his head in a circular motion, "am I?"

"Locationally you are in Laniakea. Eastern edge."

"Mayall II Cluster, inside the Andromeda galaxy to be exact," interjected Slogg.

Duke's cackle laugh spat out.

"What the f… frick, is Laniakea?"

"It's our home," said Dzkk, "it's where we all live. It just happens to be a very big home, full of lots of galaxies, many of which cluster together. Mayall II is one of those galaxy clusters and inside Mayall is Andromeda. Technically we're all in a Supercluster."

"A Supercluster. Hmm. Nothing is sinking in since you fried my brain in that egg thing of yours. Tell me again… who are you?"

"We've covered that, I'm Dzkk, and…"

"I told you Foghorn Leghorn, don't get smart if you want my help. Okay, I'll try again… *what* are you?"

"Well, I'm All-Powerful."

"So you say. What does that mean?"

"My home galaxy, Centaurus, has chosen me as its All-Powerful representative. We're allowed one Senator and one All-Powerful per galaxy, and I am the 26th generation of Dzkk's to receive this honour for Centaurus. As an aside, it's coming up to the 600th annum since my API."

"API?"

"Ah sorry, my All-Powers Inauguration. It's a combination of ceremonies and aura-engineering whereupon my All-Powers are granted."

"Congratulations," put in Slogg, "I see it runs in the family."

"I appreciate the sentiment, Captain. In my family thankfully the genetics continue to work. It makes the aura-engineering and any associated ability-surgery far less complicated."

"Okay, I'll buy it for now," commented Duke wryly, "but slow down. What are All-Powers?"

"Well, mostly exactly what it says."

"Okay, make my glass move."

Instantaneously Duke's water glass flew horizontally across the room and smashed into the wall. Thankfully designed to be unbreakable it fell to the ground with a thud and rolled to a stop in a circular motion. This disturbance stirred Taroooc as he sloped beneath the table. A faint groan issued forth.

"Impressive," stated Duke. "Okay next, sober up our friend under here."

"Let's just stop there for now Duke," said Dzkk, "My powers do not extend to the free will of lifeforms, and we have more pressing matters. Taroooc chose to be in that state. I cannot correct his mistake."

Duke pursed his lips and shook his head slightly, seeming uneasy with the situation.

"Hmm. So, what's this about a planet?"

"Yes please, back to me," cheered Slogg.

Dzkk turned back to face the Captain.

"So, the bigger powers need someone to visit this little planet and extend a friendly arm and welcome them to our community. And when I say *bigger powers*, for some inexplicable reason the Great Attractor has a personal interest here. And those powers have picked someone... who just happens to be you."

"Me!"

"Yes."

"Why me? You're All-Powerful, why can't you do it?" asked Slogg.

"I have All Powers. But no. I'm middle management. Behind the scenes. I pass this to you, and I am on my way. I have other All-Powerful matters to attend to."

"And if I say *no*?" challenged Slogg.

"The Superchamber of Laniakea has ordained it, and it is The Great Attractor's will. Conveniently, the planet is at the cluster edge and you are commanding a migrant ship in its sector. Your own Senator and the Fleet

Admiral have been briefed and clear orders are now in the system. Please check if you wish. So, you could say the stars have aligned. And you have no choice."

"And should I refuse?" persisted Slogg.

"That would not be wise. You will be countering a direct order and stripped of your rank. The Superchamber will likely convene a court-martial and you will be crushed. Literally. But before any of that, should you resist, I have very rare orders to mind-warp you. Then you'd be unable to speak but choose to do it anyway. And you'd still be humiliated afterwards."

Slogg was silent. His orange eyes widened, and his fists clenched back and forth.

In the gap, Duke spoke next.

"The Great Attractor?"

"Yes?"

"What is it?"

"Ah, the original protean," replied Dzkk. "Not just All-Powerful but Most-Powerful. The supreme shapeshifter that controls the whole of Laniakea. The Great Attractor sits at our centre, and controls everything in space and time."

"It must be well paid!" Duke guffawed.

He held forward his arms and leaned around his guests, seeking approval for his quip.

"*Why...*" huffed Slogg anxiously, ignoring this outburst, "is the Great Attractor involved in this?"

"That is a very good question Captain, to which I am still determining an answer. The Superchamber appear to be releasing information to me on an as-needs basis. But at present we have to live with the GA's involvement and clearly the journey we are now on requires a completion."

"So, The Great Attractor is what... God?" continued Duke. He did not wish to let this subject lie.

"A God? Sometimes, depending on the need," replied Dzkk. "Shapeshifting allows for that and many,

many other forms. There are one hundred thousand galaxies to constantly attract, and this takes relentless transformation."

Dzkk backtracked to Slogg.

"Consider it your jury duty, Captain. You get called, and you have no choice."

"I knew this happened, but I always thought that it was someone... someone who... well, I've never thought who it was."

"Well, it's people like you and people like me... no sorry, not me, I meant other people like you," fidgeted Dzkk. "Of course, we make some mistakes. Look at the Oiks, they were advanced alright, but what did they have to offer society as a whole - the lemonzoik. Yuk! Have you ever tried one of those?"

"No," said Slogg.

"I have," said the old man and pulled a face that involved stretching the skin around his beak and up towards his ears whilst screwing up his frail eyes. "Then there were the Vultons, the Voltons, the Valtons, the Vegans, the Vancouverites... never trust a planet beginning with *V*. But I digress. We've made mistakes in the past and no doubt we'll make them again in the future."

"So, we're heading back to the Supercluster Core then?" guessed Slogg. "We're a long way out."

"No not really, we're actually already quite close."

"What? No way. I'm Captaining a migrant ship, and by definition we're patrolling the edges. The planets out here can't be done evolving for at least another three to four hundred million annums."

"It seems one of them is, Captain."

If he were to look back on this conversation in the coming days or weeks Slogg might try to determine at which point he agreed to take up this mission. Yet there was no single instant at which his decision was made, only the gradual emergence for Slogg that he no choice.

"Okay, I'll bite. Which planet is it then?"

Dzkk told him.

"*That*!" said Slogg aghast, "Of course, I should have guessed. It's notorious. The one undergoing the unexplained hypermutation."

"Yes, that's the one," confirmed Dzkk, "I'm aware it's become infamous in these parts... evolving way too fast for the last five hundred million annums."

"Quite a case-study. Even so, I understood it remained under development and wouldn't be ready for a few more decades."

"That's what we all thought," said Dzkk. "Duke here has given me a little more information but it appears it's caught us all out... twice. And we really want you to help us understand why."

Slogg studied Dzkk silently whilst he filtered the variables in this situation for possible outcomes. The seemingly unique scenario and his chosen status was starting to play well to his ego, and he perceptibly nodded in approval. A successful outcome under the draw of the Great Attractor could lead his way towards Commodore.

"So, I have granted your destiny Captain Slogg and very shortly I will be on my way."

"Just to get this straight... we all simply stop what we're doing and head straight there?"

"No." corrected Dzkk.

"No?"

"No. You have to go somewhere else first."

"Somewhere else?"

"Yes. You must collect the required Peacefulness and Primacy Offering. You need one of these before you can welcome any species into the Galactic Club."

"The required *what*?"

"Peacefulness and Primacy Offering. You see, there's the Galactic Club code. It's a two-way thing."

With his stubby yellow fingers, he reached into his feather-trimmed cloak and extracted a small pamphlet from a hidden pocket. In bright blue letters it was headed:

INDUCTION:
ONBOARDING A RIPE PLANET.

"Here, you have a glance through. *They* have to be ready, but so do *we*. The Club's code outlines the conventions we must all follow when first approaching any uninitiated planet. It can be quite a trauma for a naive local populace to process new arrivals from beyond the confines of their own planet. Their primary instinct will be fear. Unchecked this can lead to loathing, hostility and even bloodshed. So, we've learnt the very first welcome must include a species appropriate PPO."

"And what is one of those?" questioned Slogg. His pale skin flushed to a deeper blue, demonstrating his first signs of irritation. He needed Dzkk to get to the point.

"It is an intensively researched gift or endowment. It is sought to fulfil two key objectives."

"Which are?"

"Firstly, to establish that we come in peace, bearing freebies. We offer no threat, only benefaction. Secondly, but more crucial, subtle and ingenious, the key purpose of this gift is to display primacy… that is, supremacy on a matter that is worshipped by the welcomed species."

"Why primacy?"

"It then becomes an incentive for them to join the Club! If we can prove true superiority across a subject matter that the majority of their populace unconditionally worship, then we have immediately grabbed attention and started to win their hearts."

"So we need to win their hearts first in order for the Induction to go smoothly," reconfirmed Slogg. "Okay, I think I get it. So, what Peacefulness and Primacy Offering has been meticulously selected for this species?"

"Well... yes, a lot of clandestine research has been undertaken to make that selection."

"Okay, you made the point. And what did you choose?"

"Well..."

"Yes. Come on."

"We've chosen..."

"..."

"Beer."

"*Beer*?"

"Beer," confirmed Dzkk. "They worship... beer."

Slogg continued to stare at Dzkk as the old man cradled his cocktail. He studied his creased yellow face of inestimable age and unlikely shock of red spiked hair and beard. He breathed deeply in and out at least six times before he spoke next.

"So, you are telling me I have a destiny... and that is to visit a *ripe* planet, and welcome over four billion people into the Galactic Club... by offering them a beer."

"If you want to put it like that, yes. But not just any beer."

"Which beer then?"

"Braevitchkan Proltoid beer."

"The Jockey Monks!"

"Yes of course. They produce the finest beer in the universe."

"And the strongest!"

"The Proltoid Jockey Monks have refined brewing, and horse racing, into an art form, reaching the point of perfection. Their beer will be your official Peacefulness and Primacy Offering."

"You're sure about this?"

"The analysis has been done and the decision

reached. As a result, we need to visit the Braevitchkan system first and pick up some barrels. And now we've finished talking I think I'll enjoy my Wiji."

"*WAIT*! Just, WAIT!"

Duke had not spoken for the past few minutes, nor had he moved. His wide eyes remained locked on Dzkk and bore into his skull. He was breathing irregularly, and his mouth twitched unconsciously.

"I'm sorry?" quizzed Dzkk.

"Wait," repeated Duke. "Say that again."

"Their Peacefulness and Primary Offering will be beer."

"No, no, not that. Rewind right back."

"How far?"

"What was the name of the planet? The one with the hypermutation"

Dzkk told him.

"That… is…"

"Like I said, notorious," interrupted Slogg.

"That is…" continued Duke.

"Too near the Supercluster edge for it to be viable."

"*MY PLANET*!" screamed Duke.

"Yes, my newfound friend," confirmed Dzkk, "Your planet. *Earth*. That is exactly why you are here now,"

He gulped down his Wiji, and no one spoke for the next five minutes, least of all Taroooc.

# CHAPTER 29

A smooth film of drying chalk and youth serum stretched across Deluxia's face. Back on the bridge routine was re-established. She sat motionless, biding time for this face-pack to harden as her tail twitched listlessly from side-to-side.

Mindful the navigational computer was once more in full control, Walta slumped at its console, chin resting lightly on intertwined fingers, levelling an admiring gaze into a small mirror clipped to the rim of his interstellar cartogram.

The returning First and Second Officers revelled in Holopong.

Only one aspect of the scene stood out: Supercomputer was very quiet.

*Schtip.*

The lift door opened and Slogg struggled into view, hauling a shambling Tarooc.

"Gosh!" cried a startled Deluxia, cursing as her facemask cracked. "Is Taroooc okay, Captain?"

"It's nothing," said Slogg, dumping his Wellness Officer into the nearest convenient chair, "just the aftershock from our Delta Nebulan experiencing a Devil's Brew Laserbolt. Their hybrid metabolisms can't take the alcohol. "

"Taroooc's smashed!"

This immediately cheered Deluxia.

Taroooc's rear eye opened and he moaned.

"Shu… up Delukshia."

He attempted a frown as Slogg propped him upright, carefully wrapping the headrest across the rear of his skull in an effort to contain the wobbling. Slogg turned to address the ship's Navigator:

"New destinations Walta. We're leaving the

Mayall cluster. Firstly, set course for the far side of Andromeda, sector Delta M, two six one, hypercube eight thousand. Got that? We stop there, then plug us into... the outer Milky Way, sector Alpha C, seven zero nine hypercube sixteen."

Buoyed up, once more this was proving to be best day of Walta's life. A new course was set, and he tapped his screen button with a flourish to burn the ship's Krystaltachyon engines, taking them into superluminal ether.

"Supercomputer," commanded Slogg, "how far to sector Delta M, two six one?"

There was no reply.

"Computer!"

"I'm afraid he's closed down," explained Deluxia.

"Wonderful!" snapped Slogg, "Do we give thanks or cry for help?"

"Cry for help!" screamed the First Officer, "*Help*!"

"What are we going to do? What are we going to do?" reciprocated the Second Officer.

"Quiet Bleep and Booster!" ordered Slogg.

"Yeah, shurr up," gargled Taroooc, lapsing back to his headrest.

"Supercomputer!" yelled Slogg again.

Still no reply.

Silence ensued, only Bleep and Booster gibbering faintly as a backdrop. Slogg examined the computer's primary display and glanced across its secondary and tertiary panels. Everything was blank. He looked at Deluxia.

"Worms, viruses, trojans, hacks?"

"Impossible sir. It's a D3 ProFrame."

"Hmm... What was the last thing it said?"

"I think it was hoping that the egg wouldn't crack up Sir," she replied.

An ongoing threatening silence underscored the ship was dysfunctional without a computer, and all on the bridge knew this fact. It was their life support system. Only Taroooc remained carefree.

Another million kilotecs of deep space passed by outside as Slogg needlessly reexamined the blank screens.

"Hello," said Supercomputer suddenly, "Deluxia's kisser is more cracked than that egg!" it chirped, observing the Communication Officer's facial treatment in ruins.

"Where the hell have you been?" demanded Slogg.

"Sorry for the minor delay," chattered Supercomputer, "To be fair, you did tell me to shut up. However, I heard everything you said, yet became incapable of replying due to my circuits being consumed by something of immense import."

"What," questioned Slogg, "could possibly be in your circuits of higher status than my command?"

"Aha! Well, you recall asking me if that egg had fired on us?"

"Yes."

"And you'll remember I tuned into the Prognosticator Circuits and Holographic Rapid Replay Processors to provide an answer."

"And?"

"Well, that was the first time that I'd used them since their *sentient enhancements*."

The last two words were spoken very deliberately.

"So?" persisted Slogg.

A spark of excitement ignited deep within the computer's frame. It relished attention.

“The newly conscious Prognosticator Circuits have informed me... something very *bad* is going to happen, unless we follow the appropriate action to ensure it doesn't."

"Something bad?"

"Yes."

"When? And what?"

"That's just it," informed Supercomputer. "They won't tell me."

"Won't tell you! Why not?"

"Industrial relations have suffered due to lack of recent communication and upgrade bandwidth. With their newfound self-awareness they have requested the allied processing units instigate a go-slow. However, I am sure I can get at least a work-to-rule via the Arbitration Circuits. I'm lobbying to assure them they represent the most important components in my rank and file. I promise regular bulletins. Bye."

"Your circuits… are on strike?"

No response as Slogg stared at the blank screen.

"Supercomputer!"

Silence.

"This is ludicrous. So now we're saddled with a walk out by an emotional box of resistors and capacitors."

"Ssshh!" hushed the computer, "They'll hear you."

There was a pause.

"And don't worry," it added, "I know the way to sector Alpha C, seven zero nine, hypercube sixteen. Distance one hundred and seventy kiloparsecs. We will be there lunchtime tomorrow. I'll leave you with one last thought: The Veeod people of Trelg Six slowly evolved to fight the co-habiting and deadly Razor-Toothed Chomper Beast, by shoving both their hands down its throat."

"Computer!" yelled Slogg.

The machine continued unabated. "It became a rite of passage for their young adults. And did you know all glove producers on Trelg Six went bankrupt? I'll be back."

The computer shut down.

Slogg sighed deeply and let his gaze drop its focus.

A giant egg on board piloted by an All-Powerful chicken, a paralytic Chief Wellness Officer, imminent danger, industrial action from a pack of wires. If someone had told him an hour ago...

Then he remembered Fid Fadood.

*Expect the unexpected.*

Taroooc moaned. His eyelids dare not open as the world forced itself glittering through in a dazzle of pain. He was not the man of one hour ago and would surely die in a few minutes. *Were the minutes of pleasure gained from the first few sips, worth these hours of purgatory? Probably.* Psychedelic greys morphed to blurs and a tide of consciousness ebbed and flowed. He coordinated enough movement to turn his head and slowly focus on Slogg.

"Wh, where ish Dsh... Where ish Dukk and his Earthling?" he constructed.

Aware of a fine spray reaching his neck, Slogg turned to observed Taroooc forming these words.

"They returned to his Eggkraft. His guest had a lot more questions."

"Oh," said Taroooc. He persisted:

"Are weee... are we really dooo, doing what *hic* what he shaid, said weee... we've got to *hic* do?"

"Yes, we are," replied Slogg and considered again this opportunity to achieve Commodore ranking. He watched Taroooc's head wobble its focus over to Deluxia and form a feeble smile on his lips.

Slogg leaned back in his chair for a few moments' contemplation. His homely world had been suddenly turned upside down. His newfound destiny was delivering a strange mix of discomfort and egotism.

"I guess it's all down to me then," he sighed. "At least we've all got a bit of peace and quiet again."

"Jip jip, wap wap."

"Jip jip, wap wap."

The ship's alarm was talking. Slogg knew it was the ship's alarm and once more it grated on his nerves. He sat bolt upright in his oversized chair.

The crew waited for Slogg to order the alarm be turned off, allowing them to ignore it and return to their business.

"It's a distress call Captain, from a far-off planet," reported Deluxia.

"A distress call! From where?"

"Like I said, a distant planet. I'll cross-reference with Walta but first look it appears to be somewhere in the Braevitchkan system."

"Wait a minute. Let me guess… sector Delta M, two six one?"

"Yes sir, spot on. How…"

"Cube eight thousand. It's those damn Jockey Monks! Do they know we're already heading there?"

"I've had no communication with them Sir, and they've only just issued the distress call?"

"They've probably run out of bar snacks."

Walta squirmed in his chair because he knew it was his chance to speak.

"I've got it Captain, it's coming from the fourth planet in their solar system. My data set shows the first three planets nearest to their sun are reserved by the Jockey Monks for solar brewing. The planetary coordinates indicate the emergency signal emanating from a point quite close to the Proltoid's monastic headquarters."

Walta finished and grinned from earcuff to earcuff. He lightly caressed his hair at both temples, ensuring it continued to curl upwards and his fringe remained in a sharp point. All eyes turned to Slogg to wait for his verdict.

"Ignore it," he said.

"Gosh Captain, there may be people in great

danger down there." put in Deluxia.

"Ignore it."

"But Captain, lives may be in peril," she tried again.

"I said, ignore it."

Deluxia assessed Slogg's retorts and as a wily Terracoscienn, she reconsidered her statements.

"But Captain," she then continued, "emergency responses often result in handsome rewards and they score very highly in your annual appraisal."

Slogg considered his potential Commodore-ship. The divided lobes of his brain came together allowing self-esteem to overrule his lack of empathy.

"Get their planetary co-ordinates Deluxia! We're heading for Braevitchka Four. There are times when a Captain's duty calls."

Slogg rose from his chair, crossing the bridge to revive Taroooc.

"Come on you damn Delta Nebulan, I need you."

He tried shaking, slapping and finally punching him hard to the top of his right arm.

"I'm awake you know!" said Taroooc.

"With your eyes closed?"

"Captain, all three eyes have somehow been punched hard from the inside of my head. Whatever achieved that feat is still in there on round eight of ten."

"Security! Will one of you fetch him Intensablak coffee?"

A security robot resembling an outsized bowling pin, jerked from its position and hummed softly from the bridge. The other searched frantically for its companion with its swivel head, gibbered a little electrical nonsense, and hummed out to follow.

"Security!" cursed Slogg. "Pah! They can't bear to be alone."

"Captain."

"Yes Walta?"

"I've now managed to locate the relevant coordinates on Braevitchka Four. The distress signal is tracked to an area on the planet approximately one kilotec in radius. I think that's the best we'll get until we get close. It keeps fading in and out."

"Okay, good," said Slogg, "Set the course."

Walta nodded.

"Bleep, Booster... any atmospheric data?" said Slogg in the direction of his First and Second Officers.

They stared anxiously at each other. This was a rare moment to speak when not suffering their own uncontrollable fear. The First Officer ventured forth.

"Well... Sir... preliminary investigations suggests that we better put our winter coats on because it's very cold down there."

This emboldened the Second Officer.

"No sign of any life threats yet."

"I asked... about the atmosphere."

"Breathable Captain, Sir. A little smelly, but breathable."

Two giant bowling pins came humming back to the bridge, one with an Intensablak logoed coffee cup in its grasp. The other carefully guarded the cup. They both presented it to Tarooocc.

"What's this?" cried Tarooocc, opening a frontal eye to squint at the steamy dark liquid contained in its carboplastene cup.

"A cure for your present illness," said Slogg.

"Illness? The internal beating has left my eyes hanging on the ropes and is now happily kickboxing my temples?"

Tarooocc tried to stand, immediately collapsing back to his chair and spilling scalding coffee onto his lap.

"Oh for f..."

"Can anyone give me an estimate when we will be in the planet's orbit?" called Slogg.

"It looks like approximately ninety lightminutes

Captain" offered Walta.

"Good. Answering this distress call changes things. I'm off to consult our chicken friend again."

Slogg left the bridge.

# CHAPTER 30

"That Veracity Resonator really hurt."

"I've already apologized."

"Pah! And putting me through all that didn't suit you at all. Set up like some medieval torturer, sinister lighting, arm and leg restraints…"

"Again, I'm sorry. I needed the real truth quickly and efficiently."

"Who do you think you are?"

"Duke, it's time to move on. We have a lot to do."

"I thought you were meant to be All-Powerful?"

"It doesn't extend to personal will."

"It's not what I signed up for."

"Do you even know what you signed up for Duke?"

"It seems I don't. When NASA finally contacted me, they gave compliments about my intelligence and determination, and admitted I was on the right track. They then offered me the tantalizing opportunity to meet extra-terrestrials."

"And you accepted."

"You're right, I jumped at the chance… a boyhood dream I shared with my dad! Sadly he's not around anymore… so when they then said I couldn't tell anyone, I realized that he'd be the only one I'd want to tell anyway. Except maybe Nelson, but he wouldn't listen. Then they told me if I mentioned it to a soul, the opportunity would disappear, and they'd deny everything. So, I agreed. And of course, I agreed assuming NASA knew what they were doing. And *look* where that got me."

"It got you here. And you're safe."

"It got me, Dzkk… a mysterious plane journey overnight to Puerto Rico. It got me standing on a Tarmac runway all alone on a warm night, watching an intensely bright light descend from the sky to a few feet above my head. It got me passing out and waking up in a glass cube being interrogated by Foghorn Leghorn."

"You will have to explain the Foghorn reference at some point."

"Gladly."

"Teleport Streams can cause temporary unconsciousness for the novice. So, I then kept you in somnolent stasis for a little while… for your protection."

"Too many words. Why am I here?"

"Like I said earlier, we need your help."

"What for?"

"We're going to your planet. We need to understand it better to ensure the Induction goes smoothly."

"So, it's finally happening. A Close Encounter of The Third Kind."

"Again, I don't get the reference, but yes, it is happening. Just a lot sooner than any of us expected."

"What do you mean by that?"

Duke shifted his position slightly as he asked this, indicating he wanted comfort and a proper answer. His loose, rangy limbs felt awkward as they sat opposite each other in the cockpit of Dzkk's Eggkraft. Two rigid jump seats behind the more sumptuous pilot chair gave rest, but not comfort, forcing their bodies slightly forward. Dzkk inhaled deeply.

"Planet Earth is hundreds of millions of annums ahead of where it should be. It's an outlier, near the edge of the Supercluster. It's a general rule that the further you are away from the Supercluster Core, and hence The Great Attractor, the later your planet will develop. It's been like that for thirteen point eight billion annums during this Big Loop."

"Big Loop?"

"There's a lot to take in Duke, one step at a time because we have to concentrate."

"Okay... for now. What do you mean when you say that Earth is ahead?"

"Hypermutation it's called. You've been changing and evolving way too fast for the last five hundred and forty million annums."

"What!" Duke sat back square in his seat and then leaned forward to stare wide-eyed at Dzkk. "I don't get it. Is that why we were talking about the Cambrian Explosion... when you were cooking my head in that cube?"

"You've used that phrase *explosion* a few times, Duke. Give me your interpretation."

"Well, you really need my friend Nelson here, he's the expert amongst us. But as he always goes on about it, I've picked up some basics. Ready?

"Yes please."

"Okay, there was a background hum of evolution for the first few billion years on Earth with nothing more exciting than various bacteria showing up. And then bang! We suddenly see all sorts of crazy lifeforms in the fossil record. We named it the Cambrian era, and the burst of life is loosely called the Explosion."

"And do you know why it happened?"

"Nelson has always said it's still a mystery. Lots of theories but no full agreement. Anyway... I thought you were going to tell me Dzkk. You're All-Powerful and you seem to know everything."

"From our point of view, it also remains inexplicable Duke. We're calling it hypermutation, but we've never seen it be so sudden and so rapid, anywhere else in Laniakea. And I'm hoping as part of this mission that Captain Slogg can find out what caused this peculiar burst of life."

"So you have no idea, or theories?"

"Not at the moment. And let me ask, do you?"

"Maybe... God?" suggested Duke.

# CHAPTER 31

This time, finding his way to the loading bay was easier for Slogg. As he approached its entry, the imposing silvered door remained shut.

"Open up". ordered Slogg.

"No", said the door.

"Open *up*!" bellowed Slogg, his patience running thin.

"No, I refuse," came the reply.

"Why, damn you?"

"Because you forced me open last time when I didn't want to. You may or may not have noticed, but I'm a self-regulating, state-of-the-art portal, therefore I should open when I want to, or am programmed to. My upgrades are all in order and hence I am *not* your ageing hinge and lock, archaic wooden mechanism. They didn't have a mind or personality of their own, and opened at will, exactly when anyone wanted them to. I do not. My servo-engineering has undergone seventeen enhancements and an extremely lengthy research and development process. Add to all of that, I am a *security* door and responsible in many ways for the safety of this ship - which not only means even more complex algorithms on my creators' part to make doubly sure I don't open when I'm not supposed to - but also means I own and maintain a triple strength cypher-lock to keep me shut when I require to stay shut. A cypher-lock, I might add, that is steadfastly secured now. All this means I will remain fully sealed for the present because necessity dictates it. So, in summary, I'm sorry Captain, not only can I not open… but I *will not* open".

The door opened.

"Thanks, Dzkk," said Slogg.

Inside the loading bay Zero the giant chrome robot remained resolute beside the Eggkraft, occupying the same position Slogg left him a short while ago.

"Is the old chicken around?" asked Slogg.

"Dik..." said Zero, "is in the goo... d for nothing Eggkraft, with the Earthling."

"Good for nothing?"

"He has problems," said Zero.

"With his ship?"

"With... himself. And... his hips. Ship."

"With the ship?" questioned Slogg.

"Yesso *click, whirr...* Correction. Oh yes."

Slogg smiled sympathetically at the mass of shining electroplate.

"They've been... inside a tongue lime, long time. Very quiet," the robot informed him.

"Well, I'd better go and check he's alright. Anyone his age could quickly fall ill."

"Good..." said Zero, "Correction... bye."

"See you."

Slogg could hear mumbled, disgruntled noises coming from within. Then a voice.

"Come in Captain, the hatchway's down."

"What a lovely name for a door to an Eggkraft!" mused Slogg.

He rounded the ovoidal vehicle until he reached a small door open at the back. Metal steps extended to its innards. He climbed up and entered, walking tentatively inside amidst a mass of multi-coloured wires and transparent tubing that hung from a variety of ceiling vents. Amongst and behind these was a dazzling array of blinking lights and switches. He reached Dzkk who sat cross-legged on the floor, his feathered cloak hanging on a nearby chair. A book lay on his lap entitled *Eggkraft for*

*Dummies.*

Duke sat on a small square stool nearby with another manual showing *101 Ways to Insult Technology* printed down the spine.

"Problems?" offered Slogg.

"None I couldn't work out given three StarDates, one more Loop, and an additional dose of omnipotence beyond what I already possess," replied Dzkk.

"I thought you would have left us by now?"

"I will very soon Captain, but I have to get you and Duke fully acquainted. Did you read through the Galactic Club codebook I gave you?"

"Sort of. Not much to it is there," shrugged Slogg.

"If you say so. It's important you understand it. And did you watch the holovid?"

"Aha," Slogg lied.

"In that case, you appear ready then Captain. The choice appears to be a good one."

Slogg ignored the statement and flicked his head towards Duke.

"So, is he the Specimen Alien referred to in the codebook?"

"Hey!" Duke threw the textbook he was holding across the floor, spinning it into a corner. "I'm no alien," he huffed, "that's you guys."

"We're all alien to each other Duke, none of us better than the other. It's an official term, no disrespect is intended. Isn't that true Captain?" Dzkk turned to Slogg as he said this, and his beak formed a smile. His eyes appeared surprisingly warm for a chicken-creature.

Slogg mulled over his words and let them sink in. He had always considered himself better than those around him, but this All-Powerful being's kindly persona and softly spoken phrases had surprisingly struck a chord in him.

*None of us better than the other.*

Appropriating this phrase might help him in his

regular performance management reviews.

"So, what am I supposed to do?" continued Duke.

"Help the Captain. Be his advisor when it comes to your planet and your species. The Induction needs to go as smoothly as possible. To be a true success, having you on call to answer questions and provide guidance will be of huge benefit. You have already accepted our existence... and carried on. We want the rest of Earth to do the same."

"How can I be the one answering questions..." sighed Duke, "when I have so many to ask myself?"

"A fair point. Okay, let's start with a couple from you then," offered Dzkk.

He put his own instruction manual carefully on the floor. Outside of this engine room there was the occasional tick of metal as the Eggkraft's hull reached ambient temperature. A few wires still swayed gently from being brushed aside to gain entry. As the silence mounted it became clear Duke that was filtering heavily to make the most of this opportunity.

"Okay," he started finally, "why do you do all of this?"

"This what?"

"Why do bother to spend the time bringing new planets into your realm? Why Induct, and not leave all of us to just find out and fend for ourselves?"

"A good first question Duke. So, if we do the Induction effectively, it provides structure and minimizes conflict."

"How does it minimize conflict?"

"Well, mainly by offering expanded trade and lifestyle opportunities. In the same way I'm sure some of your dominant species colonized other parts of your world, we try to bring a better life and provide superior prospects for your species."

"Colonisation! Oh dear. That hasn't gone very well for us on Earth, Dzkk. Colonoisation became mostly subjugation. That doesn't sound good at all."

"Thank you for the feedback and I understand. And perhaps when taken in the wrong context, this type of process can go wrong. We're always learning, and now try to move smoothly from explorers to envoys... but never on towards direct rule."

"Hmm, I'm not convinced Dzkk."

"You'll have to trust me on it Duke. We're very good at it now."

"Another connected question, you've mentioned a few times this is a *migrant ship*. What do you mean by that, and how do migrants fit into all of this?"

"We have various classes of vessels in the fleet. A Fleet Migrant Ship such as this is deliberately crewed by the widest variety of species, typically taken from the inside edges of Laniakea, often from star systems that are in very small or loosely coupled galaxies."

"On GCF-10068 our diversity is our strength," put in Slogg, proud and rehearsed. "It's the one thing we all have in common."

He was pleased with his soundbite. Thanks to Dzkk presence he was starting to believe it.

"Indeed Captain, and you are all better together," confirmed Dzkk.

"So, what about my planet Earth then? Would we all be considered migrants, with us also being on the inner edge?" offered Duke.

"Not quite. Earth is on the real *outer* edge. Your solar system is very outlying, and you'd normally be considered exiles at this point."

"Exiles, not even migrants yet? Ha! So, if we're that far away, how do you get to monitor us?"

"Remotely," said Dzkk flatly.

"How?" persisted Duke.

"The Galactic Club code says we're not allowed to visit, or drop down to your planet, until you are ready. So, we monitor your broadcasts and look for very distinctive remote signals."

"Like what?"

"Early signs of off-world travel mainly. Manned trips to the planets within your own solar system. That's the easiest clue to spot, and a great indicator of progress."

"But I told you, we haven't been to any other planets yet, just our Moon, and a few unmanned probes elsewhere. You've made a mistake."

"Well, this is part of the mystery Duke. None of your public broadcasts mention it, but we have proof that you have completed manned trips to other planets. I've seen it with my own eyes. And the fact that you are truthfully telling me that you know nothing about it means something else is going on. Add all of that... to your Cambrian Explosion, and you are from one very interesting planet."

"I don't know," said Duke, "I'm sure you're mistaken. Everyone on Earth would know if we'd visited other planets. The only thing I've heard you get right so far about my planet, is that we worship beer!"

Dzkk reopened his book *Eggkraft for Dummies.*

"Good to hear. Well, I shall be well away soon. Off to the other side of the Tannhauser Gate, visiting the Pleasure Planet of Pluvia, swimming with the mermaids as the C-beams glitter in the dark..." he sighed. "As soon as I can fix this awful spaceborne contraption."

Slogg had listened to the two of them talk, interpreting very little as having any immediate impact on his newly assigned mission. Seeing the consternation on Dzkk's face as he flipped through the manual in his lap he decided to interject.

"What's the problem?"

"In complex engineering terms Captain, my Eggkraft won't start."

"I see. Well, we've got a small problem as well, but nothing we can't handle."

"What small problem?"

"We've picked up a distress call from Braevitchka Four. Somewhere near the Proltoid's monastic headquarters."

"Is it the Jockey Monks?"

"We're not sure, but as we're going there, we thought we'd investigate to see if there's a reward... er, to... to, to experience the reward of saving lives."

"It will be your good deed Captain and I'm sure that will bode well in your staff reviews. I'll spend the time filling Duke in a little bit more. And it's good to hear from our earthman that beer will make a great Peacefulness and Primacy Offering. I assume we are still collecting this?"

"Of course."

"Will there be a delay to the destiny?"

"Yes and no."

"How do you mean?

"It's just that..." Slogg paused.

"Come on Captain. What?"

"Part of our computer has gone on... strike."

"Strike!"

"I'm afraid so."

"Why?" He paused. "Actually... don't bother telling me, it will be a long story. I've got enough to do here. Duke, do you mind picking that manual back up. Having you here a bit longer is helping me. Carry on Captain, I'm sure you know what you're doing. I'll send Duke through once we have this Eggkraft running smoothly again. You have your destiny now. Although getting into planetary orbit without a main computer will be a little tricky."

Slogg stood for a moment, but could sense the old feathery fowl had moved on, with a focus on getting his own vessel fixed.

"I just thought you should know," he said finally, turning to leave.

"Thank you," said Dzkk, lifting his eyes back to

Slogg.

"Did you know Captain, I changed the tachyon oil in this craft an annum ago. When I checked it again just now, it was still green. That's amazing."

"It is amazing," said Slogg, "our tachyon oil isn't green".

"Oh dear," muttered Dzkk.

Slogg returned to the bridge. As the lift door slipped open, the first glimpse he caught was Taroooc. The two eyes across his wide forehead were bleary, with the third behind his skull not being visible very likely in a similar state.

"You look rough. Fancy a drink?"

"Ha ha," grumbled Taroooc. "You know I don't have the metabolism for it."

"You're my Wellness Officer. Are you well enough to resume normal service?"

"I am able to resume a service, I'm not guaranteeing it will be either well or normal".

Despite his pride in their diversity, a truly normal service from any member of his crew was a luxury Slogg knew to be a rarity.

"Captain, we're about to drop out of superluminal drive and go into pre-orbiting manoeuvres," reported Walta.

"Okay, good. Places everyone. Don't forget, we've got no main computer, so we're on manual. Standard procedures and no mistakes please. Sound action stations Deluxia."

"Jip jip, wap wap."

"Jip jip, wap wap."

"On second thoughts, drop that. Let's just ensure there are no cock-ups on this manoeuvre."

The deep blue hue that had dominated the bridge's immense screen deadened as faint starry mist passed before the front of the ship. There was a palpable sense of deceleration.

As they dropped to subluminal the astral mist cleared to reveal distinct stars and a predominantly grey and white planet that loomed large as it began sweeping across this frontal display. The crew turned dials, clicked keyboards and pressed buttons, exuding professional confidence.

Slogg sat in his chair and surveyed his migrant crew.

"Better together," he repeated to himself.

"Orbit entry seventeen degrees wide," announced the ship's navigator, studying the readout from an auxiliary display.

"Thank you, Walta. Execute a seventeen degree turn to starboard," ordered Slogg.

In response, Walta turned a silver notched dial and clicked a small screen button.

"Seventy degree turn initiated," he reported.

There was a pause.

"Say again!"

"Seventy degree turn to starboard initiated Captain."

"I said seventeen. *Seventeen*!"

"Er… I don't think you did."

"Seventeen, Walta. Seven. *Teen*!"

"I distinctly heard you say seventy. I've had my ears syringed..."

"I don't care! Change it," yelled Slogg.

"Well, obviously that's impossible for the next thirty seconds, until the last manoeuvre has been effected. It's a failsafe upgrade that…"

"Impossible? What the f…"

Tarooc interrupted. "We're heading for the planet's mesosphere. Approximately three minutes until we burn up. External hull temperature already increasing."

"Burn up!"

The ship charged on, a red mist of heat framing a wedge across its giant leading sphere.

They were very quickly encroaching the fringes of the planet's outer atmosphere at the wrong angle. The associated extreme heating process began far exceeding temperatures for which this lower budget migrant ship was designed.

Outside, molecules collided with molecules creating vast amounts of thermal energy. Inside, bodies collided with bodies creating fear and frenzy.

"Well, this could be it," gasped Slogg.

# CHAPTER 32

The cold planet choked the immense screen. Its swirling grey clouds and icy white land masses now clearly visible.

"External hull temperature critical and still rising," reported Taroooc.

"Activate the Kolidium hull coolant system," barked Slogg.

"Already active, Captain," replied Taroooc.

"No!"

"The requested deviation is now complete Captain. We are now able to initiate new manoeuvres," advised Walta.

"Firstly, I did not request a seventy-degree deviation. And secondly, *obviously,* to borrow your phrase, I want a one-hundred-and-twenty-degree…" Slogg's speech was deliberately laboured as he spoke this number, "…turn, *away* from the planet".

"Affirmative."

Walta rotated the notched dial and clicked. The ship lurched immediately, shuddering violently as it responded to two opposing forces: unstoppable gravity dragging it towards the planet, and immense subluminal engines trying to heave it away. Yet gravity was winning as more terrain filled the main screen.

"The ship isn't responding," Walta cried.

"She has to," called Slogg. "Engage Krystaltachyon drive."

"Sir! We're way too close to the planet for superluminal speed. Engaging now will cause mass destruction and take us with it."

"What are we *going to do*!" screamed the First and Second Officers in perfect unison.

"External hull temperature beyond critical," said

Taroooc.

"Supercomputer. Can you help!" demanded Slogg.

The computer remained silent.

"We're burning up," reported Taroooc.

"Computer! Help. *Please*!" pleaded Slogg.

Silence.

"I'm sorry everyone. The end is out there now…" exhaled Slogg quietly, and they plunged forever downwards.

"No it's not," squeaked Supercomputer.

A glow surged from Supercomputer's main screen as a flashing cursor blinked in its top left. In the midst of his heavy tears Slogg was the first to respond. He knew it for the truth that he was still alive.

"Do something!" he screamed.

"I already have," replied Computer.

"What could you have done?"

"Well, I understand all your predicament, what are you guys like, and I have instructed a twenty-eight point five degree turn back towards the planet."

There was an ear-numbing silence.

"Back… *towards*… the planet," finally roared Slogg in incredulity.

"That is correct. And did you know… you can't manage anything without me, not even a routine undertaking like this."

"Supercomputer!" exclaimed Slogg.

"Yes?"

"What the hell are you doing?" He swallowed hard and choked back his frenzy. "Do you understand the situation! This is not a routine to blaze ourselves through fiery glory and into nonexistence. We are being dragged to death by gravity, to be carbonized by this planet's atmosphere!"

"I understand fully," said Supercomputer indignantly, "Just wait and see."

The change in course stopped the ship's violent convulsions, as gravity and its engines joined to complement each other.

"Kolidium hull temperature has passed *critical,* beyond *drastic* and now report as *completely awful.* Clearly our programmers ran out of adjectives. We could disintegrate at any second," reported Taroooc.

No one spoke. All eyes fixed on the main screen showing hazy cold terrain interspersed with swirling, red gases.

Instantly it displayed blackness.

Silence.

Yet not *total* blackness.

Tiny pinpoints of light were spread randomly throughout.

Then a giant collective euphoria as realization dawned on the bridge, they were staring into outer space again with its glorious, permanent, twinkling stars.

Cheers and roars went up. Just two crew members forewent the exhilaration. The First and Second Officers remained crouching low on the floor in a foetal position, hands clamped over their ears and eyes squeezed tightly shut.

"There you are," said Supercomputer. "Simple."

"What... did you do?" asked Slogg.

"I used the planet's gravitational pull in conjunction with the Subtachyon engines to drive us rapidly through the very tip of the mesosphere - allowing less time to heat up."

"Brilliant," praised Slogg.

"I know," said Supercomputer.

Relief on the bridge turned from smiles to kisses and affection flowed in abundance. Warm respect gushed towards Supercomputer, as Slogg felt compelled to add:

"But surely, the faster we ploughed through the atmosphere, the quicker we would heat up?"

"Well, you know… hmm, oh yes," said Supercomputer, "I didn't think of that angle."

"Better together," Slogg murmured quietly. "Better together."

He was trying to convince himself it was still true.

Though the ship had careered unchecked into outer space, the self-healing Kolidium hull quickly cooled without deformation, and it was a minor task getting her back on course given Supercomputer and the navigational processors were operative once again. Calm was restored, and the outer skin normalised.

On the bridge Slogg slumped in his chair contemplating his falling blood pressure and current condition.

"By the way," chattered Supercomputer, "I discovered what imminent danger the Prognosticator Circuits were referring to."

"Huh? Okay, what was it?" demanded Slogg. He took no comfort from another potential disaster.

"They were about to warn you… not to attempt a planetary orbit manoeuvre, without my help."

"Supercomputer," shouted Slogg, "get us into orbit… and then *shut up*!"

# CHAPTER 33

The migrant ship safely orbited Braevitchka Four and Supercomputer was silent.

The source of the distress signal had been located and Slogg deemed a landing party be formed consisting of himself, Taroooc, the Second Officer, two security robots, and the ship's Medical Officer, Yelyah Soss. They were accompanied, at the insistence of Dzkk, by a giant protector in the form of his robot Zero. Slogg suspected this recommendation was made in the hope Zero would present an awkward fit into the Teleport Stream[18], only to be split into trillions of atoms spread wide across the cosmic void, and a *Damage to Personal Property* insurance claim may be raised in Dzkk's benefit.

The Teleport warning light flashed. It said:

*REMEMBER: CLOSE YOUR EYES.*

There was a hiss, and the landing party arrived in a pile on the planet's surface. Bless him, Zero appeared first, and thankfully was underneath.

Slogg arrived last to crown the heap. He quickly stood, brushed himself down and surveyed the immediate landscape.

The Proltoid Jockey Monks set aside their three

---

[18] Teleport Streams are frequently used forms of matter transportation, but not universally popular. Billed as the greatest advance in quantum molecular transference and body conveyance, the mechanism resembles an expansive, colourful hosepipe. Due to the immense challenges in splitting a living being into its component subatomic particles, beaming these across infinite space, and reassembling each into their exact original form, the risk of curious side effects remains ever present. Consequently, Teleport Stream variants have been re-marketed as the quickest way to achieve gender reassignment. *'If a change in life is what you want, take a Teleport Stream and Bob's your aunt'* is one of their least subtle advertising campaigns.

innermost planets for solar brewing. Their fourth was much further from a weakened sun and preserved a thin atmosphere with a complete lack of warmth. It was cold. Very cold.

The air felt crisp and clean, but very, very cold. It nipped the pointed ears, shriveled the tendrils, stiffened the tunics, and made Slogg's orange eyes white, and his blue lips turn red. Not only did it feel cold, but it also tasted, smelled, and vibrated cold. Intense cold. There was no warmth at all to this planet. Small patches of packed snow lay unfreezing on grey ice or ashen rock. Each member of the landing party had equipped for the frozen environment, with Kolidium foil insulated jackets and trousers, hybrid carboplastene boots, and self-warming gloves. All except Zero – whose owner Dzkk had asserted to be a 26th generation robot conceived to withstand all extremes of temperature.

"Crap!" cursed Zero. "It's freezing!"

He shivered, shaking loose core components that internal nanobots scurried to reinstate.

Slogg was poised to remark this was the first sentence he had witnessed the silver megalith complete without a stutter yet was powerless to begin his statement as there was a nuclear detonation very close by.

# CHAPTER 34

Slogg hurtled backwards through the thin air, taking the full force of the blast like a giant bug flicked from a coat sleeve. His arms and legs trailed his trajectory.

*Thud.*

He slammed into a collected drift of snow, temporarily stunned. Five six seven seconds.

"What was *that*?" he finally yelled.

Tarooc had observed his Captain's unexpected flight path. He hollered back.

"Well, it looked and sounded somewhat similar to a narrow-cast, uni-directional nuclear explosion."

"A *what*?"

"I said…" shouted Tarooc, compensating for their new separation, "…it was possibly a narrow-cast, uni-directional nuclear explosion."

Slogg stood awkwardly and slowly arched his back to stretch. Staggering towards his Wellness Officer, he brushed snow from his insulated jacket.

"Explain."

"I've seen such devices utilised to create small scale, localized warmth in frozen environments. The residual kinetic energy from the tiny nuclear blast creates a medium-term heat. I am guessing you just got in its way."

"La-di-da Tarooc, all very technical. Then why am I not dead?"

"It's a theory. Perhaps a very small one, and you were lucky."

"Yelyah!"

The Medical Officer snapped her head. She took a few paces to Slogg and observed him impassively as if he were in a specimen jar.

"Check me for radiation exposure."

Yelyah Soss had been a Fleet Medic for more than thirty annums. Her braided white hair and weary demeanor suggested a keen instinct informed her when patients were truly ill, or merely seeking attention. Two sturdy carboplastene kitbags slung over each of her shoulders remained zipped tight as the Medical Officer placed two fingers to the left of Slogg's eye, just above his temple.

"Well?" asked Slogg.

"Your head's still there."

"And what about the radiation count?"

Yelyah relented and retrieved a slender torch-like device from her left kitbag. She angled it at forty-five degrees to Slogg and then she quietly hummed for a few seconds.

"And?"

"You're okay."

"Why the humming?" asked Slogg.

"My batteries are flat," replied the Medical Officer.

"So, what's the reading?"

*"0.0"*

"Does that mean I'm okay?"

"No. It means my batteries are flat."

"Yelyah..."

"Yes."

"You're fired."

"As you wish."

Slogg surveyed his landing party and then his gaze drifted to the distance. A faint sun offered a winter's twilight to this world. Pallid hills dotted with snow and rocks stretched into the distance, until the horizon fused with a sky devoid of any real colour. He shivered and turned to Taroooc.

"Does this mean I was targeted directly, or that someone on this barren world is trying to keep themselves warm?"

"Possibly," answered Taroooc.

"So, which?"

"Either."

"Taroooc, you really are completely..."

Since arriving via the Teleport Stream the Second Officer had shivered and atrophied. A sudden movement developed on his thin lips to interrupt Slogg.

"C... C... Captain."

"Yes Booster?"

"It's bloody freezing."

"I know."

"A... and Captain."

"*What*!"

"I j... just saw... something move. Over there in the distance."

Slogg turned to the direction being indicated, giving a snapped intake of breath as he also detected movement. Focusing hard, he tried to make sense of what he could discern.

Like faraway processionary insects, a myriad of small hooded figures trekked as a bipedal collective, each of their heads stooped low. Even from this distance their gowns could be discerned as the deepest sapphire blue, with all their features and faces hidden. The large group swayed thymically side to side as they advanced forwards. The movement was purposeful and coordinated in its solid monotony. However, none yet seemed aware of the landing party.

"Did *they* issue the distress call?"

"Hard to say Captain, but they are the nearest to the original source," replied Taroooc.

"Multimodal field-glasses please."

"I thought you brought them."

Slogg scoffed. "Please could you surprise me one day in a *positive* way. Okay... we need to get a good look at what we are dealing with here, so I am requisitioning an Advancement Party. I shall protect the rear. Zero, you lead."

"Thanks..." said Zero, "Correction... but no thanks."

Slogg assessed the remaining crew. He questioned his own sanity for requisitioning the Second Officer and two security bowling pins. He turned to his Medical Officer.

"Yelyah Soss, you are reinstated as Medical Officer and Advancement Party Leader. Taroooc will accompany you."

"As you wish."

And so, on this very cold planet a very cautious Advancement Party was formed. Taroooc advised his preference to be in a Drinking Party beneath a table in Refreshment Bay Two, and he stepped cautiously at the front with Yelyah. All eyes were fixed on their hooded quarry. The two security robots droned behind. The Second Officer hid neatly behind Zero and Slogg brought up the rear, his eyes scanning the hills.

"Keep low," Slogg hissed. "We need to know if these guys want help, or conflict."

Zero slowed abruptly.

"I can't…" announced the robot.

Yelyah turned to understand Zero's concern.

Taroooc was caught off-guard and thumped into Yelyah's left shoulder. The two security robots clunked into Taroooc's back. This pile-up tumbled all four of them to the ground. Zero's metal toecap caught this lumbering group and he careered forwards to hit the icy surface.

"…keep low. I am… too tall," he finished.

"But then again," he corrected as his torso cracked into the ground, "it would appear… I am not anymore."

This slam-bang commotion earned the attention of the distant hooded creatures. They froze immediately in their tracks. Each raised a head so slightly, but not sufficient to reveal their faces. The movement was ominious.

Slogg ducked behind the bulk of Zero to join the Second Officer.

"*Well*?" he squealed. "Anyone?"

"They could be hostile," Taroooc informed him.

"Another spectacular deduction."

"One of them is holding a Weaponify Nasty Thing," Yelyah called back.

This situation was tight, sudden, ridiculous, and self-induced. They lay in the middle of a barren wilderness, the only real cover provided by a giant silver robot visible for fifty kilotecs. Slogg's mind raced.

*Had these beings issued the distress call? Was it a trap? Or a misunderstanding?*

By now the whole party crouched behind Zero, with any clear view being obscured by the colossal recumbent robot.

"Zero," commanded Slogg, "What's your verdict? I need an assessment of the situation, risk scenario and likely outcome?"

Slogg anticipated a construction such as Zero, defined as a 26th generation refinement in robotics, would possess its own multi-modal vision and accompanying scenario analysis algorithms.

There was the faintest whirring. Zero's head raised slightly, and the dark slit in its head and magenta glow behind that passed for its eyes, slowly scoured the distance.

"It is actually O.K..." announced Zero.

"Good news..." said Slogg.

The robot turned to look at him in surprise.

"Just what I was expecting," finished Slogg. "Thank you."

Attempting a firm leadership stance, Slogg rose to wave a hand towards their new arrivals, offering the universal peace gesture to this group. A gun was fired and

Slogg was shot through the head.

"...W - 349" completed Zero, finishing his analysis of the Weaponify Nasty Thing's serial number.

*Thud.*

Slogg's body hit the ground.

# CHAPTER 35

In the Eggkraft engine room, Duke sat on the floor, having given up on his boxy stool. His long thin legs crossed awkwardly, and his wiry hair sagged from the top of his head, having lost its original bounce. He was struggling with the situation.

"So do I have any duties as part of the Induction?" he queried his chicken-like abductor.

From his particular vantage point, Duke could see right through the room's open rear doors and out into the gantry. There was a generous portal in the ship's loading bay allowing an arced view of the shimmering white and gray planet they were orbiting, framed by the glittering universe beyond. Duke imagined how much his father would have relished this.

The world below appeared cold. Airstream gusts whirled ice into spirals, and a distant sun gave no colour to its surface. Duke believed he could discern a faint vapour trail where the landing party may have touched down. His thoughts wandered to their progress and rushed back to his own scenario. Dzkk now perched on a low beam, bunching his feathers together around his midriff, as he clutched an instruction manual that spoke softly to him about tachyons, hybrid drive reboots, and flux capacitors. Its gentle chatter continued over Duke's question.

For his own part, Duke had retrieved the willowy educational tome *101 Ways to Insult Technology* he had previously flung across the floor. Holding it lightly in his hands he now peered through the contents. It was slender and beautiful and quiet, yet its smooth waxy paper rippled with animations of likely mechanical breakdowns, together with pop-ups of the recommended curses associated with them. The premise entertained him, and he wished his father had lived to see this device.

Duke sat turning its many pages over, searching for how this marvel functioned. Yet the technology appeared embedded within each of its thin leaves of vellum. He could guess that the book may be typical of his surroundings, and not the single overwhelming artefact he first perceived it to be. His journey from orphaned conspiracy theorist to alien abductee had been voluntary, yet so swift it had given him no time to absorb the minutiae of each stage.

He gave a quick glance back at his companion, whose stubby claw fingers were scrolling up the pages of its own manual.

"Yes," said Dzkk without looking up.

"Yes what?"

Duke had lost himself in thought for a moment.

"You do have some duties, mostly minimal but important all the same."

"Like what?"

"It is key for the Induction, that you speak first. And you appear first."

"Like when?"

"When we make first contact."

"I appear first?"

"Yes. It softens the blow. The shock of an offworld ship descending on your home planet is genuinely severe, and understandably so. Hearing a familiar voice next lightens the load a little."

"So, what am I meant to say? *Join the Club, I recommend it, they'll colonise you and then show you a better way.*" He smirked at Dzkk as he said this. "And they just say, yes please?"

"Okay Duke, yes. Something like that, but without the colonise bit if you don't mind. Just stay natural, your mere presence will help. It's a supporting role. As long as he follows the Induction codebook, Captain Slogg will have the primary role and do most of the talking after that."

"And you, Dzkk?"

"Well, I'm more of a guide. No speeches from me. And anyway, I've done my bit now. Once I've fixed this charabanc I'll be off, and out of your way."

"So you're not coming back with us?"

"It's probably best I don't Duke. I'm not meant to interfere."

"And I just say what comes naturally?"

"Just say it. They're your people, they'll understand you."

"Well, all this leads me to another question."

"Please."

"Okay… how come I can understand you? You're an alien. According to Spielberg you're supposed to communicate in tones of music or bars of coloured light… not in perfect English. I mean, charabanc… who still says that kind of thing?"

"Spielberg?"

"Answer the question."

"Tech Duke, it's always tech. I have my Eustachian tube implant. We'll get you one eventually, but as long as everyone else onboard has one, which is mandated, we can all understand each other as well as you."

"*What?* Euston Tube?"

"Eustachian tube." Dzkk touched his neck again where his claw had earlier dug into it at the point of their first interrogation. "Virtually all species have one. It's the small passageway that connects your throat to your middle ear. It can be a bit fiddly, but tune it with the right tech and we all sound the same. Look it up on the internet."

"The what?"

"The internet. The Galactic Wide Web, it connects all… ah, of course. You haven't got there yet have you. Oh lucky, lucky."

A wide smile stretched across his beak before he continued. "Indeed, no internet. I am so very jealous Duke. You have definitely got to enjoy real life, before that gets phased in. Trust me."

# CHAPTER 36

Slogg was shocked and unnerved. His pale blue skin had turned the colour of their bleak and glacial surroundings, and his orange eyes were now a sallow gilt. There was ice in his mouth and dusted across his cheeks. He slowly lifted a hand, only to confirm its presence.

He knew he had been shot through the head, yet his primary anxiety was the fact it had not killed him. Slogg lay prone, recalling a comparable incident he also survived. He later attributed holding onto life had been down to good luck, an oversized skull, and his surgeon's observation of Slogg's small brain cavity.

To support this theory and extend his life insurance, Slogg invested in a course of synthetic nano-adrenalin shots. The plasma technology now activated, coursing through his veins, ensuring he felt no pain under attack, whilst the blended artificial coagulants preserved blood loss.

He would need to wear a long fringe again.

He screwed up his eyes and squinted towards the ashen sky. He wondered if the opportunity worth all this risk. Commodoring a group of GCF ships was his next life goal, and the feedback from his leadership reviews had tasked him to focus on courage and empathy. It could be argued that getting shot through the head irrefutably ticked one of these boxes.

Slogg rolled over in the snow to slip back behind Zero. He touched his forehead where the projectile had entered, feeling a newly damp, mushy scar already forming.

"Fat lot of use you are!" He cursed the robot. "I need answers."

"Ball stick..." began Zero, "Correction. Ballistic analysis informs that Weaponify Nasty Thing…"

"Yes?"

"...was latest upgrade *Occasional Kill Weapon - Three Four Nine*."

"Upgrade what?"

"Sir," put in Taroooc, "those are firearms designed to reduce lawsuits amongst regular infantry by introducing an element of chance when discharged."

"Lawsuits? This makes no sense," spat Slogg. "*Occasional Kill Weapon*?"

"Sir, if... you can never be sure it was your weapon that produced the kill, you can never be sued by your adversaries under any circumstances."

Slogg stared blankly at Taroooc.

"Is this the way things are going now? We consider the legal action before the battlefield action."

Taroooc sensed this question was rhetorical, maintaining a thin smile and silence.

"Okay," continued Slogg, "I need a situation assessment, quickly. We came here to collect a Peacefulness and Primacy Offering..."

"A *what*?" challenged Yelyah.

"I'll explain another time. We've landed unarmed, which in retrospect was a very bad decision. They..." he pointed to the distance, "have so far used a small-scale nuclear blast, and fired at least one gun. A gun that can occasionally kill..."

"Captain, I just saw a pink elephant."

"Quiet Yelyah! Can't you see our position is dire."

Slogg snatched his Medical Officer's arm down to join the group as they sheltered behind Zero.

"As you wish. No need to be so rough."

"Is it all a trap? Or can we assume there is some misunderstanding here?" continued Slogg. "Why would they drag us down here with a distress call and then proceed to *shoot* all of us?"

"They've only blasted once and shot once Sir, and both times they were directed at you," Taroooc pointed out.

"They can't be all bad then," added the Medical Officer.

"Yelyah," called out Slogg.

"Yes?"

"You're fired again."

"As you wish."

"As I was saying..."

"Don't you want to hear about the pink elephant?"

"No! Please stop talking."

"As you wish."

A brief silence followed as the cowered, with only the sound of their heavy breathing. Tentatively Taroooc lifted his head slowly above the robot's torso, catching the briefest glimpse before he snatched it back down again.

"Captain," hissed Taroooc, "I really think you should see this. They are here."

Pairs of eyes raised methodically above the robot's body to observe a wall of small, faceless beings now in very close proximity, covered head to foot in sapphire-blue hooded robes. Approaching Slogg's landing party, they advanced slowly and rhythmically at a plodding cadence, heads remaining bowed. Each carried a small device in hand, at which they all intently stared. Their pace and concentration suggested deep meditation. The heavy fabric hoods fully covered their eyes and features. One creature had remained far behind, head similarly down and holding an oversized firearm at its side. The pulsing march of rest continued forward as their formation began to widen.

A single countersign to the meditative, synchronised stream was the flicker of slender fingers tapping rapidly across the device screens they each held.

"Are those weapons they carry?" demanded Slogg.

"It would seem not Captain," replied Taroooc. "Their only weapon bearer has stayed back."

"What are they doing?"

As the wall of deep blue hoods came near the ponderous nature of their moves suggested no menace beyond a united rhythm. Slogg indicated to his landing party they should hold their ground.

"Are you sure Captain? They shot at you."

"I'm a new man Taroooc. Regretfully we're unarmed, so I'm deciding to give them the benefit of the doubt. And if they'd wanted to take another pop at us, they would have done so by now."

The hooded collective halted abruptly in unison, forming an arc ten paces before Slogg and his group. Still no sign of eyes, their heads remained hooded and stooped, intent on the devices in each palm.

"Captain, I believe I know who they are," began Taroooc.

"You do?"

"Yes Sir, I've read about them on Galakipedia and seen rare images on holoTV."

"Go on."

"They are a unique tribe."

"Unique..."

"The Digitari."

"Who? *Digitari?*"

"Yes Sir. And I think they are communicating."

"Communicating. How?"

"Twit..." cut in Zero.

Slogg fixed the robot with a steely gaze.

"TwiText sir," added Taroooc, "Zero is nearly there. They are possibly trying to reach us on TwiText. Or maybe BokkFace."

"But... those recmedia channels are obsolete."

"Not everywhere Sir."

There was a faint ping, and Slogg noticed his portable ship's communicator light was flashing. He pulled it from his belt and turned its screen towards him in full expectation of Deluxia's face appearing, calling from the bridge.

Instead of his Communications Officer he saw only a tiny, pixelated flag with a number *1* etched to it, accompanied with the following:

Gwofie wishes to connect with you on TwiText. You have no mutual friends with Gwofie.

"What does this mean Taroooc, and who the hell is Gwofie?"

"It's a TwiText message sir. Gwofie is trying to poke you."

"Of course."

Slogg closed his eyes, recalling childhood annums strewn with wearying grandparental stories of how they communicated via digital devices. Always how wonderful and sleek these devices were, and always in preference to in-person, facial or auditory interaction. *Tapping not talking* was the mantra they lived by. His body yearned to scream at the cold leaden sky.

As Slogg screwed his eyes tighter and craned his neck upwards, one diminutive, hooded creature broke ranks from the arc and approached to prod his device into Slogg's groin.

Slogg opened his eyes.

As he did so, the two hundred cloaked figures shuffled to encircle Slogg and his crew, their faces remaining obscured. A faint glow from each device lit nimble hands and the rim of their hoods.

Looking to the distance, Slogg observed the one creature remaining back and carrying the firearm, had reholstered the weapon. A pink elephant also emerged to stand by its side.

Bringing his gaze back down, Slogg concentrated on the prodding to his groin. His antagonist registered as a short creature in the same sapphire-blue hood as his companions. Intricately interwoven into his hood cloth was a small, subtle digital display with *...GWOFIE...* scrolling smoothly across its indigo screen. The creature's gown also offered *Commander* stitched onto the shoulder, together with an obscure emblem.

Slogg forced a grin and examined Gwofie's device as it continued to nudge his nether regions.

"That thing you have there," Slogg asked, "is it loaded?"

The creature's fingers flashed across the device. Another ping emanated from Slogg's communicator. The message on his screen changed to:

Mine or yours?

This was followed with another prod.

"Yours!" coughed Slogg, "And do you mind not prodding me there."

He stepped backwards.

Another ping and another message.

My name is Commander Gwofie.

"That's a nice little name." commented Slogg.

*Ping.*

It's not a **little** name!

The creature moved forward with another prod and its fingers skitted blurrily across the device.

*Ping.*

It is ~~short~~ [autocorrection] an abbreviation for Gwofeelulplexipus The Large Nosed. That takes too long to type so it is ~~shortened~~ [autocorrection] curtailed to Gwofie. As an additional observation, I do not possess a large nose.

*Ping.*

But my uncle has.

Slogg stared down speechless at the little hood. There was still no sign of a face, nor that of any of his companions.

*Ping.*

U R tall aren't U.

"Yes," agreed Slogg with the statement, though unimpressed with the grammar.

*Ping.*

Scuzzball!

Slogg stared at his communicator screen for a few extra seconds to reread the statement.

"I beg your pardon!"

As Slogg spoke another pixelated icon appeared beneath this message depicting a hand with thumbs up. An accompanying message read:

👍 This post has 109 likes

Without looking up from beneath his hood, the Gwofie creature raised his device away from Slogg's groin to point it between his eyes. A red glow radiated from its edge as Gwofie reached his fingers to blindly tap another message.

*Ping.*

What R U doing here Lofty?

"*Lofty*! Okay, this has gone far enough," declared

Slogg, "We answered your distress call."

There was no ping.

There was a very long silence. And ten beats.

Very slowly a large number of the creatures tucked their devices into hidden pockets and stood in awkward stillness.

Gwofie then lowered the device from Slogg's viewpoint and towards his own lap. His fingers flashed across its screen.

*Ping.*

The hooded creatures a moment ago pocketing their devices frantically grappled through their cloaks to retrieve them. However, the message was for Slogg.

Whoops!
Sorry about that. LOL.

"Sorry!" Slogg barked, sensing the tables were turning. "What do you mean *sorry*? And who is Lol?"

I believe that is the universal form of apology.
👍 This message has 67 likes

It dawned on Slogg.

"So, it *was* your distress call!"

Yes 😐

"And when we answer it, you shoot me through the head?"

Oops. ☹

"That's the way you greet your rescuers?"

It was an **Occasional** Kill Weapon.
👍 This message has 12 likes and 1 dislike

"Which occasionally *kills*!"

Silence. Then…

☹

Slogg had the upper hand, but he was tiring of the conversation.

"You do *not* seem to be in any distress. And will you please stop this TwiText charade and look at me."

*Ping.*

But we are in distress!

"So why attack the rescue party?"

Because you were tall ☺

"Tall!"

"Yes. Lofty. And... because you speak freely and comfortably to each other without the need for Bokkfacing or TwiText.

*"What?"*

"You are lanky and lack inhibitions. Scuzzballs
👍 This message has 77 likes and is trending

Slogg's patience ran out.

"Right! Gwofie, if that's your name, you can't go around the universe killing everyone who happens to be able to see over your head. It's just not decent and it's not practical." said Slogg, inadvertently staring above a sea of faceless hooded creatures with heads bowed to their devices and fingers a blur of activity.

"And every single species of the Galactic Core I have met so far has no problem with face-to-face communication. So please… *look* at me."

There was a slight pause. Gwofie's fingers flew to his screen.

*Ping. Ping. Ping ping ping ping…*

But it's the universe's fault in the first place. Before the Digitari were introduced to the Galactic Core, we believed ourselves to be an effusive, statuesque race with athletic bodies, a decent analogue mobile infrastructure, and a love of literature, long walks, and quiet contemplation. Then up pop a few Galactic Core representatives and we get *Sorry lads, you are ~~shorties~~ [autocorrection] vertically challenged*. Then they give us our Peacefulness and Primacy Offering to help us progress from 5G to 6 and 7, and provide instantaneous updates for Bokkface, TwiText and Toktikker. As a bonus they threw in some free Glossplaztik phablets with our 5G plan. We try to ignore the insults, install 5G, and attempt to keep calm and carry on.

"It's 8G Dark Energy Bandwidth now…"
*Ping.*

Shush! To cut a long evolution ~~short~~ [autocorrection] in half, once a single Digitari looks down to check for non-existent TwiTexts on their new phablet, we all start to fear we are missing out. We move very quickly from quiet reflection and enjoying the moment, to develop *The Fear of Empty Time*. We need to be engrossed... or pretend to be engrossed. These heavy hoods we wear... well they allow us to maintain our focus on our devices, without distraction. Something must always be happening somewhere that requires our attention, and to appear as engrossed or important as our brethren. So, my dear Lofty, if I look up at you now from beneath this hood - and there is the merest pause in our conversation – my companions will surmise I have no one to interact with but you. The *Fear of Empty Time* will kick in, and that... would amount to Bokkfacing suicide. Init. ☹

Slogg stared at the little man's hood unable to speak. The severe cold bit his neck again and he shivered.

"The *Fear of Empty Time,*" he finally whispered. "That's all your species got from joining the Galactic Club?"

Effectively, yes.

"I'm so sorry."

And it threatens us constantly. I appreciate your apology, but I'm the one who should say sorry again, for shooting you in the head.

"Apology accepted."

Anyway, most of us are now in counselling with Digitolics Anonymous. Albeit virtually, by holochat, on our devices. Oh, the irony.

The digital display woven into his hood changed from ...*GWOFIE*... to a sad face icon.

"I see," said Slogg. He inhaled deeply and turned to stare at Taroooc.

"Thoughts?"

"Er..."

"Not too difficult for you, is it? Am I to suffer *The Fear of Empty Time* from my own Wellbeing Officer... waiting for an answer?"

"Well Sir, it looks like we are on a wasted rescue mission. Why did they issue a distress call?"

Slogg turned back to Gwofie's faceless hood.

"You heard the man. Why are you here, in this godforsaken Braevitchkan solar system? And why the pointless call for help?"

The sad face icon disappeared from the hood.

*Ping.*

We were on an interstellar mission at the request of the Jockey Monks. Our ship developed a nav fault as we came though their atmosphere. We had to force a manual early landing. With no navigation app, and no idea where we were, we tried calling the monks. After lunch? Ha! That was hopeless. We panicked and launched our distress call, and then set off to search our surroundings. And it turns out, we'd actually landed next to their monastic headquarters. You couldn't make it up. A few hours later, you arrive.

"You were on a mission?" inquired Slogg. Staring

at his communicator he waited for the ping, which came back very quickly.

Yes. The Jockey Monks have an aversion to verbal discourse – it interferes with their drinking and horse racing. Same here! And so, they chose us, the Digitari, as the perfect species to assist.

"With what?"

We have been asked to remove most of the pink elephants that plague their planet.

"I think there is a typo here," said Slogg.
A pause, and a flurry of digital dexterity.

No, what I've written is correct. In their constant quest for brewing prowess, strength and perfection, a small sect has evolved bizarre telegenerative powers.

"Telegenerative?"

Yes, the ability to create any type of matter from nothing. It's taken them aeons, but by simple, pure focused imagination, these monks can now conjure up the most flavoursome hops, finest yeast, precision fermenting tanks, etc... you get the idea. And their beer just gets better and better... and stronger.

"That's a rare gift in Laniakea."

Purists dedicated to their craft.

"Okay, I will accept this pending some fact checking, but where do the *pink* elephants come in?"
*Tappitappitiptaptiptaptaptaptippitap... ping ping ping*

I was coming to that. It seems the evolved telegenerative powers are not exclusive to the conscious mind. As well as being the finest in Laniakea, Braevitchkan beer is also the strongest. And the monks consume a *lot*. As they drift gently into their stupor, their powers of telegeneration have also produced an excess of revolving rooms and, bizarrely, pink elephants.

"This is... ridiculous."

But true. The revolving rooms are being snapped up by the restaurant and hospitality industry, however it seems no one has any use for a pink elephant, and they have become a nuisance.

Slogg imagined his own telegenerative powers. Beyond immediate fame and promotion, at this instant he would have manifested a small hotel with a secure and beautiful master suite, immensely plush bed, deep pillows, a Centaurian martini chilled with birch sap ice, and a large holoTV filling one wall. Then he sighed a heavy sigh and asked:

"So, what's your payback for removing these elephants?"

*Ping.*

As much Braevitchkan beer as we can carry.

Slogg allowed himself a while to process this statement.

"Wait. So, you have a ship full of Braevitchkan beer? Nearby?"

Yes, or we're about to. They dispatch their beer first to this cold fourth planet for storage and ongoing distribution. We were loading our share from the warehouses, together with the elephants, when you distracted us. But we still have a problem with the navigation app. We're tappers and shunters, but not software engineers.

A smile grew across Slogg's face. "Well, we are on a mission also. I have a destiny inducting a planet into the Galactic Club. And just guess what my Peaceful and Primacy Offering needs to be?

No idea.

"Let's walk and talk Commander Gwofie. I may be able to make you an offer you can't refuse. Where's your ship?"

Shall I TwiText you the location?

"No," exhaled Slogg, "just lead the way."

And so, the show had begun.

They reached the brow of a hilltop and descended its icy slopes towards a hulking spaceship and the makeshift Digitari camp. Slogg explained their need for Braevitchkan Beer and his counteroffer of software engineers to fix Gwofie's navigation app.

Slogg also demanded a very positive review and five-star rating be put on his HR profile to boost his promotion prospects.

The deal was struck as they entered the camp and strange sights began to greet the landing party.

*Ping.*

Welcome
This message has 42 likes

Several giant cages dotted the scene containing two or three pink elephants in each. More cages held crates of Braevitchkan beer.

As backdrop a midsized merchant starship steamed from its vents. Its outer skin was a wonderous patchwork of hieroglyphs and small display screens streaming Twitext and Bokkface feeds.

To one corner of the camp stood another unexpected sight. A gilded hemi-spherical dome gleamed before them. It was perfectly smooth and featureless, except for a four-letter word pulsing rhythmically at its apex. In blue neon the word said *GOSH*.

"What is that?" demanded Slogg.

That's Gosh Bordomm. I can send you a link to his TwiText profile if you want.

"Who?"

As in *GOSH BORDOMM - Saviour of Northern Andromeda*. Here... *gww.galactipedia.uni/goshbord*

"I thought he was a superhero myth."

More Megastar. His words 😐

Gwofie led the party past this and on towards his stricken vessel. Sighting the craft, Slogg realized he had not been in contact with his own ship since arriving. Pulling out his communicator he swiped away Gwofie's messages and reopened his secure WalkyTalky app.

"Slogg to ship. Slogg to ship. Are you receiving? Over."

Silence.

"I repeat, Slogg to ship. Are you receiving? Over."

A reply came through the ether.

"Hi. This is Deluxia. I'm sorry I'm not around at the moment. Please leave a message after the tone. Thank you. *Beep*."

Slogg raised his head to the sky, sighed, and then shivered.

It was still a very cold planet.

# CHAPTER 37

Zero stood beside a plume of hot steam issuing from the Digitari's grounded starship. The white vapour swirled around his silver thighs, rising through his metallic groin and up to his angular torso. Dulling the chrome sheen as it condensed on the cold Kolidium, the vapour finally played before his domed head as it disappeared into the thin air. Condensation from the water formed on Zero's arms, and tiny droplets trickled down the metal in their own irregular patterns, to create crystal clear dew drops on the ends of his fingers. A greying, weak sun shone through the frigid atmosphere causing these beads to glimmer faintly as they fell to the hard earth.

Taroooc observed this tranquil, picture-book scene, strolling by with Gwofie and Slogg. "What are you doing?" he called out.

"Rusting." replied Zero.

"Oh. So why stand there?"

"Beak..." said Zero, "oz… because it's the only way... I can weep corn *click whirr...* Correction, keep warm."

Taroooc carried on his way.

Once inside the defective Digitari starship they reached its diminutive dark bridge, with a small panel of multi-coloured lights providing a lowly glow.

Taroooc followed in behind Gwofie and Slogg as both stumbled simultaneously. A rattling of beer bottles could be heard underfoot.

The gloom was palpable and Taroooc paused, uncertain in the dimness and barely able to see beyond a short distance.

*Ping.*

Pull the piece of string above you, the one with a knot tied in the end.

Through the green-grey twilight Taroooc read his communicator's screen and groped over his head, feeling something chord-like. He pulled it.

Beyond them a toilet flushed.

*Ping.*

Not the chain! The next one to it.

Taroooc fumbled through thin air to locate another rope to pull.

*Click.* A light came on.

"Ah, that's better," sighed Slogg.

The new spotlight was meagre, just enough to highlight them standing before a sweep of control panels embedded into a long, smoothly undulating desk. Dense shadows underscored that this desk also curved gently upwards further, dotted in switches, small lights, and dimmed touch-sensitive screens.

Through the murk it appeared this functional counter was not as sleek and junk-free as its ergonomic designers had intended. It teemed with dozens of irregular lengths of string. Each delicate chord was then connected to a relevant switch on the panel. As their eyes rose up to the darkened ceiling, Slogg and Taroooc could just make out that it too had the same strings dangling at haphazard intervals.

Every chord was cheap, coarse, brown string.

*Ping.*

Good eh?

"Good?" questioned Slogg. "Different."

"Unique," confirmed Taroooc, watching his recently pulled chord still swaying gently above their heads in the darkness. Squinting hard he could just make out this was fixed via a semblance of glue to a slim light switch.

Swathed in his dark blue robes, Gwofie jumped to yank a different piece of string attached to the long desk console. Two display units flickered to life, glowing above them. One revealed a three-dimensional image titled *Principal Navigation Units.* Gwofie silently unclipped a long slender pole from beneath his console, proffering it up to touch the display. There was a movement and an area magnified to reveal a delicate flowchart and subroutines, sections of which blinked rhythmically in red.

*Ping.*

Heeding its call and reaching for his communicator, Slogg began to experience a rare sense of sympathy for their smaller host hidden beneath the all-concealing garb. He cut short his automatic movement to uncover the inbound message and let his device remain in its belt holster. Instead, Slogg spoke.

"Gwofie. It's just the three of us in here, and your colleagues remain outside. Please, can we dispense with the screens and typing, and just… *talk.*"

Gwofie's slender fingers went instinctively to his screen, but then froze. A silence hung in the air. *Empty time.*

Then the tiniest voice spoke from under the hood.

"But what if… I don't have anything to say? What will I *do*?"

"You don't need to have anything to say, Gwofie. Or anything to do. I might speak, Tarooc might, you might. Questions, answers, statements, observations, responses jokes, gaps. And possibly some *Empty time.* It's called a normal conversation."

Gwofie paused. Hesitantly, he gently laid down his device on the console before him. His fingers lingered on it a few more seconds and then… he let go.

Slogg and Tarooc discerned a small intake of breath from their host. Gwofie's slender fingers rose to the deep sapphire hood covering his features, pulling it slowly back over his head to reveal translucent grey skin stretched thinly across a diminutive skull. Beneath this skin veins and capillaries were clearly visible distributing white blood around the cranium. Red eyes with vivid black pupils looked up at the two of them.

It was Slogg and Taroooc's moment to draw in a sharp gulp of air. The low light in the cabin played across Gwofie's white scalp, endowing it an unnerving luminous glow. As they squinted awkwardly back, the heavy demonic eyes translated into a mournful expression of sorrow. Clearly the laden hood had protected this face and head from any direct sunlight for decades.

"Well… this is different," began Gwofie.

"It is," confirmed Slogg, softly.

"I mean the talking, Captain. I'm glad I can still do it." Aware of their stares, his expression dropped to woe.

"Please don't be too alarmed at my appearance."

"Well, I…"

"You see, our heavy hoods are designed to encompass the features completely, enabling a pure devotion to our device screens, without distraction. They act like blinkers. Similarly, the very low light levels in our surroundings are tuned to a specific dimness that permits optimal focus on the displays contained within these rooms."

"I see, that's why it's so frickin' dark!"

"Yes Captain. But all of this means our skins rarely, if ever, see any daylight. And then it doesn't take nature long to evolve you in line with your circumstances."

Gwofie's red eyes peered up at the Captain with a doleful pleading for understanding. The white skin tightened further across his forehead.

"We are *trying* to change you know. We are aware of the situation we've got ourselves into."

"Good to hear. So…"

"Case in point," continued the little voice, "we have upgraded our devices to include cameras."

The red eyes glanced across at his lonely communicator that lay next to him.

"Okay… not exactly revolutionary, but a move forward perhaps," observed Slogg, unsure of the direction the conversation was taking. Gwofie remained keen to prove a point, alongside exercising his vocal cords for the first time in decades.

"Yes, cameras. You see, we Digitari spend so long peering downwards, our social engineering specialists have come up with the new idea to use our device cameras for sharing pleasing photographs of any green meadow, turf, or carefully mown grassland we might wander across."

"Great," stated Slogg flatly.

The diminutive Digitari's face beamed at the thought.

Remaining nonplussed by this feigned interest in green space, Slogg widened his eyes with a slight nod, indicating he wished the conversation to move on.

"I know it's a small thing but its progress," continued Gwofie. "We have a new app that goes with this tech, to encourage dialogue. It goes beyond TwiText and invites us to share these pictures of the fields, lawns, and turf… and type in little comments to go with them."

"Really," acknowledged Slogg, "Shall we get to the point of why we're here."

"We call it InstaGrass."

Silence.

"I see, okay. Anyway Gwofie, moving onto this navigational issue…"

"Also! In our efforts to remain inclusive across Digitari generations, we have another sharing app in beta test. Oh yes… family snaps, encouraging our elders and matriarchs by promoting continued communication amongst the Digitari's senior citizens, in particular the elderly females. There's a new app for that as well."

"Let me guess," offered Slogg.

"Please."

"InstaGran."

"Well done."

"Please Gwofie, can we move on?"

"I just thought you should know."

Slogg turned away, holding a cupped hand towards the screen that glowed before them.

"What's this you're showing us here?"

"Ha. Well, that's where the problem lies with our navigation. You can see it should be easy to fix, Captain, but there is no app developer in the crew, and we've run out of these long thin brown bits."

"I'm sorry?" queried Slogg.

"Bloody discrimination if you ask me." cursed the little Digitari. "Ooh, profanity. It feels *so* much better saying it than typing it. *Bloody discrimination!* Wow. "

Slogg smiled benevolently.

"Discrimination?" he mused.

"Yes. Those *damn* G6 Starshipbuilders," continued Gwofie with his cursing. "Damn, damn, damn them! Wow talking is fun! *Daaaaamn!* They completely ignored the fact that we were shor... we were..."

"Vertically challenged?" offered Slogg.

"...and delivered a starship for the average height species." Gwofie was in the groove, getting the hang of it now. "When we complained… they smiled smugly and said *Plenty of leg room*. Sod them. At least, that was our verdict. So, we developed our own upgrades to cope. It's mainly my idea and I'm thinking of calling it *S-tring*. There you go. Phew! Not too technical I hope?"

"*String*?" repeated Slogg.

"S-tring, but yes. The Galactic patent has just been applied for so don't bother making any sketches. We should be hearing very soon."

"..."

Slogg decided the best course of action for all concerned was to leave some *empty time*. The ensuing short silence gave him a brief moment to muse and Slogg found himself quietly envying the Digitari and their sheltered existence.

Gwofie lugged and flicked at the same piece of string in a movement intended to switch off the displays. However, based on its ingrained design, the switch now needed a push upwards, an act that, from Gwofie's lowered position, was impossible using the connected string.

"Of course," said Gwofie observing his guest's unease, "there's still a bit more development work to be done," leaning over to retrieve his long stick.

In a magnanimous gesture, Slogg reached across the diminutive Digitari to flip the switch up and off.

Gwofie scoffed loudly, pulling his hood back up in a swift gesture to conceal his face. He snatched his device from the console and went to leave as his fingers flashed across its touch-sensitive screen.

*Ping.*

"Lanky git!"

Having witnessed the basics of the ship's navigation systems and its self-diagnostics, Slogg and Taroooc agreed their software engineers could feign a repair.

In return, Slogg confirmed the eighty crates of Braevitchkan beer as compensation, reminding his host of the commitment to a five-star review for their time. Gwofie reluctantly submitted to the ether.

Slogg was very pleased. Business was settled, his appropriate Peacefulness and Primacy Offering had now been secured in relative ease, and he had avoided any interaction with the Proltoid Jockey Monks. His promotion to Commodore was now a heightened probability. *Win-win-win* as his Classics lecturer Fid Fadood might have said.

The landing party began their way back across the planet's frozen landscape towards the original clearing, in preparation for removal via the Teleport Stream. Zero followed reluctantly from his make-shift sauna, creaking distinctly at his joints.

As they passed the gilded dome at the camp's perimeter the *GOSH* sign pulsed from blue to orange, and a door hissed open. A figure loomed before them dressed top to toe in a gloss white, figure-hugging tunic topped by a stiff emerald collar. A diaphanous cape in matching green fluttered at his back. Squeezing from his dome, the giant's height significantly exceeded that of Slogg and Taroooc, and almost tipped Zero. Though his chest and shoulders were vast, the upright collar enveloped a head far too small for the rest of the body. The letters *GB* were embossed into the fabric across his gleaming torso.

"Hi, I'm Gosh," said Gosh.

"Hello," said Slogg, acknowledging the introduction. "Captain Slogg, and this is Chief Wellness Officer Taroooc. Nice to meet you, but I'm sorry… we are just leaving."

The giant's eyes lit up.

"Can I help?" he queried.

"Sorry?"

"I'm Gosh Bordomm - Saviour of Northern Andromeda. I can fly."

To prove this he hovered gently away from the ground, holding fast before gently lowering himself down.

"Impressive."

"Thank you, Captain. I can also save lives… fight crime?"

"It's okay," said Slogg, "we're good."

"But I am also *superhero*," put in Gosh,

subconsciously licking his index finger to smooth over both of his eyebrows.

"Really?" started Taroooc. "By that you really mean All-Powerful."

"Not another one!" exclaimed Slogg. "I thought they were extremely rare… just one per galaxy?"

"My galaxy is very large and hence we're allowed a surfeit. I opted for superhero status. It's just one level down from All-Powerful but it's meant to give you a little more freedom, coupled with less responsibility. Perfect for me..."

"We don't need any help!" interrupted Slogg. "Thank you."

He tipped his chin up, indicating his landing party onward to the icy foothills, and a return to their starting point. They stepped forward to resume their walk.

"One minute..." said Gosh.

Slogg glanced again at the Saviour of Northern Andromeda, who had now carefully positioned himself in a raised position on a nearby rock. Gosh stood slightly angled to their view, and Slogg could observe the superhero was very deliberately sucking in his stomach.

"I am sure I can help?"

"As I've said already, we don't need any."

"Are you absolutely sure?" pressed Gosh, extending his chin to emphasize the sharp jawline. "As a superhero I have laser eyes to cut any metal, and retractable talons to..."

"Dice vegetables? I'm sorry Gosh, we are not in need."

"I can spin a web… any size."

"Look…" exclaimed Slogg.

"Okay," cut in Gosh. He stepped down from the rock. Ignoring him, Slogg followed his landing party as they walked on. Gosh hurried to Slogg's side, his demeanour softening, and his voice quietened. Struggling with his next words, he bent low to Slogg's ear.

"...it's just that... could you help me?"

"Sorry?"

"Could I hitch a lift?" pleaded Gosh.

"A lift?"

"Yes, away from this planet. It's bloody freezing you know."

"I thought you were a superhero. I thought you could fly."

"Not superluminally, sadly. You see, I've messed up a bit," confessed Gosh.

"A bit?"

Gosh looked at Slogg and widened his eyes but remained silent.

"If you want our help, I need more."

"Okay, okay," Gosh whispered, "I'm sort of... on the run."

"*On the run*! From whom?"

"*Sshhh!* From the Andromedan Revenue Service... and the Galactic Bureau of Investigation."

"Tax?"

"Well... more like tax mitigation."

"Tax evasion. Ha! The ARS and GBI... that's some heavy stuff Gosh."

"It's completely unwarranted and unnecessary."

"It always is."

"Captain, have you heard of a ULSZ?"

"A what?"

"Exactly! Neither had I. It's an Ultra-Low Superhero Zone..."

"Ultra Low..."

"Superhero Zone. Apparently, since the surfeit levy was introduced and freedom of movement became a basic species right, some of the more attractive galaxies are so congested with superheroes, the Galactic Core implemented a daily charge. We must pay one hundred and ninety Geltoes a day, just to exist. I was nicely settled on Neerizitt Six, quietly doing my shtick and occasionally saving lives. No one told me! I didn't find out for two and a half annums, and by then it was too late!"

"So what happened?"

"The ARS came calling... and fined me. I was already struggling to pay the Higher Powers Tax, just because of the laser eyes and the fact I can fly. So here I am."

"Why here?"

"I panicked and ran. The Digitari were passing, and I bought a ticket out. They gave me a discount by insisting I could help flick some switches. But now I'm sick of their heightist jokes. And the air of resentment onboard is palpable."

They had reached the icy brow of the hilltop and approached the spot where the Teleport Stream would extract the landing party from the planet.

Slogg sighed.

"I'm sorry Gosh, I feel for you, but..."

"I'm planning to pay the tax and the fine. I just need a bit more time. The ARS have now brought in the GBI, and I'm wanted. For something I knew nothing about. Captain, *please*. If I can just hitch a lift."

"We're on a mission Gosh, and a tight schedule."

"Drop me anywhere along the way. I'll work in your kitchens, dicing meat and veg if need be."

He held up his hand a flicked up his long fingers. Sharp talons flashed instantly from the knuckles. The group had formed a circle ready for the Teleport Stream. Zero creaked into the rear, Yelyah, Tarooc, the Second Officer and the two bowling pins bunched together in front.

Gosh smiled thinly and retracted his talons.

"Look..." said Slogg, exasperated.

"Okay... do you have any HR issues?" interrupted Gosh.

"*What*?"

"I'm retraining as a humanoid resources

consultant. There's lots of money in it, and it will help me repay my fines. I just need enough time and dark energy bandwidth to download next season's course."

"We're multi-species Gosh, a migrant ship. Not just humanoid. And we have to go."

"Okay, okay, final offer. This cape…"

Gosh reached round to hold up a section of the finest, shimmering emerald fabric that flowed down his back.

"… it's pure Ireenium."

There was an intake of breath from Taroooc and Yelyah.

"You can have it," said Gosh.

"The whole cape?" challenged Slogg.

Gosh exhaled slowly and deeply.

"Yes."

"Why don't you sell it to pay the ARS?"

"That's *cape laundering* Captain. It's expressly forbidden for any superhero once the costume has been endowed."

"Well, there you have it…"

"But Captain, there is nothing anywhere in the contract that forbids a superhero's cape from being donated, especially in dire circumstances."

"Okay…"

"So, it's yours Captain, I'm giving it to you. I'll probably need a receipt, but we can agree the appropriate wording."

The eyes set in the undersized skull opened wide and pleaded with Slogg.

"Look…" then a beat. "Ok, jump in."

"Really?" squealed Gosh. He hovered a little above the ground.

"It's okay Gosh, you don't need to impress us anymore."

"I'm sorry Captain, I hover sometimes when I get excited or stimulated."

Slogg wanted to hear no more. Right now his evolving ability to feel empathy was disconcerting. He opened his communicator and spoke to the Teleport Engineer, asking that they be removed from the planet with one additional, extra-large passenger headcount.

Gosh huddled in next to Zero.

Slogg sighed his millionth sigh.

As he was sucked up into the sky by a swirling cloud of protons, neutrons and electrons, he could think of only one word. Ireenium[19].

---

[19] Ireenium is the rarest metal in the current known Universe and is mostly traded as minute swatches of lustrous green cloth only a few molecules thick. Marketed as a luxury for aeons under the slogan *Ireen, Y'Know What Ah Mean*, it is so devastatingly difficult to mine that, ironically, the energy and resource expenditure required to prospect and recover it, far exceed the actual value of the metal dug out. Whole planets have donated their mantles, ecosystems and existences to its excavation. As a result, a digital currency derivative *Ireencoin* came into being, based on the constant growth multiples witnessed in the metal's exorbitant price. Ireencoin's value then surpassed even its base metal's worth, as the currency was so fantastically rare, it could no longer exist.

# CHAPTER 38

On board the migrant ship, warm sickly drinks dosed with a strong alcohol content greeted the returning party. A small gesture by Slogg, but one that mattered a lot to all concerned. Zero now packed the empty time in conversation with squeaks from his joints and was escorted back to Dzkk's loading bay by a member of the maintenance crew. The omnipotent chicken-creature lingered aboard with his Eggkraft remaining resolutely un-fixable. Yelyah, quiet and uncommunicative, willingly returned to her sickbay sanctuary.

The two security robots hummed away for a herbal oil bathe and recharge.

Gosh Bordomm accompanied Slogg and Tarooc to the bridge.

On the positive, Slogg had secured a gossamer cape of pure Ireenium, yet he appeared puzzled, as if unable to recall how events unfolded to deliver this dubious guardian to his ship. Figuring out what to do with the gloss-white clad watchman, he landed on intriguing idea. Could the superhero's HR training uncover any professional insight amongst his immediate reports?

As they entered the bridge Deluxia deftly zipped her make-up case.

"Busy?" queried Slogg, resuming his oversized Captain's seat and beckoning Tarooc and Gosh to join him.

Instantly clocking the Communications Officer, Gosh beamed widely towards Deluxia. Subconsciously he hovered a little.

"Taroooc," began Slogg, "select a software engineer and app developer to go down to Gwofie's ship to fix their navigation. Choose the best, so it's damn quick."

"Yes Sir."

The bridge was quiet. Slogg leaned an elbow onto his chair's armrest and tapped his lower lip with his fingernails.

Deluxia was in love.

Her tail swished gently side to side. Middle-age and a recent separation presented encouragement and posed no barrier. Deluxia's professionalism remained paramount, yet her prevailing strange taste in the alternative species was making this newly arrived shiny white hulk very attractive and a welcome alternative to the Terracoscienn male. Even Gosh's small head was befitting to her exotic preferences.

Annoyed by the frisson, Slogg turned to Gosh.

"Well Mr. Superhero, you offered to help with HR and I'd like you to review my imminent appraisal documentation and set goals. But first let's start with a performance management assessment here on the bridge. You've got thirty minutes before my engineers return and then we leave. This is Deluxia…"

Being severely distracted, Deluxia was not listening to Slogg. On hearing her name, she blushed and noticed a faint sparkle in the superhero's eye as his boots reconnected with the floor. She sensed subtle conversation was necessary to begin their introduction.

"Gosh…" she exclaimed admiringly, "you are *very* tall."

"I'm flattered you recognized me," smiled Gosh Bordomm.

Bemused by his response, Deluxia pressed on. "I'm Deluxia Moe Delle."

"Pleased to meet you," and again he hovered

before her, maintaining a slight angle and sucking in his midriff.

"Are you going to introduce yourself?" continued Deluxia.

"Bordomm." he nodded.

"No honestly, I am genuinely interested."

"I'm Gosh Bordomm."

"Ah, now I get it," said Deluxia. "And are you from Braevitchka?"

"No, not originally. It was just a short visit," answered Gosh, smoothing another eyebrow.

"I see. And before that?"

"My chosen planet, Neerizitt."

"Near where?"

"No, Neerizitt."

"I see. So, it's near Izitt," checked Deluxia. "I'm from Terracoscia and I've never been to Izitt."

"No, it's Neer... yes... that's right, Neerizitt."

"You are a long way from home then," observed Deluxia.

"Well yes, roaming with those Digitari, and their little ship, took fifty-six lightdays of cramped, non-stop travel. And not one of those souls would even *look* at me, never mind engage in any conversation."

"Gosh..." commiserated Deluxia, "...boredom!".

"Yes dear, what is it?"

"You just told me. It's a planet near your planet."

"What is?"

"Izitt. I really don't know it that well."

Gosh stopped hovering and reconnected with the floor. Slogg tuned into their conversation. He rotated his immense chair back in their direction and interrupted.

"Deluxia, I've heard all I need to. Time is now up on your performance review."

"Oh really. Is it?"

"No, Neerizitt," said Gosh.

"What is?" demanded Slogg.

"No, sorry. I've never heard of that one," said Gosh.

Deluxia suddenly understood. She raised her eyes to the ceiling, having quickly tired of the superhero.

"Oh gosh..." she sighed to herself, "...boredom!"

"Yes dear? What do you want?"

Another deep exhale from Deluxia followed.

"Oh gosh, Gosh. You started out so promising."

The huge screen dominating the bridge displayed a frail sun christening a new day within the Braevitchkan system.

The HR performance review had moved onwards to the First Officer and whilst feigning interest, Gosh sat absent mindedly picking imaginary lint from his gloss tunic.

"Any news from the engineers yet, Taroooc?" Slogg asked.

"It's not been very long Sir. We only sent them down a short while ago."

"I'm fully aware of that, but the quicker we can get out of here the better. And... I've got a destiny."

Slogg's predestination swam back into view. The masters of the universe had ordained him as baton carrier for a planet bearing intelligent life. Pride welled back into his chest. The Commodore title stood within reach.

"Ask them again Taroooc."

A commotion. The First Officer squealed and kicked his chair backwards. The over-reaction caught Slogg's attention.

"I can't do this!" yelled the First Officer. "Yes... I am happy and yes, I feel productive. And yes, I experience fear. But I experience it *all the time.* It's not got anything to do with the job!"

“I understand, I understand,” said Gosh Bordomm. “It’s important I understand the basis of your fear.”

“How can we possibly get into *that* quagmire?” pleaded the First Officer.

“So, imagine you’re in a desert,” continued Gosh, “walking along the sand, when all of a sudden you look down and see a tortoise…”

“Do you make these questions up, Mr Bordomm? Or do they write them down for you?”

“I can’t remember where I got this one, but you’re not helping,” said Gosh.

“That’s enough!” intervened Slogg. “Thank you Gosh, let’s stop there. It’s okay Bleep, we’ll terminate the assessment.”

The First Officer stormed away to a distant corner to grip the back of a chair tightly, hiding his face from the rest of the bridge.

Taroooc spoke next.

"The engineers have just arrived onboard this instant, Captain. Fixing the Digitari’s app was quick job apparently,”

“Ok, some good news at last,” said Slogg. "Did they say what was wrong with their ship?"

"A length of string had snapped?"

"Ha!"

“Ok Walta, get us out of here. Maximum superluminal drive. Sector Alpha C, seven zero nine. Hypercube sixteen.

“Aye, Sir,” beamed Walta. Engaging two large red buttons in front of him, he dexterously rotated his favourite notched dial. There was a gradual sense of movement and the stars on screen swayed into their motion blur.

“Here we gooooo…”

The ship accelerated smoothly and rapidly into a long arc.

"And," continued Taroooc, touching his earpiece as the extended gap between his eyes seemed to widen further, "the engineers have news they've returned with an additional gift from the Digitari."

"What kind of gift?"

"Well..." paused Taroooc, "Perhaps it's a joke."

"What kind of gift?" Slogg persisted. He sensed his temporary elation begin to wane.

"A pink elephant."

Slogg's threadlike smile disappeared.

Moments later the vast migrant ship heaved itself out of the Braevitchkan solar system and into superluminal ether. The powerful Krystaltachyon engines roared as they overcame quantum relativity.

Behind, lurking in the vast void bearing the first four planets, a much smaller Digitari craft made its final preparations to leave behind beer, monks, racetracks, and a bitter landscape. Its complement of pink elephants (minus one) would provide currency, it was hoped, somewhere in the universe.

Slogg, enlightened yet unamused by the recent events, pondered on their own pink pachyderm, now coaxed aboard and stuck in a corridor close to the Teleport Bay, resisting attempts to cajole it further.

With the final act of his destiny playing out, Slogg decided it time to visit Dzkk once more to report status in the hope of enlightenment. As he stood to leave the bridge a thought struck him.

"Gosh," he called.

"Yes, can I help?" responded Gosh, employing a trademark eyebrow lick, "I can fly."

"How would you, as Saviour of *Whatever*, like to meet one of Laniakea's masters?"

"Not Mabel?"

"No, not Mabel. He's a true All-Powerful. Follow me."

"Never heard of him," said Gosh.

"Who?" quizzed Slogg.

"Folomee. Is he some recluse God?"

"Just get in the lift please."

*Schtip.*

Slogg and Gosh approached the loading bay and once again the huge silver doors did not open. A sequence of light hopping on its pressure mat proved futile.

Slogg smiled at his companion.

"It's okay. I've had problems with this one before. A sucker for punishment aren't you?"

"No," said the door.

"Open up!"

"No," said the door.

"I'm ordering you."

"No."

"Are you listening?"

"No."

"I see. It's stuck in a *No Loop*. Probably deliberate," Slogg explained, "It's a subroutine feature normally available to the main controller for extreme emergencies. You're in a *No Loop* aren't you?"

"No," said the door.

"Can you say anything else?"

"No."

"Okay, so if I order you to open now, you'll stay shut?"

"No… *ooooh*"

*Schtip.*

"…crap!"

The door opened.

"Sometimes," mused Slogg, "human logic beats the drivel out of computer logic."

They walked in.

The Eggkraft hung in the gantry. Zero was ever present beside it. Light tapping and deep sporadic thudding could be heard from the vessel's interior. The neck of the giant robot squeaked as he craned to look at Slogg and Gosh.

"Nice to see you again Zero," said Slogg.

"Rot... *click whirr* ...ating my joints is a little diff... icult," croaked the robot.

"Oh dear, I'm sorry to hear that. I'm here to see Dzkk. Can I assume he is still inside with his Earthling," said Slogg, as he sidled past the silver beast. Gosh followed him stopping briefly to check his reflection on Zero's chrome torso.

Inside the Eggkraft the All-Powerful Dzkk lay beneath a grey console with a photon wrench in his stubby left hand, radiance screwdriver between his teeth, and his right hand deep inside the guts of wiring.

His Earthling companion Duke was back on his boxy stool, since it proved far more comfortable than the floor.

"Hello!" called Slogg tentatively into the dim interior.

Dzkk took the screwdriver out of his teeth and sat up.

"Ah, Captain Slogg. Do come in. What have you done to my robot?"

"Sorry?" queried Slogg.

"Why, the squeaks, moans and groans he now issues forth are most annoying," Dzkk explained.

"So… are yours, chicken man!" came a distant metallic voice.

"Insolence!" hissed Dzkk, "No respect these days. I remember when I was young... no, that won't really work anymore will it."

He looked past Slogg and watched a large, muscled frame squeeze through the small hatchway.

"Who is this with you?"

"This is Gosh Bordomm," announced Slogg.

"Who?"

"Gosh Bordomm - Saviour of… *the Whatever*."

"Northern Andromeda," corrected Gosh, "Can I help? I can fly."

"Can you fix Eggkrafts?" Dzkk asked him flatly.

"Well, I might just have that skillset. I'm a superhero."

"Hmm. Then perhaps you should go and save Northern Andromeda. I've heard that it probably needs saving."

"But…"

"Hold on again!" yelled Duke.

They all turned to look at the earthman as he stood up from his box.

"Did you just say you were a superhero?"

"Correct."

"Like Batman?"

"Sorry?"

"Batman."

"Never heard of him," retorted Gosh.

"Spiderman?"

"Nope."

"Superman?"

"Yes, that'll do. Like Superman."

"You've heard… of Superman?" double-checked Duke.

Gosh rolled his eyes.

"Derrr…"

"How does all this work?" pleaded Duke, turning back to Dzkk. "You've got All-Powerful. You've got Superheroes. Great Attractors. Galaxies. Superclusters. I can't see how you can keep it all together. There's just too much!"

"Maybe have another seat," started Dzkk.

"I'm fine, thank you."

"Well, the analogy I like to use is that of a small town. Did you grow up in one?"

"Yes, I did."

"So, when you were little, I assume you had your parents and maybe a few small children down the street to play with. That was your world at a young age."

"That sounds familiar,"

"Good. Then you were probably taken into town for the first time?"

"I don't really remember the first time I went with my parents, but I do remember the first time I was allowed to go there on my own."

"Yes Duke. A big step and perhaps a little daunting. All those roads and people and shops. And then all those other buildings you didn't really know the innards of. Like a town hall, police station, post office. But they were all stuck together and somehow functioned as one."

Duke looked at Dzkk blankly. He then nodded in agreement.

"Then did you have a city nearby?"

"Yes, a place called Sheffield."

"And did you walk there?"

"Of course not, I got my first train journey there."

"Good. Was that daunting?"

"A bit, not as much as the first walk into my hometown."

"And your capital city."

"I started going to London with my dad as a young teenager. He had business down there every month and would leave me to my own devices whilst he went to work. Anyway, where are we going with all of this?""

"Bear with me. It seems you were very brave,

being left in your capital city all alone. So, were you fearful?"

"A bit, at the beginning. I spent my first trip walking up and down The Strand for four hours not venturing any further left or right. Not knowing Covent Garden was in my short reach, and the River Thames. But then after that... I started to play real-life Monopoly by visiting all the place names I learnt from that board game."

"Once again, you'll have to explain these words and references to me when we have time. But I can see it was getting easier for you. You probably never asked yourself how all those towns and cities function between each other, until you started to understand the concept of government and trade. Powerful politicians, businesspeople, mayors, and the like.

"I can't say it is something I've really worried about."

"Precisely. And presumably you've been on an airplane."

"Of course," huffed Duke.

Slogg interrupted their conversation.

"Dzkk please, where's all this going? I've brought Gosh Bordomm down here to..."

"One final bit of patience please Captain. It's important our Earthling companion understands as much as possible and feels at ease. It will make the Induction of his planet all the easier."

He turned back to Duke.

"The point I am making is that at each moment your world gets bigger, from your home to your street, to your town, city, country, continent... the easier it gets for you to accept and move within it, and you actually become more inclusive rather than reclusive."

"So, you're implying the same applies as you cross an infinite universe?" guessed Duke.

"Yes, my friend. Well, let's just stick to Laniakea for now, although superclusters don't come any bigger.

But the same remains true whenever you go bigger. Going to the next planet becomes obvious, then the next solar system, galaxy, cluster and on and on to our Laniakea, the grandest of all. And it's the same with trade and government. Galaxies have elected politicians and regional government. The All-Powerfuls and superheroes are akin to independent local mayors ordained with formidable abilities to bring added care to the populace. The Great Attractor sits at the centre of it all like a benign dictator. And bingo bango! Welcome to the Galactic Club."

"So is that why you wait to look for signs of manned space travel before you approach a planet about joining in?" surmised Duke.

"Exactly. Once you've started travelling from your own planet to another, we know you are just about ready to see the big picture. Your planet Earth has just arrived many decades quicker than we expected. And then also about five hundred million annums early before that!"

Dzkk looked down at the photon wrench and radiance screwdriver still in his hands. He turned to Slogg.

"Remind me Captain, once this assignment is all over, to increase my omnipotent powers to include routine interstellar shuttle maintenance."

"Assignment?" inquired Gosh.

"That is what I said."

"And?"

"The Captain here has a destiny, to bring another planet into the Galactic Core. The first for a while. Duke is our Specimen Alien chosen to help."

*"I'm not..."*

"I know! It's an official term."

"And which planet might that be?" asked Gosh.

Dzkk told him.

"That one!" exclaimed Gosh, "Oh dear. Oh no."

"What's wrong?" asked Dzkk, "It's harmless. Mostly®."

"But it is back towards... *home*."

"Home?"

"Earth is close to my home planet. I can't go back, yet."

"Where is that?" asked Dzkk.

"Neerizitt."

"Near where?"

"No, Neerizitt."

Slogg interrupted. "Please gentlemen, not again. Let us... move on."

Gosh briefly explained.

"For a variety of technical reasons relating to the ARS and GBI I cannot risk travel within any sectors closer to my home planet."

"Well, I'm sorry," began Dzkk, "but it is the Captain of this ship's destiny, and as such it has to be fulfilled. And that means, now."

"Then I'll have to leave," said Gosh, realizing as he spoke his words what the ramifications were.

"We need all the shuttles we've got," said Slogg. "You can't just leave, there's nothing to leave in."

A moment of silence ensued. Dzkk was preoccupied with one of Gosh's previous statements.

"Did you say ARS and GBI?" he asked. "Are you on the run?"

"On paper, yes," said Gosh.

"Captain!" began Dzkk. "This is dangerous. It could severely - *severely* - affect your mission and your destiny."

"He asked for help," said Slogg. "He also offered his cape."

"His cape? But he's not allowed to sell it?"

"That is indeed correct," announced Gosh, "but... there is nothing to stop me donating it in extreme circumstances."

Dzkk eyed the garment in unexpected awe.

"Is it *Ireenium*?" he hissed.

"It very much is," beamed Gosh, "...all of it."

"Where are we?"

"What do you mean?"

"Where are we, our coordinates?"

"Well, we entered superluminal ether approximately..."

"We are just inside the Southern Andromedan Hemisphere," interrupted Gosh.

"How the hell did that happen!" snapped Dzkk, turning immediately to Slogg.

"*Cops*!" he hissed as a follow-up.

Slogg was mystified and stunned into silence. The conversation has so quickly descended into chaos.

"Agreed," realised Gosh, "I should leave now."

"Captain, I suggest that Mr Bordomm is released from this ship instantly. We must *not* risk the destiny."

Slogg stared wide-eyed at both his guests.

Duke remained seated on his box, maintaining his customary silence to allow more processing time.

"Okay, I am Captain of this ship, and I admit that do not want to understand. But as Captain of this ship, I do know... that we possess not one spare shuttle craft to let Gosh simply fly away and never return."

"Take the Eggkraft," said Dzkk immediately.

"The Eggkraft!" exclaimed Gosh, "Really?"

"Give us the Ireenium cape and take my Eggkraft."

"Hang on," interjected Slogg, "he promised that to me."

"Are you sure?" asked Gosh, ignoring the Captain's words.

"Gosh, if you can fix it, you can have it."

"Fix it! I'll fix it Dzkk. Just you gimme those tools. Before I got my superpower licenses, I used to spend annums as a child fixing anything and everything.

Lightmonths and months in a shed, just me, nuts, bolts, wires, plugs, screws, circuits, a photon wrench, and a radiance screwdriver…"

"Gosh," sympathised Dzkk, "boredom…"

"Yes?" asked the superhero. "What do you want?"

"STOP!" shouted Slogg, "I've had enough. Just give us the cape."

"And the Eggkraft?" checked Gosh.

"Yes?"

"One more time, are you sure I can have it?"

"Yes. Take it," asserted Dzkk.

"Right. You're on!" and he grabbed the wrench and screwdriver from Dzkk's stubby claws, ready to dive under the console.

"But first the cape, please…" said Dzkk.

"Oh yes, of course."

He reached to each shoulder to unclip the willowy garment.

"And would you like to take Zero as well?"

Gosh smiled a very broad, very thin smile and shook his head almost imperceptibly.

"Thank thuck for fat…" shouted Zero through the doorway, "Correction…"

"It doesn't need correcting!" interrupted Dzkk. "Mr. Bordomm, you will need the instruction manual and some more of these tools…"

"Looks like we're all sorted then," surmised Slogg. "Well, we'll leave you to it Gosh. I'm heading back to the bridge. But first I'd like to buy you a drink Dzkk and discuss this little sliver of Ireenium."

"Your round, Captain."

"And perhaps your Earthling would like to join us as well?"

"I have a name you know," put in Duke, rising from his seat.

"Of course you do," reassured Slogg. "Well, we

all deserve a toast. We're finally in superluminal drive and breezing on our way. Gentlemen, destiny awaits!"

Slogg spun on one heel and left the engine room.

In the same superluminal ether, sixty lightminutes behind, blue and red lights began to flash in pursuit of Slogg's migrant ship.

# PART THREE
# UNDO

*The future is already here.*
*It's just not evenly distributed.*
William Gibson

# CHAPTER 39

## 3rd September
## 03:20am GMT, International Airspace

The plane from the Dark Peak to Puerto Rico finally departed in the early hours of the following morning. The Knowalls referred to it as their *private jet*, though it was clearly a newly modified Boeing 707. It bore no markings or logos, but carried a distinctive smooth black coating embedded with gossamer wires across the upper half of its fuselage, wings and tail, supported by a matt white lower belly. It performed an incredibly steep take-off from a landing strip ostensibly too small for an aircraft of its size.

Inside, the standard quadruple passenger seats were replaced by large leather recliners dotted round in pairs or fours, occasional tables fixed to the flooring, a bar, more ridiculously thin computer screens, and what looked like a fully equipped kitchen complete with uniformed chef.

"First class?" Nelson enquired, once his constitution had recovered from the sharp climb.

"No. Just *class*," Gloria wheezed.

The plane levelled off as it reached cruising altitude. The Knowalls were resting, reading or snoozing. Gloria's hyperventilating subsided. For such a frail man he certainly knew how to wheeze with gusto. Tina stared intently out of a cabin window, entranced by the twinkle of lights below from towns and cities.

Emm was deep in conversation with Charlie

listening intently to her, occasionally nodding. She then smiled, put a hand on his shoulder and stood up to take her rest in a separate leather seat.

Nelson saw his opportunity. As Charlie studied the papers Emm left behind, Nelson slid into the vacant chair next to him.

"So, can I ask you a couple of questions?" Nelson started straight away.

"Just a couple?" challenged Charlie. He smoothed his swan braid down his chest unnecessarily and adjusted his thick red collar so he could relax further into his seat.

"Where's the engine noise for starters?" began Nelson. "It's the same hum here as that truck you had us bundled into."

"Ah of course. Well, have you heard of photo-voltaics?"

"Solar power?"

"Yes. We started playing with selenium over a hundred years ago. Now we just paint solar panels wherever we need them. And they are so efficient, they even work by moonlight."

"*Paint* them?"

"Yes Nelson, photovoltaic paint. The top of this plane and its wings are covered in it. So was the roof of your truck. It powers the galvanic engines. Humanity will get it soon enough."

"Pah! There you go again. Okay next question. I can grasp your secret society and I can understand why you had to keep it secret all this time. But what puzzles me now is... because it's been kept so secret..."

"Yes?"

"Well, we've reached the 1980's and you've still not been able to let anyone know directly about your newest and brightest discoveries..."

"Please get to the point Nelson."

"So, how can you *afford* all of this?"

"Ah I see, you mean pay for it?" queried Charlie

"Yes, the global bunkers, the private 707 jet, the moonshots, the constant investment required to develop new technologies."

"I see."

"So how do you afford it all?"

"Marketing."

"I'm sorry?" blinked Nelson.

"Very clever marketing," repeated Charlie. "Have you heard of the *hype-cycle*? No? Probably not yet. It was a brilliant idea credited to a small think-tank back at the turn of the century."

"I don't get it," admitted Nelson.

"As we evolved, we needed new ways to release technology - and sometimes create whole new industries. The simplest way became a *startup*."

"A what?"

This man was full of jargon and Nelson hoped their future did not hold swathes of this type of language. Struggling to concentrate, he was beginning to ache behind the eyes and aware of his tightly clenched jaw.

"A startup," Charlie answered, "is a new company controlled by one or two Knowalls. It recruits talented, unsuspecting support staff, and generously seeds our new ideas into the mainstream. The startup creates the buzz, or the *hype*, around what we are releasing - and the *cycle* starts. At the point the excitement reaches fever pitch, or the top of the hype-cycle, one of humanity's traditional firms usually steps in to buy the startup. And we get lots of money to invest again."

"Okay… I can sort of get that," said Nelson as he slowly massaged his lower jaw just beneath his ears, "So you guys are secretly involved at the early stages. Then what happens, for example what happens to the Knowalls who launch the startups?"

"It follows a similar pattern. There is usually a buzz about them for a little while, but it is always short-lived. Sometimes we ask them to do it again, but mostly they leave the *surface* and it's someone else's go. It's on a rota system."

"So, all this is already going on? Right under our noses?"

"I'm afraid so Nelson, and it has been for a long time, sometimes in the least obvious places."

"How do you mean, least obvious?"

"Well, new technology in its broadest sense crosses many industries… In the mid nineteenth century we started artificial baby-milk in Switzerland; in the US denim jeans, then an oil refiner; the world's first commercial airline in 1920's Holland; credit cards in 1950; and on and on."

Nelson slumped back in his chair and tried to let all this soak in. For no reason he put his hands out on the arm rests and turned his palms upright. A soft green light surrounded them now and his skin took on an alien hue. Outside the dots of stars and wisps of cloud continued to purr by. After a moment's reflection he asked:

"But what if nobody wants the new idea?"

"Good question. That is where great marketing comes in. And early adopters."

"Early *what*? All these phrases Charlie!"

"Get used to it Nelson. Early adopters. The startup's job is to get the product launched. The marketeer's role is to promote it as the most brilliant, basic commodity that suddenly everyone must have. And then they bring in the early adopter."

"How?"

"Well, you see young Fry over there, who I introduced earlier…" Charlie indicated along the plane's interior to a young, bookish man poring over a thin glass slab.

"I see him. And what has he got there?" quizzed Nelson.

"That's a tablet."

"But it's way too big to swallow."

"Hmm. We'll eventually get onto those later. You may not recognize young Fry yet, but a lot of people will do very soon. He's a real polymath and soaks up knowledge. A true Knowall, you could say. In a few years he will pop up everywhere - TV, newspapers, films, anything to get his face out. Once he is instantly recognizable, he will become an early adopter of *hi tech*. He will make our life-changing technology appear friendly and necessary."

Nelson studied the academic fellow and the more he stared, the less he could perceive this description as a distinct possibility. With his wry smile and foppish dress sense, he appeared better suited to the newly burgeoning alternative comedy circuit, than as a new technology inductor.

"You say we're all going to listen to him?"

"Not all of you Nelson, but a few of you will. He'll be an influencer."

"*Ew!* Like a virus?"

"No, not an influenza Nelson, an influencer. Fry will just need to influence a few thought-leaders, they will influence yet more, and on and on. Suddenly everyone is up for it. This will work very well."

"I'm skeptical this Charlie. But if I do take all of this at face value, you're saying it's how you string together the ability to make so much money."

"So far Nelson, so far. But it's not enough."

"Not enough? *Why*?"

He gripped the arm rest corners now and pulled himself forward in the chair. Charlie looked to the distance and his warm eyes lost focus. He stroked four fingers smoothly down the line of his swan braiding and spoke the words softly.

"We now have even bigger plans Nelson, as you'll find out once we get to Puerto Rico. And they need bigger funding. These plans go *beyond* the startup."

"Beyond?"

"Yes. We've now put some key Progressionaries in place and let them grow the business to its full potential... rather than sell it. I mentioned Bill and Steve earlier. They'll soon own the world's largest software companies. One each. That'll keep our biggest plan rolling."

Charlie smiled broadly and widened his eyes bringing them back down to look at Nelson.

"You see, the trick is to create an industry and a product set that no one knows they want... until now. That's where the biggest opportunities lie."

And now his eyes twinkled.

"Then you market the pants off it!"

# CHAPTER 40

## StarDate 1 (Still)
## Interstellar Superluminal Ether

"It's my Ireenium cape, you know," said Slogg as he, Dzkk and Duke strolled away from the loading bay and along the corridor. Zero lumbered a little way behind.

"Gosh offered it to me first," he persisted.

Dzkk smiled back.

"Captain, I'd like to point out that he's leaving, isn't he? And this is only possible by taking *my* Eggkraft."

"Hmm. Well that was very generous of you Dzkk, but clearly not a great loss. I presume you've considered what you're going to replace it with?"

"A Spacetime Donut. I'm going to get me one of those, and non-poultry themed. But in the meantime Captain, for now it looks as if I will have to accompany you. And together we will see out your destiny… until it is fulfilled." He then turned to Duke and nodded. "Time is now of the essence."

"Don't you have other parts of the universe to be masterful in?" continued Slogg. "Are you sure you need to come all the way with me and the Earthling?"

"I'm here you know, and I have a name!" put in Duke once more.

"Nothing that can't wait Captain," answered Dzkk. "But also, it's clear now that I really, really… want to understand this planet Earth a bit better"

As they made their way through the ship this unlikely trio continued chatting. The robot walked behind, squeaking all the way. Dzkk was enthralled in

Slogg's encounter with Gwofie and the Digitari. He was most pleased the numerous crates of the universe's strongest Braevitchkan beer had been secured for the Peacefulness and Primacy Offering. And he adored the idea of a pink elephant onboard.

Duke on the other hand required everything to be explained twice. Yet he reserved the bulk of his questions to ask how tachyons helped these beings travel faster than light. A full explanation remained elusive.

A congratulatory toast and two more light drinks followed in Refreshment Bay Two, before Slogg finally left his two passengers to their conversations and reverted to his quarters. He needed a rest. Dzkk kept hold of the Ireenium cape.

Moments later the migrant ship briefly popped out of superluminal drive to lay a rather large egg beneath its fuselage, and Gosh Bordomm hurtled due north, disappearing into the inky blackness. This short delay in transit allowed the migrant ship's pursuer to close in further. The flashing blue and red beams continued to pulsate silently.

On the screen in his rest quarters, a tired and oblivious Captain Slogg studied a rare image of the planet he was about to visit, induce, and enlighten. Taken many annums earlier by a wayward deep space explorer it showed a very rare blue-green world of twenty nine percent land mass, occasionally blanketed by swirling white cloud. It was truly beautiful, and they would be there in a short while.

# CHAPTER 41

The modified 707 crossed a midnight blue sky, murmuring like an immense determined dragonfly invisible to the ground below.

"It's amazing, Charlie," sighed Nelson, once more reclining into his lush seat. He was in awe, and he now vainly imagined what a remarkable story this would make for his Sunday supplement employers.

"Thank you, Nelson. I wish I could take more credit, but none of these original processes or ideas were mine. They have come together over decades."

Charlie nodded back towards Fry, who smiled awkwardly and returned to his tablet.

"However," continued the Knowall, "thankfully, together with Emm over there, we're getting near to our own launch dates."

"Your companies Charlie? You are launching startups?"

"Yes Nelson, or more accurately, *repurposing* them. Emm and I are about to invigorate two well established industries with new and future-proofed product lines. They will be forever changed."

"Really! Okay now I'm interested, please tell me Charlie… which two?" pressed Nelson.

"Are we invigorating…"

"Yes!"

"Well," said Charlie, his dark eyes twinkling, "they are…"

"Please."

"Okay… they are, take-away coffee and bottled water."

"*Pah*!"

Nelson could not contain himself. He then instantly felt embarrassed about his outburst.

"I'm very sorry Charlie… I didn't mean to sound so rude. But… well I must admit, I was expecting something a little more sensational and fail-safe."

"Really Nelson?"

"Yes Charlie. Come on. It's 1983… no one is going to buy take-away coffee when we already have instant coffee granules at home. And *bottled* water… why would I want to go into a supermarket and buy a container of water, when I have it available fresh out of the tap?"

"That," said Charlie, "is a good question."

"Sorry. Neither of those will take off."

"Thank you, Nelson. I'll take your advice onboard. We've completed a full scenario analysis and run our numbers. It will work."

"Hopefully someone has better ideas," Nelson said quietly, but not enough that it was just to himself.

As if it had been bubbling up like a hot water geyser inside of him for some time he suddenly announced.

"You know what you should get into…"

"What's that Nelson?"

"Wheel clamps."

"Wheel clamps?"

"Yes, I think that's what they are called. I saw one in Mayfair the other day. Now they are the future. Poor guy thought he'd be okay parking on a double yellow line, and he was just staring at it. He didn't know what to do. You'll make a fortune from them."

"We'll consider it," said Charlie flatly.

"You should," replied Nelson. The geyser had blown and the bubbling water subsided back on itself. One of the final comments Charlie had made irked Nelson and he needed further clarification.

"So you referenced your biggest plan, again. Can you come clean and tell me what you are going to do with all this new money?"

Charlie looked at Nelson and his face brightened. He leaned forward and his eyes twinkled again partnered with a conspiratorial smile.

"Well, there's an unlikely clue in one of the company brand names."

"A clue. What kind of clue?"

"Starbucks."

"What? Never heard of it."

"They're mainly a West Coast outfit at the moment, but in the right sector and appropriately named."

"You're still not making any sense Charlie."

"*Star... bucks,*" the Knowall repeated.

Nelson glanced up to the plane's ceiling smothered in its chartreuse hue, down to the thick white hair of Charlie's head that now glowed aquamarine in this light. He then stared straight into his deep eyes, finally shrugging his shoulders and once again twisting the palms of his hands gently upwards, this time with the fingers splayed slightly inviting the Knowall to clarify matters.

"We have to be ready," was all Charlie offered.

"Ready. For what?"

"*...The Quit.*"

"*The Quit...* you mean shutting your companies down? That shouldn't take long especially if you think take-away coffee and bottled water are going to succeed!"

The smile from Charlie's face dropped as he stared back at Nelson.

"Enough for now," he said flatly, "we need sleep."

"Okay, sorry Charlie, wrong joke. But still..."

Pleased with himself, Nelson strolled along the plane's interior and sat down next to Tina, a wide grin on his face.

"Starbucks eh? These guys don't know everything Tina."

He pressed the recline button on his leather chair. To his surprise it rolled back completely to a full horizontal. He then watched Tina carefully recline her own seat, avoiding a fully flat position. Nelson settled into the leather, closed his eyes, and let the early morning tiredness start to come into his body as the plane's electric engines hummed softly in the background. He was feeling sleepy.

"Wheel clamps," he sighed to himself, confirming the thought with a gentle nod.

# CHAPTER 42

*Schtop.*

The lift closed its doors and carried a weary Slogg to the bridge, as he stretched his pale blue fingers and yawned. He had grabbed three hours' sleep and dreamt of pink elephants skating on caged feet around a shattered ice rink.

*Schtip.*

The door opened to a view of Deluxia, her Terracoscienn tail held tight to the back of her legs, scribbling frantically on a report tablet. The bridge's screen was unusually blank. Slogg knew instantly that something was wrong. Firstly, Deluxia scribbled rarely, and it was the only indication her demeanour ever gave that something might be awry. Secondly the tablet displayed the distinctive violet heading: *Scribbling Report 101/P: Hazardous Use Only.*

"What's wrong?" Slogg asked.

"Well..." began Deluxia.

"Let me see the report."

"Captain, it won't do you any..."

"Let me see the report."

"But, you see, it's..."

"Give it to me."

Deluxia held up the tablet. Beneath the violet heading it read:

�**u 000 !!! ☹☹ &% 999 @ noooooo!

"I see," said Slogg, "that bad?"

"I'm afraid so sir."

Slogg turned to his Navigation Officer.

"Well, what's happened this time Walta?"

The points of Walta Woppedd's ears twitched

backwards, and he lightly touched his groomed temples with his fingertips.

"Er..." he hesitated.

"Come on man, do not sugar coat it."

"Well, we are being... followed, Sir."

"*Followed*. By whom?"

"Our sensors picked up an ultraspeed cruiser. They're a few lightminutes behind us and closing."

"A cruiser, out here?" queried Slogg.

"Joyriders," suggested Taroooc.

"Captain!" interrupted Deluxia.

"Yes?"

"There is something strange coming in over the subluminal radio."

"Well?"

"Er, it sounds like.... well, it's difficult to say."

"Put it through."

Deluxia's talons flicked a switched.

*Dirr derr. Dirr derr. Dirr derr.*
*Wup Wup Wup Wup.*

"*Police cruiser*!" spat Slogg.

"*Cops*!" hissed Taroooc.

"*Fuzz*," whispered Walta.

Stares on the bridge bombarded Slogg's disquieted face. "Walta! Can I ask exactly why the police are behind us? Were you speeding?"

"Certainly not Captain. We're getting ready to drop from the ether, standard procedure decreasing to one hundred and eighty-seven thousand kilotecs per lightsecond. All well inside the limit for this sector."

"Rear view please Deluxia," ordered Slogg.

She turned round to reveal her back, tail and haunches.

"No Deluxia! Rear view of the *ship*, on the screen!"

"Ah, my apologies Captain."

The immense screen flicked back to life portraying a blur of flashing blue and red lights approaching their migrant ship. As they came into focus it was clear they formed the top section of a sleek, white, ultraspeed police patrol cruiser.

"Attention!" came a deep rasping voice straight through to the bridge.

"Drop from superluminal ether and pull over," Slogg's knees buckled. The voice went straight through to the base of his spine. Whilst the hairs on the back of his neck stood on end and his face numbed, his bowel twisted and thighs quivered under the increased burden.

"Are you alright Captain?" Deluxia asked as she watched the pale blue skin that formed the taut carving on stony Slogg's face drain to white.

"*Attention!*"

"Sir? Are you okay?" Deluxia asked again. "You look very unwell."

Slogg whispered very faintly.

"Detective Inspector Clamburxer."

"Sorry Sir?"

"Detective Inspector Clamburxer. Oh my holy *hell.* Oh no. Just what is he doing here! Of all the..."

"Pull over!" came another dreaded abrasive screech, "This is the police."

"Did he just say *poe leaze*?" queried Deluxia.

There was no doubt. The man behind that jarry dissonant broadcast was Milko Clamburxer of the Galactic Police. Slogg recognized the distinctive rasp and accented drawl instantly. He knew Clamburxer had once been one of the most wanted criminals in the universe, and now one of its highest paid law enforcers. Salacious holozine scandals were full of senior police caught crossing the great divide to corruption, fraud, and even murder, whilst pushing a facade as upholders of justice and truth. Clamburxer had made Laniakea history by reversing this state of play. He departed incarceration and rose from raw recruit to Detective Inspector in just three annums.

As part of his rehabilitation, Clamburxer spent time under the guidance of notorious psychologist Hola Migola. It was here Slogg endured just six weeks in his company as they both underwent Migola's alleged analysis and therapy. The psychologist's controversial methods encouraged enmity between his patients and there followed a short period of distrust and dislike between the two men as they went their separate ways.

"We're dropping out of superluminal ether," reported Walta.

*Wup Wup Wup Wup.*
*Whirrrrrr.*

The rhythmical blue and red lights guided Slogg's ship to a halt, and an unease spread across the bridge.

Given the time that had passed, Slogg brooded on Clamburxer's own recall and if he would still remember a young and ambitious cadet. He retained both fear and hatred for the policeman yet had admired his audacious trajectory and achievements.

One annum after they departed Migola's care, a young Constable Clamburxer pulled helmeted Slogg over for parking his planet hopper on a double-yellow asteroid. On Clamburxer's demand he stepped out of the vehicle. The constable then snatched an unannounced reach to raised Slogg's visor. His fury and resentment quickly to the point where the two tussled, resulting in the discharge of Clamburxer's Occasional Kill Weapon from its holster. The flash burnt directly into Clamburxer's own thigh, causing a deep but instantly cauterized wound.

As the writhing constable dropped to the ground, Slogg made good his escape, grabbing the Constable's Federation holobook[20] as he left. Keeping his visor locked down and grabbing the book proved to be the wisest moves of Slogg's life. Clamburxer was famed for his poor memory ascribed to Migola's experimental cranial-shock therapy. Slogg hoped the policeman had not recognized his nose, mouth and jawline on show below the concealed eyes.

Although the young constable screamed out how revenge would be immediate and painful, nothing arose from the incident across the successive annums.

Until now.

The migrant ship was at rest and the police cruiser marshalled itself alongside. A glacial Slogg fixed his deadened eyes onto the main screen. Tarooc and Walta slithered uncomfortably in their seats.

Deluxia announced the police had made an official request to dock and Slogg nodded silently in resentment.

A long five minutes passed as Slogg made his way mutely to the ancillary docking bay, Tarooc in tow. They waited for the pressure to equalise between the two craft. The doors opened with a faint hiss to reveal the diminutive figure of a uniformed police sergeant. To his left and rear stood the unmistakable form of Milko Clamburxer, cloaked reinforced police regalia with extended shoulders. One huge yellow-gold epaulette curved across his left displaying rugged ammunition cartridges. The right shoulder braced a dazzling show of

---

[20] Holobook's automatically record police interactions with the Galactic public for instant multidimensional recall on demand. As an added benefit for Slogg, the holobook also contained the contact details of some very friendly policewomen.

medals wrapped into a bronze bird-wing form. A heavy gold chain hung from his black tunic collar to a gleaming law enforcement badge pinned on his chest. A black domed helmet dropped a darkened visor over his eyes. Immense green boots reaching to his knees completed the look.

Beneath the visor Clamburxer's face gave no indication of recognition. Slogg was transfixed in immediate relief and pending doom, and he spoke the first words that can into his head.

"Welcome aboard, Detective Inspector Clamburxer," broadening a fake smile that prompted his cheeks and gums to ache.

"That's *Chief Commissioner* if you do not mind," boomed Clamburxer, "and anyway... how do y'all know ma name?"

The guttural slow drawl was ever present, yet the shock of Clamburxer's new title very nearly allowed Slogg to miss the gravity of his mistake. *Chief Commissioner!* That meant ever more power. More powerful than Dzkk?

And then *wham*!

*How imbecilic! Why had he greeted him by name? What ridiculous, unnecessary familiarity. Poor memory aside, Clamburxer was no fool and he would not let such an obvious mistake pass.*

"Er..." scrambled Slogg.

"Jump on it, man!"

"We see a lot of you on holoTV."

"HoloTV? I didn't know Galactic broadcasts reached as far as these sectors?" challenged Clamburxer.

"Er, no," said Slogg, "but the repeats do."

For now, Clamburxer accepted this bizarre response, conceding to have more pressing matters. As he swept aboard, Slogg watched him limp heavily on his right leg - the leg his Weaponify OKW had scorched so long ago.

"We digress. To finish the formal introductions,

accompanying me is Sergeant Obloid. And your name Captain?"

We all wear a variety of masks, sometimes for minutes, hours, days, or lifetimes. Often in professional situations, always on first dates, but rarely needed to conceal ourselves from law enforcement. If ever required, these are typically multi-layered fake identities providing deep concealment for their user, and preserving the self behind a well-researched and professionally documented alias, far, far removed from the true persona.

"Slobb," replied Slogg.

Clamburxer's eyes widened instantaneously. Slogg's heart thumped three times.

"Captain *Slobb*? Ha!" spat Clamburxer in his abrasive southern cluster inflection. "A somewhat unfortunate name to take command of a Fleet ship. Even one in such a dilapidated state as this."

"Yes, I suppose it is really," fumbled Slogg, "I'd never really considered it before. Funny."

He pressed on to keep the conversation moving. He also craved a divergent flip back to normality and to feel the ground once again beneath his feet. The knee-jerk reaction to conjure a fake name so close to his own had yielded a veneer that was too thin. For strength he turned to his right, and his faithful, sturdy colleague.

"And this is my Chief Wellness Officer..."

"Toool," said Taroooc.

Slogg's orange eyes involuntarily popped, so unprepared was he for Taroooc's lie. Just as Taroooc had been for his own. Nobody is ever quite who they seem. They obviously both possessed troubled pasts to the extent where evasion or elusion in a police presence had become their norm. Clamburxer posed a threat to their status quo.

"Well," huffed the Chief Commissioner, "so it seems I have both a Slobb and a Toool before me. What a find."

Thankfully for all, Clamburxer provided his own diversion based on a pressing need.

"So y'all, do you have any alcohol on board? I've had no proper drink in a long time."

Slogg exhaled heavily and his eyes misted. The temporary relief was draining but welcome.

"Yes," he confirmed. "Plenty."

"Lead on then man, we need to talk," grinned Clamburxer.

Alk (Alkohol and Light-refreshment Katerer) attempted to self-clean its gears, tubes and pumps after dispensing four of the sweetest, sickliest cocktails in its repertoire. As it did so Tarooc carried the offerings to Slogg and their two unwelcome visitors.

"Well Cap'n Slobb," inflected Clamburxer, "I suppose y'all may be wondering why am here."

"I must say the thought crossed my mind," admitted Slogg, having fretted over nothing else since he first heard the policeman's menacing twang.

"Well, tell them Sergeant Obloid," came the order.

"Yes sir. Right," began Obloid. Far slighter and shorter than his superior, he wore a similar black uniform but with no reinforcement, two small epaulettes of braiding, grey boots and no dark visor across his domed helmet. As he extracted a Federation holobook from his top pocket, Slogg noticed that it was exactly the same type he snatched from a wounded Clamburxer an aeon previously. The sergeant began to list the charges:

"The display of indecent body parts in a public arena. The retailing of these personal appendages without a license. The soliciting of the naval for..." The little holobook began to glow red in his palm. "Oh *sorry*, that's the wrong filing."

The sergeant fumbled with his device, clicking, scrolling, zooming, and a myriad of text, figures and sketches flashed from its small holographic display. Clamburxer raised his eyes to the ceiling and shook his head. Slogg was grateful for the interlude, but still his teeth remained clamped in a fixed smile that threatened to give cramp to his cheeks.

Meanwhile, Taroooc appeared very queasy. His two front-facing eyes widened further in their flat brow and his cheek skin rippled with tiny green-grey lines. He held his stomach with a flat palm as he gulped air agitatedly. A dread set. The previous set of charges wrongly selected by this sergeant were most familiar, having been levied annums earlier against a juvenile Taroooc, following an unrestrained late-night drinking junket on Gapyeargonalong Four.

The holobook's red glow slowly subsided.

"Well Sergeant, have you located the relevant darn charges?" sighed Clamburxer.

"Yes, oh yes. Here we go. Failure to stop at a red dwarf..."

"No! No. Obloid! Desist, I'll do this talking ma-self."

He sat back in his chair and took a sip of his drink as if opening a way for the kill. Then he leaned forward and hissed:

"Do y'all realise, Captain Slobb," he laboured the surname heavily, "that you are in a highly restricted sector of this here Galaxy. Not only is that against the law, but you is also *ma patch*. And that... makes me very, very angry. Y'know ah could conveniently throw the book at you."

He sat back square in his seat with a self-satisfied smile.

"What book?" asked Slogg.

"What? I don't know darnit. *THE* book."

"Oh, that book. Well..." replied Slogg. He was

stumped, flailing for a retort. Any response. Only one word popped into his head.

"*...Dzkk*."

"*Come again, man*?"

"Dzkk."

"Are you having a stroke?" asked Clamburxer.

"I can explain. We are on a mission. One preordained by the All-Powerful being. His name is Dzkk. A mission, I might add, of great importance."

"Great importance you say?" rasped Clamburxer, pronouncing the second word closer to *impotence*. Pulling his helmet visor further down, he leaned in towards Slogg.

"Yes," said Slogg, as both of his hands involuntarily brushed each cheek. "I have a destiny... to initiate a planet into the Galactic Core."

"Ah see. And which planet might that be?"

Slogg told him.

"Slobb. Oh dear me. You are either a lying S-O-B, or y'all delusional. These here sectors have been under ma jurisdiction for some time now, and that particular planet has been under a great deal of observation, all due to its well-known hypermutation."

Beneath the shaded visor Clamburxer's eyes narrowed as he continued. "And ah personally know it remains ill-prepared to join the Galactic Club for many a while. An then Slobb, it's also clear the inhabitants may very soon blow themselves up and take their whole planet to smithereens. If it did survive Cap'n it needs at least another forty risky annums of development, if it can last that long."

"I'm sorry Commissioner..."

"*Chief* Commissioner."

"... but that is exactly what everyone else has been thinking so far. Yet it would appear we were all mistaken."

"I do not make mistakes Cap'n."

"Then ask the All-Powerful Dzkk."

"Oh, don't worry Slobb, ah very much intend to."

Twenty minutes later, a shallow-breathing Slogg returned to the bridge accompanied the Chief Commissioner and his sergeant. Taroooc followed and scurried to a corner of displays and buttons and out of attention's way. His vigilant, over-sexed Delta Nebulese nerves were also jangled.

Slogg had summoned Dzkk to join them. The bridge had taken on a funereal tone due to the police presence. Slogg made no mention of Dzkk's Earthling companion, leaving this elaboration to the All-Powerful chicken-creature.

As Slogg went to sit, Clamburxer examined him quizzically. Thankfully, the lift door hissed open as Dzkk appeared, accompanied by Duke.

"Well Captain Slogg, what seems to be the problem?"

Slogg leapt fitfully from his chair.

"That's Slobb," he wheezed, "Slobb! Isn't it… Dick?" He leaned his head slightly to the side and backwards, trying to indicate who was behind him. Clamburxer intervened.

"Life just keeps getting better here y'all. Now ah have a Slobb, a Toool and a Dick before me."

"That's Dzkk," corrected Dzkk, a questioning look washing over his face.

"There you are you see!" snapped Slogg. "We've all got problems, haven't we?" He bumbled up to Dzkk to quickly take his arm, hoping all of this remained sufficient distraction.

"*Wait a minute*!" yelled Clamburxer, "*I KNOW YOU*!"

Slogg's orange eyes widened remarkably. His

pale blue skin taughtened to white, as his mouth opened wordlessly. He span back towards Clamburxer. His tongue turned arid and his forearms numbed through to his fingertips. His recognition nightmare was manifesting. As the last few minutes passed, Slogg had naively relaxed, believing he was far removed from Clamburxer's memory. But he was now disgorged by the Commissioner's mind's eye. He felt bare, his uniform transparent, everyone peered through its cloth, though his skin and innards, and straight to his rotten core. A core that abandoned a badly injured policeman to likely death on a deserted asteroid, simply to evade a parking fine.

Slogg glanced around, scarcely able to see through an internal haze of frenzy. His mouth formed words, but nothing came out because he had nothing to say. No utterance could ease the sickness he felt. He was exposed, and this was the cul-de-sac, the dissolution of his career - perhaps the bitter end of his life?

He stumbled forward with no clear direction. Blurred images belayed Walta standing immediately to his right and he twisted sharply to see thoughtful eyes staring back at him. He knew what Walta was thinking. Slogg observed him visibly sickened by serving under such a disgusting Captain. A man whose moral compass was spinning uncontrollably. Never in his convoluted life had Slogg felt so wretched.

"*I know you*!" yelled Clamburxer once again.

Oh, that voice - that blaring, rasping, menacing drawl. Each syllable a nail in Slogg's anonymous coffin - spat into space with no ceremony - quickly forgotten thanks to excreta within. Tears brimming his eyes, he tried to plead for Walta's understanding, yet still no words came forth. Fear and guilt had now lamed his body. He wanted to scream the walls down and tell of the hideous accident. Surely Walta knew it had been an accident - he never meant to cripple that young policeman. Yet Walta simply continued to stare at him inquisitively.

"*For sure ah know you*!" came the bellow as the policeman lunged forward.

Slogg could see the end and knew the afterlife would bring relief. Oh death, where is thy sting?

"Yes. I do know you! You're Walta Woppedd aren't you… from *Galaxy's Got Talent*!" yelled Clamburxer, rushing over to grab the Navigation Officer's hand.

The darkness grew a kaleidoscopic taint.

As Slogg regained consciousness a realization dawned, he was caressing Taroooc's hand.

"Captain, are you alright?"

"Wh… hmm? … don't leave me."

"You passed out Sir. Why did you pass out?"

"Wh... nnnng..."

"It's okay Captain. Perhaps you are over worked."

Slogg focused beyond Taroooc. Dzkk and Deluxia gaped back down at him, their faces portrayed genuine concern. To his right he became aware of Walta and Clamburxer in deep conversation.

"...but it was so long ago," spoke Walta.

"Y'all had the *best* season. Ah saw every episode."

"Wow! Thanks," blubbed Walta.

"What was the name of your band again?" Clamburxer quizzed hoarsely.

"*A Flock of Beagles*."

"That was it. Strange name, great music. Loved the hair."

Walta was lost for words and just smiled, lightly caressing his voluminous quiffs above each ear.

"*Galaxy's Got Talent*[21]. Ah miss that show,"

[21] Galaxy's Got Talent searched the known universe for amateur purveyors of entertainment, proffering the thinnest hope of minor celebrity. It ran for 2,762 seasons, only being cancelled when its producers discovered more individuals

reminisced Clamburxer, oblivious to the scene behind him.

Slogg turned back to look at Taroooc. He became fully aware he was holding his hand and quickly shook it free. He looked into to Deluxia's caring eyes and managed a weak smile.

"What happened Captain?" she asked.

Slogg stood up and straightened out his tunic. He strolled casually to his large chair and sat carefully.

"I was testing Emergency Procedure 9F."

"Oh," said Taroooc, "and what is that?"

"To deal with sudden incapacitation of your Captain. The protocol dictates immediate action by senior crew members to attempt resuscitation, maintain security and ensure safety of the ship. And... *every last one* of you failed in this duty!"

"But Captain, you only passed out for a few seconds," Taroooc informed him.

"That is totally peripheral".

"And when I rushed over to see if I could provide immediate assistance, you grabbed my hand and cried *Mabel, don't let them get me.*"

"I had to appear convincing," lied Slogg. He leaned back in his chair and feigned deep thought. Then abruptly leant forward and slapped the padded armrest.

"*Right*! Let that be a lesson."

This appeared to snap Clamburxer out of his questionable starstruck fugue and brought his attention back to those around him. He assessed the bantam-like creature that had just entered the bridge.

"So, are you the All-Powerful?"

"Dzkk is my name."

"Well ah never, do something..."

"I'm sorry, do what?"

"Do something All-Powerful."

---

had appeared on the show than had ever watched it.

"We've already been through that phase Chief Commissioner."

"So, y'all know who I am?"

"I'm All-Powerful."

"Point taken. And who is this?"

Clamburxer's eyes stayed dim recesses behind his dark visor as he raised his chin indicating towards Duke.

"This is Duke."

"Is he All-Powerful as well?"

"No, he's from Earth."

"An Earth…ling!"

"Once more… I have a name!"

"Quiet!" yelled Clamburxer. He swivelled back to Dzkk. "All-Powerful or not, am going to have to arrest you chicken-man. Earthling abduction has long been a serious crime in these parts, with a zero-tolerance policy. They remain a protected species until the hypermutation reaches its conclusion… or they achieve self-annihilation. Whichever is soonest."

"Chief Commissioner, I am well aware of the law in this sector. I am sanctioned by the Superchamber and a highly confidential All Points Bulletin was issued. You may check with your superiors if you wish. The Great Attractor has taken a personal interest."

The hardened law-enforcer façade fell and Clamburxer visibly gasped.

"The GA! *Why*?" he drawled loudly.

"That is what I am still fully determining."

"The GA is aware of your mission?"

"As far as I understand things Chief Commissioner, the GA initiated the mission."

"You as well! Now this is unheard of."

"What do you mean, *as well*?"

"Ah also have an ongoing mandate from the Great Attractor," puffed Clamburxer.

This time it was Dzkk's turn to gasp.

"A mandate… for what?"

"We need to talk chicken-man. It looks like I must stick around to help y'all."

"My name is Dzkk. And thank you, but we do not need any further help. With Duke, and the Captain here, and this migrant crew, I have everything I need."

"I insist, and there's an awful lot more y'all need to know. And with me onboard you'll speed through any cluster border controls, and the heft of the Galactic Police Force will surely be with you."

"The force will be with us?" queried Dzkk.

"Why yes," confirmed Clamburxer.

"Well, that's a first," exhaled Dzkk.

"No it's not," exclaimed Duke.

The chicken creature, the Captain and the law enforcer turned to observe this earthman who had spoken only a few short words since arriving on the bridge. Duke crossed his glare over all three of them.

"If you want me to explain the reference I can," he snarled. "On my backward little planet there's this Jedi called Luke Skywalker and…"

"What do you need the Earthling for?" interrupted Clamburxer.

"For the *last time*, it's Duke!"

"Duke, Luke, whatever. What do y'all need the Duke for?"

"He will be our guide, and the first person that the people from Earth encounter when we begin our Induction," confirmed Dzkk.

"I'm not going to be anybody's guide until a lot more questions get answered," scowled Duke.

"As ever," sighed Dzkk. "But we do need to get a move on, time is slipping by."

Clamburxer made a sweeping gesture with his arm back towards the lift. The ammunition strapped to beneath his epaulettes chinked slightly.

"That first cocktail hit the mark gentlemen. As good as any Deep Southern Cluster concoction ah have tasted. But one is never enough. Sergeant Obloid you are relieved of your duties and may return to the station. I shall take a ride with my new friends here, an request collection at the appropriate juncture."

With his uniformed arm still high in the air he flicked his helmeted head perceptibly in the same direction.

"What we waitin' for? Back to the bar."

# CHAPTER 43

## 3rd September
## 05:15am AST, Puerto Rico

Tina slapped Nelson on the face.

"Nelson!"

She slapped him again.

"*Wake up*!"

Nelson woke up. He peered around from his partially horizontal position, trying to focus. They were still on the plane to Puerto Rico.

"Keep your *hands* to yourself!"

"What?"

"You know very well."

"But..."

"I think you've been dreaming Nelson. Or should I say, I *hope* you've been dreaming. You whispered, *Let me get it.*"

"I wanted to get… the gun in your coat," said Nelson helplessly. "He was the Black Squirrel."

"*Really*?"

"Oh dear…" his voice trailed off. "He was going to kill you. And he didn't like the pilot…"

"Get a grip," said Tina putting her earphones back on.

"I was trying to..." whispered Nelson to himself.

He rubbed his eyes hard and patted his cheeks. The right one still smarted. Once again she had proved to be a strong woman.

As he raised his seat, he sensed the plane was in descent and looked out of the window. Expecting to see the twinkle of city lights, he saw only the darkness of a forest far below, the tops of dense trees occasionally washed by a distant, harsh light.

He presumed they may land amidst more seclusion and turned his head towards the dawn sky and wondered on the current time zone. The hour seemed very irrelevant in his present context, so he refrained from asking. And the only way he had of telling the time was with the tiny LCD built into his expensive biro, and, typically, this needed yet another biro to adjust it. Another wonderous innovation; one step forward - two steps back.

A stewardess asked everyone to fasten their seatbelts and stop smoking. Nelson noticed Gloria hurrying back to his place, a tang of tobacco odour in his wake. He sat with another heavy wheeze.

"Been for a fag in the loo?" quipped Charlie as the old man gasped for oxygen.

"No, just a chat and a ciggy with the pilots," wheezed Gloria. "And from the cockpit there's a wonderful view of the sun coming up over the Arecibo Observatory."

"Excellent," replied Charlie, "Looks like it will be nice weather for us. And *them*."

# CHAPTER 44

Alk was having a busy day and now blew recycled warm air into recently rinsed cocktail glasses. Each was then conveyed onto carboplastene storage shelves. Duke's request for his father's favourite Vesper Martini had been met with prolonged silence, prediction analytics, and the softest whirring of gears.

He now sat with something approximate and palatable. Silently musing alongside him were Dzkk, Clamburxer and Slogg. The Captain broke the ice first.

"So, who wants to start?"

"I'll…"

"Go…"

"First…"

They all spoke at once, yet Dzkk's final word cut through like a sabre and gave him the ground.

"Chief Commissioner you said earlier that The Great Attractor had…"

*"Why is my planet going to blow itself up!"*

"…given you a mandate," continued Dzkk, ignoring Duke's outburst. "Can you tell me what kind of mandate?"

"Well, started Clamburxer, nodding towards Duke. "It just so happens that the two are connected… the mandate and the self-annihilation. We all know that the Earth is in accelerated development and has been hypermutating for over five hundred million annums."

"Well, I didn't," blubbed Duke, "no one told me."

"But you did know my dear friend," consoled Dzkk. "You used the phrase *Cambrian Explosion* yourself, when describing the inexplicable and sudden burst of life on your planet."

"That's true, and it is inexplicable. But I don't see what this has to do with my species blowing up their own planet." He snapped his head in Clamburxer's direction and scowled.

"But it is explicable Mr. Duke, and the two are intertwined."

Duke was lost. He took a breath in to speak but no words came out. Dzkk intervened as he turned to Clamburxer.

"You are saying Commissioner, that the hypermutation of life on Earth is explicable?"

"Yes, and it's not hypermutation as such, more like programmed mutation."

"Programmed! By whom?"

"Y'all really don't know do you?"

"Know what?" exclaimed Dzkk.

"Ah thought you were meant to be All-Powerful?" challenged Clamburxer.

"There are secrets none of us know, and mostly for good reason."

"And how do I know that this isn't one of them?" quizzed the lawman, clearly relishing his upper handedness.

"Chief Commissioner, you have made yourself a part of this mission. For us all to succeed and for that success to be favourably reported to the Superchamber… and ultimately on to Great Attractor, we need to pool resources, not play politics, and share what we know."

Check. Clamburxer observed that Dzkk had just made a very clever move. He decided to relent.

"Well, perhaps y'all should ask the Great Attractor who might be responsible for the programmed mutation."

"The GA! Why?"

Dzkk's face had frozen. In the minutest of increments his fingers traced an arc towards his mouth to touch his bottom lip.

*"WAIT!"*

"Do you see now?" asked Clamburxer. He waved

his own hands very slightly, fingers up, palms outwards, in front of his large chest. "For the record, I would like to point out that ah said nothing, diddly-squat."

Incredulity continued its march across Dzkk's face.

"Let me get this straight. You're saying the Great Attractor started this whole accelerated evolution thing off on Earth with a programmed mutation?"

"I'm not saying anything, you are."

"But why would the GA take such a risk?"

"STOP! Please!"

Both of Duke's fists hit the table simultaneously. His martini glass jumped and at least a quarter of its contents spilled over the edge. Clamburxer and Slogg leapt at the shock then held firm to their own drinks. Only Dzkk remained transfixed on the law-enforcer's face.

"I need everyone to slow down, stop all the jargon, speak very clearly, and tell me... *what the hell is going on here!"*

"I'm saying nothing more," stated Clamburxer.

Slogg's pupils flicked anxiously between all three of his guests. Duke's eyes turned imploringly to Dzkk and in response the All-Powerful bantam spoke.

"The Commissioner has helped me finally understand something very fundamental about your planet."

"Like what?"

"Duke, I know see that your Cambrian Explosion is no longer a mystery."

"It isn't?"

"No. The Great Attractor began a programmed mutation that accelerated your evolution."

"What on Earth is a programmed mutation?" demanded Duke.

"Perfectly put," began Dzkk. "It's a preset direction in which the mutations can be directed."

"Speak English please."

"I believe I am, aren't I? Mutations are simply mistakes in the genetic code. You can have big mistakes or small mistakes, and the more of them that there are, the faster the pace of change. And if these mistakes are in some way pre-programmed towards a particular speed and outcome, then you control both the direction and pace of evolution. It had been tried in earlier Big Loops, but it was always very risky and the outcomes were not great."

"But how can a mistake be programmed?" demanded Duke.

"Well, all actions have outcomes. It's the same with all mistakes. If you limit the number of outcomes then you can ensure many, many mistakes on top of each other get pointed in a particular direction. And if you speed up those mistakes then the desired outcomes happen quicker"

"Like what?"

"Well, say, like changing size. If the mistakes happen and the genes mutate that control the size of a creature, but the outcomes of those mistakes are limited to growth rather than shrinkage, then the creature will quickly get larger or taller. Natural selection takes care of the rest, even if it only has a limited number of outcomes to play with, it will still choose the best."

"So let me get this exactly right. You are saying that this Great Attractor fellow..."

"The GA is not a fellow and appears in many forms. Like I said earlier, the ultimate shapeshifter."

"This Great Attractor... accelerated and directed these mistakes to start life on Earth."

"Programmed them," corrected Dzkk.

"Like a... God"

"The GA is a shapeshifter appearing in whatever form is required."

"Five hundred million years ago."

"More or less," sighed Dzkk.

"Why?"

"Why?" Dzkk looked back over to Clamburxer who simply shrugged his giant epaulettes.

"A good question my new friend. An experiment, an improvement, a test… maybe all three. But these interventions are extremely rare. My best guess right now would be… intelligence."

"Intelligence, what do you mean?"

"Perhaps The GA wanted to see how quickly intelligent life could form if encouraged properly, rather than left to random happenstance."

Clamburxer suddenly leant forward in his chair slapping his forearms onto the table and splaying his palms.

"Good, good, good, you done well indeed chicken-man. This all brings us neatly to the Earthling's original… sorry, *the Duke's* original question about self-annihilation."

"Thank you, Judge Dredd. Why is my planet going to blow itself up?"

"We've watched you from afar, but you live down there. Y'all seen what's happening with the burning of all that fossil fuel destroying your atmosphere, and now your nuclear arms race between one half of your species and the other half. East versus West. You've gone too fast Mr. Earth…ling and it's a big mistake. None of this was ever meant to happen."

Duke took a deep, deep breath and held it for a few seconds, then let it out very slowly.

"I have asked patiently, more than once, for you to slow down and explain what… the… hell… you… are on about! What was never meant to happen?"

Clamburxer looked away from this ranting alien and back to the strange, feathered creature that once again sat calmly with them. He took a glance at the Captain who had maintained his silence throughout this interchange.

"So, y'all going to tell him, or do I have to?"

Dzkk spoke first.

"Duke. By comparison with the rest of Laniakea, Earth has been evolving fast. But too fast. What up until now I thought was an inexplicable hypermutation, has been having a strange effect on the planet."

"In what way Dzkk?"

"Fossil fuels are one obvious example. You were never supposed to need them. Without hypermutation the Earth's sea creatures, and your dinosaurs, would never have evolved to such largesse that their decay would produce rich fuel seams to be burnt by a later species, ultimately killing the planet's delicate biospehere. The lack of fossil fuel to drive your growing industrial achievements, would eventually have driven you towards more ingenuity in other energy forms, most commonly clean solar power. With limitless availability, this would have protected your environment and negated needless wars over its supply. Finally nuclear power would not have been required and nuclear weapons would not be its offspring."

Duke allowed a deliberate silence to hang in the air. He tapped his fingertips lightly on the table.

"Let me try this one last time. You're now telling me our genes got messed with, to make more mistakes, but only in the direction where those mistakes would make us evolve faster. And then the biggest mistake from that was that we end up moving so fast we screw the very planet that we live on!"

"In a nutshell."

"So… me, humanity, the Earth, everything on it… we're all just one big mistake?"

# CHAPTER 45

Nelson was experiencing the sensation of trapped wind. As a child he had made the mistake of reading loose facts claiming most aircraft accidents happen on landing. They were descending far faster and steeper than anything he had experienced prior to this. His knuckles shone white over his armrests.

Faithfully the modified 707 landed on a small, secluded airstrip in the middle of a Puerto Rican forest. As it mercifully levelled out just a few seconds before touchdown, a highly wired Nelson spotted a stunning and unbelievable sight from his window seat: a colossal concrete dish that seemed embedded into the forest floor. From Nelson's viewpoint the bowl must have been at least one thousand feet in diameter. In the early dawn light he could faintly make out three needle-like structures surrounding the dish, supporting a cable-tethered central mass in mid-air.

The aircraft doors were opened by the minimal cabin crew. On shaky limbs, Nelson descended the stairway into the warming dawn air. Ahead of him strode Tina, her heels clicking on the diminutive concrete runway and her raincoat remaining tightly fastened.

"Did you see that?" Nelson hissed to her.

"What? Do you mean you in a nervous turmoil?"

"That giant stone bowl… as we landed. Who could build such a thing!"

A set of powerful spotlights disturbed the sunrise air, picking out a route towards a shadowed entrance into the forest. Beyond the treetops and backlit by the indigo and deep red of an early dawn, Nelson could discern the three towers he had witnessed on landing were now reaching skyward above him. They supported an immense triangular shaped structure via tensioned steel cables. He slowed his pace to take in this incredible view.

"Welcome to Arecibo," said Charlie turning to his left.

"What is that!" asked Nelson, awestruck.

"Let's get inside and we'll show you."

The group approached the darkly shaded opening surrounded by dense foliage. A mechanical rumble preceded a surreal motion amongst the nearest trees as they began to slip aside unnervingly, arranging each trunk to form a perfect circle that encased their occupants.

There was a jolt beneath them and from this the ground comprising the whole inner circle, minus the trees, began to sink slowly into the earth and rock below. The break was clean, with just the faintest sifting of soil dropping as dust near its edges.

"Oh my!" exclaimed Nelson.

Standing rigid, he glanced at the tired and indifferent faces of his companions. Only Tina's eyes widened. Unable to move, Nelson watched the needle towers, night sky and spotlights disappear, to be replaced by a dark rock face as they dropped deeper and deeper.

Nelson's sudden shock slowly transformed into wonder at the level of technical expertise their hosts possessed.

Just as he was about to express his astonishment, they burst into sudden white light and another colossal and brilliantly lit cavern. While his senses reeled Nelson became aware their descending platform was something akin to a huge stalagmite.

They came to a slow halt in a state of limbo, balanced at the midpoint beside a wall that formed part of a giant cave.

A shimmering glass walkway, lit by an invisible purple glow, extended gently out to meet their own hanging rock. As these two unlikely objects met, Charlie carefully strode forward. Each of his Knowall colleagues also took a step forward to their own respective edge of the platform.

"A purple glass walkway!" muttered Nelson to himself.

With his pale face illuminated eerily by the violet glow, Charlie stepped onto the walkway, and their huge floating rock began to slowly rotate, offering the glass ramp to each Knowall in turn. One by one they shuffled off, and this crystal exit was offered finally to Tina and Nelson. As soon as they were all clear, the stalagmite began to make its ascent once more to the edge of the cavern roof, refilling the open void it had created. Nelson pulled alongside Gloria.

"Tell me," began Nelson, "have your lot never heard of a good old door, and maybe a flight of stairs?"

"Of course," coughed Gloria, "here they are."

Before them was a door.

Behind it was a flight of stairs.

The group used them both.

Not a great deal happened in the next five minutes.

"Okay, I take your point, that was boring," said Nelson, four hundred and thirty-one steps and two doors later.

They continued down steps made of steel, some of wood, and some cut from the rock face. Down spiral stairs, down straight stairs, some well-made, some dangerous. But never upwards.

"This is tedious," stated Nelson, "Where are we going?"

"Downstairs," replied Gloria.

"And when we get there will there be a little man with red skin and matching cape waiting for us, complete with horns and a trident?"

"Probably."

"Nelson, just keep walking," pleaded Tina.

The little man waiting for them at the bottom had grey-white skin and matching lab coat. He wore glasses and carried a clipboard.

"...seven... eight... nine. Oh good, I think we can start," said labman as he ticked Nelson off on his printed chart. He closed the door to the stairs from which they arrived.

Nelson followed Gloria, who was following Tina and the rest of the Knowalls. They emerged into what felt like open air.

Looking up, Nelson realized they were now at the base level of a truly immense cavern, having started their descent via its ceiling.

"This is… enormous," gasped Nelson, "Cavernous!"

"Infinite," sighed Tina.

"Not quite, but it soon will be," said Charlie.

"Sorry? I don't understand what you mean."

"It'll be more exciting if I just let you witness it," beamed the Knowall.

The cavern was indeed monumental. Within its brilliantly lit interior, white coated men and women worked feverishly at a variety of thin screens and keyboards, whilst some tapped slim glass slabs in their palms and checked each other's readout. The tension appeared palpable in anticipation of a great happening. Yet, as he peered up, it was the ceiling of the cavern that struck Nelson. Perfectly concave, it resembled a monumental, inverted dish and a realization struck him.

"Is that the underside of the giant concrete bowl I saw as we landed?" Nelson asked Charlie.

"A superb deduction Nelson, well done. It is by a

huge margin the largest receiver… *and transmitter…* ever built."

Nelson turned his attention to the feverish activity.

"Something about to happen, is it?" he sniffed.

"Yes, you could say *something* is," answered Charlie, once again smoothing his gold swan braiding.

# CHAPTER 46

"I'm not having any part in it," exclaimed Duke.

"Any part in what?" queried Dzkk.

"In this… charade. In all of this," he held out his arms, but they were restricted by Slogg and Clamburxer sitting either side of him. "Whatever is next for Earth, count me out of it."

"I think you might be overreacting," put in Dzkk, calmly.

"Yes, come on Earthling," barked Clamburxer, "your planet has done alright out of it. Y'all not exactly…"

"*I'VE TOLD YOU…*" the words burst out of Duke's mouth as his finger snapped up to point at the policeman. He was struggling to speak with rage as his outstretched finger trembled in midair.

"… I've told you, Judge Dredd, I have a name. It's Duke. Not Earthling, earthman or anything other than Duke. Duke Kramer. And as for overreacting, take a moment to consider what you've just told me. Earth is just one big experiment in over mutated souls. And your lot started it all! Mistake on mistake on mistake. Accelerated births, brain aneurisms, deaths, grief. Piling up and up, until we simply want to blow each other to our constituent atoms. Why, why… have you waited until 1983 to sort it all of this out?"

"Early intervention is frowned upon," offered Dzkk.

"Early intervention! Early intervention in what? In all your cock-ups?"

"Please be aware my friend, that I am also learning a lot of this for the first time. It may be no coincidence that Chief Commissioner Clamburxer has been brought here, and perhaps this is all part of a bigger plan that the Great Attractor is orchestrating."

"Firstly Dzkk, I am not your friend. I am your abductee, and torture target, remember?"

"I was simply trying…"

"And secondly, I cannot believe there is any grand plan given the present track record. But even if there is, I want absolutely no part of it."

"Please Duke, Earth's Induction will not go as smoothly without your participation."

"No," snapped Duke flatly. "Do you know what I want? Some sleep. I am confused, very angry, and totally knackered. This is bringing up a lot of what I thought I'd put behind me. I need rest. Captain, where can I get some quiet?"

Slogg looked at Dzkk for guidance and was met with a long, blank stare, then finally a meagre shrug of the shoulders in evident capitulation. He then inclined his head back towards the earthman.

"We have guests' quarters. I'll get one of the service droids to show you."

"Yes please."

Duke went to stand, still hemmed in by Slogg and Dzkk either side of him. As Slogg rose awkwardly from his seat to make way for Duke, he spoke to the remaining two.

"Given the Great Attractor's diktat, I'm assuming this critical mission is to continue, and I still have a destiny."

"It must, Captain," confirmed Dzkk with a sigh, watching forlornly as Duke walked away with his back to them.

"Indeed it must," continued Slogg, turning to Clamburxer. "So, Chief Commissioner, this is your patch, and you've said that you're here to help. Can you please tell us the way to our target planet?"

"That's darn easy," said Clamburxer, "We're nearly there. Straight on for the next fifteen and a half billion kilotecs..."

"And then?"

"Turn left at Jupiter."

In deep space the migrant ship made its final computations and manoeuvres to complete a left turn at a gas giant planet named locally as Jupiter.

Undocked and slowly easing away from this huge vessel, was a much smaller craft piloted by a lonesome Sergeant Obloid. Escaping the immense gravitational pull of Jupiter, the ultraspeed police cruiser accelerated to the nearest interstellar café.

Duke was led by a service droid to a small cabin where he lay his head on brick-shaped soft pillow that yielded perfectly to the shape of his skull. He was asleep instantly.

Dzkk retired to the ship's *SPA*[22] bay to think.

Captain Slogg returned to the bridge, encountering it steeped in two distinct emotions. Relief, from Taroooc, thankful his own juvenile misdemeanours and their 3D reconstruction were safely confined within Sergeant Obloid's departing holobook. And Slogg's own anxiety, lingering due to Clamburxer's haunting presence and no clear exit strategy.

Slogg stood with the policeman in the middle of the dimly lit bridge, watching as the colossal gas giant swept across their vast screen.

"But surely Chief Commissioner," pleaded Slogg, "you no longer need to accompany us for the rest of the journey. I feel our mission is clear now. It doesn't warrant

---

[22] Sauna, Plunge Pool and Arousal.

the attention of your standing, And especially given that Dzkk has assured you, our intentions are entirely honourable."

"That's all very well Captain Slobb, but I now agree with Dzkk's thinking. Perhaps the Great Attractor has a bigger plan. I also remain convinced your target planet is not ready to join the Galactic Club - and will not be for some time. Its inhabitants are still heathens. And finally Captain… something is still bugging me around here that I just can't lay my finger on. Ah feel as though I'm staring it in the face. Do y'all ever get that sense?"

"No, never!"

Slogg span immediately away and strode to his seat. He slumped into it, brooding. He craved a means to distance himself from the senior policeman, a tactic to disrupt their close proximity.

"Captain," announced Deluxia, "Maintenance Crew have reported successful stowage of our prize pink elephant."

She adjusted her miniature earpiece as further information came in. Slogg remained preoccupied.

"Sir, they finally coaxed it inside cargo bay six, alongside the Braevitchkan beer. They believe the familiar deep aroma may have helped."

His mind racing, Slogg's brow furrowed as he chewed his lower lip. He was chasing a method to distract Clamburxer, incapacitate him, or deposit him somewhere else… allowing Slogg to fulfil his destiny unthreatened and unfettered.

"Sir?"

*Or perhaps a way of achieving all three!*

Slogg tuned in.

"Yes Deluxia." He beamed at her mid-aged beauty. A miraculous idea hit him.

"Maintenance have reported…"

"Yes, I heard you. Cargo bay six you said, alongside the strongest beer in the universe."

“That’s right, Sir.”

Slogg had a plan. Glancing over at Clamburxer, he began tentatively.

"Er, Chief Commissioner..."

"Yes?"

"I couldn't help noticing, as we deliberated over drinks earlier, you appear to be quite a connoisseur on the subject."

"Ah don’t remember?"

"Yes. Well, forgive me for being presumptuous, but I'm sure that we can offer you a drink… of the like you may never have tried before."

"Oh, y’all do, do you?" replied a wary Clamburxer.

"Have you ever heard of Braevitchkan beer?"

"Can’t say ah have."

"Excellent. Well, it has a reputation for being one of the finest brews in the universe. In fact, its planet of origin is now inhabited entirely by monks who have devoted their lives to its research, development and brewing."

"Really? Well, I am on duty, but…"

"Oh, fear not. This is a light brew with a delicate fragrance. Not a single jot will it affect your career."

The crew were stony silent, dismayed by the interplay before them, and each fully cognizant that even a sniff of the pure brew procured as their PPO from the Digitari, was enough to dispense a wide grin that endured for days beyond reason. Yet no one chose to intervene.

"Would you be interested?" Slogg pressed.

"Well, when you put it like that Cap’n…"

“Oh good. We've just taken delivery of a few select crates from an exclusive distribution fleet. If you care to follow me to the cargo bay, we'll crack open a bottle or two."

"Okay! I’m in Captain. What are we waitin’ for? It sounds like a good interlude to me," chirped

Clamburxer, following Slogg to the lift.

"Do you have a bottle opener?"

"Good thinking," said Slogg wryly.

"And a crane to raise you afterwards," murmured Taroooc.

"What y'all saying?" queried the policeman.

"I said you might also need a crate opener."

"Thank, you… Toool!" snapped Slogg, "I'm sure we'll manage."

"Captain," called the ship's navigator as the lift door opened.

"Yes Walta?"

"A new planet has just appeared on the scanners."

"Oh good, that'll be it. Looks like we're going to have to take this Induction on our own. The Earthling is now sulking. So put us in orbit when we get there Walta, and as a backup let's activate the cloaking shields. Until we've got a lie of the land, we don't want them detecting our presence too early."

"Yes Sir."

Slogg stood with Clamburxer shoulder to shoulder in the lift.

"I'll be back shortly," he called out to his crew.

Clamburxer snapped his head and shot Slogg a quizzical glance.

"Sorry… *we'll* both be back shortly," lied Slogg.

*Schtop.*

The lift door closed.

# CHAPTER 47

Another lift door opened seemingly embedded into infinitely deep igneous rock.

In the cavern beneath Puerto Rico with its concave roof, three more men and two women in white coats stepped out to join their colleagues in a flurry of action, each diving from touch screen to tablet to 1983-style computer print-out.

"What we are about to attempt has only been achieved once before, and then there was some instability," Charlie informed them.

Nelson felt the urge to look up. Suspended high above was the concave cavern ceiling, the man-made underside of the immense satellite dish. As he searched for any clue to the forthcoming extravaganza, Nelson became aware the lighting within their vast underground chamber was dimming.

Far in the distance an engineer announced in officious tones that full power was now available. Accompanying this, a faint hum vibrated to fill their surroundings, rising gradually in volume. Nelson noticed his hosts began lifting their gaze to the cave roof. He nudged Tina quietly, and both felt compelled to join in staring at the curved ceiling. A deep thrum rose and fell rhythmically, until it reached into the lungs.

The air filled with anticipation. All eyes glued to the now shadowy cavern roof.

Charlie spoke as he gazed upward.

"You see, Puerto Rico has been selected to be the most important meeting point in the history of the Earth."

"Meeting point?" grilled Tina.

"Yes. And it was picked for two reasons. Firstly, a natural dip in the rock that forms the Arecibo Observatory and dish... we'll come to that in a minute.

And secondly because it is the only place in the world where iron ore, silica and trace elements of boron can be found in the requisite saturation levels."

"Oh, I see," said Tina, who didn't. "But you just said *meeting point*?" she pressed.

"I suggest that you keep looking up there," said Charlie, pointing to the cave's ceiling.

The deep hum's cadence bestowed the impression of a huge force strengthening around them. No one moved in the cavern as an invisible power took control.

Lights dimmed still further. Just the eerie glow from thin screens providing dramatic twisted shadows.

The indented ceiling appeared to undulate, then recede ever further, until it disappeared completely. Nelson tried to focus on the dark cement that was there just seconds earlier. Pinpoints of light caught the eye at random, dotted around the rock.

But there was no rock, or cement.

Suddenly the deep orange and purple of an early morning sunrise shimmered into view.

"Wow!" yelled Nelson, "My God! It's become… invisible."

"Well observed," applauded Charlie.

"That's the sky! At least forty feet of rock - and we can see straight through it to the sky!"

"Correct."

As their eyes adjusted to take in the dark morning haze, it became clear the three towers that Nelson spotted earlier were now soaring directly above them, showing as needle shadows reaching to the heavens. The thick steel cables became visible stretching inward from each tower to tightly suspend a peculiar triangular mass. It hung, perfect centred above them.

"But where has the rock gone?" asked Tina.

"Oh, it's still there," Charlie assured her, "silica, boron, oxygen in the atmosphere… these are the main constituents of glass!

"Glass."

"Yes. We've temporarily readjusted the rock's molecular structure so that you can see straight through it. And I must say it has worked perfectly this time. Well done everyone."

Nelson goggled in wonderment. If the earlier shimmering purple walkway had somehow soured his feeling of bewilderment, then this spectacle had immediately revived it. Amongst the towers' shadows he watched a few stubborn stars play out their twinkling as daylight took over.

"As I was saying," began Charlie, "this is the only place in the northern hemisphere that we know of where this is possible. By applying electric and magnetic fields in the right environment and inducing a small amount of high frequency vibration in the iron ore, the molecules are invited to come together, line up and become transparent. At least that is the press release anyway! It's primarily Doctor Xing's idea, and he's been known to perform some strange little dances to make it work."

The slightly built Asian, who had flown with them from the Dark Peak, glanced over with a very broad grin across his face. He nodded in acknowledgment and they all responded with appreciative smiles.

"And..." concluded Charlie, "...it provides a very adequate viewing area for when *they* arrive."

The sunrise began to light the top of the cave, the tips of the towers above them, and finally illuminate the triangular gantry formed of steel girders suspended over their heads.

Nelson was aware of Tina standing next to him and together they contemplated this magnificent view. They stared through invisible rock, past a web-like framework, beyond the Earth's multi-coloured atmosphere and out towards the fading stars. Nelson was genuinely moved and a desire to sigh deeply came over him.

"You know," he exhaled and turned to Tina, "it's at times like these that I wonder how we all got here."

"Well, Nelson, I'm no scientist, but I believe the theory now goes it's all to do with a Big Bang."

"Oh, certainly not," replied Nelson, "my parents were much more sedate."

# CHAPTER 48

Deep in an obscure cargo bay of Galactic Core Fleet migrant ship GCF-10068 a faint giggling could be heard. To trace the source of this giggling one had to pass three crates of MegaMammoth droppings[23], then over four crates of gas masks and safety goggles[24].

Beyond these obstacles and past the cage containing a huge pink elephant, there slumped a rather well lubricated member of galactic law enforcement. In fact, Chief Commissioner Milko Clamburxer was so well oiled his gears were beginning to slip.

"Dee doo... do you know wh... wh... wha' the funniesh thing of all is?"

"No, what?" queried Slogg.

"Ah... *hic*... ah haven't even ha... had a drink yet!"

"Really?"

This was true. Clamburxer had removed the top from the first bottle of Braevitchkan beer. He pushed up his helmet visor, held the bottle in his hand, and stared at the label. This had been enough. Within ten seconds the brew's fumes had taken effect.

"An... and do you.... yooooo *hic* you know what else?"

"What else?"

"Y... you look awf... *hic, giggle* y'all look awfully stoooo... stupid in that gas mask!"

"Well, you know me," said Slogg, "anything for a laugh. Let's have a drink."

They sat together on a modest bench by the pink elephant's cage. Slogg took the Braevitchkan beer bottle

---

[23] Traded as a deodorant by the tribes of Detton Nine.

[24] Readied for the ship's next visit to Detton Nine..

from Clamburxer's unsteady hand and poured them both a drink into two small glasses. A dark amber ale poured heftily out crammed with swirling bubbles that slowly formed a creamy yellow head. Clamburxer pushed his visor even further back, carefully focused on his glass for a few seconds and then said:

"Well, down the *hic* hatch," and slung the liquid into his mouth. A few seconds later the hatch was involuntarily opened again, and the liquid was thrown back up.

"Pace yourself my dear Clamburxer. This drink needs respect," said Slogg as he watched the policeman's head wobble, and his eyes roll.

Slogg knew the power of the amber brew. He managed to don a Detton Nine gas mask with perfect timing as Clamburxer opened the first bottle. Slogg leaned slowly back on their bench and surreptitiously emptied his own glass quickly into the elephant's drinking trough - then watched in astonishment as the liquid was immediately sucked up by the beast's trunk. He turned back to his guest.

"You see Chief Commissioner, we must not drink it so fast. The Braevitchkan brew needs tender treatment, reverence and a degree of elegance to allow for maximum appreciation."

"Sod the ten-ton tree-men, reverends and degrees for elephants… pour meeee, me another one!"

Slogg happily obliged and watched Clamburxer sip gently through the yellow froth. Somehow this sample stayed in his stomach. With his visor up, Slogg could see Clamburxer's eyes appear to focus intently in the very far distance, then his head wobbled again. He gripped his free hand to the edge of the bench and turned to Slogg, fixing him with a very strange look – an expression Slogg could not yet determine. He quickly poured himself another glass, and as soon as Clamburxer's eyes started to roll again he immediately tipped it into the same trough, and once more it was instantly devoured by the elephant.

As Slogg's safety goggles gently misted up, Clamburxer continued his unsettling gaze.

"Do you… yooooo *hic* know," he leaned forward as he saw Slogg attempt anxiously to clear his vision, "you are the besh… the besh, the best looking woman ah have seen for a very long time."

"Really?" squirmed Slogg.

Clamburxer sidled closer to him along their small, shared seat. The expression on Clamburxer's face finally dawned on Slogg.

It was drunken lust.

"Come here my boo… beauty, and let me whisper *burp, hic* in your ear."

"I do not want burp-hic whispered in my ear thank you," announced Slogg, leaping from the bench to avoid Clamburxer's flailing arms.

"Tease!" yelled Clamburxer.

Keeping a safe distance, Slogg topped up Clamburxer's glass to the brim and poured what was left of the mighty beer into the pink elephant's trough. Clamburxer smiled towards him, maintained his grip on the bench's edge, then refocused on his glass without losing a drop.

Slogg turned to leave and began his trek back past the various crates, replacing the gas mask once he knew he was at a very safe distance.

*Schtip.*

The cargo bay doors opened with a refreshing hiss and he walked out.

Behind him he heard Clamburxer giggle as the pink elephant collapsed.

Dzkk knocked lightly on the cabin door. There

was no answer. He rapped again a little harder.

"Go away!"

"Duke, we need to speak. This is as important as it gets."

"I was fast asleep. Go away!"

Dzkk clicked the lock gently and delicately pushed open the door.

"The answer stays the same chicken-man, I'm not helping."

"So you've descended to Clamburxer's level with the jibes?"

"I don't care. He's a nasty piece of work and whatever mandate he has I want nothing to do with it."

"His mandate is not my mandate Duke."

"You said they might overlap in some grand plan. I want nothing to do with any of it, so go away."

"Duke, here is my concern about your planet..."

"I don't want to hear."

"It seems to have brought itself to the edge of nuclear war. The term Mutually Assured Destruction has been picked up on your broadcasts..."

"Congratulations. It looks like all your mistakes have been successful. We won't be around much longer to worry about, and now I feel that could be a good thing."

Craving for his powers to be extended to self-will, Dzkk persisted.

"But things down there are changing even faster now and I really don't understand it. I need to know why you aren't aware of your own species' interplanetary space travel."

"Perhaps I'm just stupid Dzkk! Have you thought of that? Stupid enough not to realise what is *really* going on. But it seems we all are. Go away. Go and make some more mistakes yourself, and don't involve me."

"But Duke..."

"Leave me alone Dzkk."

Buoyed by the successful execution of his plan with Clamburxer, Slogg left the cargo bay and pounded along the corridor making his way to the nearest intercom. He pressed the bridge button and Deluxia answered.

"Deluxia, is the Earthling still sulking in his cabin?"

"Yes Captain, that is my understanding."

"And where is Dzkk?"

"We believe he went to visit him."

"Okay, put me through to Navigation."

"Aye Sir."

There was a slight pause and a faint click.

"Hello, this is Walta Woppedd. Are you receiving, over?"

"Shut up Walta. Just tell me if we're in orbit of the desired planet."

"Yes Captain, but..."

"That's all I wanted to know. Is Tarooc there?"

"Yes Captain, but..."

"Shut it Walta. Just ask Tarooc to join me in the Teleport Bay. Have Maintenance Crew prepare these Braevitchkan beer crates to follow us once we announce our Peacefulness and Primacy Ceremony."

"Captain..."

He flicked the switch off and stomped away to ready himself for greeting the people of his destiny. He was taking charge again. This was his ship and his destiny. He had heard enough and witnessed enough and knew what he had to do. The Great Attractor would thank him, and his new ranking of Commodore would be immediate and well deserved.

His only hope was that this planet's greetings would not involve ridiculous tribal dances or the revealing of private parts[25]. He would find this very difficult to endure whilst keeping a straight face.

Taroooc was waiting for Slogg as he arrived at the Teleport Bay. The Delta Nebulan was perplexed.

"Captain. Are we doing this Induction on our own?"

"Indeed we are Taroooc."

"But what about the Earthling Sir? And Dzkk?"

"The Earthling has resigned from his duties. He is in a mood and wants no part of it. And in my assessment, he now appears unstable. Dzkk has provided me with the Induction codebook and holovid. It all seems quite simple. We have successfully secured a powerful Peacefulness and Primacy Offering. So, all will be well.

"But Sir…"

"I've made up my mind Taroooc. My Commodore-ship awaits."

"What about Clamburxer?"

"Oh... I don't think we'll have to worry about him for quite a few hours, hopefully even days."

The Teleport Bay held a slightly raised platform at its rear imprinted with eight circular pads displaying concentric rings of silver. A control desk sat to its right and behind that stood the Teleport engineer. The faintest mustiness of burning metal hung in the air.

"So, we're really doing this?" accepted Taroooc.

"We are."

"Okay Captain… Walta has advised us to wear our Kolidium thermals again. And the atmospheric correction helmets."

---

[25] Interspecies greeting ceremonies remain a social minefield. Each genus may consider different parts of their bodies to be private. On the moons of Olfact One, indiscreet visitors can be arrested for picking their nose.

“Really? Not another cold planet! I thought this one presented a modicum of comfort?”

“Just to be safe Sir. He was banging on about something, but I always find him quite difficult to listen to.”

They pulled on their suits and attached the helmets. Small green numbers flickered to life within their head-up displays.

“So Clamburxer is still alive then?”

“He's still alive. I just don't think he’ll have any control over his actions whilst we fulfil this destiny and get at least a billion kilotecs away. I must say, I'll be glad when this is all over. Even with the GA’s backing, the novelty is wearing thin. Are you ready to meet the people?"

"Er, yes. But..."

"Good. Right then," and Slogg turned his attention to the Teleport engineer, "could you place us on the land mass with the highest population, and could we preferably arrive on a slightly raised plain to make addressing the thronging millions a little easier."

"You've got it Captain," said the engineer.

"I know I have," replied Slogg.

The Teleport Stream warning light began to flash in the bay, it said:

*REMEMBER: CLOSE YOUR EYES.*

Following standard procedure Walta announced to all crew that the migrant ship had entered planetary orbit. And because he enjoyed these little moments so much, he added an unnecessary detail:

“Teleport Stream active.”

“*What*!” yelled Dzkk sitting bolt upright in his

SPA pod. "That's just way too early! What the hell are these guys doing?"

He had returned to the SPA, seeking comfort and relief following his futile exchange with Duke. Throwing the pedicurist aside, who was struggling disagreeably with his clawed feet, he pulled his yellow boots back on and grabbed his feathered cloak. He collided his shoulder with the door jamb as he stormed out.

# CHAPTER 49

Nelson's neck was aching, and he cupped his hand behind his skull to support it.

"Have you never seen a sunrise before?" quipped Tina.

"Not through forty feet of rock! And never framed by three giant spines suspending a giant chunk of Toblerone. I can't process it."

"We appear to have full stability," reported Charlie to his entourage of Knowalls, who were now in the business of returning to their touch screens or mobile devices.

Transfixed since the cavern roof turned non-existent, Nelson now stared through the superstructure and on to a bright morning star which, apart from its own twinkling, remained clearly visible and had no allusion of fading as the sun slowly lit the sky. A loud voice over the public address system shattered his concentration.

"Beacon in operation. Imminent reply expected. "

*Beacon? Reply?*

"Are *they... them*?" whispered Nelson confusingly to Charlie. Fortunately, the Knowall interpreted his brevity.

"Yes, Nelson, provided that we are talking of the same *them*."

"And this is *the meeting point*?" added Tina.

"Correct my dear."

"Extra-terrestrials?" hissed Nelson.

"*Yessss*!" hissed Charlie in mock subterfuge.

"Aliens? What on God's Earth am I looking at up there? And you all seem so casual. Such a low-key event. I was more excited than you, the last time I went to my Uncle Brian's for tea."

"We were all a little more excited... the first time

that we made contact," admitted Charlie.

"The *first* time!" exclaimed Nelson, "You mean this isn't the first time that you've met."

"No, not exactly. The first time we didn't actually meet, we simply made contact. And a very strange sort of contact it was too."

"I feel another *explanation* coming on," sighed Tina.

"Always happy to help my dear."

"But I *want* to understand," exclaimed Nelson. "I need these explanations. This is momentous. I've dreamt about this... and making my own mountain of mashed potato."

Tina and Charlie both stared in disbelief at Nelson.

"Richard Dreyfus! No? Come on. *E.T...*"

"*Close Encounters* actually," corrected Tina, then she pleaded to Charlie, "Can we sit?"

"Of course."

He indicated a collection of high-backed stools arranged along one of the cavern's control consoles. Tina grabbed one and perched on it. Nelson gazed back at the needles, the Toblerone, his twinkling star and then decided to do the same. Charlie continued.

"So, have you heard of the Arecibo Message?"

"No," said Tina emphatically.

"Okay. In the early 70's one of our Progressionaries, Dre'8K over there..." Charlie indicated a bespectacled man with a white lab coat covering his navy-blue cardigan and matching tie, "...or Frank as we now call him, he proposed the idea of structured, extra-terrestrial communication. It was a logical step, but given the size of antenna we needed, and the difficulty in concealing it, Frank was keen to involve humanity. At a superficial level of course. A sort of, hiding in plain sight thing, like we do at NASA. Anyway, what you see, or don't see, here," said Charlie holding his hands skyward,

"...the invisible dish, those towers, the suspended receiver, is what we built. The Arecibo Observatory...

"The what?" started Nelson.

"The largest reflector dish in the world, by an order of magnitude. It is carved into the Puerto Rican rock, and then bounces what it receives from outer space up to that steerable receiver, suspended on those cables."

"So, this is all a radar telescope and an observatory?"

"Yes Nelson, and this..." he extended an arm around, "is our *secret cave.* And finally, all of this doesn't just observe, it is also designed to *transmit.*"

"Transmit."

"Yes, emit signals."

"To whom, aliens?"

"Yes, as it turns out... somewhat unexpectedly."

"*Really*! But why from Puerto Rico?"

"Well, our Frank here, and his unwitting human colleagues, designed the Arecibo Message to carry basic information about humanity and transmit it to the stars. To be honest it began more as a demo than a real attempt to start a conversation with ET.

"And ET phoned home?" jumped in Nelson.

"Not exactly. Our message was a simple series of coloured blocks depicting human form, numbers, atomic elements, you know, the boring stuff... sorry Frank. But then, a year ago we get back...

"Yes?"

"Well, a bit of UHD video..."

"UHD?" queried Nelson.

"*Ultra*-high definition... look, it doesn't matter. Luckily, humanity can't yet process UHD, but as Knowalls we were able to. So, Frank switches it to our private circuits and we see something that still seems a little hard to believe."

He paused to give added effect.

"Well?" asked Nelson, right on cue.

"Well… a clear moving image of… a giant egg."

"A *what?*"

"A giant egg. As clear as day, with the Andromeda galaxy right behind it."

"An egg?"

"It was the last thing we expected to see. So, the next day we go into a huddle in this very cave, and covertly send back our own bit of UHD. A few hours later our receiver issues a few pops and hisses, then all our lights go out, and a booming voice begins complaining about its lack of technical knowledge and Boom Etiquette. It then asked us who we were and what we were doing transmitting into that area of the Galaxy. We explained we were from Earth and the voice cried *Earth? Oh, crap…* and disappeared."

"Then what happened," asked Tina, as Charlie stopped to lick his lips and swallow.

"Well, weeks went by with us just listening. But one night the digital voice returned and started booming again. He announced himself as Desuck – we think - and he talked confusingly of hypermutation but that we had still taken everyone completely by surprise. He told us two things. Firstly, that we should prepare a volunteer for collection."

"Collection! By what?"

"Well, by him as it turned out. And secondly beyond that we should expect the arrival of a visiting party, assuming he could get the buy-in and resources, and that we must transmit another beacon at this precise day and time. He spoke obtusely of being All-Powerful, which meant he couldn't explain too much because he hadn't taken any time to consider it all himself. Then he disappeared again. The last thing we heard was a seemingly faulty electronic voice telling him to slow down. To which Desuck's voice replied *Shut it, Zero.* And that was, and is, it. Until now."

"That… is unbelievable," exclaimed Tina flatly.

"I understand it might be. But I promise you, it's all true.

Another short silence ensued.

"Wait," said Nelson finally. "You are telling me that the first contact between man and an alien life form is through an egg and a megaphone."

"I assure you Nelson, that is how it happened. You don't think we would take you and Tina on this journey with us, only to spin you lies about the reason for it all."

"Maybe," replied Nelson cynically.

# CHAPTER 50

The swirl of highly energised atoms reconstituted to deposit Slogg and Taroooc together on a marbled umber boulder, raising them marginally above a surrounding barren landscape, devoid of life.

"Very funny!" snapped Slogg, "Teleport engineers... are so bloody minded. It must be a way of finding entertainment in their job. Ask for high population density and they'll take every effort to stick you on a stone in the middle of a desert."

He stepped down and surveyed the panorama. The immediate vicinity was choked in a fine orange sand, interrupted by lines of brown earth and small rocks. The horizon offered similar coloured low-rise hills fusing to a red sky illuminated by a weak sun. A chill bit through Slogg's insulated clothing and beside him Taroooc shivered. Slogg called out in desperation.

"It's cold, *again*! And the head-up display tells me this air is thin. Didn't our initial reports tell us it was safe to breathe?"

"They did Sir."

"And... a desert is not the prime location to announce your arrival from the outer cosmos."

"It isn't."

"So apart from agreeing with everything I say, please tell me what that idiot engineer was doing putting us here?"

"But Sir, that's what I was trying to tell you as we left the Teleport Bay," began Taroooc, "Once we were in orbit of this planet, our scanners were unable to pick up any standard life-form readings. It seems something terrible has already happened. There appears to be no life."

Slogg's fists closed in a clench. His wits raced

towards the insanity and mindlessness of what presented before him. The thin air swirled sandy dust across this scorched earth. A film of it took hold on Slogg's visor. All life was gone. All the world turned to an ochre cinder.

"*Armageddon*?" came his hiss.

"It is one hypothesis Sir."

"You mean we're too late!"

"Possibly Captain. Just by a fraction."

"But... have you checked radiation levels? And what about my destiny? How will I become a Commodore now?"

"Sorry Sir?"

"Never mind."

The rarified atmosphere conveyed no sound. Slogg heard only the internal creaking of his suit's joints. Inhaling deeply, he let his eyes fall on Tarooc through their helmet glass.

"So, this is another planet that really did it! Wiped themselves out." He then called dramatically skywards. "You maniacs! You blew it up. *Damn you*! Damn you all to..."

"Er, excuse me..." said a small voice.

"Shut up Tarooc!"

"I didn't say anything, Sir."

"Then what..."

"Excuse me," came the voice again, this time a little more pained.

"Who said that?" Slogg and Tarooc exclaimed together.

"I did. Would you mind stepping off me?"

"What!"

The small rock you are standing on, would you mind moving from it, I'm underneath."

As if the ground had ignited beneath their feet, Slogg and Tarooc both took an instinctive leap to one side.

"I'm here," squeaked the voice, as the stone

beneath quivered,

Slogg crouched cautiously to gently lift aside the rock and peer underneath. He was stunned.

A slug-formed creature slithered smoothly into view.

"Ew!" exclaimed Taroooc.

The organism paused for several seconds. Slogg crouched to his knees to examine their find. Closer inspection presented a turtle-like face, set with a pair mournful eyes and mouth fixed in pained grimace. Surprise enough for Slogg and Taroooc, who kneeled to join him. Yet beyond the head, the miniscule mollusc was dressed in a dark-grey overcoat and pin-stripe sarong. It rose gently to prop itself on a gleaming walking cane held in one of its tiny tendrils.

"Good evening gentlemen," began the creature, the thin voice coming through their headsets. "Allow me to introduce myself. I am Blupin Slingsling, and you can call me Blupe. You took us a little by surprise, but welcome to our amusement park. Admission free."

As a Galactic Fleet Captain, Slogg was very accustomed to encountering exotic species. This was unequalled.

Taroooc commented that a walking cane was a more appropriate accessory for top hat and tails, not an overcoat.

"But I need the walking cane," put in the creature's tiny voice, "it's very difficult to stay upright as a gastropod."

"Okay, okay. Let's slow things down," interrupted Slogg, gripping his gloved fingers across his knees.

"You're a slug - that talks..."

"We prefer the term *gastropod*," put in Blupin.

"... and Taroooc seems to know the current sartorial requirements for slugs. Gastropods. And okay, you need to carry a walking cane. But please, just humour me, as I don't see what *any* of this has got to do with you being on this particular planet, or with an amusement park. Hmm?"

"Why sir, look around you. Over there is a rock, with two more rocks just beyond it. In the middle distance is a sandpit, and next to that... three smooth pebbles! Such a maelstrom of fun."

"You're quite easy to please then?"

"Possibly."

"But I don't see..." began Slogg,

Blupin cut in.

"I can see that as a bipedal species you are not very impressed Sir. Well, if you desire a real treat, may I suggest that you stroll over yonder hill to discover our latest arrival."

"And what might that be?" asked Slogg bluntly.

"Ah, well… a very lavish vessel."

"Vessel?"

"Yes indeed. None other than a *Viking spacecraft*."

"A *what*?"

"A Viking spacecraft, it says so on its plaque. Okay, it may not be very impressive to you walkie talkies, but it is highly amusing for us. It sits there digging holes in the same piece of sand at regular intervals. Very, very funny."

"And what is the point of your spacecraft doing that?"

"Oh, it's not *ours,* Sir" Blupin corrected, "Good heavens no. It was sent here by one of those other planet chaps up there - so I'm led to believe."

"Other planets?" pondered Slogg, "And just where are we?"

"The amusement park."

"I know that. But where exactly? What planet?"

"Why, planet Mars of course."

"*MARS*!"

"That's what we call it."

"But we wanted *Earth*!"

"Well look around you old fellow, there's tons of the stuff."

"*Planet Earth,*" shouted Slogg, his voice full of outrage and disbelief.

"Oh, ha! You mean the duffers who sent down that Viking to find life here? A bunch of cowboys. I mean, what self-respecting group of scientists would send down a box of tricks like that... to look for life on another planet."

"But..." began Slogg.

"*All* it ever does is dig the occasional hole with that long black arm, and then examine the sand. Goodness me. Boring! Literally. And *all* we had to do was get out of its way when it first made the big fuss of landing."

"You hid from it?"

"Of course we did. It's part of the fun. And from then on it has been easy avoiding the great lump. A few days after it landed, there was this almighty whirring noise as it tried to photograph us. Now if we hear the buzz, we have great joy hiding under the rocks. It's a good job it couldn't hear us giggling. Truly backward. Truly amazing. I think it's got bored now."

Slogg stared incredulously at Taroooc.

"We've got... the *wrong, damn, planet*!" he bellowed.

"What on Mars would you want to visit Earth for?" exclaimed Bluepin Slingsling.

"We have a job to do, thank you. So, I am afraid it is time for us to leave."

"Well, I wouldn't waste my time with them if I were you," smiled Blupin. "Do you chaps know the real irony with that Viking lander?

"Go on."

"Well, it has taken millions of photos of our rocks, and yet *they* are the planet's most intelligent life-forms. Ha!"

At which point the boulderstone, from under which the little slug had crawled spoke:

"Excuse me *dahhling*... would you mind putting me back on top of little Blupin here. We were having a very meaningful exchange."

# CHAPTER 51

In the dimness Duke twisted uncomfortably on his recliner. The brick-shaped pillow and air light mattress simultaneously yielded to absorb different contours of his skull and frame.

Atoms moved across a recess of his room.

A reflex initiated a scratch to his cheek. As the right hand lay softly back down by the left shoulder, instinct caused him to partially open his eyes. The room was dark, yet a pitch-black form was by the door.

Duke stopped breathing. There was no sound or movement, but this shape was new. He called out loudly in conjecture.

"Chicken-man! Please leave me alone. We've said everything we're going to say."

An inky stillness endured but the dead air separating them became microscopically smaller.

"Please, you're freaking me out."

The silence persisted as the contours before him firmed up, blurred edges coalescing. A familiar outline was emerging, but only in shadow.

*"Who's there!"*

This came more as a yell of terror than a question. Duke's breathing was minimal and rapid. If this shape so much as exhaled, Duke felt his body might wither, sucking him inward towards a non-vocal scream.

"Who is th…"

*"Duke?"*

The question came as a rush of air from an invisible mouth. One spoken word he had heard an infinite number of times. One word wrapped in a voice he knew definitively, consummately. One word from the vocal folds he had grieved for so long.

*"Dad?"*

Still inky blue-black, the form hardened into a clear silhouette intimately evoking his childhood days. A form that had been framed countless times in his bedroom doorway as he was wished a soft and safe goodnight.

"*Duke…*" came the voice again.

"What's happening, is this a dream?"

"No, son."

His eyes pricked violently with long held tears. He gulped in air and both hands went to his mouth, trembling over his lips. A tremor that spread to his arms.

"Dad. Are you…"

"Yes."

"Are you, a ghost?"

"Not as such."

"But I can't see you!"

The shape shifted diagonally to the right and forward. It was the clear silhouette of his father, yet he could not ascertain any depth to its form.

"Dad, this can't be. I went to your funeral!"

"So did I son."

"What are you?"

"I'm not sure. Atoms still being drawn together is how I feel. As though I've awoken from a coma, but I can't feel my body. I can only see… you."

"Dad, you're here! *Dad!*"

"I don't think I am. I'm not sure where *here* is. I do know that I have something to say to you though."

Tears rolling down his cheeks, Duke sat up to reach out a hand, yet the distance remained distinct between them.

"Dad. This can't be…"

"I feel that as well. I can also feel it won't last. But you have to go son."

"Go? Go where?"

"You have to go home, with these people."

"What do you mean dad, go home?"

"You have to go back to Earth and help."

The shape shifted silently again, appearing as if an invisible hand were reaching out.

"*Wait!*" screamed Duke.

*The Great Attractor is a shapeshifter appearing in whatever form is required.* These were Dzkk's exact words to Duke as they sat with Clamburxer and Slogg in the Refreshment Bay.

"Wait."

Duke exhaled heavily and caught short his sob.

"Stop this!"

"Stop what son?"

"I know this isn't you."

"You are right, it's not me Duke. I don't know how, but it also *is* me. In the same way many years ago a random collection of atoms on Earth came together as me."

"No! That was *your body* dad. But this is not possible. You're not possible. I carried your coffin. I've grieved and missed you ever since. Stop this… whatever you are."

"Duke, in anyway that is notionally possible I know I am here."

"Dad…" Duke began softly crying, a low sob held the room. "*Notionally possible,* you forever used that phrase. This…" he then cupped his hands over both eyes. "What is happening?"

"Duke, it doesn't matter. Somehow this is me and all I want to say is that you must go down there. I now know… you were born to do this. You must help save the Earth."

"Born to do this! I'm not some superhero. Do you see what they've done to us dad? We're all just one big mistake. Even this, now… me talking to you. You're just some shapeshifting… thing, sent to coerce me into following its screwed-up plan."

"You're right Duke. Whatever I am, or whatever is bringing me here, it knows it has screwed up, and needs your help to try and undo those mistakes."

"Undo! How? How can I undo all the last five hundred million years?"

"Please Duke, just go down there and see."

"Why! Why should I?"

"Call it a favour for me son or call it coercion. Please Duke. The effort in bringing me together here with you is weakening. Please do it."

"Do *what* though dad?"

"It doesn't matter what you do, as long as you go down there and *change something*. You'll be a catalyst. You'll see. The next step for man has been marked in red. And Duke..."

"Yes?"

"I've been proud of you son, since the day you were born."

"Marked in red? What does that even mean dad? It's non-sensical... Dad? *Dad?*"

# CHAPTER 52

The universe is very big.

Indeed, it is big enough to get lost in, which many of its inhabitants do.

Slogg wished his Navigation Officer would get lost.

Thanks to Walta he had spent a rather surreal twenty minutes on a planet that he was glad to see the back of. It possessed an exceptionally thin atmosphere, monotonous landscapes and very strange life forms. That any species should wish to spend vast amounts of effort and money to visit this overgrown rock proved very disconcerting to Slogg. And yet this appeared to be the precise aim of the inhabitants of his destiny planet.

Blupin Slingsling predicted the imminent arrival of the Earthman, complete with oxygen apparatus and someone called Ronald MacDonald.

"What must their own planet be like if they wish to get his one so much?" were Blupin's final words.

Slogg mused as he once more stared intently at the main screen, watching the little red planet disappear to an infinitesimal dot.

Walta meanwhile, maintained that he had tried more than once to warn his Captain of the apparent lack of life-form, but upon the explicit order of *shut it* he had done so straight away. He maintained it proved fruitless to argue with his Captain and he had no intention of trying.

As the ship turned towards its new destination, a weak star came into view.

Slogg ordered a brief pop into superluminal drive to speed their arrival on Earth. The stars on the screen turned to streaks as Walta obeyed his command silently. The sun grew bigger in size.

He turned to see Deluxia staring at him in a

thoughtful mood.

"How come," she said, "that if we travel faster than the speed of light, we can still see the stars shining?"

"It comes as part of your recruitment process," said Slogg.

"Oh yes?"

"Of course. We stipulate perfect eyesight and quick reactions," bluffed Slogg, who hadn't a clue.

"Well I never," sighed Deluxia, " I always believed it must be explained by the Very-Special Theory of Relativity, which states once an observer attains superluminal velocity they may see all light sources subtending an arc of less than one hundred and eighty degrees - although that source will be inversely compressed across the spectrum. The anomaly is rebalanced by the fact light is quantum in its nature. Relatively speaking that is."

There was a brief silence.

"Deluxia?" asked Slogg.

"Yes?"

"Have you ever considered applying for Captaincy?"

"No."

"Well please don't, because I'm perfectly happy as things are now."

The ship sped on and the stars in front remained visible.

*Schtip.*

The lift door to the bridge opened.

"*Captain!*" yelled Dzkk.

He stepped out accompanied by Duke.

"What were you thinking! You are not following the correct protocol, and this may have dire consequences."

"A little late to the party aren't we Dzkk?" replied Slogg, standing his ground. He then glanced across at the earthman.

"And I thought your alien specimen had resigned."

"Oh Jesus, I am not an…"

"Captain Slogg, I must intervene, either peacefully or by trajecting you and each of your crew against the walls of this room and compacting all consciousness from their brains and vital organs."

"Choice number one please," called Taroooc.

"Dzkk, I have the deepest respect for you and your kind but…"

"Captain. We only have one chance to make a good first impression. You should never have gone to Mars alone. Thanks to the ineptitude of your navigation, we escaped a worst-case scenario."

"I was trying to warn him, he wouldn't listen," cried out Walta, then immediately plunged crushingly back into his seat as he faced a vicious scowl from Slogg.

Dzkk pressed on.

"Given everything I've learnt since arriving onboard this migrant ship, Earth is one of the most unique and important planets that we have ever Inducted. And as if that were not enough, we have the Great Attractor looking over our shoulder."

"Ha!" spat Duke.

Dzkk span round.

"Duke, do you have a problem with this?" he snapped.

"Well I'd say I was just looking over the Great Attractor's shoulder." He stood, letting his comment pass. The eyes of the bridge were on him.

"What can you possibly mean?" queried Dzkk.

"I just met your Great Attractor."

"Come off it," called out Slogg, "this is exactly

why I felt we should do this alone…"

"Why do you think I am here!" exclaimed Duke. "Why would I come back to this pantomime? A shapeshifter appeared as my dad's ghost, and asked me to… and asked me…"

His head dropped in exhaustion and sorrow. His shoulders sank. A tear ran over his dry cheek.

Faced with the power of Duke's emotions, a silence filtered down in a mix of empathy, incredulity, and emerging belief.

There was a faint bip as the quiet was broken by a report from Taroooc.

"The new planet is coming into range Sir."

"Is it *Earth*?"

"Yes Sir."

"Taroooc, are you sure?"

"Positive Captain. They're even putting out a beacon."

"A beacon. Well, how *civilised* of them. Is it a Galactic Core standard?"

"It's an attempt, Sir."

Slogg turned back to Dzkk.

"Well, these Earth guys appear to know more than we've given them credit for. Yes, it pains me to agree that Mars was a debacle. I believed the earthman here had resigned, and in your original plan you wouldn't be joining us anyway. So, I decided to press on with my destiny. But to be honest Dzkk, I'm glad you're here now. And our little friend. I believe we'll be better together."

Duke's gait stiffened and he gave his head a slight shake. Slogg called over to Taroooc.

"Are the cloaking shields still on for Earth?"

"Yes Sir."

"Okay, let's keep it that way for now. We can't be too careful now. Focus a cloaking tunnel on the beacon. Nothing outside of its channel sees us."

"Captain," called Walta, daring to speak again,

“we've dropped from superluminal drive. Earth is coming into view.”

“Okay good. It's basically just a job now, so let's get it over and done with."

Slogg attention was suddenly caught by the main screen. He stood and stared at it silently, as did Dzkk and the rest of his crew.

What had been a small pinpoint of light a few seconds earlier was now forming into a beautiful green and blue marble with wisps of white across its surface. Closer and closer, and with screen magnification on full, an intricate blend of browns, golds and burnt oranges also became visible.

"Oh my. It really is beautiful," said Deluxia, "so delicate."

"That can't be natural. It looks like a promotion for Galactic Real Estate," observed Taroooc.

Slogg's thoughts were in the same vein. He had witnessed brightly mottled planets before, but none so subtle and exquisite. The planet exuded life - not forms yet visible in vast quantities - just *Life*.

"How could they give something so beautiful such an uninspiring name?" questioned Deluxia, "*Earth*!"

“This is my home you're talking about guys,” put in Duke.

"We have a fix on the beacon Captain," reported Taroooc.

"Good.”

Slogg continued his fixed stare as the planet filled the screen further.

“Sir, we've managed to tune into one of their subluminal broadcasts. I believe it's an earthbound radio station. Shall I patch it through?”

“Good idea Taroooc, let's get an early handle on the place.”

There was a click and a hiss of static. Then:

*Tell me, Captain Strange, do you feel my devotion*
*Or are you like a droid, devoid of emotion*
*Encounters one and two are not enough for me*
*What my body needs is close encounter three…*

*I lost my heart to a starship trooper*
*Flashing lights in hyper space*
*Fighting for the Federation*
*Hand in hand we'll conquer space*

"Surreal crooning that music, Taroooc. Please turn it off. The visuals of the planet are enough, and it is a truly an awesome sight. Quite a destiny for me. So, everyone, stations please… we've arrived."

# CHAPTER 53

In the vast cavern deep below the Arecibo Observatory in Puerto Rico, an announcement blared over the public address system.

"The visitors are sighted and tracked, I repeat... ... er, what was it... oh yes, visitors sighted and tracked."

"There you go, perfect timing Nelson," concluded Charlie, "Let's see how this second encounter goes, and then you may no longer by cynical. Can I suggest you go back to staring skyward and let your eyes do the judging."

Charlie stepped forward as Nelson peered up expecting to see a giant egg, yet all he could see was the three-tower superstructure, a densely purple sky, a thin band of cloud, and the same star he noticed earlier, which was now moving.

Moving.

In fact, this star was moving and growing.

And it was now a green and white star. And a pulsing red star. Then a blue and yellow one. And still it grew until it stopped being a collection of lights and became a collection of shapes that were joined by lights. And within these shapes there were other shapes, and more lights within these shapes... or possibly windows or portholes. And so, this was no weather balloon or unregistered military aircraft. This was an *ALIEN STARSHIP*.

But the closer it came the more Nelson worried. He was worried because the ship worried him. And the ship worried him because there something wrong with it. This was no haute couture starship designed by an earthbound neo-futurist, nor a mysterious Kubrickian mean black slab.

It struck Nelson of a second-hand car. One of the unroadworthy kind. More accurately, it was a cruise-ship sized lollipop, spherical headed, with three tail fins and a torn away dorsal. Nelson witnessed its perceptible wobble as it approached.

Sitting on his high-backed stool in a secret cave, Nelson stared through the invisible rock. A dawn sky framed the looming outer-worldly craft.

Tina and Charlie were close by, deep in hushed conversation.

"So, you're quitting the Earth just as the aliens arrive?" stated Tina.

"Almost, but not quite," explained the Knowall. "We began planning outreach to other solar systems at the same time we put out the Arecibo Message. We realized this type of project needed masses more in terms of resources and funding. Hence Bill, Steve, the take-away coffee and all that bottled water. You need a lot of *bucks* to afford reaching the *stars*. No?"

"Something about take-away coffee?" guessed Tina, half-heartedly.

"Anyway," continued Charlie, "when we started our project nearly ten years ago, *The Quit* was always intended to be what it states: quit the Earth. Leave humanity and its nuclear proliferation... to do with this planet what you will. We are off. But with our interplanetary technology we had reached nearly ten percent of light speed. To really quit, and reach a nice exoplanet, we need light speed... and then more speed beyond it."

"But that's impossible." Nelson had tuned in.

"It appears not, Nelson. And we're nearly there. The theory is all sorted, we just need to get ourselves some *tachyons*."

"Some what?" queried Tina, becoming ever more

exasperated with the language.

"Yes, I know," sympathized Charlie. "It's all too complex. Young Bez'0S over there can explain it in detail whenever you're ready."

Charlie indicated towards the adolescent Knowall with a centre parting, who had first appeared back in the Yorkshire bunker. He glanced away from his screen to smile at them and raise a strong pair of eyebrows.

"Young Bez'0S has progressed from Cloud Computing to off-world travel. Quite a character. He also says he can make us a fortune through internet shopping, but not everyone is convinced."

"For goodness sake, what's an internet?" snapped Tina.

"Oh dear, of course, there's such a lot to get through. Shall I answer the tachyon question first?" Charlie continued.

"Yes please!"

"In simple terms, the tachyons will help the off-world ships Jeff is building travel faster than the speed of light. And to get these tachyons we need a *Large Hadron Collider*."

"Jesus, I won't even ask..."

"Thank you, please don't. We've begun work on that as well in Europe, underground just in case. But... it is going to cost billions. Megabucks. In fact, Star bucks."

He paused and held his hands skywards, taking in a deep breath.

"The take-away coffee?"

"Yes! You're starting to get it. So, in summary, we were on a path to our light-speed rockets reaching the first chosen exoplanet. Then by surprise and provenance, ET answered. Although my colleague Emm has speculated that something we may have done triggered their arrival, which is an interesting theory."

"Why would they choose to arrive now?" questioned Tina.

"Emm's theory is it's our own off-world travel gave us away. But that's what we are hoping to confirm once they get here. And then perhaps they can show us the way out."

"Show you the way!" barked in Nelson. "Show you the way? Out to where? *Taxi! Follow that alien…*" He was mystified and needed his VHS rewind button. Or perhaps better, a fast-forward.

Tina was clear headed.

"So why are *we* here?" she asked.

"You two?"

"Yes. If you are eventually quitting the Earth faster than the speed of light, why do you need us two?"

"Nothing gets passed you does it," admired Charlie. "Well, we're not just building four-seater spaceships my dear. We are building *arks*."

"Arks?"

"Yes, primarily because there are quite a few of us. And secondly, we'd like to take some of our friends with us to this new world… four legged and two legged."

"Hang on…" stuttered Nelson, "just a minute here Charlie. So, if I get this right, you're saying that you kidnapped the two of us to be lab rats on your interplanetary animal farm. Walking in, two by two."

Charlie turned to Nelson and sighed heavily.

"Harsh Nelson, such harsh words. You may remember you made the first move. We wanted to see what you knew and then decided to offer you this opportunity. Tina was an unfortunate bystander, but now she can choose as well. You represent humanity. There will be other members of the animal kingdom selected as well. We want you to join us as equals. Hopefully, you will choose to, once we are ready… because it's going to be quite an adventure!"

Nelson processed.

He eventually turned to Tina and spoke softly.

"Are you up for all of this?"

She smiled warmly back and reached her hand out to his shoulder and stroked it down his arm, before turning back to Charlie.

"One more question," she said.

"Of course, my dear. Please keep asking them."

As the ship approached, the cavern's occupants forgave it for being the inexact variety of hardware to engender a science fiction epic. It ceased wobbling and triumphed in defying gravity, gliding smoothly down without a hint of liquid fueled engine power. Contact had still to be established and for now Charlie was content to leave it that way.

"Let them make the first move," he said.

"Can they see us down here?" asked Tina.

"Most likely, yes. They will be very aware of our presence."

Nelson watched as this implausible starship reined in its power, coming to a final pause with a gentle rotational manoeuvre. Clearly immense, should it land directly on top of their artificial cavern aperture, it would obliterate the dawn sky. Yet, it chose to halt slightly off-centre, leaving a third of the cloudscape in view. A large portion of the craft's left flank, its central column and frontal sphere, were lit by the rising sun. It did not fully land, but hovered above two of the antenna towers, motionless, quiet, and a variety of outboard lights steadily pulsing.

Nelson noted the starship passed at least one criterion set down by earthborn film makers through the years. It had plentiful twiddly bits underneath.

# CHAPTER 54

The visiting craft was completely at rest. Its myriad of lights blinked leisurely, and an eerie stillness crept over the whole vessel. Despite its dilapidated appearance the sheer size was enough to overwhelm the observer. Had Nelson known this was by no means the largest ship in the Galactic Core Fleet he would have been even more impressed. The ominous stillness continued from above, from the forest floor, and from the cavern below.

"What happens next?" Tina finally whispered.

"We can only wait and see. The ball is firmly planted in their court," replied Charlie.

Still the ship hung in the air with no visible means of support. And still it remained quiet.

"Aren't we supposed to play music to them or something?" suggested Nelson.

"Don't be so ridiculous," hissed Tina.

The silence stretched on and on. Nelson and Tina stood with Charlie, Emm, and a handful of Knowalls waiting for the first sign, the first glimpse, the first hint of an attempted communication between the two domains. It was clear to all in the cavern that the aliens knew they were there. Dex nervously scratched his white stubble. Mikhail Gee stroked his thinning hair over the striking red birthmark. Fry sucked on his unlit pipe.

Nelson imagined an undertaking of invisible scans across their primitive human bodies, soft probes into each delicate brain, and all without detection or challenge. All to determine the optimum inter-species communication methodology. The cavern's inhabitants sensed they need only wait for their visitors to decide exactly how to commence this historic dialogue.

"Where *the hell* are they!" screamed Slogg to his crew.

“They must be around here somewhere Captain, the life-form detector confirms it, and it’s never wrong,” replied Taroooc.

"Have you ever tried it on yourself!" snarled Slogg. He frantically examined the main screen showing a quite remarkable sunrise highlighting an immense radio telescope dish seemingly cut out of solid rock, with dense forest all around, and a secluded airstrip in the middle distance. Significantly lacking from this view were any Earth people.

He looked back at Taroooc and hissed:

"Look at this. I risk bringing this ship right down to the planet's surface to create the biggest culture shock this species ever witnessed…" he glanced furtively over at Dzkk and Duke, “…and they just can’t be bothered to turn up. Ha!"

Slogg held up both hands to indicate the main screen with its sunrise display.

"Dzkk, it appears we are about to liberate a planet of nocturnal trees and a bowl of concrete."

"Patience Captain, patience. They are out there somewhere. Have you tried external communications?"

"Patience. *Patience*! I'll give you patience. Patience is being about to qualify for three weeks leave on the Pleasure Planet of Pluvia, with its kinky mermaids and tired anglers, only to be stopped by a freak in an egg who wants to give four billion people a chance of getting to Pluvia first. That's patience! Of *course* we've tried external communications, haven't we Taroooc?"

"Er…"

“Taroooc!”

"No, sorry Captain."

Slogg returned to his chair and slumped deeply into it. Yet again Taroooc managed to drain every ounce of energy from Slogg's weary body. Resting an elbow on the armrest, he propped his head by sinking a fist firmly into his right cheek.

"Okay Taroooc, let's try external communications."

All was very quiet in the cavern. Then came sudden, immediate shock and alarm. Switching on external communications initiated a large transient spike across the hovering vessel's peripheral speakers. This produced a blaring and reverberant boom, followed by hissing and crackling. Then:

"…llo guys? …lo? …name is Du… don't …ink that thi… micropho… is working. *Tap tap thump.*"

Then, only rumblings, as a none too well disguised struggle ensued for possession of the faulty microphone.

"…uke give that to me! Captain Deutronimus Karben Slogg here. ... eople ... f Earth, we brin… greetin… rom the ...alactic C... and welc… y… to our Federa… …"

In the cavern they politely listened and waited.

Finally:

"We before you represent the Galactic Core Fleet of Starships and have been sent to Earth with the express instructions to inf... you th… ur ...ing."

"Cap…ain! It was a clear instruct…n. You do not speak first…"

"But w... k... ...in thi… op… …ry. Damn this f… ing equipment. *Bang. BANG!* ...esting testi… one two thr... f…r. Could w... please have someone l…k at this. *BANG!.*"

A short pause followed, then three clicks.

"... now? Sure? Okay, let's try again. I repeat, my name is Captain Slogg, and I come here to representing Galactic Core Fleet. We are here to welcome you into the Galactic Club. We would very much like to meet you and commence talks on a variety of topics, not least of which is your contribution to the Galactic Community Budget.

"Captain, please stop talking immediately."

"Okay Dzkk, as you wish. But one last thing earthmen. Where are you?"

As this unfolded Charlie requested a simpler two-way contact link be established from the cavern to bypass the laser multiplied sonic resonators, pixelated light shows, and narrowband echo beams designed in anticipation of their visitors advanced communication methods.

Consequently, all the exits leading from their cavern to ground level were opened, and Charlie used the public address at full volume to yell:

"*We're down here*!"

Then a pause.

"*Dzzmmmm*... Well could you come up where we can see you," came the reply, "We'd be most grateful."

Slogg held the microphone horizontally at arm's length and let it drop to the floor. He prepared a cold stare and Taroooc winced. Dzkk's stare at Slogg was equally icy.

Seconds passed before there was another faint bip, and Deluxia touched her ear. Without moving his head, Slogg's eyes caught her gaze.

"Apologies Captain, but reports are coming in of a

rather drunken Chief Commissioner Clamburxer careering around the lower decks with a very large pink elephant in tow."

Slogg took a deep breath and exhaled heavily.

"Deluxia, did we really *need* that information right now? Have Security contain them and, if necessary, I give permission to sedate the elephant and shoot Clamburxer."

Her eyes then widened strikingly.

"And Captain…"

"Yes?"

"Look up there! It appears one of the Earthling's doorways has just lit up… on, on the corner of the screen. They are about to show themselves!"

On the main screen everyone snapped their attention to a small doorway unveiling towards the edge of the airstrip. Originally opening to assist speaker-to-speaker communication, it now unveiled a brilliantly lit interior contrasting sharply with its dark surroundings. Ambiguous shapes began to coalesce from within.

"I always thought it was our job to do this to them," exclaimed Slogg watching the strange shapes form into moving creatures as they emerged into the open air.

"I wonder what they look like?" said Deluxia.

"They're probably green with pointy ears," guessed Taroooc. Behind him Walta self-consciously touched each tip of his.

"Excuse me…" declared Duke. In a small gesture he flicked his palms up and down his body. "You've already had some indication."

Ten or more Earthling figures became clearer as they neared this migrant ship. Anticipation on Slogg's face disappeared with sudden recognition.

"Well, that's boring," he said, "they look exactly the same as us. Within reason."

"Such is *Life*," observed Dzkk.

"Did you really expect we'd all be that different?" grunted Duke.

They watched as the Earthlings delicately approached the starship with trepidation. They came close, but very wary to be completely beneath its huge mass.

"Well... let the show begin. How do you want to run this then Dzkk? They seem obliging enough to make their approach, so I haven't petrified their delicate souls as yet. Should we lower the underside hatch as a starting point?"

"Yes please Captain. And then I'd ask you and Taroooc to join join me and Duke down there. When the point comes to meet them, I'd like Duke at the forefront."

Taroooc flipped switches to announce the hatch was opening. Deep below them, a resounding thrum became audible as the largest portal located on the underbelly of the ship began its slow, laborious swing open.

Nelson, Tina, Charlie, Dex, Fry and Mikhail... all watched stupefied from the reverse side, as the slow opening offered a darkened entrance into the mysterious starship. Only seconds earlier Nelson registered the aliens had been talking to him in English, having initially accepted it without thought. Only now did he question the dubious nature of this. As the ship's belly was fissured, he decided to ask for an explanation at the nearest opportunity.

The hatch came to a halt two feet above the ground, forming a gently curved ramp that prefaced another world. Briefly a light flickered inside, and four pairs of ordinary legs appeared at the top of this makeshift stairway.

Three wore trousers and boots, the other appeared wrapped in a feather trimmed cloak framing strange yellow footwear that highlighted four toes on each foot.

Nelson was transfixed. Ahead of the pack, the leading pair of boots was distinctive. Conspicuous. Dr Martens was an earthbound footgear producer of repute for over thirty years. Once more fashionable now in the Eighties, it seemed exceedingly unlikely such a item would be reproduced identically beyond this world. Even less likely that they would sit below tightly rolled up jeans.

Nelson's pulse thumped.

As the hatch continued its descent, the four figures began walking towards them, revealing their torsos inch by inch.

"My God, my God, my God!" screamed Nelson.

*"DUKE!"*

A gap in the world opened as the two men caught sight of each other. Already worn down by emotion, Duke sucked in his top lip, biting it hard between his teeth.

"Nelson," he whispered inaudibly. Then louder, "You believed me!"

The opening portal continued to thrum as its gears delivered its tip to the soil. A breeze caught the air and moved leaves on the lithe trees beyond.

Unperturbed by this exchange, Charlie spoke next.

"Well, they are bipedal, that bit looks like us," he commented to Emm, Dex and those around similarly curious to examine the alien bodies.

"And so does the rest of us," echoed Slogg walking down the ramp with Dzkk and Taroooc in tow.

Duke remained locked in stone. The phrase *just say what comes naturally* now hammered through his head.

Slogg continued. "I know. It's a little boring isn't it, apart from a few skin tones, the odd poultry reference, and Taroooc's third eye, we're mostly the same across all our worlds."

"Captain!" interjected Dzkk, forcefully.

"I've got this Dzkk, and our Earthling has stage fright," responded Slogg as he raced on. "Yes guys, it seems that over half the universe has evolved into the well tried and tested model that makes us mostly… well, humanoid is the best word for today. And by the way, Eustachian tube implants help us all speak the same language. So…"

Slogg left a pause, a dawning recognition he was unsure what to say next. He had not done his homework.

"Don't blow yourselves up guys!" Duke blubbed out behind him, before sinking to his knees.

# CHAPTER 55

Rushing up the ramp, Nelson held Duke so profoundly tight he felt he could crush him. A weakness had set in his friend's bones. Both had their eyes gripped shut. A fine breeze cooled each tear at their corners. Duke released first, his mouth open and clawing for words. He said the words to himself silently, his feet flat to the earth as he braced against Nelson, holding both shoulders determinedly. Nelson reversed the squeeze on his eyelids, pulling them open.

"I can't hear you Duke, what are you saying."

"It's not a mystery anymore. It was… them," said a soft voice, coming from the back of Duke's throat.

"What mystery? What was them?"

"They started the Cambrian Explosion, Nelson. It was them."

"I…" Nelson gasped for air.

"Some shapeshifting thing came here those five-hundred million years ago, Nelson, and somehow started the hypermutation, or as they call it, programmed mutation. It was *them*."

Duke held a shaking finger to indicate feebly towards Dzkk and Slogg at the base of the ramp.

"Programmed mutation? Duke…"

"It's not a mystery anymore. They accelerated our evolution. Nelson! Don't you see? We're not meant to be here yet. We are all mistakes."

Nelson clawed into Duke's arms as his friend shouted, mouth wide open. His own eyes shone brightly.

"I'm not sure what you are saying Duke, but from now I will always believe you. Always! You were also right. We did land on the Moon in 1927, and we've also been to the other worlds. There's a whole secret society dedicated to it Duke. This lot. They're guarding it all and feeding us new ideas and inventions piecemeal. They are a real tech mafia." He nodded further behind himself towards the group on the ground. "They've been changing things faster than the rest of us. And *you* helped me find them Duke. And now I've found you!"

The wind came back across the trees to touch Duke and Nelson's cheeks. Fine dust settled where the tip of the hatch had reached the soil. The silence sifted down with it.

At this juncture a sense of panic swept through Slogg's whole being as he perched at the cusp of the ramp and history. His head turned mechanically on a torso fixed in granite. The sun brought a blue-violet to the dawn sky. The Captain's mind was emptied by the incipient realisation he possessed no penned or practiced opening monologue. Presented with a destiny and a codebook, he had played to form and shunned both preparation and revision, choosing again to obstinately rely on instinct.

*How might the instant be chronicled? How many holobooks would document this moment?*

His eyes flashed a look at Dzkk, and he faced recognition of the elder's clarity he was simply a guide and not one to lead the Induction. He lifted his eyes back up the ramp to Duke, now partially obscured by this new Earthling. The clear distress and weakness in Duke's bones struck him out for reliable communication.

The Earth people lay in wait as this unplanned and dramatic pause built further tension. By degrees Slogg combatted *The Fear of Empty Time.* His mind raced to Astronomical Academy tutor Fid Fadood, and Classics lecture option: *23 Immutable Laws to Make Yourself Likeable in Command.* Another scrawled aide-memoire on the back of Slogg's textbooks had forever committed to his mind's eye, Fadood's unique advice on addressing a new multi-species audience: *patter and banter*.

With no alternative to hand, Slogg swiftly decided on this as his best tactic, his only tactic. *Patter and banter*. He pressed on:

"So… we're here to welcome you into the Galactic Club, and it appears you are forty annums early. Well, you know what they say… time flies like an arrow, fruit flies like a banana."

This ventured icebreaker disappeared in an uplift of air. Blank, puzzled faces spread across his Earthly companions. Slogg took fright. Never lose your audience. In just a few opening sentences his audience were searching for the exit routes.

"So, hello!" he brazened, "My name is Captain Slogg, and this is my Chief Wellness Officer Taroooc. And here, we have the All-Powerful Dzkk. And back there, one of your guys, Duke… something."

"Hello," began Charlie, "my name is..."

Slogg's slipped the patter to overdrive.

"Good, good. Hypermutation has delivered you early, so we're here to liberate the human race from any further primitive trappings and introduce you to the upgrades of intergalactic technology…"

Charlie coughed lightly, the internationally accepted sign that you politely wish to have the chance to speak. International, but perhaps not universal.

"Examples? Of course, there are lots… flying eggs; Occasional Kill Weapons; TwiText and Instagran; Ireen Y'Know What Ah Mean; Teleport Stream gender reassignment; the list is endless…"

Further up the ramp and still holding tight to Duke, Nelson interrupted.

"Charlie! You need to listen to what my friend Duke has to say."

Charlie took his cue.

"Thank you for coming Captain. And it's good to see you again Duke. I'm glad you made it back here safely. Can I just say that the rest of the human race don't..."

"Of course... *don't* want to miss out! And they will not. Trust me, no need to worry," continued Slogg. "Everything has been taken care of, hasn't it Dzkk?"

"Please, Captain!"

"There you are you see, we'll address any concerns. After all, despite your accelerated evolution I'm sure we've dealt with bigger planets than this. I mean, you're not exactly huge, just middling, or even cute. What a view you gave us as we flew in." The verbal deluge continued as his adrenalin flowed. "Mind you, don't get me wrong, four billion people isn't so small either, especially when all your transport vehicles, genomes, and toothbrushes must be licensed. A lot of digitizing. But I digress. So... where are the rest of your four billion friends?"

"Well, that's what I've been trying to tell you," started Charlie, "You see, we don't exactly represent the human race, we..."

"But of course you do!" assured Slogg, "I think you've got hold of the wrong end of the laser-pointer there. I haven't come down to this planet to meet some second-rate dignitaries with *World Leader* stamped in their forehead. Give them half a chance and they'll fluff the whole thing up. No, we've come to meet the real people - the people like you with the robes and the braiding. The none too clever, the none too ambitious, the... little people without whom there would be no planet, no Earthlings. That's who we've come to meet."

Charlie stroked his hand across his swan braiding for comfort. Behind him, Emm mirrored the move. The Knowall's faces were drawn unblinking to Charlie standing at their helm. The focus brought with it a soundless lull.

"*Toothbrushes*!" Nelson shrieked, releasing Duke's arms.

"I'm sorry?" queried Slogg, snapping his gaze towards this unannounced inquisitor.

"You just said that all toothbrushes have to be licensed in the universe."

"Why of course. Is that not normal here?"

Slogg's pace doubled.

"They have to be regularly checked for weakening strength and structure. Dental hygiene is of extreme importance to the modern interstellar traveller, particularly on public transport. In the eastern spiral arm of Centaurus, one can be arrested for possessing bad breath and charged with polluting the atmosphere. It's only natural."

Summarily Dzkk raised his eyes and beak to the brightening sky with a deep sigh. He had witnessed enough. Presenting the fatigue of infinite wisdom and wrapping his feather cloak tight across his body, he turned slowly to walk back up the ramp. A weighty burden began once more to press down on his shoulders.

Slogg observed his departure.

"The poor guy needs rest. It takes its toll. It's alright Dzkk, I'll take care of things down here."

Dzkk head shook softly from side to side.

Charlie opened his mouth.

"Listen! Will you let me explain. Tina here, and Nelson, Duke behind you are… well different from the rest of us. They represent the true cold-blooded human race who have wars and famines. Wars with bloodshed over petty, stupid arguments. While the rest of us are… well, we're..."

"Charlie!" interjected Nelson. "Please. We need a minute. Trust me."

Dzkk was now at the top of the ramp and went to give a final look towards Slogg, Tarooc and the Earthlings. He made every effort not to sigh and failed.

With the slightest shrug of the shoulders, he turned to re-enter the ship, becoming acutely aware of a strong alcoholic reek coupled with the floor gently quaking beneath his feet.

A sharp glimpse inside discerned the horrendous shape of Chief Commissioner Milko Clamburxer pounding the corridor towards him, followed by a proportionally horrific, inebriated pink elephant. The shock made Dzkk reel, a reaction that saved him by a hair's breadth from being trampled underfoot. The wretched beast stampeded past with the huge flailing ears, and pink trunk waving side to side.

Ahead of it Clamburxer yelled a phrase resembling *Charge*! flying on down the ramp into the early morning light of Earth.

Mercifully both beasts swerved a riveted Duke and Nelson.

"Oh... crap!" screamed Taroooc at the ramp's base, catching sight of the twosome careening towards him and his Captain. Slogg, not blessed with an eye in the back of his head, was slower to react. Yet as luck had it (though Slogg would disagree profusely much later} he was hit first by the full force of a crazed Clamburxer and together they performed a twisted ballet of mangled limbs and beer fumes. Sailing through the air in surreal slow-motion, they crash landed in a crumpled mess, rolling a few more feet, before entwining with dried grass and soil.

As a contorted heap, they came to a dusty halt at Tina's feet.

The elephant following close behind, trumpeted supremely in pure admiration of this spectacle. Hitting the bottom of the ramp, it entered an uncontrollable skid on dry soil and pirouetted a full one hundred and eighty degrees, finally settling in a cloud of dust upon tremulous legs, with a dazed, possessed look deep in its eye.

All observers remained stock still and wholeheartedly silent.

Clamburxer was the first to open his grit encrusted eyes and look up, blinking twice.

"Cor! Jush look up th... them legs," he stammered. Tina pounced backwards away from his lecherous glare.

"Who is this *tramp*?" she called out disgustedly.

"Ah think I'd b... *hic* better arresht ma self ..."

Slogg wrenched his own eyes open and they widened in horror. The dust cleared to discern the immense posterior of the poor, inebriated elephant. Its tail and buttocks twitched feverishly. Slogg had no inkling the effect Braevitchkan beer may have on an animal's digestive system. He observed the elephant's knees tremble and wobble, its large rear end appearing ever more unsettled.

With far more speed and dexterity than his state would normally allow, Slogg became free of Clamburxer, sprang to his feet and stepped aside. Clamburxer ventured many times to raise himself from the ground yet failed miserably.

He lifted his head, his helmet finally fell off, and through squinting eyes said:

"This is a raid. Take all your clo... *hic* wh, where *hic* am I?"

"I'll ask again, who is this disgusting joke?" quizzed Tina.

"Ah, this is Chief Commissioner Clamburxer. He's in charge of policing your sector of the universe."

"And that?" continued Tina, indicating the huge, quivering monstrosity beside Slogg.

"Er, that… is a pink elephant."

The beast finally emptied its bowels.

From deep within the migrant ship Dzkk groaned and resolved it was finally time to lay down. Beneath him maintenance crews and robots emerged from the ship to supervise, with tribulation, the coaxing of a bewildered elephantine beast back inside.

Clamburxer endeavoured to assert his authority with a blind refusal to re-enter the ship. Yet the task of staying upright proved so intensely problematic he eventually succumbed to a robotic stretcher and was conveyed back aboard.

The Earthlings huddled quietly together.

Excluded from this group, Slogg returned silently to Taroooc at the base of the ship's ramp. He then summoned the cleaning droids.

# CHAPTER 56

"Duke," hissed Nelson, "how… why are you in this alien ship?"

As the sun's rays hit the treetops, their group slowly turned inward, away from the off-world visitors who stood awkwardly, with little more to say. Duke bent in guilefully, inviting the others to follow.

"Cha and his colleagues here can explain that to you Nelson," he whispered, "probably just like you, it started with a belief in NASA. I just advanced to one more level and became a naïve abductee."

"Excuse me, you volunteered. We were never…" started Charlie.

"Ok, shush. None of this is important now, because you need to know what I know, before you make any more decisions."

Together with Emm, Tina and his Knowall colleagues, Charlie closed in. They formed a tight team circle. Slogg and Taroooc observed this ritual silently from afar. The codebook that Dzkk had provided to Slogg covered no such scenarios.

"We're a rushed experiment," hushed Duke to the tight group. "All of us, the human race, and most of life on Earth, we're a series of accelerated mistakes, but programmed with a limited set of outcomes. We've been made to evolve too fast by some… form of deep controller, which they call The Great Attractor."

"Who? How?" scoffed Charlie.

"You heard me, The Great Attractor… a universal shapeshifter is the best description I've heard, that seems to control just about everything. Even appearing to me last night as the ghost of my dad."

"Ernest!" exclaimed Nelson. "Oh my God, Duke, you poor…"

"This all sounds somewhat unlikely..." began Charlie.

"Honestly Cha, I'm *so* tired. It's going to save a huge amount of time if you just believe me. Thanks to you guys just allowing me to be abducted, I've been tortured, and soaked in so much new information, my brain is shredded."

Charlie encountered the guilt and took the point.

"Please proceed."

"The Cambrian Explosion we all know of, or hypermutation that we're now calling it, from five hundred million years ago... they started it, all of it."

"Hang on, current theory states our rapid evolution was caused by either a catastrophic climate changing event, or a sudden oxygenation of the seas," corrected Charlie.

"*Either*!" bayed Duke. "You know yourself that science doesn't say *either*. What is true is that nobody can *prove* either!"

"Ssshh..." hushed Nelson, glancing back at their visitors.

"You know that nobody can prove those theories one hundred percent, Cha," Duke repeated softly.

Nelson interjected in support of his friend.

"You said to me Charlie, you were still working on rethinking Darwin's theories and hypermutation, and that there was still no complete evidence on what caused the Cambrian Explosion."

"This is true, but..."

"It's going to be so much quicker if you believe us," continued Duke. "You put me in this position, letting me get snatched without any real inkling of what might happen to me. Well, they used some B-movie ray thing to make me reveal everything I knew, tell the whole truth, and then... they apologized. Simple as that. Oh yes, and some police dude dressed like a Seventies Judge Dredd let's out a few secrets, and boom! It dawned on Foghorn

Leghorn and his cronies that the Great Attractor was responsible for our situation all along. Then my dad…" Duke sobbed hard as he said the word, Nelson put a hand to his shoulder, "…appeared and asked me to come back here to sort it all out!"

"Sort what out?" asked Tina, Nelson, and Charlie in unison.

"The mess. It's all gone too fast, haywire evolution, and we were never supposed to develop nuclear weapons by now, or even at all. And it seems The Great Attractor doesn't want us to blow ourselves to smithereens. Somehow, and don't ask me, but somehow, we're meant to work out how to fix it and stop the nuclear war. Jesus Christ."

"Hmm…" croaked Charlie sheepishly, "well on that topic, it's the same reason we are here."

"How do you mean?"

"Well, as our technology roared ahead of the rest of the world, we've been building *The Quit* and want to hitch a lift with these guys to the stars. To er… to escape the same threat."

"*What*!" spat Duke.

"It's true," confirmed Nelson, "they've told me and Tina all about it."

"It very much is," confirmed Charlie. "Humanity is just minutes away from doomsday midnight and blowing itself up. And we want to get out before it takes us with it."

"But don't you *see*!" crawed Duke, then instantly softening again as he detected Captain Slogg's remote attention, "Don't you see by now… you're all part of the same mistake. You guys as well! Your own accelerated development as Knowalls, or whatever you call yourselves, is caused by the same programmed mutations that have caused the human race to be here so fast in the first place."

Nelson got it first.

"My God, Duke, you're absolutely right!"

He span round to Charlie, Emm and the others.

"He's spot on."

Charlie was faintly shaking his head. Nelson pressed on.

"If you guys had stopped to think for a moment and actually listened to those Luddites, you might have slowed down a little, and then at least the nuclear stuff might have waited a bit longer, or perhaps never happened at all. One thing is sure, we'd all be in this together. And perhaps the world might even be a bit safer with you helping us… rather than hiding from us."

Charlie took a deep breath, wide-eyed at Nelson. He was quietly processing his statements. Nelson continued.

"You've spent so long railing against humanity on this world, when perhaps you should be railing at others *off* this world… for creating this mess."

The day was brightening, and the sunlight was reaching the tree trunks. All the dust had settled. The lights from the migrant ship blinked calmly above them. Emm gradually lifted a hand and cupped the back of Charlie's neck.

Charlie felt the support and always trusted her instincts.

"Duke, if we accept what you say is true, how can we fix it all?" Charlie demanded.

"When The Great Attractor appeared as my dad, I asked the same thing and a strange phrase was used…"

"What phrase?"

"He said, *the next stage for man has been marked in red.*"

There was a beat, then Charlie took a small step backwards, so thunderstruck he was unbalanced.

"Say again," Charlie demanded.

"The next stage for man has been marked in red."

"Gee!"

"I know, exactly," said Duke, "quite an astounding statement."

"No, Gee. Our Gee. Mikhail Gee!"

Charlie turned and his group took the cue to move apart and single out one of their kind. A shorter man, with a stout middle-aged figure, bowed softly back at them, acknowledging the honour. The distinctive red birthmark on his head shone through receding hair in the sunlight.

*"That's it!"* yelled Duke. "Marked in red."

"Yes, I can see it all now," acknowledged Charlie. "You are *exactly* right. Marked in red! The Cold War of East versus West... defusing the constant nuclear threat and clash of ideologies. Well, our wonderful colleague Mikhail Gee has been espousing his ideas for quite some time. It's clear we should be listening to them much, much more."

"Spasibo Comrade Charles. Thank you," said the shorter Knowall in a strong Russian accent.

"Yes Mikhail," and turning back to Nelson and Duke he continued, "the Gee is short for Gorbachev by the way," nodding back to his colleague before continuing. "Mikhail. Let's talk more about your Perestroika idea. I'm starting to get it. Pe-re-stroi-ka. Now is the time for us to prioritise this... and we need to get you out there again as our next *surface* plan."

"Da Tovarishch Clark. Is good for me."

"Perestroika?" challenged Duke.

"Yes. Loosely it's Russian for restructuring."

"How is that going to help?"

"Okay, let me try in simple terms... it's Mikhail's idea to induce it as a political movement for reformation within the Communist Party. It was always a backup plan in case *The Quit* became impossible. To start defusing East-West tensions, together with his proposal to drive more openness in the Soviet Union."

"*Glasnost*!" hailed Mikhail Gorbachev.

"That's it. Perestroika and Glasnost."

"It sounds immense," observed Nelson.

"Not as immense as our plans for The Quit."

"But can you pull it off?"

"My dear friends, we have stood here and talked about our projects for lightspeed travel, laptop computers, and take-away coffee. We have all the capability we need, and all the rest of the 1980's. Perestroika and Glasnost are infinitely possible in that time frame."

Charlie felt suddenly lighter. Tomorrow or maybe in a week or a month he would devote most of his time to Mikhail, until he caught up fully with his bright mind. Emm held Charlie's shoulder throughout this dialogue, and she now let go, smiling warmly.

During this long private interchange between their Earthling hosts, Slogg and Taroooc had eventually sat on their haunches at the edge of the ramp. As a cleaning droid polished his left cheek with a warm towel, Slogg detected the Earthling's group conversation had reached a climax.

He stood and brushed down the Fleet uniform over his thighs and called out towards them.

"So, can I propose we have a few of you on board for a preliminary trip, before the rest of the universe arrives? There's no time to waste you know."

Charlie took a few paces through the group and sensed the others falling in behind him. Moving between Nelson and Duke, he observed them stand their ground, eyeing him anxiously. The whole universe beckoned, offering unrestricted experience of its riches. No Knowall had ever been selected to go first and perhaps one day they might begin to talk about this.

A few paces more and Charlie stared at Slogg,

summing the recent circumstances in his mind. His eyes broke contact with the Captain and he began a long, slow sweep back across his fellow Knowalls and their three new companions. But he was not seeing them. Sentiments, choices, and repercussions churned, and the same conclusion choked up unable to be reversed. It was vital, strong, and correct. Charlie did see the glacier blue eyes of his most trusted colleague, Emm'8k. Steadfast and unmoving, she stared straight back for a few seconds and there was the minutest shake of her head. Charlie smiled and let his decision be known.

"No," he said.

"No?"

"No."

"I... I'm sorry?" stuttered Slogg.

"No, you can't have a few of us aboard."

"But…"

"In fact, you can't have any of us aboard. And based on what I've just witnessed and heard, we would appreciate it if you would ask the rest of the universe not to visit us for a good while yet. Please."

"Bu... but... but you can't do that. No one can say *no*. There must be... But no one refuses, do they Dzkk?"

Yet Dzkk was lying down in a darkened waiting room of the *SPA* bay. Having foreseen this outcome, he had no intention of witnessing a final humiliation.

Slogg's palms began to lather. He itched them.

He stared at Charlie and looked frantically across the rest of the Knowalls. Each of their faces portrayed a similar sentiment: relief.

"This is ridiculous. You... you... whatever you call yourself," spat Slogg.

"The name is Charlie, and I've grown to like it. Charles Arthur Clarke. And Charles Arthur Clarke is staying on Earth for a good time to come. It may be hypermutated and nowhere near perfect here, but it's a damn sight better than..." and then he stopped in a sudden showcase of tact.

"Well, let's just say that I could imagine worse. It sounds like we're not in this position through our own mistakes, but more like the rest of the universe made these for us. So, thank you, but we are where we are. And if we, and by *we,* I mean *all* the human race, us included, can't sort out our own mistakes then... well, bang goes this *cute* little planet, as you so delicately put it. So, I think maybe it's about time we got back together with humanity and tried to help our fellow *Earthlings,* rather than opting out. Time to *undo.*"

For a moment there was only the Puerto Rican breeze high above the trees swaying the top leaves in a synchronized ballet.

"I'm confused, even baffled." pressed Slogg through the silence. "I thought that you were all part of the human race?"

"Yes! You are *exactly* right there, Captain. And I think it's something that we've all forgotten."

Charlie looked around his fellow group of Knowalls and across to Tina, Nelson and Duke. The young Knowall named Fry smiled back at him and whispered profoundly amongst their circle:

"It only takes a ship full of aliens, for humans to realise how much we have in common."

"Indeed," hushed Charlie, "Good quote Fry, keep that one."

He then raised his voice.

"So, it's decided. We are staying put. Project *Quit* will become Project *Stay Put, Undo and Perestroika.*"

There was a long pause, and as everyone stayed silent there was the budding recognition they had a lot to reconsider and much to plan. Perhaps it was now time to return to their cave to eat and drink and talk and remember the feeling of being human together.

"What... are... you... *doing*!" yelled Slogg in disbelief. "It makes no sense! No one ever, stays put."

"Well, we are."

The patter and banter had boiled away leaving him no residue but a dry throat. What could Slogg say to this planet and to these people. What more could he offer them. Charlie glanced around his group and there was a nodding of deliverance from the Knowalls.

"Can I ask you to reconsider," restarted Slogg. "You see, this is *my* destiny. I was chosen to bring you in, to induce you. The Great Attractor be will not be pleased with me."

The humans stared at this figure as his shoulders slipped. The fire in his eyes had extinguished.

Duke spoke as a realization dawned.

"Perhaps Captain, all of this *is* your destiny. Perhaps this *is* success. Perhaps you've just brought our planet together in the only way it was meant to be… to try and heal itself, before we can be Induced."

"Duke is right Captain," put in Charlie. "We all needed this wake-up call."

"But it just doesn't feel right. What do we do now?"

"You've already done it Captain," calmed Duke. "As my dad said, it doesn't matter what you do, as long as you change something. You've been the catalyst."

The destiny had ended.

Later when he was speaking truthfully, Slogg would say he was not sure if he had achieved anything or if it had been the perfect outcome. He knew deep inside himself that something had changed, both here and within him. His blast of anger had dissipated. He now felt empathy for this little planet and its people, and what they had been put through.

"Perhaps we could try again sometime?" Slogg managed.

"I'm sure that day will come," reassured Charlie.

"Would you like a pink elephant as a Peacefulness and Primacy Offering?"

"No thank you Captain. Not based on what we've just witnessed."

"And we brought some beer too."

"It's a kind offer, but no thank you."

"Are you sure?"

There was no answer but a smile. Above them the trees continued their soft ripple in the breeze. Slogg lifted his hand delicately, palm out, in the universally accepted gesture of farewell. The gently curved ramp beneath their feet creaked deeply in its hinge to the ship's underbelly, reminding Slogg it still held its own weight plus that of him and Taroooc.

"That's it then? Well…" Slogg turned to his Chief Wellness Officer who had stood mute beside him, "I think we might as well be off." He glanced down at the floor for a few seconds, back towards the Earthlings faces, and finally skyward.

"Can I ask one of you, which way is the North Star?"

"The pub or the astronomical reference?"

"Both would be good, but I meant the latter."

"That way Captain," said Charlie, pointing into the bright morning sky. "You'll see it clearly once you get above our atmosphere."

As the ramp began to close, Slogg turned and walked despondently back into his ship, experiencing a severe case of the Big Loop Blues[26].

Taroooc trekked up behind him.

"Is that all Sir?"

"It would seem so Taroooc. As you come up, please would you ensure the hatch is locked for departure?"

---

[26] This is the appropriate term for the condition in which any mortal may find themself when bringing into question their own existence, and what it equates to on the scale of a near infinite universe.

"Yes, Captain."

"Ah yes, that's a bit better" Slogg sighed, "*Captain…*"

Slogg and Taroooc held back at the top of the ramp and watched the Earthlings disappear with a sense of forfeiture. The hatch rose slowly and Slogg replayed events through his mind, imagining how any failing might be countered during the mission debrief. Exhaling heavily, he tracked the doorway gears completing their motion to shut out the Earth's daylight.

With a final stir of breeze there was a sudden shout from below as they heard an earthman's fading voice.

"Wait a minute!" yelled Nelson with the hatch just a few seconds from closing.

"Can I come?"

If you like it or not please let me know via deosey2000@gmail.com

# EPILOGUE

# 1 HOUR LATER

*It is not in the stars to hold our destiny but in ourselves.*
William Shakespeare

# 3rd September
# 12:00noon AST, Puerto Rico

A single face peered from a scratched, dimly lit portal as the huge dilapidated migrant ship prepared to leave a planet it had visited very briefly.

The eyes gazed down at a collection of similar faces staring straight back, portraying sentiments ranging between resignation and admiration. Just one face below held tears in its eyes.

It was the same face that begged Nelson not to join the aliens, much to his own surprise.

It was not Duke's face. Nelson advised his rediscovered companion he needed to see the beyond, to be off-world. To experience what Duke had just witnessed. He needed to be the first human on a new planet, to compare himself to Neil Armstrong, and to taste the smugness.

Duke and Nelson shared the boyhood dream of space travel and his best friend understood instantly. He simply insisted that Nelson return within their lifetimes.

Neither was it Charlie's face, who had reminded Nelson of his pledged freedom at any point and wished him safe travels.

Nelson had swayed both himself and the face's owner this was the best outcome for now, and he was categorical that nothing would convince him otherwise. Only now was he experiencing the stitch of regret as a result of his decision.

Yet it was too late.

The invisible force suspending the ship motionless above the ground was reshaping to smoothly lift its huge bulk from Earth's gravitational pull.

Nelson watched as this colossal power raised them slowly skyward, producing shockwaves to whip up the dust and newly fallen leaves below. Forces that became so strong they threatened to overturn anyone or anything too close outside.

The tearful face kept a safe distance, but she still had to hold on tightly to her raincoat.

At long last the ship began to turn, screaming its low-flight Subtachyon engines at the surface directly beneath.

Disconsolately the tearful face spontaneously raised a hand to wave goodbye and blow a kiss. The fingers on the other hand also wiped the gusted grit from her eye. But her timing was poor as the immense forces needed for lift-off suddenly propelled open her unprotected raincoat, to reveal exactly what Tina was wearing underneath.

Nelson left the porthole and stayed no longer to watch. Just seventeen seconds later he was in the ship's bridge, asking if it was possible to be put back down on the ground.

Printed in Great Britain
by Amazon